Praise for

A MILLION OPEN DOORS
by JOHN BARNES

Chosen Best SF Novel of 1992
by *Science Fiction Chronicle*

A 1992 Nebula Nominee

"Such zest, narrative energy and critical intelligence that readers across a wide spectrum of tastes will be charmed....A consistently enjoyable read, one of the most inventive and diverting SF novels this year."
—*The Washington Post*

"Barnes's unusual combination of romantic adventure and high-tech SF succeeds in capturing the atmosphere of a story that features derring-do, revolution, and the clash of cultures."
—*Library Journal*

"Barnes once again demonstrates his gifts for giving high technology a human face and creating worlds that we can't help but enjoy visiting (even if we wouldn't necessarily want to live there). *A Million Open Doors* is the kind of SF novel that general readers, as well as fans, will savor."
—*The West Coast Review of Books*

"As hard science and an emphasis on storytelling have returned to favor, John Barnes and a number of other 'neotraditionalists' have been favorably compared to the late Robert A. Heinlein....[*A Million Open Doors*] is engaging, reflecting a great love for its characters and a carefully stated humor."
—*Atlanta Journal-Constitution*

More praise for

A MILLION OPEN DOORS

"Persuasive and well-realized."

—*Kirkus Reviews*

"*A Million Open Doors* plays with some of the central motifs of Heinlein's *Beyond This Horizon*....The result satisfies William Tenn's description of science fiction as jazz: take some riffs somebody else has played and put them through your own horn to see what you can make of them. Barnes, it turns out, blows up a storm....*A Million Open Doors* and *Orbital Resonance* represent both the fulfillment and the fusion of the Heinlein juvenile and adult traditions."

—*Locus*

"John Barnes just keeps getting better. *A Million Open Doors* gives us a tour through just a few of the Thousand Cultures. I am looking forward to seeing all the rest of them. No other writer that I know of is as interested in the question of how societies work—and fail to work. Pick this book up and read it. You will be too busy enjoying it to notice how much Barnes is teaching you."

—*Roger MacBride Allen*

Science fiction novels by John Barnes

Orbital Resonance
A Million Open Doors
Mother of Storms
Kaleidoscope Century
One for the Morning Glory
Earth Made of Glass
Apostrophes & Apocalypses
Finity

A MILLION OPEN DOORS

JOHN BARNES

A TOM DOHERTY ASSOCIATES BOOK
NEW YORK

This is a work of fiction. All the characters and events portrayed in this book are fictitious, and any resemblance to real people or events is purely coincidental.

A MILLION OPEN DOORS

Copyright © 1992 by John Barnes

Cover art by John Harris

A Tor Book
Published by Tom Doherty Associates, Inc.
175 Fifth Avenue
New York, NY 10010

Tor Books on the World Wide Web:
http://www.tor.com

Tor® is a registered trademark of Tom Doherty Associates, Inc.

ISBN: 0-812-51633-8
Library of Congress Catalog Card Number: 92-24132

First edition: October 1992
First mass market printing: November 1993

Printed in the United States of America

0 9 8 7 6 5 4 3

A MILLION OPEN DOORS

PART ONE

CANSO DE FIS DE JOVENT

ONE

We were in Pertz's Tavern, up in the hills above Noupeitau, with the usual people, ostensibly planning to go backpacking in Terraust and actually drinking on Aimeric's tab. With fires due in a few weeks, we thought we might see the first herds of auroc-de-mer migrating to the banks of the Great Polar River, beginning their 1700 km swim to the sea. Aimeric had never seen it and was wild to go. For the rest of us, the pleasure was in watching his excitement—like his bald spot, it was always there to be made fun of—and in the red wine that flowed freely while he bought.

"Perhaps on the last day we can spring to Bo Merce Bay and see the first ones head out to sea. They say that's *really* a sight. Last chance for twelve stanyears, we shouldn't miss it, *m'es vis, companho*." Aimeric laughed, looking down into his wine. The bald spot was bigger than ever. I enjoyed pitying him.

Aimeric slid his arm around Bieris, his *entendedora* of the time, and pulled her closer to him. She raised an eyebrow at me, asking me not to encourage him.

Garsenda, who was my *entendedora*, squeezed my arm and whispered in my ear, "I think he really means to go. Are you going to?"

"If you wish, *midons*. My father took me when I was nine. I wouldn't mind seeing it again."

"Giraut's seen it," Garsenda said, very loudly. "Giraut can tell you all about it."

Everyone stopped talking and looked at us. If Garsenda had not had long, thick blue-black hair, bright blue eyes, and big heavy soft breasts over a taut belly, she'd never have been my *entendedora*—I surely hadn't chosen her on her personality. Sometimes I thought of getting rid of her, but she so impressed my *companho* that it was worth tolerating her many lapses. I only wished that the laws of *finamor* did not demand that I think of her as perfect.

She giggled when she realized they were staring, and rubbed my thigh in a long stroke under the table. "I thought we were talking about going backpacking to the South Pole," she said. "You know, to see the aurocs-de-mer turn their legs to flippers or whatever it is they do."

"Yes, we were," Raimbaut said. He was grinning, enjoying watching my *entendedora* embarrass me.

I grinned back. Since he had none of his own, if he wanted to get insulting, I held trump.

"Have you actually seen it?" Aimeric asked.

Bieris hit him on the shoulder, giving him her don't-encourage-Garsenda glare.

"*Ja*, my father took me the year before you got here, Aimeric." I took the carafe and helped myself to another glass of wine; Aimeric flagged old Pertz, behind the bar, who started to pour another. I had lost count of glasses, and didn't care. "And what actually happens is that they have these pockets that their legs and flippers fold into. They just disjoint whatever they're not using and tuck it up into the pocket is all. The *toszet* who designed them must have been a real genius—not just having the organs, but having the instinct to do that, is really something." I sipped the wine again, and noticed I had everyone's attention—maybe they really did want to go. "But let's just go and see them get into the river. The going out to sea doesn't look like much—just a lot of big gray-brown backs in the water. Not nearly as impressive as the levithi you can see from Bisbat Head."

Aimeric said, "Giraut, you could make a dance on the clouds on gossamer wings sound like going down the hall to spring your laundry to the cleaners." Raimbaut and Marcabru both laughed a lot more than it was worth—they were as drunk as I was.

Marcabru, who rarely went out of the city if he could help

it, said "But I'd like to see the whole thing—as Aimeric says, not for another twelve stanyears . . ."

Raimbaut nodded vigorously and refilled his glass.

Aimeric beamed at them. "Consensus is against you, Olde Woodes Hande." That was the nickname he had given me when I was twelve and he was new to the planet, on the many family trips my father had taken him on. "I think we should stay the extra days."

I shrugged. "It's a little more dangerous. While we're there, I'll show you some of the graveyards. The auroc-de-mer only *usually* beat the fires to the river. Each year some of them—sometimes a lot of them—burn to death, piled up in box canyons or at the foot of bluffs. Then after the snowfields form and melt, the charred aurocs-de-mer get swept into streams and piled up along some of the river beaches in meters-thick banks of white bone and black carbon. You shouldn't miss the sight—but I don't want any of us to become a permanent part of it."

Marcabru smiled at me. "Very prudent of you, Giraut. You're getting old. Hey, Garsenda, you want a fresh young *toszet* when Grandpa Giraut gets tired?"

It was nothing of course—mere banter between old friends—but then a big brawny Interstellar, sixteen or seventeen and far-gone drunk, bellowed from the next table, "You're a coward."

Every table in Pertz's went instantly quiet.

Ragging among friends is one thing, but in Nou Occitan *enseingnamen* is everything. I slid sideways away from Garsenda. "This won't take long, *midons*."

"You're a coward, Redsleeves," the young lout repeated. From his voice, I guessed he had stood up. I glanced at Marcabru to make sure the young turd wasn't about to rabbit-punch me as I stood, a trick that was very popular among the Interstellars, as anything low, dirty, or *ne gens* tended to be.

Marcabru raised and slowly lowered an index finger, so I kicked the bench backward hard and spun into the space where it had been. Beside me, Marcabru's epee uncoiled into rigidity with a sharp pop, its neuroducer tip almost in the face of that young clown. Between the flickering glow of the neuroducer in his face, and the slam of the bench against his shins, he took a big leap back, giving us a moment to assess the situation.

It didn't look good. Five young Interstellars, all dressed in the navy-and-black style patterned on Earth bureaucratic uniforms, sneered at the four of us. All of them were big and muscular, and none were hanging back. Probably they were all dosed on a berserker drug.

The smart thing, if possible, would be to avoid a fight.

On the other hand, I detested Interstellars—traitors to their culture, imitators of the worst that came out from the Inner Worlds, bad copies of Earth throwing away all the wealth of their Occitan heritage; their art was sadoporn, their music raw noise, and their courtesy nonexistent—and spirit and style were everything. Anyone could be graceful with nothing at stake. Here was a real test of *enseingnamen*.

Everyone speaks Terstad everywhere you go in the Thousand Cultures, but it doesn't offer the powerful, compressed imagery of Occitan, so it was that in which I insulted him; a few musical, rolling syllables sufficed to point out that his father had dribbled the best part of him onto the bathroom floor and he needed to wash his face of the stench of his cheap-whore sister. It was a fine calling-out for spur of the moment and half-drunk.

Aimeric and Raimbaut rose to their feet, applauding with harsh, ugly laughs to make it clear that it was everyone's fight.

"Talk Terstad. I don't understand school talk."

He was not telling the truth, since all instruction is in Occitan after the fourth year, but it was a point of pride with Interstellars to speak only Terstad, because they were determined to reject everything about their own culture and tradition.

"I should have expected that," I said. "You *look* stupid. All right, I'll translate—please let me know if I'm going too fast. Your father (that's one of those drunks your mother called 'customers,' though god only knows *which* one) dribbled the best part of you—"

"I don't give a shit what the Octalk meant. I just want to fight you."

His epee banged out into a straight line pointed at me. Mine replied. There was a fast flurry of pops as all those involved extended epees, and crashing and scrambling sounds as everyone else in Pertz's tried to get out of the way.

He grinned at me and glanced at Garsenda. "After we get done with all of you, me and my underboys will share your slut."

It was a dumb adolescent trick, which probably worked pretty well on dumb adolescents. I drew a sharp breath and dropped my point a hairsbreadth, as if he had actually broken my focus. He lunged—straight onto the point of my epee, which tapped his exposed larynx, bending like a flyrod under the force of the collision.

He fell to the floor, bubbling and grasping his throat. The neuroducer had made solid contact, and it would require sedation and several days' slow revival to convince him that he did not have blood gushing from a hole in his throat. We all stood watching him as he quickly hallucinated himself dead and went into a coma.

I sort of hoped I had actually bruised him with the force of the blow, but they'd be able to fix that too. On the other hand, a really good zap with a neuroducer is almost impossible to erase with anything but time, so probably a decade from now his throat would spasm hard enough to choke him every now and then.

The situation was satisfactory as far as I was concerned. "An apology, on behalf of your friend, would settle this," I said.

"I wish we could," the biggest of them said, "but then we'd all have to fight him as soon as he got out of the hospital—with fists, too. Gwim is strict with his underboys."

Two more things I hated about Interstellars—they liked to give and take orders from each other, and they contracted fine old Occitan names like Guilhem down to ugly grunts like

Gwim. "Then let's get on with it," I said. "The odds are honorable now."

The two in the back gulped hard, but to give them credit, they all nodded. Maybe there was a little *enseingnamen* left in them despite the clothes.

"Let's do this in the street," I added. "Pertz doesn't need any more furniture broken up, and a stray hit with a neuroducer can wipe a vu."

I glanced at the Wall of Honor, memorializing Pertz's dead patrons, and all the vus were smiling and nodding as if they'd heard me. It was an eerie effect, but in a moment they were all out of unison again.

When I looked back, the Interstellars were nodding, and so were my seconds. Aimeric had that lazy, bored look he got just before some intense pleasure. Marcabru, best of our fighters after me, was solidly ready and balanced, his face almost blank—he was already in that state where thought and action are identical, a state I could feel myself settling comfortably into with each breath.

Raimbaut had a crazy gleam in his eye and was rocking back and forth on his feet, almost bouncing—I never knew anyone who loved a brawl or a wild adventure better. His face was distorted in a dozen places, and his left shoulder and right ankle were stiff, where muscles could not be convinced they weren't scarred, and there must have been internal effects as well.

If I had been thinking I might not have let things go the way they did, but of course he and I were both twenty-two stanyears old. Everyone seems immortal then. Besides, Raimbaut would tell me later that he wasn't unhappy about how he died, only about when.

With a fierce little nod, he signalled for me to get on with it. I said, "Well, then, gentlemen, the street. Will it be to first yield, to first death, or without limit?"

"First death?" one of the ones behind squeaked, and the brawny blond boy who now seemed to be their leader nodded.

"I think we'll have to, to satisfy Gwim."

"All right then, to the street, *atz dos*," I said.

We walked out to the street in side-by-side pairs, one of them with each of us—it's the position for honorable people, and given that they were Interstellars it might have been some risk, but they had shown real *enseingnamen* since their vulgarian leader's dispatch, and so I extended them the courtesy.

The street was empty—everyone was down at Festival Night in Noupeitau. From far below, we could hear the clash of a dozen brass bands playing in different parts of the city, mixed together by distance.

The redbrick villas up here were the color of heartsblood in the warm glow of the sunset; the little red dot of Arcturus, a bloody period, was sinking into Totzmare in the west, and the surf was running fast and big. The skimmers riding them in (on the western coast of Nou Occitan, waves are ridable as much as two hundred km out to sea) were just putting on running lights, and a few were tacking and putting on sail to work their way back out to sea so that they could start another run next morning. Those last few weeks before a Dark, when the sky was still deep purple and the long evenings still warm, always seemed to hurry by too fast.

It was a good night to be alive, and a fine setting for a brawl.

"Let's get on with it." It was my responsibility to say that, for though I had challenged originally, the boys' taking up their friend's quarrel had made me the challenged, so timing and protocol were mine to decide. I might have chosen the issue fought to as well, but, under an imputation of cowardice, I preferred to defy them by letting them choose. When I saw how young and scared their faces looked in the sharp black-edged shadows of the red street, I thought of softening it to first yield—but no, their *ne gens* behavior had begun it.

Let them bear the consequences.

I spoke the traditional words then: *"Atz fis prim. Non que malvolensa, que per ilh tensa sola."* It meant "to the first death"—that to remind everyone when we were to stop—and "not from rancor, but merely for the sake of the quarrel"—to remind us that this was not a blood feud and would not become one, that this fight would settle whatever question there was for good and forever.

Then I flicked my epee upward in salute, the boy facing me did the same, and all the seconds saluted in unison. Their epees had barely returned to ready when the boy was on me.

Our epees had clashed no more than ten times—I had not yet formed any impression of him—when Aimeric cried *"Patz marves!"* to end the fight.

All the safety locks clicked, and the epees coiled back into their hilts, the guards folding in last. I dropped mine unconsciously into my pocket, looking to see who had died. Raimbaut was on the ground, not moving.

At first it was nothing we hadn't seen before—we were getting ready to move him to the back room at Pertz's with the young clown who had started all the trouble, for pickup the next morning. And it even made sense that it was Raimbaut; much as he loved a fight, he was slow and easily fooled. I had seen him dead three times before, and there had been other times as well, when I hadn't been there.

Then the banshee cry of the ambulance froze our blood. Raimbaut's medsponder had triggered.

We set him down in the street, backed away, and got no more than a dozen paces before the ambulance dove in from directly overhead in a thunder of reversed impellers, lowered the springer box over him, and sprang him to the emergency room. The impellers flipped to forward with a click and a whine, and the little robot, for all the world like a cylindrical tank on top of a coffin, lifted slowly and flew away. In the pavement where it had been there was a rectangular depression, two meters long by one wide, a centimeter deep.

By the time we got inside and commed the hospital's infocess, they knew. At the bottom of the report, beneath all the aintellect's terse notes about liver and kidney damage, and hysterical distortion of the heart, someone human had noted "one shock too many."

* * *

The burial took forever. His parents didn't show for it, and that was the best thing that happened.

Raimbaut babbled all the way through his funeral, too. His will named me as recipient, so I had struggled through carrying his body up the mountain, along with Marcabru, Aimeric, David, Johanne, and Rufeu, with the added difficulty of pain from the fresh scar where his psypyx had been implanted in the back of my neck.

Raimbaut watched through my eyes as we lowered his naked corpse onto its bed of roses at the bottom of the grave the nanos had shaped in the raw granite of Montanha Valor.

Each *donzelha* present climbed down and kissed the corpse, rubbing her face on his to anoint him with their tears. There were a lot of *donzelhas*—which surprised Raimbaut so much that he couldn't stop talking about it in my head.

Garsenda made a truly spectacular show of her grief, though she'd known Raimbaut only through me, and not well. Raimbaut appreciated it, but I was embarrassed.

Bieris, who had known him longest of any *donzelha*, was oddly quiet and restrained in the grave, but when she climbed out her face was drenched with weeping.

Then, as each of the jovents nicked a thumb to drop blood on Raimbaut's body, Aimeric sang the *Canso de Fis de Jovent*, perhaps the great masterpiece of Nou Occitan verse. Written by Guilhem-Arnaud Montanier in 2611, first sung at his funeral a year later, for two centuries it has been what we buried our young, brave, and beautiful to—under normal circumstances it brought tears to my eyes, and now it tore my heart like a claw.

Guilhem-Arnaut himself had said that all four possible meanings (*fis* means either death or end, and *jovent* either a young man or the time of first manhood) were equally intended, and there is nothing in the song to make one choose between them; my mind skipped wildly from one idea to the next, while Raimbaut marvelled at the quantities of roses and girls.

At last, when it was over, we walked the six kilometers back in silence. Even Raimbaut was quiet.

It had been hard and heavy going up with the body, but this was worse.

"Are you still there?" I subvoked to Raimbaut.

"Still here." His voice was more tired and mechanical than it had been, and my heart sank with what that portended, but he did say, "Burial was nice. You're all very kind. Thank you."

"Raimbaut thanks you all," I said. Everyone turned and bowed gravely toward me, so he could see through my eyes.

"Where am I? I must be dead!" his voice cried in my head. "Deu, deu, this is Montanha Valor, but I can't remember the funeral! Giraut, were we there?"

"*Ja, ja,* yes, Raimbaut, we were there." I subvoked so hard that Garsenda, beside me, heard the grunts in my throat and stared at me until Bieris drew her away. "Reach for the emblok, try to feel it through me," I told him. "Your memory will be in the emblok."

It was no use, then or any time later. Only a rare mind can continue after losing its body. Like most, he could not maintain contact with the emblok that would give him short-term memory, or the geeblok that would allow him his emotions, though each was a scant centimeter away from where he crouched in his psypyx at the base of my skull.

Days passed and he forgot his death, and then that we had ever been at Pertz's Tavern, for he could not recover what he downloaded.

And as my emotions separated again from his, and he was increasingly unable to reach his geeblok, he felt colder and colder in my mind. His liquid helium whisper raved on endlessly, trying to remember itself, trying to wake up from the bad dream it thought it was in.

After two more weeks—about eleven and a half standays— they said there was no hope, and took the psypyx, emblok, and geeblok off me. Raimbaut sleeps now in Eternity Hall in Nou Occitan, like so many others, waiting for some advance of technology to bring his consciousness, memories, and emotions together again.

The good-bye had taken so long, and so little of him was

left at the end of it, that I felt nothing when they removed him.

TWO

Marcabru and Yseut had some appointment they were very secretive about, so only Aimeric, Bieris, Garsenda, and I went to the South Pole that day. Because it was so late in the summer, we made only a day trip of it, springing there right after breakfast to walk the six km to the observation point. At this season Arcturus was very low in the sky as it wheeled around the horizon, its red-orange light glinting off the huge pipelines that ran up to feed the distant mountain glaciers that in turn fed the Great Polar River.

"Those must really be a nuisance to a painter," I said to Bieris. "You can't paint what the landscape really looks like because it's not done yet, and you can't even see what it looks like right now because all those pipes are in the way."

She sighed. "I know. And they expect it to be at least another hundred stanyears before Totzmare is warm enough to make enough rain fall here. Not to mention that several of the bamboos and annual willows they'll be planting in the river bottom aren't out of the design stage yet, so all I have of those is 'artist's conceptions.' And since the 'artist' is an aintellect, their conceptions are really flat and dull. But all anyone wants to see is what Wilson will look like when it's done. By the time it really looks that way, people will be bored with it."

That was a strange remark to make, especially for an artist, but this was a strange trip, anyway. My only strong reason to come had been so that Raimbaut could see this, but they had taken him off me two days before, and since he had no memory, why should he have seen it, even if he could?

By then, though, Aimeric had gotten Garsenda and maybe even Bieris infected with the idea, so I had to go too. Bieris's bush-sense was as good as mine, we'd been on most of the same trips, but of course they would not listen to a *donzelha*, and it was too dangerous this time of year for them to be in Terraust without someone who could tell them what to do in an emergency.

The tower at the observation point was made to look like a weathered old castle keep, with no mortar in the joints between its granite blocks. It must have had internal pinning, to have held together through several grassfires, freezes, burials in snow, floods, and thaws.

Obviously I was in a sour mood if Bieris had infected me with that tendency of hers to wonder how things were made instead of just appreciating their beauty.

As we climbed the stone steps, it surprised me how hot the tower was to the touch. Aimeric winced away when he brushed a shoulder against it. "Six stanyears of continuous sun will do that, I guess," he said. "Think what it must be like when the sun first comes up!"

"You're welcome to find out for yourself," I said, "and then you can write and tell me about it."

He laughed. "Don't forget I grew up in Caledony. I know all about cold—it's all they have on Nansen."

It was just a passing remark, but it did startle me; Aimeric so rarely referred to his origins, and almost never spoke of his home culture. That and his age were the two topics he would never discuss.

When we reached the top, the sun was almost directly behind us as we looked down into the river valley. Broken by irregular cliffs, the wide steps of the valley slope were brown with dry grass in the sunlight; Arcturus was a deep-maroon clot in the thin blood of the sky, for the fires were already burning in many parts of Terraust. To our right, the pipelines and glaciers sparkled; to our left, the plains reached into the valley, a flat intrusion that made a steep cliff facing us.

We put on distance glasses and adjusted them. "There," Aimeric said, "by that sharp bend—"

I focused in on it. Far below us, there were a few hundred aurocs-de-mer at the water's edge, wading in.

As I watched them, they would suddenly drop into the water, heads almost submerging as their legs folded up, then swim strongly and smoothly as their flippers extended. With so many entering the water, the river rose almost to its normal midseason depth.

But not quite far enough. "Look downstream," Garsenda breathed.

In one wide, shallow place, they were floundering, at least a thousand of them. The more fortunate ones on the edges extended their legs and ran to deeper stretches downstream; those in the middle were mired hopelessly, some of them already drowned and forming an impassable barrier.

"What will happen to them?" Garsenda whispered to me.

"The lucky ones will drown. The weak ones will starve. And in a couple of weeks at most the fires will finish the rest." With the sky already red-brown with smoke, her question had been stupid.

"I wish we hadn't seen this part of it."

I did too, and put an arm around her, sorry I had spoken so cruelly. I noticed a couple of odd scars when her hair pulled back from her ear, and was going to ask about them, but then my attention was taken up with Aimeric and Bieris.

They were also watching the doomed herd, still as statues behind the masks of their distance glasses. A fine film of soot covered their cheeks; it was streaked with pale tear-trails.

I looked from them to the plains, and down into the valley again, and felt Garsenda's warm body against mine—our puny lives in the middle of the annual death of a continent—and was about to start making a song about the grandeur and horror of everything when suddenly we all jumped at loud hooting that erupted behind us.

There on the level ground behind the observation tower was a retriever, just landing. Some aintellect somewhere in the bureaucracy had decided we were about to be in too much danger, and dispatched it.

We hurried down from the tower—delaying your own rescue is very bad form, aside from being a misdemeanor—and as we ran to the retriever, we could see flames and smoke on the horizon behind it. The stranded aurocs-de-mer below us would burn, not starve.

We stepped through the springer entrance on the side of the retriever and sprang into the huge, cold, echoing Reception Concourse of Central Rescue.

To judge from the many people in hiking clothes, fire must have been spreading wildly all over Terraust that day. Some people in mountain gear, a shivering couple in bathing suits, and one extremely irritated-looking diver completed the crowd in the nearly empty concourse.

"Amazing," I said sarcastically. I really would have liked to have seen the fires, at least a little, before the aintellect yanked us out, and no doubt if I filed an appeal they'd give me cash compensation—but they couldn't give me back the sight of the fires. "This place was only built in the six stanyears since we got springers, and already it's the ugliest building on Wilson."

Garsenda giggled and stopped to pick something up; it was a strange little object, a metal ball with pointed spikes of irregular sizes coming off it.

"What's that?" I asked.

"Just an earring." She dropped it in my hand; it pricked me, its little points needle-sharp.

It seemed strange again, somehow. I'd never known anyone with pierced ears. Moreover it was odd she hadn't told me. Your *entendedora* is supposed to tell you everything. And the little thing gleaming in my hand looked more like a tiny weapon or instrument of torture, not like any of the recognized traditional styles. Primitive, even brutal—

"Look," Aimeric said. "The springer is opening to the Main Station in the Quartier des Jovents in six minutes." He pointed at the board. "It says we spring from Entrance E-7. Where is that?"

Bieris checked one of the maps and snorted. "Other end of the concourse, naturally. We'd better run."

We made it, barely. After everything that had happened, I wanted Garsenda to come up to my place, but she said she had things to do. I watched her till she turned the corner, all that long dark hair swaying like a horse's tail, brushing the top of her full long skirts. It gave me an idea for a song, so I went upstairs to work on that.

That night for some perverse reason the four of us, plus Marcabru and Yseut, all met at Pertz's to drink. It was thirty nights, just about twenty-five standays, since the night Raimbaut had died.

"Forecast says the Dark will start within a week," Marcabru said. He raised his glass. *"Raimbaut: que valor, que enseingnamen, que merce."* We all drank to him, and I wished again I was still wearing his psypyx, so that this could be in his emblok whenever the technology to bring him back arrived.

The amber glow of the artificial lights made all the colors painfully vivid, like a travel-vu from a G-star system. Most Occitans kept the lights in their homes tuned far toward red, the way the outside light was, but old Pertz was red-green color-blind and would never have seen any color at all if he did, or so he said.

"May every Interstellar die," Marcabru said. "After all those centuries of isolation—with the greatest adventure of all time beginning, and the Thousand Cultures suddenly linked again—the only thing it occurs to the youth of Occitan to do is to dress like petty clerks from Earth, forget every bit of their own culture and history, imitate the lowest forms that come from Earth—did you know that kid you killed was the leading artist in his crowd, Giraut?"

"At *what?*"

"He's made a couple of hundred pornographic vus and a dozen or so short subjects. All featuring him beating up and degrading young girls. That's the hot thing among them right now—Interstellar boys walk girls on leashes, or have them wear jewelry that makes them bleed. All clear-cut imitations of Earth sadoporn, completely outside the Charter—as are those stupid jackboot swagger-suits, if you ask me. But when people file charges that it violates the Nou Occitan Cultural Charter, the Interstellars claim it's a legitimate protest against the tradition of *finamor*, and go running to the Embassy to have their rights protected."

"Why do the girls *do* it?" I asked.

"Who knows? It's fashionable. And since when has a true Occitan ever claimed to understand a *donzelha*? We just worship them—as we're meant to do." He swallowed the rest of his glass at a gulp. "Anyway, they murdered Raimbaut. Reason enough to hate them."

I glanced around the table. Aimeric was coolly nodding agreement. Yseut was just leaning on Marc's arm, smiling dreamily as she thought about whatever it is a beautiful *trobadora* thinks about. Bieris seemed very sad, even upset, but I didn't see any more reason for that than for Yseut's smile. But then, who ever claimed to understand a *donzelha*, as Marcabru had said?

Garsenda was slowly stroking my leg under the table; I certainly understood that.

I hated Interstellars too, but I didn't feel like making a speech just then, and besides it was beginning to feel irrelevant. Garsenda was about as young as you ever saw an Oldstyle (to use the ugly Interstellar word for jovents who respected tradition) anymore. All the younger people were going Interstellar; in a few years, when people my age were no longer jovents, all of jovent society, the whole Quartier, would be Interstellar. It seemed such a crime, but there was clearly no holding it back.

My heart stopped for a moment. I was looking into Raimbaut's eyes, and he was smiling.

Then I realized. Old Pertz had added a vu of Raimbaut to the Wall of Honor, along with all the other permanently dead regulars. The Wall itself was real wood—still very rare and expensive, though our culture had been designed to live on the heavily forested island that Nou Occitan would eventually be, and to exploit the forests still being designed for Wilson's polar continents. "Guilhem-Arnaut never saw a mature forest. Maybe not any forest, ever," I said.

Marcabru started to make some joke, but Aimeric had followed my gaze and stopped him with a touch of the hand.

They all turned and looked, then, seeing Raimbaut and the whole Wall of Honor. It was about a fifteen-second vu of him; I don't know where Pertz got it from. Raimbaut stared forward seriously, broke into a smile, looked off to the side, seemed to hear something that troubled him, and stared forward seriously, over and over again.

I realized they were all waiting for me to explain what I had said. Garsenda was smiling, arching an eyebrow at me in the expectation that I would honor our *finamor* with some clever saying.

"Well," I began slowly, "I guess it was just the thought that the terraforming robots didn't start working this planet till 2355 or so, thirty years ahead of the culture getting here, and theoretically full terraformation won't be complete until about 3200, so we're only a little past halfway through, right? That means all this time, while we've tried to preserve the Occitan tradition that was created by the culture's authors and shipped along in the ship's libraries, the planet's actually been growing and changing. A lot of what we've done has been in anticipation of things that didn't exist yet. Outside of a botanical garden, Guilhem-Arnaut probably never saw a tree as tall as himself. So when the *Canso de Fis de Jovent* talks about the spring leaves arching over the Riba Lyones—"

"He never actually saw it!" Marcabru seemed more struck with the idea than I was. "But, *m'es vis*, his description of it is so perfect it never occurred to me he hadn't seen it."

Aimeric spoke softly. "I think Giraut means that we have all learned to see it the way we do from Guilhem-Arnaut's poem. The world is the way it is only because we've learned to see it that way. 'Terraust's ancient plain' was still under permanent ice less than five hundred years ago, and the 'waves, waves, waves / Ceaselessly beating time / Even as grandfather's little boat—' probably thawed out only a couple of Wilson-years before Guilhem-Arnaut's grandfather's grandfather got here."

I nodded. "We still do it. I've written ballads set in the forests of the Serras Verz—and I was on the first tree-planting crew there when I was seventeen. Right now there's probably not one waist-high conifer, and they probably won't plant the oak and ash that I talk about in the song for another hundred years."

It all seemed very strange. Raimbaut, of course, went right on looking at us very seriously, then smiling, then growing serious again, as he would forever in the vu.

We all poured another glass and drank some more, and agreed the vu didn't do Raimbaut justice—but none of us had a vu of him, so we couldn't offer to replace it. We drank steadily, not yet drunk but meaning to get there, and we were just about to get up and go to some place that would not drown us in melancholy, when the King walked in and headed for our table.

That stanyear it was Bertran VIII, a quietly fussy little professor of esthetics whom I knew slightly through my father. The Prime Minister, who looked much better than the King, but just as out of place in the ancient-style *suit-biz*, came right behind him.

This was stranger than anything I had seen in a long time —nobility, and a high official, walking into Pertz's, dressed as if for a Court function.

"Aimeric de Sanha Marsao?" the King asked.

"That's me." Aimeric rose and bowed. The rest of us, suddenly recovering our manners, leapt to our feet, along with practically everyone else in Pertz's. The King nodded gravely, all around, and then came forward to speak to Aimeric, gesturing for everyone to sit.

"I would have sent a messenger with this *semosta*, but with the Dark coming on they're all at home. I'm afraid I'm here to tell you you're drafted, into Special Services, and we have to talk tonight."

I was beginning to wonder when this hallucination had started. Aimeric was what we called a *tostemz-jovent: puer aeturnus* or a Peter Pan. Normally after the first couple of times the Lottery summons you into public service, which will be by the time you're twenty-five or so stanyears old, you're ready to move out of the Quartier de Jovents and up into the main part of the city, to marry, settle down, take up some serious course of study or life-project. I was twenty-two

and had already been half-consciously shopping for a small
house up there. But Aimeric had been through four bouts of
service, one just sub-Cabinet, and had always come back to
the Quartier. He was about thirty-five physically, in his forties
if you counted the years he'd spent in suspended animation
on his way here, and he had never shown the slightest interest
in growing up; he had been my crazy jovent uncle when I
was a child and now he was just one more of my jovent com-
panions.

Furthermore, Special Services are emergency non-peerage
appointments, not chosen by lot but by qualification—crisis
appointments when no one else will do—not exactly a job
you offer to an overage jovent.

But despite all the excellent reasons that this could not be
happening, it was anyway.

Oddly, the only part that made any sense was the King
having to hand-deliver his own *semosta*. When the Dark blew
in from the South Pole, and the skies went black with smoke
for two to three weeks, everyone preferred to be at home in
his own digs—and the Dark was due within a few days.

You don't dodge a *semosta*, either, so we all followed
along, Aimeric because he had to and the rest of us because
Nou Occitan law allows any citizen to witness any government transaction, and we were all dying of curiosity.

The King indicated we were going to the nearest springer
station, perhaps half a km away, and we walked there in silence. I kept trying to figure out what could possibly be going
on.

As we all crowded into the springer booth, the King said,
"I should warn all of you we're going to the springer at the
Embassy. Try not to be startled by the light."

He pushed the go button and yellow light blasted into our
faces, hot on the skin and stabbing to the eyes.

Some nervous squeaking Embassy person—my eyes did
not adjust before he was gone—guided us to the conference
room, where, mercifully, someone had thought to tune the
lights to Occitan levels.

We all drew a breath for a moment, taking in the real

wooden furniture (grain too wavy to be tankgrown) and the walls covered with vus from all over the Thousand Cultures; some of them seemed to be quite long, several minutes at least.

Garsenda moved forward—only then did I realize she had been pressed back against me—and stood in the hand-on-the-hip pose she used to tell people she was not impressed, especially when she was.

The Ambassador from the Human Council Office had gray hair and a deeply lined face; she wore a plain black uniform, not much different from the Interstellar one. It looked uncomfortable. I wondered how much choice they allowed her in her clothing, and for that matter in her cosmetic surgery. It seemed very strange to me that, knowing our local customs, they had chosen to be represented by a woman—and not just a woman, but an older and bluntly plain one.

Her first official action was to order coffee for everyone; it came in just a moment, and there was an alcohol-scrubber tablet discreetly in the saucer. I tossed mine in, and noticed that everyone else did the same.

She gained some points in grace by not asking who all these extra people were, but I suppose after six years she knew our ways.

"Please forgive my clumsiness," she said, "but to make sure—the Aimeric de Sanha Marsao I have here is the one who was born in Utilitopia, Caledony, on Nansen?"

"The former Ambrose Carruthers at your service," Aimeric said, with a little hand-flourish. His smile looked fake; the joke, such as it was, seemed intended to fall flat, as if he wanted to indicate his attitude but not to allow them to be amused by it.

I thought I saw the Ambassador stifle a very mannish grin. The PM visibly winced and the King blinked hard.

"Good," she said. "Let me explain very briefly why we've interrupted your evening. We have just made our first official springer contact with your home culture—apparently after they received the radio directions, it took them about a year to decide to do it, but Caledony now has a springer. Now, you may recall that when the first springer was built here, a few years ago, Castellhoza de Sanha Agnes and Azalais Cormagne returned from Lange to assist in the social transitions—because they had fourteen years' experience with the Springer Changes there, and they were native here. They worked for your government for a stanyear or so, mostly to help you get through the Connect Depression and the growth explosion that followed it."

As she had spoken, I had been watching Aimeric. It seemed as if another man had settled into his body—a serious, intense, and restless older man—and I had the sudden thought that those of us who had only seen him in the Quartier might not have seen all of him. "I worked with Castellhoza. So that's what you want me to do? Go to Caledony and do the same thing for them? I assume you're sending someone to St. Michael as well, at least as soon as their springer opens?"

"Yes—in fact, we're sending Yevan Petravich through the springer to Utilitopia, and then he'll catch the suborbital over to St. Michael from there. Apparently their springer won't be done for another few months."

Aimeric nodded emphatically. "Yevan's a good person for the job. He came here as a missionary, and he hasn't been happy at his lack of converts—he must be overjoyed to be returning to his Mother Church in Novarkhangel." He drew a long breath and looked around. The pause stretched out until it seemed it had to tear. Bieris was staring at him as if she'd never seen him before. Marcabru and I were looking at each other, as if one of us would have something to say. The PM had a funny, twisted smile, but the King and the Ambassador were impassive.

Finally Aimeric got up and walked over to the coffee pot, pouring himself another cup. "It's different for me, you know. Very different from Yevan's situation. My whole reason for leaving Nansen . . . well, I was eighteen then, and it's been what—eighteen stanyears of experience, twenty-five stanyears by the clock? a long time anyway—my reason for leaving was that the trip was one-way. Certainly I came, in a large part, because I loved everything I had ever read or seen about the culture of Nou Occitan, and the planet Wilson. But what I loved best about it—I confess this, *companho*—was that Nou Occitan was not Caledony and it was not on Nansen.

"So before we talk further at all—*must* it be me? Forty-two of us from Caledony survived the voyage, and almost all of us were economists—it was just about the only occupation Caledony exported. Isn't there anyone who *wants* to go back?"

The PM nodded and cleared his throat. "Eighteen have suicided since. Sixteen are married with young children, and . . . well, you would understand why I would not send a family with growing children to Caledony—"

"That's wise and humane," Aimeric said. "So eight are left."

"Three are severely ill emotionally," the PM said. "Six years in the tank, and six years in the tight confines of the ship, and then being released into a society that's much freer than the one you grew up in—not everyone can deal with that. Same reason there are so many suicides, I suppose. Of the five remaining, you're the only one with experience in either economics or government, and you're one of three without a serious criminal conviction."

Aimeric sighed. "So it's me or no one?"

The Ambassador shrugged. "We could send people from the Interstellar Coordination Corps—"

"I'll go," Aimeric said.

The Ambassador glared at him. "Those are highly trained people, and while we'd certainly like to have you, I'm sure that—"

"You've *got* to have somebody who knows Caledony," Aimeric said, bluntly. "Your bureaucrats had enough trouble here, where things are pretty open and straightforward, with accepting ordinary cultural differences—"

"Well, the ICC personnel at that time all came from Earth, Dunant, Passy, and Ducommon—" The Ambassador sounded unhappy. "That's changed a little—"

"The ICC people who tried so hard to make a mess here have all been promoted since, so they have even more power," Aimeric said. "And an interest in teaching the true way to the natives does not usually weaken with time. And let me promise you—Caledons will not tolerate one tenth of what Occitans will." He looked at the wall for a moment, thinking hard, and finally said. "No, you were right to ask. And I have to go." Then a little light came into his eyes, and he said, "Who's next in line after me?"

"Faith McSweeney."

I didn't know her, but it seemed to decide Aimeric. "I assume I depart from here? How soon?"

The three of them looked at each other and nodded slowly; for the first time I realize this had also been Aimeric's interview for the job, and that had he wanted to, he could easily have persuaded them he was the wrong man. His choosing to do this seemed very unlike him—but so did everything he had done and said since the King had walked into Pertz's Tavern.

"Departure is from here, yes," the Ambassador said. "Seventeen o'clock tomorrow—I know that's fast, but the sooner we can get you there the better from the standpoint of the Council of Humanity's relations with the Caledon government. Will that be all right?"

Aimeric laughed, the first time I had heard him do so in hours now. "*Ja, ja,* certainly!" He looked directly at the PM and said, "Remember, I run with the jovents, and there's nothing of any importance I would be doing."

The Ambassador seemed baffled, but went on. "Try not to eat or drink in the last three hours before you spring, and you might want to avoid alcohol tomorrow. Apparently springing across a difference of more than a percent or so in gravity upsets many people's stomachs. Your baggage allowance is twenty-five tonnes, so if you like we can just ship everything in your digs."

"That would be good—I've got to remember to pick up my laundry and return everything I've borrowed." He looked around the room slowly. "If that's all, then obviously I have a lot to get done. So, *companho*—"

"There is one more thing," the Ambassador said, "and it's possibly relevant to your friends. In the last few years, allowances for people doing this sort of work have gotten much more generous. You may take with you, as assistants, personal aides, or whatever you wish to call them, up to eight friends or relatives." The Ambassador's eyes twinkled, and despite her being an official, and not at all pretty, I liked her. "Supposedly that will help preserve your sanity."

"Clearly you haven't really looked at these friends of mine," Aimeric said. "Preserving my sanity is not at all what I keep them around for." There was a strange sad warmth in his eyes as he looked around the room again.

THREE

We parted in haste at the springer station in the Quartier de Jovents; Aimeric had a lot of comming to do, and the rest of us had to think.

I went home briefly and picked up my lute, playing idly as I considered.

If I went—I'd have two years in another system, and not many people had that, since stepping through an offplanet springer was still so expensive. Of course, the expense was just the problem—the Council of Humanity kept the price directly proportional to energy cost, but since that depended on the square of the gravitational potential traversed, and a simple ski lift of 750 meters cost as much as a beer, it seemed likely that going from orbit around one giant star to another, six and a half light-years away, would add up to a lot of beer. No, it was a real commitment—if I didn't like it, I would have to serve out my time anyway to get my free ride back, because I couldn't possibly afford to buy passage.

On the other hand, it would give me a highly unusual service record, many new things to see . . . romance and adventure, no matter how dull Aimeric claimed his homeworld was.

And then again—the Dark would be a time to quietly read and think and compose, and following it would come the great explosion of Northern Spring. While Terraust's blackened lands were covered by meters-thick snow, the rivers and freshwater seas of Terrbori would fill to flood with snowmelt, thundershowers would roar up its fjords and canyons, and its meadows would explode into grass and flowers.

Polar bamboo would burst up even before the soot-darkened snow could melt, hurrying to begin its climb to ten full meters before the Northern Autumn's fire could destroy it again.

At least I would see Northern Summer—surely I would be back before three years were out.

But I would miss Northern Spring, and I could only recall one of them. With its twelve-stanyear year, Wilson makes a homebody of you—a lucky person might see eight of each season, so missing one was not to be done lightly.

Also, there was my own career. I was, I had to admit, only adequate as either composer or poet, but my performances of other people's work were being very enthusiastically received—non-jovents were coming down to the Quartier to see me perform. The next two or three years could prove critical in gaining a high place among the joventry, and, though the doings of jovents weren't *supposed* to matter, when jovents hung up their epees, moved to the more regulated parts of town, and settled into the kind of quiet life that my parents led, they tended to keep their friendships and loyalties. A hero among the jovents was likely to be first in line when the best appointed positions in art, politics, or business were being handed out.

Finally, two people weighed in the balance, now that Raimbaut was dead and his psypyx stored: Marcabru, my best friend, and Garsenda, my *entendedora*, focus of my *finamor* and inspiration to my art. Surely no real Occitan could be expected to leave his mistress? Except, of course, out of loyalty to his friends . . .

The mere thought of separation from either Marcabru or Garsenda seemed unbearable, and for the moment that fact made my decision for me. All for one, and one for all. Of course, if they disagreed with each other, then I would have to make up my own mind.

It did not seem possible that my luck could be bad enough for them to disagree.

Marcabru first, I thought, since I could com him. Talking to your *entendedora* on the com is hopelessly *ne gens*, so I would have to go to Garsenda's place in person.

He had an answer, a definite one. "Giraut, I know just how you feel. Part of me is dying to go, too, but I've got something wonderful here in Noupeitau—I was going to announce it at midnight, but then we got shanghaied out of Pertz's and all this stuff with Aimeric's appointment came up. You know next stanyear is a Variety Year for the monarchy?"

"*Ja*, I occasionally com up the news. When I'm stuck in the dentist's office or something. So what?"

"They've picked the variation and the finalists. The announcement will be out in a few hours. Instead of the usual boring middle-aged fart with a bunch of scientific papers or public service awards, it's to be a *donzelha*. And among the finalists—"

I guessed. "Yseut! Marcabru, that's wonderful. Of course you're right—you couldn't possibly go!"

Images dance through my head—a young poet-queen, my best friend her Consort, thus surely a term-peerage for me and very likely an appointment to the Court for Garsenda. These were the kinds of dreams you usually waited twenty years for, and here was the chance to have them while we were young enough to enjoy them.

"With so much that could happen—" I said, and then stopped myself from saying something sure to offend him.

He laughed, having read my mind. "You're right, of course. Even if it isn't Yseut, to have it be one of our generation, a *donzelha* to give the Palace some grace and style— god, it will be exciting to be alive!"

"*Ja, ja, ja!* I'm going to talk to Garsenda now. Maybe you

and I can get together later, and perhaps even go say good-bye to Aimeric. Oh, won't he be furious when he finds out he's going to miss all of this!"

"Let's plan on it," Marcabru said, grinning at me. "Seeing him off, I mean, *and* making him furious. And now, Giraut, if you don't mind, you did com me less than an hour after my *entendedora* and I got home—" He let the com wideangle a little to show me he was not wearing any shirt, and continued to widen it down his naked torso.

"Of course!" I waved a mock salute and turned off the link.

Pausing only to throw on my best cape and pull on my best boots, I sprinted down the winding stairs, ran all the way through five blocks of narrow, winding streets, crowded even two hours before dawn with vendors, pushing and shoving my way through like a properly love-crazed jovent, and raced up the stairs to Garsenda's place.

She wasn't home.

I pulled out my com and called a location on her. She was at Entrepot, which was strictly an Interstellar hangout.

Part of the normal, even essential, stupidity of being a jovent is that you don't always catch on very quickly. One part of my mind remembered the number of times in the past few weeks when she'd been unaccountably missing (of course I hadn't called locations on her then because it hadn't been urgent, and to do so would have been a mark of distrust). Another part reminded me of that weird, ear-scarring jewelry. Still another whispered that Garsenda was very young, even for eighteen, and was always the first one onto any trend or fashion . . .

And everything else just shouted them down and headed me for Entrepot, as quickly as I could go while keeping any dignity.

It took me half an hour to walk there. When I got there I called another com and it said she was in a back room, so I followed the walkways around the dance/fight floor, enduring the catcalls and kissy-noises and shouts of "Grandpa wears a dress!" from the young Interstellars hanging on the railings, and headed for that room. Some part of me insisted on knowing.

Garsenda had always been attracted to the arts—or rather to artists. And in just that one way, the Interstellars were true Occitans—they valued their artists. So naturally when she decided to start climbing the other social ladder behind my back, she had joined their equivalent of the arts scene.

Which is why when I opened the door, there were three cameras running (one automatically focused on me as I stood there). What they were filming was Garsenda, wearing thigh-high spikeheeled boots and nothing else, her head thrown back in a pose of ecstasy while a boy crouched in front of her, sucking one nipple and clamping the other with what looked like a bright orange giant pair of pliers out of some cartoon. Neither of them noticed me, so I closed the door and left. Probably she'd recognize me in the shots from the third camera, and that would be enough.

I wasn't sure, and hadn't wanted to check, but I thought the boy might have been one of the ones who fought us the night Raimbaut died.

On my way out, I decided someone had insulted me. I drew and cut him down without any warning, a hard slash across the throat. Technically you're entitled to do that. It didn't make me feel any better, so I used my neuroducer to stab one I thought had made a face at me, right in the kidneys, and sneaked a very real kick to his head as he fell. Even that didn't offend his friends enough to overcome their terror (I suppose I must have looked pretty alarming in that mood) so I cut down two more of the cowards, but then the rest fled, and to pursue them would have been *ne gens*, so I had to leave without any sort of brawl to either work out my rage or put me into the hospital.

Striding into the street, I tried to formulate some plan of action. In the days before the springer had brought all its changes, just six stanyears back, my choices would have been fairly simple: I could kill myself, or wait and apply to leave on one of the ships that departed every ten stanyears or so. Nowadays there were no more ships. For most people, that left suicide—but not for me, I realized. I commed Aimeric. I had walked just six blocks from Entrepot.

He said I was welcome to come, and even seemed grateful. He gave me another code to com.

At that number, I arranged to have everything in my apartment shipped, my accounts liquidated to pay my bills, and that sort of thing. They told me I wouldn't need to do anything—I could just walk out of my apartment, go to the Embassy, and depart the next day. They would even pick up my laundry. They reminded me it would be at seventeen o'clock.

I thanked them, set the alarm on my wrist unit for sixteen o'clock (enough time for an anti-alcohol tab to straighten me back out), went to the tavern nearest the Embassy, and worked hard on getting drunk all that morning and afternoon. I swallowed the pill on time, and got to the Embassy okay. Apparently to make sure, they gave me a huge anti-alcohol injection—whatever it had against alcohol, it had no quarrel with hangovers—scrubbed me up, and generally made me feel like a dirty kitten pinned down by its mother.

Along the way I babbled out a confession to Aimeric and Bieris about what had happened. Bieris kept telling me Garsenda was just a kid having fun, and Aimeric kept telling me I could still get out of this if I wanted to, that all I had to do was say I didn't really want to go.

I shook them off. My head was pounding, the blinding yellow glare of the Embassy lights was making it worse, and now that I was sober I was painfully aware that I hadn't eaten all day. "So I might throw away two stanyears of my life. So what? I *was* just going to kill myself. And at least this will be completely different from Nou Occitan."

"Oh, it will be that," Aimeric agreed.

Bieris bit her lower lip. "Giraut, we've known each other since we were children. Tell me the truth. Is it really between this and killing yourself?"

I was more offended than I'd ever been before. "*Enseingnamen* demands. This is the gravest sort of violation of *finamor*—"

She turned to Aimeric, shaking her head; I noticed that somehow she seemed much older, though she was still the same laughing brown-haired beauty who had been my friend so long. "I think he means it."

Aimeric nodded. "I'm sure he does. We've both known him a long time. So we let him do it?"

"You're not *letting* me do anything," I said. "You issued the invitation honorably, and I want to take it up."

Aimeric sighed and fluffed out his shoulder-length hair. "And I certainly don't want to fight you about it. All right, then, come. You're a bright enough *toszet*, Giraut, when a *donzelha* isn't involved, and I can certainly use you. But I'm warning you one more time—if Caledony is anything like I remember, there are going to be a lot of times when you will wish you had stayed home and killed yourself."

Maybe something in his tone finally got through to me. "How bad can it be? What's discomfort in the face of shattered love?"

He didn't answer, just turned away. I think he was a little disgusted. Bieris gave me one worried, pitying glance and followed Aimeric.

When the time came, we just stepped into the springer as if it were any other springer, this time going from one group of boring Embassy people to another. There was a solid shove on the soles of my feet, and a downward tug on the rest of my body, as the gravity increased about eight percent from Wilson to Nansen, but otherwise I might only have stepped into the next room.

Aimeric staggered as if he'd been punched in the stomach. I actually had to catch Bieris, who retched a couple of times before regaining her composure. From the way they looked at my apparent immunity to springer sickness, I think they were wishing I had stayed home and killed myself.

"Welcome to Caledony," a tall, older man said. "I'm Ambassador Shan. Which of you is Ambrose Carruthers?"

"If anyone were, it would be me, but I use my Occitan name of Aimeric de Sanha Marsao. This is Bieris Real, and Giraut Leones, my personal assistants."

Shan nodded. "I'm delighted to meet you. I'm afraid staff and space are in *very* short supply here—we just grew this building in the last forty-eight hours and there's much, much more left to do, so we're sending you directly to your new homes, and we'll send your baggage after you as soon as it arrives. I'm sorry we've nothing to offer in the way of hospitality, but our talks with the government of Caledony regarding the supply of the Embassy have stymied completely."

"Meaning either they want to charge you for it, or they want you to work for it," Aimeric said.

The Ambassador nodded. "I was hoping that what they were saying was just a polite form, and whatever they really wanted would emerge from the discussion. But they really do mean that?"

"They sure do. Try not to be surprised if they tip you when the deal is done, either. Anything more than two hundred utils is excessive and might be a bribe."

"I can see you'll be invaluable here."

"In Caledony, nothing is invaluable. It's the one place in the Thousand Cultures where everything, absolutely everything, has a known value." Aimeric smiled when he said it. Shan laughed and nodded. That left Bieris and me completely mystified.

We went into the next room, where some Embassy flunkies gave us knee-length, insulated parkas with transparent facemasks. That was some warning, I suppose, but nothing could really prepare anyone for what was outside.

It was like walking into a dark cryogenic windtunnel. Water sprayed my beard and mustache and froze instantly.

I realized what the mask must be for, and pulled it down, but not before getting two searing-cold chlorine-reeking lungfuls of air. The wind shoved on my chest like the end of a post.

"Don't worry, *companho*," Aimeric shouted to us over the moaning booms of the wind. "It's just we've arrived during Morning Storm. It gets much nicer toward afternoon!"

I didn't see how it could get any worse, and I had done a lot of skiing back home in the North Polar Range.

"How much chlorine is in the air?" I shouted.

"Plenty, right now. The Morning Storm is salty from what blows off the bay. This must be our ride coming up now on the cat."

A "cat" had to be the big treaded tractor now approaching, its cab lights reflecting off the low dark buildings. "Where is everyone?" Bieris shouted. I could barely hear her.

"Inside! They aren't crazy! They'll come out when this lifts, in another half-hour of so."

She shouted something, and then repeated it in a near-scream. "I meant why are there no lights in the middle of a city?"

"Why turn on a light when nobody's out? And why have windows when there's nothing to see?" Aimeric was shouting but he didn't sound interested; it must be one of those things that would be obvious later.

The cat came up then, and I thought I knew why it had that name; all the little maglev lifters that kept its treads moving were humming and whining at different pitches, and the wind was whistling through the centimeters between the treads and the lifters. The total effect was like the wail of a gigantic cat hurled into the deepest pit of hell.

We climbed up the steps that extended down from the cab, and the outer door swung open. (I was quickly to learn that every entrance on Nansen had two doors, and that the local epitome of *ne gens* was to hold both open. It was almost the only thing Caledons and St. Michaelians agreed on.) We crowded into the cat's little heatlock. Aimeric closed the door behind us. The inner door opened.

Aimeric paid the driver. I was startled by that, and Bieris was too—she glanced at me as we shucked off the heavy coats.

Then Aimeric roared with laughter and threw his arms around the driver. "By god, Bruce!"

"Yap. Really afraid you wouldn't remember me."

"Hah! You're the first good piece of news in a while." He introduced us to the older man, who it turned out he'd been a student with.

It took me a moment to realize that Bruce hadn't been one of Aimeric's teachers. Aimeric's six-and-a-half years in suspended animation weren't all of it, by any means—Bruce's skin had a strange, leathery quality and was spotted with brown flecks, and his hair, where not grayed, seemed to have been erratically bleached to a pale flatness. I wondered if the chlorine in the air had done that.

For a long time, they talked about all the things people do when they haven't seen each other for a long time—and since they had many stanyears' catching up to do (it sounded as if their last letters had been before Aimeric had arrived on Wilson), the conversation stretched on for the full hour it took us to get out of Utilitopia. There's no city that big in Nou Occitan—by design, we build new cities after old ones reach a particular size, so that with the slow changes of architectural style, each city will have its distinctive look. Here, they just kept expanding Utilitopia.

As we drove and they talked, the storm dwindled to a freezing rain, and the outside temperature gauge climbed to almost the freezing point. The streetlights came on, revealing that most of the buildings looked like simple concrete boxes with forward-pitched roofs; all churches seemed to be identical, with a very low narthex and very high double-peaked transept, so that they seemed to be about to plunge down into the street like birds of prey.

There were a lot of churches.

Every now and then, a trakcar would glide by on the maglev strips in the streets, its headlight tearing through the fog and suddenly bringing up the color of the buildings—which seemed to be either blue-gray or brownish-red. Though I had grown up riding trakcars, they seemed quaint and old-fashioned to me now; it made me a little sad to think that here too they would no doubt disappear within a year, replaced by springers.

I wondered if they would take out the trakcar strips, or leave them in place; in Noupeitau we had made them into pathways for bicycles, skateboards, and row cars, with brick planters to control access surrounding them—but that did not seem in the spirit of things here.

I had thought that we had been passing through an industrial district, like those in pictures from other cultures who didn't have the common sense to leave that all to robots and put the operations somewhat uninhabited, but when we topped a rise and the fog was briefly up, I could see clearly that the whole city seemed to be made of these concrete blocks.

At last we were out of the city and driving along a road; to my surprise, it was simply scraped rock, the thin soil cut away and the rock smoothed to form a roadbed.

I was about to ask about the primitive look of the road, but then Bruce said, "I guess I ought to ask. Your first letter said Charlie had died."

"Yap." Aimeric said, without volunteering more.

Bruce nodded slowly, just as if Aimeric had told him a great deal. "I haven't been to church in ten years," he said, which seemed to have nothing to do with the subject. "And since you didn't come in as Ambrose—"

Aimeric interrupted. "Wait a second. *You* haven't been to church—?"

Bruce shrugged. "I—well, you know how it went. You and Charlie got to go, but I lost out—there were only two slots on the starship for preachers. And so for a while there I got to resenting God for calling me, and then giving myself the scourge for resenting God. Made me into one of those bone-mean fanatics that always seem to get hired for the backwoods. That was when I wrote the last letters you got from me . . ."

"Yap."

We came to a fork in the road; with a slight rise in the pitch and volume of the hum, a sharp pull to one side, and a wild spray of dust and gravel, the cat turned upward, beginning to climb switchbacks. In the fog, I had no idea what we were headed toward, and without the city lights, it was terribly dark again—visibility couldn't have been more than thirty meters, even in the cat's headlights.

Bruce went on. "Well, after that I got worse for a while. It felt *right* at the time, of course, because if you really think all this stuff is true, then obviously there's no excuse for compromise or even compassion. I had a congregation up by Bentham, and I spent about three years causing all kinds of misery by enforcing every jot and tittle.

"Then one morning . . . I guess it would have been around the time your ship reached Utilitopia . . . something happened. Just one of those things where I had to realize that I was causing, not curing, unhappiness. I went back to my quarters. I prayed for a while—well, a month, actually. And when that didn't work, I quit the job, bought a farm over in Sodom Basin, and I've been there since." We came around a tight turn, and gravel sprayed from under the spinning tracks, making a distant chatter against the bottom of the cat's cabin. There didn't seem to be anything at all, except dark fog far below, under my window. "I had to really lowball the bid to get to pick you up—they wanted someone more doctrinally correct."

"Sodom Basin is a long way away," Aimeric said. "You came a long way out of your way—that must have made it hard to justify your bid."

"Nop. I rationalized it by packaging the contract. I'm your landlord."

Aimeric seemed struck dumb for a moment, then burst into a delighted crow. "Brilliant, Bruce, you haven't lost the touch!"

We came over a rise and down a short, steep drop in the road. For a bowel-yanking instant the headlights pointed down into a seemingly bottomless gorge; then gravel sprayed again and we were running up a ledge on the canyon wall.

Since neither Aimeric nor Bruce was acting like anything unusual was going on, I wasn't going to. I looked away from the window to see how Bieris was taking it, and found her almost on my lap trying to see out the window.

"How far down do you suppose it is?" she whispered.

"*Non sai.* It's a long way though."

"That's the Gouge you're looking into," Bruce said. "It's a

long fjord—the bottom is sea water, almost eighty meters deep. We're probably three thousand meters above that right now, and we're going up to seventy-three hundred to get through Sodom Gap. This whole thing is a big crack in the crust from an asteroid strike."

"An *asteroid* strike?" Bieris leaned forward, toward Bruce.

Alarmingly, he looked away from where the headlights bounced and danced up the narrow road in front of us, and turned to talk to her. "Yap. But don't worry—we're not expecting another one soon. Though this one is recent. Probably less than a thousand stanyears ago. I guess you people didn't come here with much warning about what all you'd find?"

"None at all," I said. "Does it all look like this?"

Bruce roared with laughter, and Aimeric joined him. "A very polite way to voice your concerns, um—Grot?"

"Close. Two syllables—like gear-out."

"Giraut." He got it right that time. "Anyway, it's no wonder you've been so quiet. No, the Council of Rationalizers wants to keep people in Utilitopia, for greater efficiency, so they have a high tax on any activity that could be there and isn't. I wasn't really enthusiastic about farming when I started, but it was the only job that would let me live on the warm side of the Optimal Range. It'll be another two hours till we get across the mountains, but I think after that you'll be pleased with what you see."

"Why do they name it 'Sodom Basin,' if it's pleasant?"

"So those of us who insist on living there will know we're showing an irrational attachment to incorrect values," Bruce said. "We've put ourselves on the road to spiritual destruction." He sounded more tired than angry.

"For those of us with no patience," Bieris said, "just what is this place we're going to?"

Aimeric nodded at her, as if thanking her for the change of subject. "The mountain range that the Gouge cuts into, and Sodom Gap goes through, runs along the eastern coast of Caledony. On the other side is Sodom Basin, a salt-lake basin. It's one of the warmest places on this crazy planet—I'm sure you'll be appalled to know that you're less than half a degree off the equator at the moment.

"What happens is that the Sodom Sea creates a huge heat sink, and because the mountains are high enough to block most of the clouds from blowing in, it gets lots of sun. Keeps the whole valley warm– normally it only goes to freezing for a couple of hours out of each Dark."

"How do you get Darks here? Surely there isn't enough vegetation to burn—"

"Means something different locally," Aimeric explained. "Nansen only has a fourteen-hour day. It's easier to put two of them together than to live on a fourteen-hour schedule. So the day divides into First Light, First Dark, Second Light, and Second Dark. Right now we're about twenty minutes from First Light."

I looked at the dim, glowing fog outside and said "It looks very close to dawn—so where's all the light coming from?"

"The moon just rose," Bruce said.

There was a long awkward silence. I felt stupid, for not having remembered that Nansen had a big, ice-covered close-in moon.

After a while, Bruce asked, "So what prompted either of you to come to Caledony with this old reprobate? Isn't there enough fog and sleet for you anywhere on Wilson?"

Bieris laughed softly. "You could almost say that Aimeric talked me into it."

"I was trying to talk you *out* of it! I said it wouldn't be anything like what you were used to, and you wouldn't be able to do even half of the things we did for amusement in the Quartier." Aimeric sounded really distressed. "There really aren't a lot of people here who are anything like your friends back home."

She was nodding her head vigorously. "*Ja, ja, donz de mon cor.* After all the strong reasons you gave me for coming, how could I be expected to resist?"

I had a sense that she was teasing or needling him, somehow, but I didn't get the joke either.

"You're not going to meet anyone here who understands that you're a *donzelha*!" Aimeric said.

"Oh, I don't know. Bruce, what gender would you say I am, just offhand and from surface indications? Just give me your best guess."

Bruce laughed, sounding very nervous, and suddenly seemed to need a little more of his attention for the road. "I never get into arguments between people of opposite gender," he said. "Part of why I'm still healthy and vigorous at my age."

Aimeric chuckled a little, and said, "We really did need you along on the ship, Bruce. A diplomat like you was wasted as a preacher."

That seemed to lead a very long silence, before Bruce asked what had brought me to Caledony. Without too much detail—I had an idea that describing what I had found at Entrepot with any precision would probably have upset him—I sketched out how I had ended up in the springer to Caledony.

To my surprise, unlike Bieris or Aimeric, he seemed to understand at once. I warmed to him immediately—or at least I did until he added, "Yap, it was a long time ago, but I had something like that happen to me, with a girl that *I* had been planning to marry."

Aimeric sat up as if he'd been goosed; Bieris was suddenly choking; I was left having to do the explaining.

"Ah . . . marriage isn't even legal in Nou Occitan till you're at least twenty-five stanyears old. It's not common before you're thirty," I said. "This was—well, *finamor*." I had the sudden embarrassing realization that I had never actually learned a Terstad word for it. Maybe there wasn't one.

Bruce nodded emphatically. "You know, in all the reading I did about Nou Occitan, years ago, when I was trying to get to go on that ship, I never did really get a handle on the idea of *finamor*." We spun around another turn and I avoided looking out the window, knowing perfectly well that there was truly nothing to see below me. As he brought the cat around, Bruce added, "But I can surely understand that you felt like doing something big and sudden when something so importaut to you got wrecked." He hesitated. "Um—there is something I'm curious about though."

I was so grateful to be getting any kind of understanding — even from someone who apparently didn't know what I was talking about—that I said, "Of course."

"Well ... if you're *not* going to marry a girl, why do you get into an exclusive arrangement with her?"

It seemed a very peculiar question to me, but Aimeric's friend clearly meant it sincerely, so I tried to answer, and I stammered out a lot of not-very-coherent things about inspiring my art, giving me a purpose to place my *enseingnamen* at the service of, helping me to the sweet sense of melancholy ... it sounded dumb to me.

"Well," Bruce said, "actually that does sound like fun. I can see where spending a few years that way would be interesting, at least." It sounded as if I had confused him completely but he at least understood that I loved it, and again I was deeply grateful. "Uh—but what do the girls get out of it?"

The question was so startling that I blurted out the truth. "I really don't know."

Bieris broke in, to my annoyance since I seemed to be getting on so well with Bruce, and said, "Well, we get attention, and we get to feel proud of ourselves because we're doing things we've been encouraged to fantasize about ever since we were little, and every so often we get sex, which is fun."

"That's awfully cold-blooded," Aimeric said.

He had a gift for understatement; I was so angry I wanted to shout at her, but you don't do that to someone else's *entendedora*.

Something about the way she flipped her hair and shrugged, for some reason, suggest the style of a couple of Sapphists I had known; since they tended to be very aggressive and often treacherous fighters, and delighted in scrapping with jovents over any possible issue at all, I avoided them. Not that Bieris was wearing man's clothing, as they did, or even that she had spoken in the dominating, quarrelsome way they did—but something about her manner reminded me of them, of how dangerous it was to fight with them. And after all, she was Aimeric's *entendedora*, not mine. I was still annoyed about her breaking into my serious discussion of *finamor* with Bruce, but I decided I would just sulk quietly.

"Well," Bieris added, "it's also true that unless one has some special talent or study to pursue full-time, there just isn't a lot to do before you're twenty-five. So I suppose *finamor* also gives us something to do."

Bruce nodded a couple of times, and I realized that for some reason he had believed her. I would have to find a chance to give him a better, less ugly, explanation, later.

As soon as I thought of one.

I noticed that Aimeric was slumped in his seat and realized that he must be dying of embarrassment, as I would have in the same situation.

After a while, Bruce said, "Well, I don't imagine you'll find anyone here who will be interested in exactly that arrangement, Giraut, but we do have women, if it's any consolation." I think he meant it as a joke, but I couldn't think of any way to pick up on it, and neither Aimeric nor Bieris did, so it just lay there. The only sound was the hum and whine of the treads, and the faint sputtering of sleet against the windshield and cabin roof.

The conversation was now thoroughly cold and dead. The rising moon, and perhaps the sun itself, were beginning to turn the fog a pale yellow around us, enough so that we could see the many little frozen waterfalls and the heavy rime on the rocks. The temperature gauge had still not quite touched freezing.

"Something must have really gone wrong with the terraforming," Bieris said. "You must be way behind schedule for reaching planned temperature."

As we whirled around another high, hairpin turn, Bruce and Aimeric looked at each other, obviously trying to settle who would explain it. The cat slipped a centimeter or so sideways toward the edge. The gray down below seemed to be lightening and getting a little farther away; I wondered, in the higher gravity, how long it would take to plunge all the way to the sea below.

It was beginning to penetrate my hung-over, sleep-starved brain that Noupeitau had been the home of many great-looking, traditional *donzelhas* who were not Garsenda, and that I was now going to be in this icy waste for a stanyear or two. The great advantage of suicide is that no matter how stupid and short-sighted the action is, you don't have to be aware of your stupidity afterwards.

I was working up from that thought into a full-fledged depression when Aimeric cleared his throat and said, "I did try to talk both of you out of this, you know, but now that you're both here, maybe I should just—well, all right. I guess the way to say it is . . . um, I mean—"

"What Ambrose—sorry, Aimeric, I mean—is trying to tell you," Bruce said quietly, "is that most people here want it to be like this. And this planet was not terraformed. It came this way."

FOUR

They had time to tell us the whole story before we reached the Gap.

Nansen was bizarre in many ways, but the strangest feature was that it should have been a prime candidate for terraforming—potentially it could have been within one percent of the so-called Tahiti-Standard Climate, far better than Wilson was.

But a simple loophole had made it possible for the two cultures here, Caledony and St. Michael, to enjoy the wretched climate that both preferred for ideological reasons.

Technically Nansen could avoid terraforming because it had already been a living world when the probes got here. The explanation, as far as it went, was that around our stanyear of 1750, the asteroid that created the Gouge had torn a great hole in the crust of Nansen. The impact and the vulcanism it spawned had blackened the glaciers and ice sheets, and immense eruptions of greenhouse gases had further warmed the planet. In addition, the large releases of sulfuric acid had started the calcium sulfate–sulfide cycle in the oceans, turning them over and beginning the circulation life would need.

And that was where the mystery started; it was understandable, though very improbable, that Nansen had accidentally started its own terraformation without human intervention—but where had the life that continued the process come from? Exobiologists fought over the issue with great passion and little in the way of conclusions.

When Nansen's star, Mufrid, had swelled into a giant, as in practically all such cases, the Faju-Fakutoru Effect had stripped its gas giants of volatiles, leaving their habitable-sized cores in the process, and the very wide habitable zone of a giant star had virtually insured at least one world would fall within it.

But normally, after liquefying, recooling, and forming their new atmospheres, such worlds either froze, as Wilson and Nansen had, boiled like Venus, or became lifeless hell-holes with many small briny seas and an inorganic nitrogen-CO_2 cycle atmosphere. In their short lifetimes of a few hundred million years at best, they did not usually begin life—instead they waited, inert, until someone came along to seed them with organisms and begin generating the series of ecologies that would move them to human habitability.

Nansen had not waited. In the late 2100s, the first human probes to reach the planet had found a flourishing, photosynthesis-based microbiological ecology. A complete absence of any fossil forms, and cores later drilled into the remaining primordial glaciers, had shown that life must have arrived very recently, or been almost absent until the asteroid strike created the opportunity.

The theories about where the life had come from boiled down to four:

First, Mufrid's now-destroyed inner worlds had harbored a civilization, a few members of which had made it to the stripped gas-giant, where their efforts at terraforming had failed, leaving low populations of a few simple organisms in the never-quite-frozen oceans—populations that exploded when the asteroid gave them the chance. This was clearly impossible because by the time the volatiles were gone, the inner worlds would have been engulfed by the expanding star for at least two million stanyears.

Or, since that was impossible, the second theory was that an unacknowledged probe from one of many defunct Terran governments had contaminated Nansen. This was impossible because to produce the results observed by the first known probes, such a probe could not have left much later than 1825.

Rejecting those theories, a few scientists contended that the gas giant whose core had formed Nansen had been warm enough to harbor life of its own—which had then somehow survived the sudden removal of ninety percent of the planet's mass, made its way to the core, and survived in the molten iron soup for decades as the gas giant's former moons, now in eccentric orbits, socked into the new molten planet every few hundred stanyears.

Since that also couldn't be true, there was a notion that the nonhuman civilization we still had yet to find had discovered an easily terraformed planet at the enormous expense of an interstellar probe, started the process of terraformation at even greater expense, and then not bothered to move in, perhaps on a whim.

"Every one of those ideas is ludicrous," Bruce said, "but there you have it—Nansen was alive when we got here." He shrugged. "Which meant the cultures that bought land on it could invoke the Preservation Regulations—no additional terraformation, just species addition."

Aimeric sighed. "And just to make sure you both understand how grim that is—if you check the historical documents, you'll find out that a variance was theirs for the asking. Nobody who designed or founded St. Michael, or Caledony, wanted it to be any other way."

Mufrid had risen behind us by now, a bright yellow smear

in the dingy gray, and there was much more light. Little pellets of brown sleet bounced off the windshield, and I could see a couple of hundred meters down into the Gouge, and even dimly make out the far side as a dark spiky shadow. Colors were starting to appear in the rocks.

"But—maybe I'm slow," Bieris said, "Why didn't they want it to have decent weather?"

"Oh, two different reasons, one for each culture," Aimeric said. "St. Michael needed a bleak, gray place for human beings to do hard, pointless physical work, so that they could properly contemplate the essential sadness and futility of life, and therefore appreciate Christ's glorious generosity in releasing them from it."

Bruce suddenly pointed. "Hey—look. The Gap Bow." All of us leaned forward to look through the windshield. There in front of and above us was the biggest double rainbow I had ever seen, and unlike the simple red-to-green ones of Wilson, this one extended all the way to deepest violet. "You'd have to ask a meterologist how it works," Bruce said. "Something about the way clouds form in the Gouge. It only happens at this time of morning, up at this altitude, maybe one out of every twenty Lights or so."

"*Deu*, it rips my heart," Bieris said. "Surely someone here has made a symphony or a hymn of it—that would be wonderful to hear!"

There was an embarrassed cough from Aimeric. "Um, perhaps some hymn would allude to it in passing."

Bruce sighed. "I don't think they'd even allow that. Concern with appearances is the first of the Nine Indicators of Misplaced Values. And the Gap Bow is pure appearance."

I didn't ask who thought so; probably I would not be able to avoid finding out, later.

Besides, there was the Gap Bow itself to see. After the black dirty saltstorm from which we had started, and the drizzling gray climb along the bare rock walls, here in the glorious amber light under the turquoise sky was that brilliant blazing stripe like an immense, graceful bridge across Sodom Gap in front of us.

It lasted for several minutes as we climbed; meanwhile, the cabin actually began to be a bit warm from the sunlight. My eyes had adjusted—though the colors of the rock layers still seemed garish to me, the pain I felt in looking at them was only esthetic.

When the Gap Bow had at last disappeared, all of us sighing to see it go, Bruce said, "Not far now." He brought the cat around the outside of a small draw that entered the Gouge there.

The last fifteen km of road winding up into the Gap was along bare, scoured rock ledges, some natural and some blasted. At their widest they were about eighty meters, and at their narrowest only thirty, about twice as wide as the cat. By now the sun was halfway up to noon, and the clouds in the Gouge were so far down that I had to press myself against the windows to see them. Opposite us, four kilometers away, Black Glacier Fall plunged into the Gouge—"It falls only during sunlight," Aimeric said, "and it all freezes into hail on the way down. From one of the outcrops on the other side, you can look all the way down to the green sea through the hole the hail makes in the clouds."

To protect the ledges of Sodom Gap Road, great needled vines had been engineered and planted on the cliff faces, so on our side the vertical slopes were covered with tangled wood as thick as the trunks of mature trees, forming a latticework several meters deep.

"Does anything live in that? Squirrel or monkey analogs?" Bieris asked.

"Escaped chickens," Bruce said. "We'll probably see a couple before the drive is over. They were bred to have huge breast muscles and wings like condors, and to feed on the lichen that grows all over the planet. The idea was to raise them as sort of a free-range meat animal. Well, they do eat lichen, plus anything else they can get into their beaks, but they really prefer the needles on those vines—and up here they're hard to get at."

We came around the bend and two visibility-orange chickens, at least two meters in wingspan, swooped past us.

"That's them," Bruce said. "We bred them to be easy to spot. Still doesn't help when you're hunting them. Fifteen kilos of meat on them, dressed out, but it's work to get them—nothing in their genes to make them go into a trap, and if you shoot one up here he tends to drop straight down into the Gouge. Only use we get out of them is the guano."

When we finally climbed up the last slope to the top of the Gap—still between mountains that towered a kilometer above us on either side—Bieris and I gasped audibly and Aimeric seemed to get a little water in his eyes.

The last bit of the Gouge had broken into a saddle between two mighty iceclad peaks. From where our cat whirred along the rocky surface, at the top of the Gap, bare rock stretched forward a full kilometer before plunging out of sight. Beyond that rim, a broad plain of deep blue-green, broken by tawny-gold grain fields and the paler green shimmer of orchards, reached to the jagged peaks of another mountain range far beyond. I guessed that perhaps the other mountains might be two hundred km away.

"Anc nul vis bellazor!" I exclaimed, drinking in all that color after the barrenness of the journey.

"Ver, pensi tropa zenza," Bruce said.

Bieris and I giggled; Aimeric burst out laughing. "You realize you just lost your best chance to spy on our Occitans, Bruce."

"Avetz vos Occitan?" Bieris asked.

"Ja, tropa mal." Bruce sighed. "Nowadays I'm way out of practice. But I thought it was only fair to let you know I could understand your language."

"The three of us spent a lot of time practicing it," Aimeric said.

"Yap, you and me and Charlie. In fact we even practiced it up here a lot."

Aimeric sighed. "I had almost forgotten."

I had known Aimeric for almost a full Wilson-year—just a bit less than twelve stanyears—since my family had been his host family after his arrival in Nou Occitan. And in all that time, I had never heard him speak of this Charlie, who had apparently been one of those who died in the tank on the way. Yet clearly they had been very close friends, together with Bruce . . . I wasn't sure I liked knowing that Aimeric had been able to forget his friend so completely.

Bruce was nodding. "I guess I'm still pretty amazed that we got away with it."

Bieris looked from one to the other. "It's illegal to take a hike?"

"Not illegal, but irrational. After you do it you have to prove you're not out of harmony with God's plan for your life," Bruce explained, making it completely confusing.

"Why is it irrational?" I asked. "Anyone who got up here ought to be able to see why you would do it."

"Mere esthetics are beyond reason," Aimeric said. His voice had a cold, ugly edge to it and a deep flatness that sounded like some peculiar accent. Without knowing who it was, I knew he was imitating someone's voice.

"Since you can't prove it's good, it's got to be a matter of individual taste. And matters of individual taste are not supposed to be your first priority," Bruce said. "But we did manage to get around it. Once we thought of doing this, we spent almost a year establishing a walking fetish."

Aimeric laughed. "Walked to everywhere we could, every chance we got. We had them convinced that the whole culture would double its aggregate utility total if only we could get to walk more."

"The last three trips or so we made, we spoke Occitan exclusively," Bruce said. "It really is a better language for dealing with beauty. Of course, those were long trips, and harder to get permission for—it's a good five days, or ten Lights, really, to get over into Sodom Basin—so that was later on. Just as well since we were about the only people who had ever done any hiking or camping in Caledony, and we had to teach ourselves everything by trial and error. Sodom Gap would not have been the right place to try to learn—it isn't what you'd call a low pass."

"How high up are we?" Bieris said. "Or were we—I mean, how high is the top of the pass?"

"About seven km," Aimeric said. "But the temperature and pressure gradient is much less steep than on Wilson—you can breathe up here, easily, without carrying oxygen, and though it's cold it's not all that much worse higher up than it is lower down."

By now we had driven down to where we could see the way the road tumbled down in a series of steep switchbacks to the valley below.

As we descended, we left behind the heavy retaining vines and saw more long grass. "That's *wheat*!" Bieris exclaimed suddenly.

"Yap. Practically every engineered plant in Caledony, even the cover crops, is edible or good for something. Part of making it all maximize happiness," Bruce said. He threw us around another tight bend, and we lurched down the brightly sunlit road, a roostertail of dust springing up after us. Now that I could see, and had ridden with Bruce for almost three hours, I was beginning to enjoy the way the cat zoomed along the mountain road. "This whole part of the planet is one big farm. One reason we don't trade much with St. Michael is that over there, to make life more rugged, they engineered weeds. We're crazy here, but not that crazy."

As we came down into the hills that ran along the eastern side of the Optimals, I saw that all the trees had been machine-planted in long straight rows, so that what had looked like forest from far away looked more like an orchard planned by an obsessive gardener close up.

"I bet all these trees are seedless," I said.

"Yap," Aimeric said. "That way trees grow only where they're planted, and with very little genetic drift, machines can pick them on a regular schedule."

When we slowed to a stop at Bruce's house, at first glance it looked like just another bare concrete cube— "Hey, you've got windows!"

"Yap. Took me three stanyears of complaining to a psyware program that I had claustrophobia before they decided it was rational for me to want them. But you're all in luck—by a slightly elastic reading of the building permit, I had all my guest houses windowed as well."

When we climbed out of the cat, it was actually pleasantly warm, perhaps twenty degrees, and we just carried our parkas. The bright amber sun, now rolling down toward the mountains west of us, made our Occitan clothes look oddly garish and outlandish; Bruce's simple coverall, kneeboots, and shirt had more color and texture than I'd have thought possible.

"Let's all get inside and get a little food and sleep," he said. "I imagine you're tired, and we're coming up on Second Dark, when most people sleep, so you can get on the local schedule. Supposedly your baggage won't be along for a Light or two, but I've got spare rooms I use for field hands at harvest, so I made up three of those—uh, unless you'd rather use two." He sounded so embarrassed that I thought it was kind of heartless of Aimeric to wink at me.

"You're very kind," I said, *"que merce!"*

That seemed to embarrass Bruce even further, and he turned away from me and toward Aimeric, just in time to catch Aimeric reaching into his pocket. "Aw," he said, "now that we're away from the city and the cops your IOU is good enough for me."

I turned away for a moment to look around me. The land I stood in looked more like a vu to me than like anywhere real. Automatically, I reached for Raimbaut's mind to show him this, and—almost as automatically—I was shredded at the heart by the realization that he was no longer there. It had been the same, over and over, for the past four days, since they had taken him off of me; somehow, though, as I looked at the odd colors and the harsh, scoured mountains, the great open fields and straight-rowed orchards, I knew this would be the last such seizure of memory.

As I looked at my strange surroundings, I wondered what Raimbaut might have thought of all of it, and to my surprise that made me feel differently, as if the loop of these past few days had suddenly broken; I had known, even before I wore his psypyx, everything he thought about everything one might find in the Quartier des Jovents. But confronted with this . . . I had no idea what he might have felt, thought, or exclaimed.

My thoughts turned again to Garsenda, and I realized that it was much the same for her—as well as I had known her back in the Quartier, I could not now imagine what she would make of this. The same held for Marcabru, and Yseut, and all my other friends. Indeed, I had no idea what Aimeric felt as he saw his homeworld for the first time in many years, after so long believing it lost to him forever, or what Bieris might be thinking.

And Bruce, of course, was beyond comprehension.

I had lived all my life in the certainty that what passed through my mind would pass through the minds of any of my fellows, were he standing where I was. And it had been true. My wearing of Raimbaut's psypyx had only confirmed what I already knew to be true, that everyone I knew was what I was.

If somehow a springer door back to my own apartment were to open in front of me right then, it would make no difference; I could not return at all to what I had been—to the only thing I knew how to be. My mind whirled through the last two days, trying to find the moment when I had crossed over to this new life—

"Hey, Giraut!" Aimeric said. I turned to see him standing in the heatlock of Bruce's house. The others had vanished. "We didn't even notice you hadn't followed us in. You'll freeze solid out here in a couple of hours—why don't you come in?"

I shook my head, once, to clear it. "I was just thinking."

Aimeric came out of the house, closing the outer heatlock door, and approached me as slowly and carefully as if he thought I might suddenly blow up. "I was afraid you might be," he said. "Did it just hit you that you can't go home?"

"You could say that." He was now standing directly in front of me, and realizing why he had come to me, I said, "Did you ever feel that way?"

"Often, my first few weeks; off and on since." He sighed. "I wish we'd had a few more hours to talk you out of this.

Well, at least it's not quite so permanent—you will be going home in a stanyear or two."

"I'll be going *back*," I corrected him, automatically, as I picked up my lute case and followed him into his old friend's house. He turned and looked at me, perhaps trying to think of something to say, but finally said nothing.

The heatlock door closed behind us, the inner door opened, and we went inside. It wasn't until I was almost asleep, in one of Bruce's guest rooms, that I realized I had no idea of how I felt either.

PART TWO

MISSION TO A COLD WORLD

ONE

The sun was up, making the kitchen cheerful and bright. Bieris and I were sitting across from each other, exchanging eyerolls, while we listened to two people catch up on events that had happened long before we were born. Every so often she would shrug, or I would.

True, I was not feeling bad physically. For the first time in two standays I wasn't hung over, I had had some sleep, and I wasn't being rushed from one place to another. But it was beginning to sink in that I would be on this unpleasant icy rock inhabited by two unpleasant icy cultures for at least two stanyears.

Meanwhile Aimeric and Bruce went on and on about who was dead, who had married whom, who had what job, while Bieris and I waited. At least the food was good, if you didn't mind Anglo-Saxon cuisine. (Fried meats, bland boiled starches, and thick, fatty, salty sauces, mostly, if you haven't tried it. Usually I disliked the stuff, but Bruce had kept the salt and grease under control and been liberal with the spices, and the coffee was dark and properly bitter.) And since there would be no *companho* around to harass me about Garsenda, I could just shrug the faithless little slut off and enjoy life— the only problem being whether anyone could enjoy life in Caledony.

Finally, I found a hole in the conversation to ask. "Uh, Bruce—I'm sure you folks have the same technology we do—so . . . what does a farmer *do*?"

Bruce sighed. "You'd be amazed how many extinct occupations we have here. A cousin of mine is a blacksmith, his wife is a computer programmer, and their son delivers milk.

I do what everyone else does here in Caledony, except teachers and people with other jobs that require a living person. I com a central number to find out which robot I replace today. A while before I get there, the robot switches off and I do its job for four hours. And I bet Aimeric hasn't told you that everybody—resident aliens included—has to do that."

"But I thought we were working for Aimeric," Bieris protested.

"The Council of Humanity recognizes that as work," Aimeric said, "but the Caledon government issues the local money, and that's the only thing you can spend here. And the only way you can get that is to put in your four hours a day as a replacement robot."

"Yap," Bruce said. "Hell, they wanted to make the Ambassador work. The same damned stiffnecks we were fighting way back then, Aimeric, are in power now, and they've not budged a bit. Technically, the Council of Humanity is loaning you to the Caledon government, and since nobody ever gets paid for working for the government, you've got to put in your Market Prayer time, same as anyone."

"Market Prayer?" Bieris asked.

"The work you do replacing a robot." Aimeric sighed and poured another cup of coffee. He looked over his shoulder at Bruce. "There's someone I haven't asked about—"

"Yap. He's Chair of the Council of Rationalizers, now."

Bruce didn't say who "he" was. I looked at Bieris; she shrugged.

Finally Aimeric said, "Bruce, what happened?"

Bruce leaned back against the counter and scratched at a callus on one hand. "I'd been afraid you would ask that. Can't we just say interest just faded away?"

"You don't believe that."

"Nop. I don't. But I sure can't fault any of you for having gone to Wilson." Bruce looked up at him, his mouth drawn and thin. "My God, I tried so hard to go myself. But it sure tore the guts out of the movement when you all left."

"We had seven thousand members in the Liberal Association. What difference did twenty or thirty of us leaving make?"

"Almost everyone sent had some major role in the leadership of the Liberal Association—besides Charlie there were five other regional chairs in that crew."

"*Anyone* intelligent was in the Liberal Association in those days!" Aimeric drummed his fingers on the table and stared at the wall.

Bruce said, softly, "Think of it the way the PPP would see it. Here's a chance to get rid of sixty or seventy heretics and troublemakers, in exchange for being able to fill some needed slots at the university without running the risk of having to allow Caledons to read forbidden texts as part of their training. I don't say that any of you was wrong to go, Aimeric. I'm just saying we lost more than any of us realized at the time when you and the others left, and I think the peeps set it up to happen that way."

Aimeric didn't say anything for a few long breaths. Rather, he just stared out the window at nothing. Finally, a little half-smile formed, and he said, "Look at us. Dead ringers for our fathers, except that we don't apologize to Jesus for being irrational."

Bruce laughed, and began "On my honor as a Wild Boy"— and Aimeric joined him, their voices rising into mad crescendo—"I swear I will not apologize for enjoying myself, pass up a chance to get laid, or *be like my old man*."

"Charlie wrote that when we were thirteen," Aimeric explained to us. "He was the best of us."

"He was," Bruce agreed. He turned to his com to get our work assignments. "We're in luck," he said, "at least for today, it's picking apples."

For a long time, as we strolled up the road toward the orchards, the only sounds were the paltry breeze brushing the leaves and the crunch of our boots on the gravel. Amazingly, after the howling blizzard the previous day in Utilitopia, three hours away by road, it was actually a little warm.

The destruction of the land here appalled me. In Nou Occitan only those things that absolutely could not be done well hydroponically, like grapes for wine, were grown in the open, leaving the rest for wilderness, park, or city. Here, instead of open spaces or forests—or whatever there would be, given proper terraforming and species design to produce wildlife and landscapes—there were only ugly square fields, broken by stone walls, fencerows, and trees along a river, an obviously artificial landscape, made uglier by a lack of design or planning. It looked like ancient flat photos of Vermont or Normandy.

"Who exactly are we working for, Bruce? You?" Bieris asked.

Bruce took a field coffee-maker out of his pocket and said, "I don't know if anyone wants any more coffee, but let me show you something."

We stopped by the side of the road to sit with our backs to a huge, stone-warmed boulder. Bruce unfolded the cup, set the little cylinder of the maker on top of it, and pointed to the digital display there. As he pressed START there was a hiss— the machine extracting water from the air—then, after a long second, coffee gurgled into the cup.

The digital readout flashed:

COFF BEANS .0082
WATER .00005
ELEC PWR .00002
COFF MKR RENT .000001
CUP RENT 2E-8
PRAISE GOD
GIVE THANKS
THINK RATIONALLY
BE FREE

"There's a readout like that on everything here," Aimeric explained. "Whatever you get here, you're renting from someone, and you pay every time you use it."

"Right down to the fly on your trousers," Bruce said. "But you can't save money by pissing yourself—they just get it back in damage charges on underwear."

"Well, who are you buying from?" Bieris asked.

Bruce hit a number combination on the coffee maker, and the digital readout flashed:

PREV PAYMTS THIS SYSTEM:
LIBERTY COFFEE CORP
JUSTICE OF GOD BEVERAGES
CALEDONY WATER LICENSED
MONOPOLY
JESUS-MALTHUS TEA AND COFFEE LTD.
CALEDONY POWER LICENSED
MONOPOLY
ROGERS HOUSEHOLD APPLIANCE
LEASING
MARY CARTER AND CHILDREN
KITCHENWARE RENTALS
PRAISE GOD
GIVE THANKS
THINK RATIONALLY
BE FREE

"Okay, I see, but who owns all those companies and corporations? They must have stockholders and things!" Bieris seemed to take all this as a personal affront.

"We're the owners," Aimeric explained. "But all the stock earnings go into health and life insurance to prevent our being a burden on society. Then when we die whatever's left from our premiums goes to the government, which uses it to buy stock for new workers coming into the system . . ."

"So everything here is rented, leased, or sublet?" I asked, feeling like an idiot for asking once more, but passionately hoping to get a different answer this time.

"Yap. The stuff in our baggage is probably the largest aggregation of really private property ever to enter Caledony. All part of doctrine—it's the only way the market can make sure everybody always works, because work is what God wants from us."

There was a long silence. It wasn't so much that I was

afraid of working—at least I don't think so. I had always stayed in shape, between hiking, dancing, and dueling, but there was something about the idea of my replacing a machine that made me want to bash in the face of anyone who suggested it.

"Why does God want *that*?" Bieris blurted out.

Bruce laughed like it hurt him. "I can tell you what I would have said if you'd asked me while I was a preacher. *He loves us.* Work is how He teaches us to reason and become thinking beings, because in a moral society the morally correct choice always gets the largest rewards."

We didn't talk much on the rest of the walk, as we turned off the road and followed a little trail into the orchard to where four human-form robots stood still, like naked mannequins, the sun playing over their beige-pink coverings, their faceless, hairless, single-eyed heads pointed straight forward.

Bruce jumped, swung up into a gnarly old tree for a moment, and came back down with four bright-yellow apples. "Stop, thief," he said, handing one to each of us and waving off our attempts to fish out coins. "It would be polite of you to pay me, you're getting the custom right, but Aimeric and I can both tell you from our childhood that they don't really taste perfect unless they're stolen."

Aimeric nodded solemnly. "Absolutely true."

The apple was cool and very crisp, full of sweet thick juice that gushed down into my beard. "Oops," Bruce said, "should have warned you—to be freeze-resistant they have to be kind of sticky."

I ended up pulling my spare handkerchief out of my sleeve to use as a napkin; all of us were a mess.

I was forced to cheer up despite myself. On such a fine day, picking apples wasn't bad work at all. The sky was an astonishing shade of deep blue that I had never seen before, and colors were so vivid in Mufrid's amber light that it all looked like the paintings of a genius child who had mastered line drawing but still painted only in bold primary colors. The brighter light made the distant mountains leap out in startling complexity and detail, the high falls on the valley rim shining like white-hot silver.

Up in the trees, the crisp sweet scent of apples was over-powering, and at Bruce's urging every so often we'd pause to devour an unusually ripe or fine one. My skin was sticky with juice, my arms ached with the unaccustomed stretching, and my nose was beginning to run a little, for as the sun sank it rapidly got cold and damp. My throat felt a bit raw, and I had not been so tired in ages, but when the alarm bells on the robots rang to tell us they would soon come back to life I was a little sorry it was over.

On the way back, Bruce said, "You're welcome to stay with me as long as you like, of course, but I assume that as soon as your belongings arrive you'll want to move into the guest houses. They're on our way back—would you like to take a look?"

What Bruce had for us were three little bleached-white concrete cottages in a grove of apricot trees out of the wind. Each stood empty and freshly scrubbed, awaiting the robots with our furniture and belongings. They looked like tempo-rary utility buildings back home.

Aimeric looked around, smiled broadly, and said, "Your work, Bruce?"

Bruce stammered and blushed, but admitted it was. I could well understand his embarrassment.

Bieris clapped her hands, applauding him, and said, "It's wonderful! You've got such an interesting eye—I never would have thought you could do so much with simple geo-metrics."

I thought she was overdoing it.

She turned toward Aimeric and, only half-joking, de-manded, "Why didn't you say your friend was this kind of an architect?"

Bruce turned deep purple, but I don't think he was dis-pleased. I realized, with shock, that she meant it, and looked around again, trying to see what my friends saw in those bar-ren, square lines.

We had come here from the height of Nou Occitan's Second Baroque Revival, with its innumerable spires, complex suspended fabrics, and convoluted tiny detail, what one critic called "the gaudy webs of mad romantic half-spider half-elves." These bold clean lines were a shock, and not anything that any Occitan would ever have come up with. I still couldn't see what everyone else obviously did. I consoled myself by thinking that I simply preferred things warm and human, but it seemed a pretty weak rejoinder to Bieris's lightfooted dance from wall to wall and window to window, catching the way the light played on the gently curved surfaces.

When we finally got back to Bruce's place, Second Sunset was almost on us and it was distinctly cold. I looked around, saw the first bright stars lighting in the amazing blue depths of Nansen's sky, tasted the clear tongue-spiking air, and felt the cold all around me stretching out from the edges of this warm basin, hardly broken all the way to the meter-thick blankets of frozen CO_2 that lay on the ice at the poles. The others went inside, but I lingered a bit longer, watching the last pink flares above the mountains west of us.

Nansen's moon rose then, over the mountains to the west opposite Sodom Gap, blazingly bright and perceptibly warm. With a period a bit under ten hours, it swept perceptibly though slowly up the sky, waxing as it rose, the ground brightening and shadows deepening as they crept along the ground, as if sucked into their sources. Supposedly in the next few thousand years they would have to shove it back outward; if you look closely, you could see a tiny flicker in the dark part, where the huge artificial volcano was providing the thrust. It gave me a marvelous idea for a song, and I went inside to work on it.

As I was sitting practicing with my lute, the Council of Rationalizers commed us. We would first meet with them three days from now to discuss what we could do for them; at that time, we would also be expected to go by the Work Assignment Bureau in Utilitopia and choose our permanent work. Till then we could work at Bruce's as farmhands.

We napped for part of First Dark—most people took a two- or three-hour nap then, and slept through Second Dark—and ate a large midday meal. It was still a while before the sun would come up for Light, and too cold to take the walk I was starting to look forward to, so I spent a lot of time at the reader trying to find out what anyone did for amusement. At first I looked for entertainment reviews, but finding none, I started looking through the general com listings.

There were some music instructors, but no musicians. No art galleries or theaters. I had a brief moment of encouragement when I noticed a category for "Instructors in Literature," but as far as I could tell those were tutors for college students. Sure enough, there were also "Instructors in Mathematics."

There seemed to be no competitive sports, and there were fewer cafes, taverns, and restaurants in all of the huge city of Utilitopia than there had been in my little hometown of Elinorien. There were no dojos, but there were sizable numbers of "Spa-noun comf-adj-mod-spa pro-studia-adv-mod-comf" in the student neighborhoods surrounding the University. At first I had thought they might be the local equivalent of hangouts, because the "SCS" abbreviation didn't give it away and I could not read Reason. When I checked I found they were giant study halls.

I could have named twenty professional poets in Elinorien, and it would have taken me a long time to count all the people who played and sang for a living in the few blocks of Noupeitau's Quartier des Jovents where I had been living. I had always assumed that everywhere else was something like Nou Occitan, solving the problem of the fully automatic economy by employing everyone at some interesting occupation. Obviously this place had other solutions. There were more than 170,000 entries for "General physical labor," almost all of them contractors who presumably hired other people to do the actual labor.

It occurred to me that I had left so abruptly that I had not even told Marcabru about what had happened or where I was going. I dashed off a quick note to him, emphasizing the romantic qualities of leaping to another world, and adding a paragraph about Caledony as the "culture-free culture."

I spent the afternoon of Second Light wandering around with the lute, stole a couple more apples, and worked on getting used to rectangular scenery. As the sun sank opposite the Optimals—I had learned by then that the more distant range had no name because no one ever went there, but the local joke was that they were the "Pessimals"—I had the beginnings of a couple of songs and had even begun to get fairly well used to the way the land looked. Give it a decade and I might be ready to believe there was a difference between "attractive" and "unattractive" cultivation; I had to admit some stone walls and meandering streams had a certain crude charm. By the time I got back to the house for evening meal and rest, Second Dark was coming on fast. I slept remarkably well, and awoke with the guilty feeling that I had not thought of Garsenda at all.

TWO

The next day we drew our temporary work assignments. Aimeric and Bruce were to pick apples again; Bieris was to take a little electric cart around and leave supplementary food out for Bruce's herds of the local sheep-goat cross.

And I was to shovel out Bruce's dairy barn.

The obnoxious aintellect cheerfully noted that it was estimated to be a twelve-hour project, so I could put all three of my remaining shifts as a farmhand into it.

After my first four hours as a shovel propulsion unit, I was stiff and groaning. Moreover, I had not really noticed before that the gravity was a bit over eight percent more than what it was on Wilson—but now, with every three-kilo shovelload weighting a quarter of a kilo more, and every thirty-kilo wheelbarrow weighing 32.4, by the end of my shift I felt every dragging extra gram. It took me some hours to get used to the new relationship between inertia and weight, as well, so that for the first hour I was accidentally flinging shovelloads against the wall, where they splashed back onto my clothing, and then for the next hour I was dropping them short, where they coated my boots.

I wrote two more letters to Marcabru—one about the quaint revival of the archaic custom of forced labor, and one that discussed my discovery that in the past fifty years, the eighteen million inhabitants of Caledony had produced nineteen novels, about one thousand pieces of secular music (all instrumental solos for some reason I couldn't fathom), and 262 human-designed public buildings, thirteen of them by Bruce. Having looked at the photos of all of them, I had furthermore been forced to the conclusion that he was indeed the nearest thing to an architect this culture had yet produced. I then added,

> But I am encouraged because in the same period
> they have produced an estimated seventy-eight million
> sermons and one hundred thousand hymns.
> Marcabru, when I return—perhaps with great
> good luck in the last month of Yseut's reign—I shall
> be much obliged if you will follow me around for
> three straight days endlessly repeating "Now don't
> do anything stupid." That is, assuming I can walk
> after spending all the time shoveling manure; from
> the feel of my shoulders, I shall be the ideal Rigoletto.
> Bruce assures me that soon I won't feel it.

Bruce lied. I was still stiff when we were setting out for Utilitopia two days later. Maybe in atonement, he had offered to teach me to drive the cat. I had jumped at the chance.

Now, as we sat down at the controls together, he said, "These barges are complicated and tricky to work. Are you sure you want to learn?"

"Anything not to be moving that stuff around."

"Ha," Aimeric said, settling comfortably into the back. "You're an administrative assistant to a government economist. You have not yet *begun* to move it around."

"Anyone who can't see the difference between the literal and the figurative has never done the literal." At Bruce's direction, I pulled the lift switch, and the cat rose a couple of centimeters as the maglevs pushed out the treads.

"Actually I have done the literal—the whole time I was a teenager, at a feedlot in Utilitopia. My father thought it might help the career in politics he had planned for me. There's some prestige value in having done a really grubby job. God, I hated him."

"Is he still umm—" Bieris began.

"Yap. In fact he's the Chairman of the Council of Rationalizers," Aimeric said. "Kind of the same job as PM back home."

Bruce finished system checks. As the last wave of green rolled through the holographic cube in front of him, he said, "Did you call him last night, Aimeric?"

"He knows where I am. And who. He can call me. If he wants to."

Bruce seemed not to hear the non-answer, turning to me to say, "Now just remember, right foot is throttle, left foot is brake, right joystick angles right treads, left angles left, button on top of the left stick locks the tread angles together, button on the right locks them together toed-in half a degree. Double tap the throttle to set an isospeed, triple tap for isoload, then take your foot off it till you need to control directly or reset—you've got the throttle back as soon as your foot touches it. And don't worry! You've got twenty-five kilometers before there's anything near enough to the road to run into or fall off of. Keep treads parallel on levels, splay for uphill, snowplow coming down—or for a *very* fast stop."

I started with a lurch, but no one commented. I thought maybe Aimeric would talk more about his father, but he stayed silent, and clipping along at just over 150 km/hr, I was busy doing what Bruce told me to. By the time I gained any idea of what I was doing, we were halfway up Sodom Gap, and the scenery was so spectacular that conversation was reserved for exclaiming over it—not that I saw much other than the road on that trip. A half hour later we topped the Gap and headed from there down the Gouge in the winding journey into Utilitopia.

* * *

The Council of Rationalizers met in a small room with no windows or decoration. There was a large interactive screen up front and a small terminal at each of the fifty or so seats. My chair seemed to be deliberately a little uncomfortable, either digging into my back or pressing my thighs annoyingly. The dingy colors suggested that the room ought to have a nasty sour smell to it, but it had only the faint, sterile scent of soap, disinfectant, and hard cold surfaces.

They began with a prayer that sounded like a contract. "Our Father, acknowledging that it is only reasonable that . . . as beings created with the capacity for rationality therefore . . . thus assuming . . . it follows from the observed portion of Your Law therefore that . . ." and so forth, winding down eventually to ". . . for it is demonstrable that no person in the sense-accessible realm is, or can be, or ever can have been, in any statable way, greater than You."

They ran through some routine business, ratifying a wide range of price changes (plainly, market here did not have anything to do with "market forces") and an interminable set of reports demonstrating, I think, that they had gotten immorality down to the lowest possible level.

Finally, they came to New Business, which was us. They were visibly uncomfortable about Aimeric's insistence on his Occitan name, but they sat politely while he made graphs spin and leap on the screen for them. I had settled on a position in which the chair slowly ate my coccyx and my thighs gradually creased, but neither happened too quickly.

A three-hour debate followed, none of which I could follow and all of which I had to appear to be following with intense interest. After a lot of arguments that were, I think, about principle versus expediency, they decided that maybe the markets they had now would not be able to handle the adjustments all by themselves, and appointed Aimeric, Bieris, and me to be advisors to the Pastor for Market Function. I realized at once that since the Pastor for Market Function was a dumpy-looking woman named Clarity Peterborough, the job was obviously ceremonial. We were told our job would be to assist her in drawing up proposals for dealing with the expected changes.

As the meeting broke up, Chairman Carruthers said he wanted to talk with us and with the Pastor for Market Function, so we stuck around. No one bothered to speak with any of us before they left, but they didn't speak with each other either—they just stood up and walked out after the closing prayer—so I didn't feel particularly insulted.

When they had gone, Aimeric turned to his father and said, "It's a pleasure to see you looking so well, sir. I hope this will work out to our mutual benefit."

Old Carruthers's head bounced once, hard. "I appreciate your courtesy. We have much business to do. Have you been pleased with your new life?"

"Yes, quite." Aimeric's voice, utterly expressionless, sounded as if he had spent years developing this tone.

Carruthers never looked at him. He said, very softly, almost inaudibly, "Then no doubt your decision to emigrate must have been based on a strong rational grasp of the intangible factors in the situation. You have my congratulations."

"I appreciate that very much."

It was like watching people make love by semaphore.

The two of them bowed, deeply and formally. Aimeric showed a very slight trace of a grin, or perhaps it was just tension.

Then, just as if nothing at all had happened—and still without touching the son he had not seen in a quarter of a century—the old Chairman got down to business.

"Sit, everyone. Now that we're out of that silly meeting we can dispense with ceremony. Aimeric—am I pronouncing that correctly? accent on the first syllable? good—I believe you met the Highly Reverend Clarity Peterborough while you were here."

We all bowed, since that seemed to be the local custom. "Highly Reverend" sounded like a real title, and now that I thought of it half the Council of Rationalizers had been female—in fact I'd thought at first they had all brought their wives, but the women were clearly voting. I was still a bit shocked to find a woman in a job that no Occitan woman would have stooped to, but I obviously needed to get used to local customs, so I tried to look at her with calm neutrality.

Clarity Peterborough was a slim woman, short, perhaps forty years old, who blinked constantly, as if her eyes were sensitive to the light. Like most of the more religious Caledons, her hair was cut close to her head, but she had gone some time between haircuts, and it was not long enough to stay combed. The preswelds on her shirt and coverall seemed to pull a little in some places and sag in others, making odd wrinkles, as if they had been made to slightly wrong measurements or she had worn them more times than they were designed for.

She looked at each of us as if memorizing our faces and names and studying us the way a butterfly collector does a rare, highly prized specimen. "My," she said, "you're all so colorful to look at. It will delight people to see you."

We all blushed; Bieris thanked her.

I thought I detected a raised eyebrow of amusement on the Chairman, but at the time I didn't know him well enough to be sure. Did Caledons spend all their time trying to guess at each others' feelings?

"Let me make sure I'm pronouncing everyone correctly," the Chairman said. "Bieris and Grott?"

Pretty close, really. "Giraut," I said. "Short *i* between the *g* and the *r, au* dipthong like in Industrial Age German or Classical Latin."

He nodded. "Giraut," he said, getting it perfectly. "I hope you'll excuse my accent—I read several languages but I can only speak Terstad and Reason without embarrassing myself."

A flunky brought in large mugs of hot, slightly salty water, with a citrulo slice floating in each one. Bruce and Aimeric had coached us enough to know that we were to wait until Carruthers drank, then finish our mugs with him, in three long draughts with prayers in between. It had seemed a silly ritual, but no sillier than any other, as we learned it, but now I noticed that the warm liquid felt very pleasant on the throat and seemed to take a lot of the chill off. I wondered how anything so pleasant had survived in this culture.

Carruthers sighed a little and said, "Let me start out by stating the problem back to you, to see if I really do understand it. I think I speak as an unusually consistent and reasonable thinker on such subjects, with my many years of experience in the mathematics of both correct politics and correct theology. Even if you are not able to apprehend my logic immediately, I do hope that you will be able to recognize the validity of my emotions."

I couldn't decide whether he was insulting us or confessing to a personal failing.

He went on. "I don't think any of us here really wanted the springer to come into existence. In our isolation from the rest of the Thousand Cultures, we've enjoyed several centuries to develop a fully rationalized world. But we are by no means finished. As far as I can see, connection can only set the cause of Rational Christianity back. It was simply our decision that connection must come, sooner or later, and that if it came later, the situation would only be worse—hence the decision to face it immediately. And I might add that many prominent citizens opposed that decision all the same."

I squirmed on my seat—the damned thing was hurting me again—and noticed others, even Carruthers, doing the same thing.

"It seems to me," Carruthers said, "that my first concern has to be with this supposed 'assistance through the Transition Period' that the Council of Humanity is supplying us with. You may propose a solution or an internal policy that we may not wish to follow. Are we free to say no?"

Aimeric thought about this quietly for a moment and then said, "My mission is only to provide advice and technical assistance in handling the violent dislocations your economy is going to go through. The Council of Humanity has a strong interest in making sure that reintegration of the Thousand Cultures goes smoothly, and therefore they want you to suffer the least possible social pain."

Carruthers pressed his fingers to his gray-white temples

and said, "Then they really have made no study of our culture at all. Surely if they had, they would know that economic dislocations cannot possibly happen here."

Aimeric cued up three graphs on the big common screen. "In one sense you're right. This will all be temporary anyway, so no matter what you do, even if you have some perverse longing for disaster and go out of your way to cause it, in six or seven stanyears everything will be just fine. So what I'm talking about here is softening a blow."

"I don't see why a fully rational market should feel any blow at all."

"I don't have all the data on Caledony yet, and I'll be able to tell you more in a couple of days, but here's what historical experience has been everywhere: In thirty standays, the Bazaar opens in the Embassy compound. In effect that's a giant trade fair and catalog—every culture that has built a springer so far in the Thousand Cultures sends reps and goods. You don't get a choice: it's uncontrolled free trade including prices and quantities."

"Well, I see that could disrupt other cultures, but with our fully rational—"

Aimeric just kept pressing the point, as if explaining to a four year old. "No, wait. I mean the prices are uncontrolled. Not the people. You won't be able to freeze or restrict anyone's assets, or set up a structure to make people 'rationally' want what you want them to want. They can draw down their accounts, buy whatever they like, and own it rather than lease it."

His father got up very slowly, as if something under the table had bitten him and he was bleeding from the wound. He leaned forward, his hands on the table, suddenly looking older. "So in thirty standays we will have no economic self-government at all?"

"You still have plenty of powers to use as you wish—you can regulate currency and banking, expand or shrink the government budget, raise or reduce taxes—all of that. And you can still set prices and quantities on goods and services in your local market. What you can't do is prohibit or tax interstellar trade, or set prices for it, or touch any property acquired through interstellar trade. You can still control a lot about the economy—you just won't be able to stop people from getting outside of it."

Carruthers's hands twisted together in front of him like fighting animals. "I still don't—well, no matter anyway. It will still pose no problem for us, except for a test of faith, and there are always plenty of those. We just have to trust that with centuries of training in rationality, our people will want only the things that will make them truly happy."

Aimeric shook his head like a dazed bull. "What I'm saying is that people are not going to want what you want them to want. And especially the fascination with really owning things individually is going to surprise you." He sighed. "But all that can be set aside. For now at least. Because even if everyone bought exactly what you would want them to want, there would still be trouble."

Carruthers was plainly having trouble controlling himself as well; he got up and paced. Peterborough looked very worried and seemed about to speak up when Carruthers said, "I suppose you'll have to explain *that* to me too. I'm listening."

"I appreciate that." Aimeric tilted his chair back and stared at the ceiling for a moment. "I'm trying to think of the best way to explain the problem. Okay, if they're rational, they'll buy any good that's cheaper than leasing the equivalent good here. Do you grant me that?"

"You need not lecture your father. I taught you Reason."

"I know. I remember. I'm sorry if I offended you, sir."

"I accept your apology. Please proceed."

"All right. Well, the goods the imports will replace have already been produced, in many cases, and scheduled for production in others. So there will be a lot of surplus inventory, which will have to be cleared by lowering production and prices—but lower prices at one end of the system means lower wages at the other end, and lower production means fewer hours. So everyone will have less money, and there will be a smaller market, and of course the less desirable domestic goods are the ones that people cut back on. Meanwhile money is pouring out to pay for the exports, which drives up your interest rates and thus domestic production costs. So it costs more and more to produce goods that are selling for lower and lower prices in smaller and smaller quantities . . . and the whole thing spirals downward. Those are usually called Connect Depressions."

Peterborough nodded eagerly. "This makes perfect sense, even though nothing quite like it has happened in the last five hundred years or so. So how do we get out of a Connect Depression? Does it self-correct, like a classical free market?"

"Right. With your prices so low, all of a sudden you've got the cheapest exports in the Thousand Cultures on some items, and you're paying the highest interest rates. Money pours in—and you get rocketing growth and explosive inflation. The system might bounce once or twice through the whole cycle again, but there's a lot of 'drag'—every surge and depression reshapes your culture's economy into better accord with the macro-economy of the Thousand Cultures, so that in a little while, six or seven years, you restabilize at a higher level of production.

"So in short, the Bazaar will open, and in a few weeks the Connect Depression will start and last two years or more; then after that the Connect Boom will give you towering inflation, for several years following. It's going to be a rough, bumpy ride before things finally settle out.

"With the right measures we can make sure that everyone just notches the belt a little and gets through. On the other hand, if we just let it go its own way, a few people will do very well and many people will get savaged—which means widespread envy, misery, and anger."

Aimeric's voice had risen to a very loud, firm tone by the end of that, and he was staring directly at his father. The old man stared back squarely. After a long while, he said softly, "You can prove this?"

"*Yap, stip-subj tot-dob prev-mod-tot,*" Aimeric replied. I never got good at Reason, but a rough translation would be "Hell, yes." At the time, I thought Aimeric had developed

some unaccountable speech defect; my ear had not yet
learned to tolerate so many full-stop consonants juxtaposed.

"Then," Carruthers said very slowly, "the purposes of the
Council of Humanity are at least partly rational, in the technical sense, and I think we have to respect the possibility that
they have real help to offer us. Under those conditions it's
quite reasonable to make all the arrangements immediately—
and let me add I am looking forward to your report." He
stretched and yawned. "I also think it's fully rational of me
to wish that all of this had come up during someone else's
term as Chairman, and for a man of my age to feel the need
for his First Dark nap."

Aimeric smiled a little at that and said, "Sir, if the meeting
is officially over at this point, might I ask when you won the
decision? I confess to not having looked it up."

Old Carruthers nodded crisply. "Perfectly correct. It would
have been irrational of me to be offended by your not looking
up information for which you had no immediate need."

"Dad," Aimeric said, "it was thoughtless of me to mention
my not having looked it up. It was graceless and tasteless. It
would have cost me only a second's effort to have looked it
up, and by expressing some interest in your affairs I might
have given you some pleasure. Please accept my apologies—
and then do tell me about winning the decision!"

His father stared very steadily, with no response or connection, into Aimeric's face, until any normal person would have
broken away in anger and embarrassment. Aimeric looked
back coolly.

At last old Carruthers said, "By your rules I suppose I
should accept your apology. It would cost me nothing and
may do you some good. But any pleasure I might take in it
would be irrational; and such pleasures are temptations to fall
away from the path of Rational Christianity."

The silence stretched on longer than before. At last the old
man said, so softly that I might have missed it, "But I do accept your apology."

"Thank you," Aimeric said.

The old man was already headed for the door. "I am afraid I do not feel comfortable with a rush of emotions. I do hope you will all forgive me, but I really do need that nap."

He was gone before anyone spoke.

"Extraordinary," Reverend Peterborough said. "I've never seen him like that before, and we've been friends some years." She got up. "I would suspect that choosing work is going to take up the rest of your time in town today. So let's just exchange schedules by com after you get home, and then we'll get together sometime in the next couple of days." She looked around again, smiling at us all. "I am so delighted to have you all here—Caledony so often forgets the good things that are not rational, and I think you will help us remember."

"Good things that are not rational?" Aimeric asked. "I thought that was—"

"Heresy." Her smile grew wider. "Quite a few people think so." There was a twinkle in her eye that made me grin foolishly back. I had never liked a plain woman, let alone a slovenly one, so much before. She left with another polite bow.

I wasn't quite sure how I was going to explain this morning to Marcabru. Maybe I would just wait for his letter, which surely would be along in a day or so. In fact, I was a bit surprised Marcabru hadn't written yet.

I turned to say something to Aimeric, but he was now staring at the wall, his arms twined around himself, lost in thought.

No one said anything until Bruce came for us; then Aimeric stood up slowly, and sighed. "Some day, *companho*, over a great deal of wine, I will do my best to explain to you just what was going on there. But not now. Now we put on ultra-calm faces and go to be interviewed by the Work Assignment Bureau. The people there have no sense of irony, as I recall, so be very sure you don't say anything you don't mean to be taken literally."

Bruce snickered. "Charlie had to spend four weeks in Morally Corrective Therapy, over and above his work assignments, because he answered the 'describe your ideal job' by telling them he wanted to be a Viking and his lifelong dream was to pillage and burn Utilitopia. So, be very careful."

THREE

The Work Assignment Bureau was a big clean space, lighted in cheerful pastels. The only place I had ever seen like it in Noupeitau had been the visitors' lounge in a mental hospital.

Somewhere in the middle of manure-shoveling the day before, I had come up with an idea, which Bruce had helped me to refine—but no one had told me I would have to find a way to explain it to an aintellect, not to a living, breathing Caledon official. I suppose it had seemed so obvious to Bruce and Aimeric that neither of them had thought to mention that.

Of course, from what I'd seen at the meeting this morning, the difference between an aintellect and a Caledon official might not amount to much.

After I answered all the initial questions by keyboard, the microphone extended down from the ceiling, and the aintellect asked me what my most preferred job was.

I thought for one instant of saying something silly—"well, I think I have the looks to be a gigolo," or "do you have any openings for gladiators?" and mentally cursed Bruce for telling me that story. Then I made myself relax and began. "What I would like to do is to open an experiential school of Nou Occitan culture."

"Please define experiential school," the aintellect said.

"A place where students learn primarily by experience and by skills practice rather then lecture. In effect, the coursework consists of behaving like Occitans in some specific area of endeavor, for the duration of each class."

The aintellect paused for a moment. Somewhere back in the electronic chaos, a thought formed. "Objection: no real benefit to students or to Caledon society. Occitan thought is not rationalized. Expected results are contamination of Caledon thought with uncanonical premises and an eventual unnecessary heterogeneity of Caledon thought."

Since this was the one objection Bruce had been sure I would face, I was prepared. "Occitan culture is very complex and it's east to give insult. A Caledon is only safe there because he's tolerated as a kind of social idiot." That had certainly been true of Aimeric's first stanyear. "The only way to function safely in the Occitan culture is to be able to follow the complex cultural system by habit rather than try to remember all the rules at once."

"Objection," it began. Obviously it had been thinking ahead. "Trade has historically been much smaller between the Caledon and Occitan culture than was economically feasible, amounting only to a slow exchange of economists for art historians and literature instructors. This tends to indicate that very few Caledons will have any desire to do business with Occitan, and there will not be enough rational demand to support your school."

That sounded like I had carried the previous point, so I allowed myself a little hope. "The historical case is irrelevant," I said, "because it pertains to exchange of information. You can expect material goods to flow in quantity once springer charges come down. Reference interstate trade theory, key names Ricardo, Hecksher, Ohlin." Those were the names Aimeric had given me—he said they'd trigger such a sweeping search that the aintellect probably wouldn't bother to read it and ask me anything about it. Just in case, I kept talking quickly. "You can expect that instead of scholars who've spent years studying Occitan, you'll have lots of naive businessmen going there. You don't want them to establish a reputation as boors." I didn't actually have any facts to back that up with, but it sounded pretty good to me.

This time the pause went on for a very long time. I looked all around the little booth for any sign of decoration or desecration, but there was none. Maybe they cleaned it after each interview.

I thought about the ten million people of Caledony who came through here to have an aintellect tell them what to do with the rest of their lives, and not one of them had left any mark on the space. It gave me a cold, shivering feeling, and I thanked every god I could think of that I would be gone in a stanyear or at most two.

When the voice came back, it said, "Final objection: The introduction of Occitan culture may create irrational patterns of thought, which in turn may significantly diminish the overall rationality of Caledon society, economy, or polity."

I didn't know whether "Final objection" was the last test before saying yes or whether it meant that my suggestion had been rejected and this was the grounds. In any case it was the same point as the first one, and I wasn't going to let the aintellect get away with it. As soon as they think they can fool us they start all this nonsense about getting the vote again. "Look," I said, "anyone who is going to become crazy or irrational from going to a Center for Occitan Arts is awfully damned weak in his rationality to begin with. If I'm a corrupting influence at least you'll find out who's ripe to be corrupted. Think of me as an early warning system or something." *Deu*, I didn't want to spend two stanyears shovelling shit!

"Clarification request: Expression 'awfully damn' means strong emphasis of what follows?"

"Awfully damn yes." Well, no doubt I had blown it—having any normal feelings in front of these people seemed to upset them, so no doubt having a full-fledged outburst would convince the aintellect that I was much too crazy to be allowed to teach anything, let alone to offer open access courses. Maybe they'd let me pick through the rotten vegetables or something.

"Proposal accepted in principle," the aintellect said. "Benefits to include social prophylaxis of irrational and sin-prone individuals, creation of a skills base for possible expanded commercial contact, and validation of existing policy." A panel slid back, revealing a workscreen. "Please enter all requested data so that this agency can establish capital and resource requirements plus make necessary arrangements."

Still in a mild daze, I answered a lot of questions about

floorspace and equipment needed for different activities, numbers of students I was willing to take in the various classes I was planning to offer, and so forth. It took a long time. As I noted in my letter to Marcabru that night, apparently aintellects were more sympathetic and reasonable than people here.

It was lunchtime—late in First Dark—when we finished and Bruce picked us up. Aimeric had gotten a post as a professor of Occitan literature at the University. Bruce and Aimeric tried to explain to me why the University of Caledony would have such a thing as literature studies. I never did understand it really, but it sounded as if since there had never been a high culture without some interest in literature they were keeping it around to see what it might be good for.

Shouting all that information to each other over the thunder of hail on the cab took up most of the short cat ride through Utilitopia's dark, ice-slick streets to Retail Food and Eating Space Facility Seventeen, which they claimed had good local food. During all my arguing and their explaining, Bieris was quiet.

As we slipped into the entrance tunnel of the restaurant, I turned to her and said, "What will you be doing?"

"Bruce is taking me on as a permanent farmhand. I've really enjoyed working on the farm and I just thought I'd keep doing it."

"You're not just doing this to avoid working over here in the fog and the cold?" I asked. "I know it's gloomy, but—"

"Well, of course that's a consideration," she said. "But yes, I really do like it."

There was a long, awkward silence, and then Aimeric began to talk with Bruce about a bunch of people who had been dead for a long time. Bieris didn't look happy with me, but fortunately just then the food arrived.

Because of the robot-replacement rule, almost every place had human waiters, bartenders, busboys, and so forth. Bieris and I thanked the young man who brought us the food. He seemed startled, so I suppose we were not strictly in accord with local custom.

It took a little effort to fish the meat out of the thick, salty fat-sauce without getting any more of the sauce onto the potatoes. That gave me some time to think—I really had not meant to offend Bieris, though it was obvious I had. Carefully, I worked my way around to saying that there were some women who simply were genuinely interested in those offbeat occupations even in Nou Occitan, and that a mere unusual interest certainly did not make anyone less of a *donzelha*. Indeed, by the contrast it might show to her own grace and style, such a job could only enhance the loveliness, particularly of a fine, spirited beauty. I thought that last a nicely done indirect compliment, just at the level of not giving offense to Aimeric while flattering Bieris.

She glared at me, clearly too furious to speak, or eat, or do anything except glare. Perhaps I had turned the compliment badly? No, as I turned it over in my mind, it had been fine, a true gem of the flatterer's art. Did she feel it was insincere? It had not been, and surely she would realize that?

She kept glaring.

Finally I said, "I'm sorry. Of late, I have been in the grip of *finamor*, but now that I have recovered from my melancholy over Garsenda, I obviously need to make some amends."

From the way she bolted the next piece of food, I could tell I had not yet said the right thing. "Giraut," she said, "that is so stupid I'm not sure it *is* worth talking to you about. Have you ever wondered what the jovents look like to us *donzelhas*? I'm just asking out of curiosity."

"Well—uh. I've read a lot of poetry by women, about men."

"Written for men."

"Ja, *verai*." When all else fails, admit you're an idiot. "You're right, I don't understand what you're talking about."

"No, you don't," she said, taking another big bite of potatoes without scraping any of that nasty brown glop off. "Why is it all right for you to act like a complete fool for weeks, with everyone required to sigh and admire you, even though we all knew Garsenda was flighty and just plain stupid besides—and then when she turns out to be doing just exactly what any ardently fashionable young woman in Noupeitau does these days—what you yourself might have expected if you'd had half a brain—we're all supposed to be in mourning because you've been tragically wronged?"

It all seemed obvious to me. "It's just fun, Bieris. Being a jovent is something you do for fun for a few years. That's all. Besides, I thought we were talking about you being a farmhand. I was trying to be nice about that." I glanced at Aimeric for support, but he was still engrossed in his conversation with Bruce.

She sighed and brushed her hair back off her face. "Have you ever noticed that practically everything the jovents do is pointless without an audience of women?"

Before I spoke again I had gobbled about half of that grim piece of greased meat. I made myself slow down and take a long drink of water, then said, "Uh, no, but it's true."

"It's true for everyone in Nou Occitan," she said, "think about your parents, or mine."

"There are a lot of women in important positions." It was pretty feeble and she just made a face at me. I tried to continue, stammering awkwardly—"I guess . . . well, certainly, verai, I know what you're going to say. Nobody on Wilson pays any attention to what the government or the corporations do anyway as long as their allowances keep coming in, so if you look at the Palace or the arts, where all the energy and intelligence goes—that's almost all male."

Bieris nodded, the first sign of approval I had seen from her. "Except for dance. Men like looking at us when we're nearly naked. And I would bet you've never noticed any of this, Giraut, before I pointed it out to you."

"No, I haven't. I'm sorry."

I ate a little more, but my appetite was gone. She brushed her hair back again. I had never noticed before that she seemed to be annoyed by having it fall across her face all the time.

After a while, Bieris said, "Giraut, I'm sorry."

"It's fine. You're right."

"*Ja*, I am, but you weren't the person I was angry with. I'm not sure who is. It's only—well, when I got here the first thing Bruce did was ask me to do physical work, and it was no special thing at all—he didn't ask me in any way differently from how he'd ask you or Aimeric." She sighed and looked around the room. "This isn't easy for me to explain, Giraut."

"You're doing fine. I think. At least it's making sense even if I don't understand it."

"This is the first time I've ever felt like a person, I suppose. Instead of like a *donzelha*. Have you ever seen any of my paintings, Giraut?"

Bieris had been at every public performance I had ever given. At that moment I died a couple of thousand deaths. "No. And I'd like to."

She opened up the small locket she wore around her neck, took out her portfolio, and handed it to me. I took out my pocket reader, slid her portfolio into the slot on the back, and raised it to my eyes.

"Look at the last ten especially," she said. "Remember the aurocs-de-mer?"

"They're hard to forget."

"That's the last ten."

I pressed the codes to see the last ten paintings; Aimeric and Bruce were gabbling on about somebody's dead third cousin.

"If you hate them and think they're really terrible—lie," Bieris said. I glanced up from the eyepiece and she had that bent grin I remembered from childhood and schooldays. When had I seen her smiling like that last? Maybe graduation day when the faculty toilets had suddenly erupted just when they were all in there putting on their formal robes. And where had that side of Bieris gone when she got involved in *finamor* with Aimeric?

Thinking of that—in my career of six *entendedoras*, what

had any of them actually thought about *me*? What were *their* memories like?

I doubt Bieris knew my thoughts, but she could see I was thinking, so she waited a long breath before pointing to the reader I still held.

I put the reader to my face. My breath slowly sighed out. The painting was extraordinarily well done; I realized with a guilty start that if Bieris had been male, she'd have been ranked with the very best of the jovent painters. And its quality was not merely in clarity of composition or simple technique, though both were superb, but in the sharp intelligence of its seeing. I could almost feel my own memory of the day slide away as this took its place. It was Bieris who had truly seen the huge herd that poured over the riverbank, the soft reds, browns, and yellows of the plains.

I flipped to the next painting and looked out across the plains to the first rising smoke of the oncoming fire; to the next and saw a terrified auroc-de-mer struggling in the mud; and on through them. It would take many repeat visits for me to really say I understood the work.

As always when praising art, I began to speak in Occitan, and then stopped, strangling conventional forms in my throat—there didn't seem to be any words for the way these paintings made me feel. There was something missing in the Occitan perception—

I raised the reader to my eyes again, and flipped back to the first one, and there in the background was the shining specular blur of red sunlight bouncing off the pipelines feeding the polar glaciers. In the next, the auroc-de-mer died framed by the scaffolding that carried the muck pipeline into the areas being planted in forests.

Her wide landscape of the great intrusion of plains into the gorge revealed, on the horizon, a blue-white plume dancing in the red sky—hydrogen from the ocean, brought five hundred km by pipeline and burned to get water into the air in the huge dry basin around the South Pole. The rocks themselves in the gorge showed the not-yet-weathered melting and glass fragments from the many directed meteor impacts that had been needed to give the basin an outlet to the sea.

In other paintings the power lines for the heaters that kept permafrost from forming, the concrete baffles that slowed and bent the Great Polar River so that it flowed like a much older stream, and even the high dams on the mountain gorges were clearly visible. You could look through four centuries of Occitan landscapes and never see one of those things. Every painting of the South Pole I had ever seen had shown trees bending over the river, little lakes and pools lying everywhere, and forests on the distant mountains—the way it would look in four hundred years when it was done, not the way it was today.

When I looked up at her, it was with the painful realization that she was more artist than I would ever be, and that if I would have anything to brag about from my jovent days, it would be my friendship with her.

"We talked about it," she said. "On Wilson, people want paintings of what everything will be like when the terraforming is complete."

"But Bieris—here on Caledony, there's no art at all, and . . . these are spectacular! Back home such an exhibit that could make your career!" A thought struck me. "Have you shown Aimeric?"

She made a face. "You must be joking."

I dropped the subject. "So—if you're painting like this, why are you hanging around here as a farmhand?"

She grimaced at me. "Then you haven't really seen Sodom Basin, either."

At least I knew the right thing to say. "No, I haven't. Tell me. Or if you can't tell me, I'll just wait for the paintings."

"You *might* have to wait for the paintings to fully explain it," she warned. "But it's the light, and the reflections off the snow on the Pessimals, and how green everything is—"

"But what is it you can see as a farmhand that you can't see by just being there in your off hours? Or do you just want to avoid the trip every day?"

All of a sudden, finally, she was really smiling at me—in

a way I couldn't remember since puberty had hit us both. I liked that more than I could have said. "You *do* understand," she said.

"A little, maybe. Explain it slowly, in little words, *companhona.*" It was a silly word to use, one that just slipped out—the feminine of our word for a close friend, but in Occitan a grown man never applied it to a *donzelha*, let alone to a grown woman.

She apparently failed to notice. "When I work in a landscape, I have to see it in more detail. To know a storm cloud I have to know what all clouds look like, to tend an orchard I have to be able to see the individual apples on the individual tree. That's all. I'm sorry. I probably could have explained all that to you in three sentences. It's just that nobody's listened to me in *ages*. You know the old saying—'If you're tired of listening to her, make her your *entendedora*.'"

"Are you people done with the fine local cuisine?" Aimeric asked, breaking in. We both jumped at the sudden noise.

FOUR

Two days later, I pulled the cat I was now leasing into the parking area of the new building for the Center for Occitan Arts, which had finished growing less than three hours before. The last freighter was pulling back out through the loading doors, and huge loads of stuff needed to stock and ready the Center for classes were piled in what would be the assembly hall. To get the unpacking and setting-up done, I had arranged for some robots, and they arrived as I was closing the loading doors.

This was my third time unpacking and rearranging furniture in three days. The day before, my things had finally arrived, apparently after some trouble with getting them packed and moved on Wilson. I had seen at once that my baroque furniture didn't go well with the smooth, clean lines of

Bruce's guest house, and had hinted to Bruce that I would be very interested in seeing any interior designs he might have for the place. That seemed to delight him—as much as you could tell with a Caledon—and for no reason I could see, it pleased Bieris too, who promptly requested the same for her place. Really, I just didn't want the contrast between my beautiful furniture and that bland, lifeless house to make me homesick.

Bruce had had quite a few designs on file, so we had them made up the following First Afternoon, put our Occitan things in storage, and did our second job of furniture moving.

Now I was about to start my third, and in a much bigger building.

In this mild yellow fog, a few degrees above freezing, with the rime on its soaring buttresses turning to shining icewater, the Center stood out against the gray concrete boxes around it like a piece of magic thrown into a geometry lesson. The first two hours setting up the place were wonderful fun; I created a snug apartment for myself out of one of the sleeping rooms so that I could stay the night when necessary, got the robots to lay and cover the mats for the dueling arts room, and had the Main Lounge turned into a pretty fair copy of Pertz's—though I purposely omitted the Wall of Honor. I had a feeling that concept might be more than Caledons would tolerate at first.

That accounted for the first cargo, and there was still more than an hour of First Light left, so I ordered the furniture for the seminar room and the little theater—since the fabrication plant was only fifteen minutes away by trakcar, and it took less than forty minutes to grow an order of furniture, I had to be careful to order things in the order in which I wanted to bring them in.

I sat down and had a sandwich and a plum while the robots removed construction dust from the upper floors—*gratz'deu* I had a springer vacuum in my baggage, probably the only one in Caledon at the moment, and the recycling plant had already built its springer, so the dust sailed cleanly out of my place and became their problem.

Now that I saw what the furniture was doing in the space, I considered some rearranging, but I was pretty pleased in general. Just as two robots moved the last table into place, one of them stopped and announced, "This unit's replacement will arrive in twenty-two minutes. Sorry for any inconvenience. Please acknowledge. This unit's replacement will—"

"I understand," I said, hoping that was the right way to acknowledge. It must have been because the robot then moved into a corner (thankfully one where I had not planned to put anything), locked its joints, and switched off.

While I waited for whoever to arrive, I worked up a grocery list and had the robots test all the plumbing, electrical, and data connections. The printer in the library was merrily turning out posters and vus, including all ten of Bieris's auroc-de-mer pieces. She had emphatically pointed out to me that they were not at all typically Occitan, and I had counterargued to her that, first of all, they were brilliant and one could hardly get more Occitan than that, and in the second place, as the director and chief instructor of the Center, I was the planetary authority on what was Occitan and what wasn't.

It was still a few minutes until the human worker was supposed to show up, so I put the robots to more cleaning (freshly grown buildings are always so dusty), took my vacuum bottle of hot coffee, and went up to the little solar on the third floor to watch the sun go down. I would skip my nap and work through First Dark, but I felt I had earned a bit of a break.

The solar, with wide, comfortable benches and a lot of cushions, was intended as a place to talk or read, but the view through its tall arched windows was surprisingly fine. They'd located me near the University, down in the low, cold, nasty part of the city. Utilitopia, like Noupeitau, had been built on hills around a bay, but Noupeitau had been laid out by the great Arnaut de Riba Brava, with every major building placed to lead your eye up to the Great Hall of the Arts on Serra Sangi, flanked by the Palace and the Forum. Here, because the local sulfur-calcium cycle gave the sea a rotten-egg stench, and areas near the sea were cold and dank, a legal requirement, called the "balance of utilities," intended to make sure that no one became irrationally attached to any particular place, forced the more pleasant parts of the human environment to be located in the nastier parts of the physical environment, and vice versa. Thus, like the University, my Center was right on the waterfront, giving me a splendid view up the hillsides to Utilitopia's two dominating structures, which capped the Twin Hills like scarred nipples: the Municipal Sewage Processing Facility to the north, and the Central Stockyards and Abbatoir to the south.

Yet west of the ugly boxed squalor of Utilitopia, the fierce amber eye of Mufrid, at last visible in the brief fogless period of last First Light, burned its way down between the high peaks of the Optimals. Light flashed from their icy upper reaches and deep shadows streaked down to the sea from them. As cooling water vapor from the glaciers drifted down into the dark sea-chilled chasms and fjords facing me, brief ferocious storms broke out, their lightning flaring in the rips and tears in the face of the range.

As I watched, the moon broke from the western horizon and shot up the sky, toward the sun, darkening as it climbed. As owner of one of the few decent windows in town, it was all mine. But perhaps, with a little training, these people would be able to see what they had here.

I realized why I was feeling better now than since I had come here. I had been doing real work all day—had in fact gotten up early to drive the cat in—and the work was toward something that really mattered, bringing a little of the light of culture to these cold, emotionless people. Sternly I reminded myself that I must not let them know that I was here to show them a better way—missionaries, even those on behalf of simple human warmth and light, are never popular, after all!—but *I* knew what I was here to do.

A trakcar slowed in the street in front of me, extended its wheels, and alighted, turning off the track to park next to my cat. I was most of the way to the door when the bell rang.

The young man who stood shifting his weight from foot to

foot in the Center's heatlock had Afro features and light blond hair. He didn't bother to look at me when he said, "Here for work duty."

"Good," I said. "Come in, please. My name is Giraut Leones."

I took his parka and hung it up, which seemed to startle him—I suppose he thought of that as work, and people don't work for robots. "This way. What's your name, by the way? I don't want to call you Unit Two."

"Thorwald Spenders." For no reason I could see, he then recited his ident number.

We spent an hour hanging posters in the hallways. Thorwald seemed a bit surprised that I cared which poster went where, and occasionally rearranged posters when I had a better idea or something didn't quite look right. I suppose he thought of them as wallpaper with inadequate coverage.

The bar for the Lounge arrived. It took ten minutes of struggle for Thorwald and me to get it up the stairs, me wishing the whole time I had put in a real elevator instead of just installing a one-person springer.

At last we had the bar in place. "You might as well stock it," I said. "The bottles are in those crates—just arrange them alphabetically."

He nodded and started on the job; meanwhile I worked on getting a tapestry up. It was a machine dupe of a handmade, and usually those hang straighter, but they still take a lot of effort to get straight.

Halfway into Thorwald's shift, it was completely dark, the clouds covering the moon again, and I had turned on the lights. I fiddled with them now, trying to tune them to get the right colors for the tapestry; what I needed was not just Arcturus's spectrum, which after all was in the database, but Arcturus's spectrum after entering through clerestory windows and bouncing off the rough surface of mica-rich pink granite vaulting. Back home I could simply have ordered a spectro of it, but I had discovered that pending the opening of the Bazaar, data was not being passed between the two cultures except in letters, and I doubted very much that

Marcabru would be willing to send me the twenty or so pages of it. If, in fact, he ever wrote.

"It's a little dim to read the bottles," Thorwald said.

I copied the best approximation I had come up with so far into the lights' memory and then switched it up the local standard, Flat Amber.

Turning back to the console, I heard something that was almost a gasp. I looked up again in time to catch Thorwald ducking, a blush spreading over the part of his forehead I could see. "Almost drop something?"

"No, I just looked up, and um—well, the cloth things on the wall are really bright. It kind of did something to me."

I walked over to the bar and studied him intensely, but he didn't look up. I turned to look at the tapestry.

I had known that the light was wrong, so I had paid no attention to it. The dark richness of Occitan tapestries comes from the combination of brilliant dyes with Arcturus's red light, the same way that some Old Masters paintings get their rich subtle shading from the darkening of their varnish.

"It's called a tapestry," I said, trying to sound completely casual. Please, please, let there be some residual traces of esthetic sense in these icy pragmatic barbarians. "Do you *like* what it makes you feel?"

He was looking, now, closely, and said, "Yap. I think I do, I really do. Is that what it's for, like a way to focus your feelings?"

"That's not a bad description." I could refine his esthetic language later; right now I was overjoyed to find an esthetic *sense*, however misguided.

He flushed a little. "I thought it was . . . well, to keep the wall warm. Not literally, I mean, like a blanket, but to insulate the room air from the cold wall. I'd heard in school that your houses were cold so I figured that must be what the travesty is for."

"Tapestry," I said, holding my voice neutral. On the other hand this might be a very long couple of years. "Did you notice it before I yellowed the light and turned it up?"

"Well, I did, but . . . um—"

Thorwald looked a lot like Marcabru had, long ago, when I'd caught him in bed with my first real *entendedora*, just before we'd fought our first real duel. I said, "Let me show you something. If you don't mind being a research subject, instead of a robot, for a few minutes?"

It was the wrong thing to say. "Oh, nop, nop, I really shouldn't do anything but the work. That's what the shift is for. I don't know what got into me." He turned back to the bar and started diligently putting bottles where they belonged. I considered kicking him.

"It's called an esthetic experience," I said. "That's what got into you. A lot of people have them—they're harmless, but I'm afraid there's no cure. At least none I know of. Here in Caledony there may very well be a cure, come to think of it."

He kept loading bottles in, but I could see him stiffen all over. "You're making fun of me."

I had been, so naturally I denied it strenuously and apologized as much as I could. "Look," I said, when he finally looked up at me. "There *are* some things I really want to show you. Can you hang around for half an hour or so after your shift if over, so we can talk about them? I'll even compensate you with a meal, in exchange for being my research subject."

"I guess so." He set the last few bottles into the bar, making soft resonant thumps. "What needs doing next?"

"Hanging the chandeliers in the Dance Room." I led him down there, and handed him the specs.

He glanced at them and nodded. "It says one tenth of a percent off spec on everything. Why?"

"Just a little bit of fuzziness gives an effect that's a little warmer and more human. If you want, set it on exact, then on the fuzzed effect, and you'll see the difference."

"Ah, nop, that's—"

"Look at it this way. It's easier to have you see it for yourself than it is for me to explain it, so you're saving me work. You aren't required to work *exactly* like a robot, are you? Because the robot would have to keep doing trial and error on it, generate twenty or thirty settings, and then ask me which one I wanted. If you can see colors at all, you should be able to get it right all by yourself—as long as you compare the exact with the fuzzed-up versions."

He hesitated for a long breath; then all the air came out of his lungs and he relaxed a little. "Well, put like that, I guess you're right. We're supposed to do the robot's job to the best of our abilities, and it's fine if those exceed the robot's. Sorry I'm such a stiffneck."

"I've met worse," I said, referring to practically every other Caledon. "Call if you need help." I thought that if I didn't hang around and press him, maybe he'd be able to enjoy it more.

My feet made an oddly hollow ring on the sprung floor, not yet detuned to deaden the sounds.

While he worked on the chandeliers, I put in the time you always do with a new building, checking for errors. Construction software is always buggy, by definition a robot can't look for trouble when you don't know yourself what trouble looks like until you see it, and with the kind of cold drafts they could have on Nansen, I didn't want loose joints caused by over- or under-growing.

I found three loose joints where the growth nanos would have to be restarted, and one big tumor in a crawl space, the concrete already pitting around the shapeless apple-sized lump as malignanos stripped the wall to feed the tumor.

I sent in the report on all of that to the construction contractor, who downloaded the right software to the building system to get it all fixed. I noted to myself that I would have to go back and see what was happening in a couple of days.

When I went back down to the Dance Room, Thorwald was just tuning the last green on the last laser for the last chandelier, and fifteen minutes were left in his shift. "Did you try putting it in and out of tune?"

"Yap. I saw what you meant, though I sure would never have known anything like that happened."

For the remaining time, I put him to unpacking caps of

books and racking them in the library, then went down to the kitchen to start the meal.

Since Thorwald was a Caledon, I held spices to a bare minimum, but since he looked young, I made the portions extra-large. When he came by, after his shift, he wanted to pay, saying that the meal was too much for just answering a few questions. I let him, but couldn't resist adding that "once this place is officially in operation, people will have to follow Occitan customs at least part of the time. Every now and then they'll have to accept getting a meal without paying for it, just because we want to give it to them."

He tried a couple of bits and then his cheeks bunched up in a smile. "This is wonderful! I've never tasted anything like it before. But I'm glad I tried it now before you're officially open. Otherwise I'd have been so put off by that guest idea that I might never have found out I liked this."

I just blurted out the obvious question. "What's so bad about being a guest?"

He shrugged at first, taking another bite and enjoying it; but as he chewed, his face became thoughtful, and by the time he had swallowed, he was obviously struggling with the question. "You know," he finally said, "I think it's just what they tell us all in school. And now that I think of it, maybe some of it is wrong, or misleading, or something."

I took a couple of bites myself. I had cooked it well enough, but it was still pretty bland; I wondered how he could taste anything but the plain ingredients. Yet I noticed he was drinking quite a bit of water with it, as if he needed to cool his mouth regularly. "What *do* they tell you in school?" I asked, after a while. I pushed about half the money he had paid for dinner back at him. "And this is for being a consultant on the issue, so I don't have to feel guilty about asking a lot of nosy questions."

He accepted it without comment. At last he said, "They say that even though you don't exchange money, you do exchange favors, and that unlike money, you can't really compare favors, so anyone in a relationship is always going to feel both guilty and exploited at the same time."

"Guilty and exploited about what?"

"Well, inequality, I guess. The feeling that you either got a deal that was too good from the other guy, or gave him more than it was worth." He wasn't looking up at me anymore; he concentrated on tearing apart a chunk of bread to dip in his soup. "That's what they told us. Sounds like it wasn't true."

I was about to agree, vehemently, that it wasn't, but it occurred to me that the most basic rule of *enseingnamen*—something I could remember my mother telling me as soon as I could understand—was that anyone truly *gens* will always try to give more than anyone else in his surroundings (though of course you're expected to be gracious about, and fulsome in praise of, gifts from others). "Let's say it's not that there isn't truth in it, just that it's not the whole truth and it really isn't the way things feel to the people doing them. It's as if people from Nou Occitan were to say that people on Caledon will do anything for money. It's not true, but you can distort the real world enough to make it seem true."

He ate a couple of bites, still not looking up at me, and I hoped I had not made him angry. I also reflected that in my last two letters to Marcabru, who had still not written back, I had said exactly that.

When he looked up, though, I realized he had been almost unable to breathe from laughing. "That's a great example," he said. "I have a lot of friends who would think that was pretty funny—you can always get a laugh by making fun of anything we learned in school."

"Since I'm a guest in this culture," I said, "I'll try to leave that to you." And I reminded myself strongly to do it. As resistant as these people had been made to art, culture, and beauty, I would have to lead them gently to it, not mock or scourge them for their esthetic inadequacy.

We finished the meal with a good sharp cheddar and a sweet pear. Thorwald, it turned out, had failed his first try to qualify for higher education, not for not being bright enough, but for lacking a command of theology. "I'm just not that mathematical," he said, shrugging. It didn't seem to be a sore spot with him, but reading between the lines I soon realized that it was fairly important to his parents, especially to his mother, who was on staff for the Council of Rationalizers.

When we had thrown the dishes into the regenner to be melted down and recast, I took him back up to the Lounge to show him the tapestries in their proper red lighting. He could see the richness of color but still liked their garish, clashing glare in amber light better. I supposed anyone who grew up in Utilitopia, with its monochrome of fog, black rock, and dingy pastel concrete, must be starved for color. Sophistication could come later. Besides, using his interest in color, I could lead him to the prints and vus, giving me a chance to lead him into giving me some unofficial reviews of the topics I was planning to offer.

In five minutes, I was back to thinking of him as a barbarian. Dueling arts repelled him as "teaching people to hurt each other." He couldn't seem to conceive of dance except as "a complete waste of motion, not even optimized for exercise." And although he had really enjoyed the meal, as far as he could see cooking classes would hopelessly enmesh everyone in mutual obligation.

At least poetry and music attracted him, and he seemed pleased that I had hired Bieris to offer a painting class, and would throw in the basic Occitan language course free to anyone who enrolled in three or more other classes.

"Well," I said, finally, having drawn as much out of him as I could, "it sounds as if I have at least one student. Thanks for your feedback. I guess I should let you go."

I walked with him back down to the door by the trakcar stop; it was now blind dark outside, the moon already gone and still three hours till the day's second sunrise. A thought came to me, and I said, "I'm going to need a janitor, according to your local labor laws. You want the job? There's a small apartment that comes with it, if you're tired of living with your parents."

He seemed startled and pleased, but he hesitated a moment. "Uh, I hate to take advantage of you. You ought to know that I don't have the money for a decent bribe. That's a good job and it would go for a lot. Just giving it away like that—the peeps might haul you in for a Rationality Check."

"No problem," I said, after thinking for just a moment. What were the peeps? I would have to check with Bruce. "It's only a two-hour job as it stands. The rest of the time I'll train you, and eventually use you, as a dueling arts instructor. Hard, painful, and morally repugnant work shouldn't look too attractive for you to afford to buy the job."

"That *will* work, no question." I liked the way he grinned. "Yes, I'll take the deal. I'll send in a credit transfer tonight, say 25:05 if you list it at twenty-five o'clock." We shook hands on it.

Much later, he told me that it was only after he got home and took the job that he realized he had been delighted to get work that was hard, painful, and morally repugnant.

As I walked into the conference room at the Pastorate for Market Function, later that afternoon, Bieris and Aimeric had six displays up on the screens. They were putting together the master model; Ambassador Shan and the Reverend Peter-borough sat in the back, watching intently and occasionally murmuring to each other.

"As the last one in," Aimeric said, "you win the honor of doing datahunt. Over on that terminal there's a list of the questions that none of the automated seekers could find answers to. I'd like you to find them. As soon as you find one, attach it to the question flag and it will autotransmit into the master program."

I sat down and got to it. Meanwhile Bieris and Aimeric completed laying in the model.

The first one I managed to get a handle on was "response time of average size of potatoes sold to change in price differential with respect to size." A couple of minutes later I found a way to get "rate of change in hem length of ceremonial kilts with respect to average hem length." This was going to be a long afternoon.

Since I was doing the harder ones last, the times between my sending in results got steadily longer. As that happened,

Aimeric and the others had more time to see what each change was doing to the model, and I could heard a lot of excited babble, but with four of them talking, and needing all my concentration for what I was doing, I wasn't sure what it was all about.

The last few pieces of information I put together took eight or ten minutes for each, burning up a lot of time on very wide-angle associative searches. As I did them, I had more time between system responses to hear the others talking. "But isn't it bizarre, Mr. de Sanha Marsao?" Shan was asking. "Why should it work out that way?"

"It does seem a little perverse to have all unknown values, when they're put in, push the system in the same direction," Reverend Peterborough added. "And perhaps a little blasphemous to have that direction be as unpleasant as it can possibly be. Do I take it correctly that there's no way this could just be a simple error in your model?"

Aimeric sighed and said it was always possible; he said something else, probably just getting the Ambassador to call him by his first name. (Come to think of it, I didn't know where the Ambassador was from originally—was Shan a given, clan, family, locative, or honorific name? I never did find out.) I had results coming in, so I missed what came next, but as the next search began to run, Aimeric was still talking—". . . entirely consistent-with-theory reason for it to do this."

The report came back and now I saw how to get this next-to-last one, raw asteroid metal prices versus value added in retarded corrosion of durable hand tools. I pulled it together, at last, and sent it in, making the model dance around again.

They fell silent as they watched it, and I went on to work on the final problem, probability of diversion of resources into terraforming as a function of rise in price of agricultural land. I brute-forced that one—simply letting it find every land sale since the beginning of the colonies of Caledony and St. Michael, and every purchase related to terraforming in every budget, figuring changes in the former and opportunity costs in the latter. With just over four hundred million values to calculate on land prices, and just under eighty billion purchases, I set up a lag nine permutation to be estimated; probably this would take a full minute, so I just sat back to listen again.

"That curve jumps like a shocked snake," Bieris said, at last.

"Yeah." Aimeric's fingers flew over the console.

"What's going on?" Shan didn't seem to be asking anyone directly.

Aimeric explained. "In some systems things don't balance; they reinforce. This algorithm was using interpolated values from other economies in other cultures to fill in for things it didn't have. It was depending on those to hold down the extremes of the function. But since Caledony's economy is actually out in an extreme corner position in the system-state space, all the estimated values were much less extreme than the real ones. So every time we got another accurate piece of data, it made the model's behavior more extreme—and increased the compensation being loaded onto the remaining estimates. So every new true value that came in produced a bigger jump, by hitting a more heavily loaded estimate."

Peterborough got up and walked over to the screen, almost pressing her nose to it as she stared at the wildly swinging curves that played through the forecast of the next nine stanyears. "You know," she said quietly, "I have said in dozens of sermons that we on Caledony have built an absolutely unique civilization. And now I find myself flabbergasted to discover that it is true." Her eyes followed the streaking curve again, and then she nodded slowly, as if it had told her everything.

"Maybe there's some basic error?" Shan did not sound hopeful.

Aimeric started to answer, but Peterborough cut in. "No, there's none. I've done the little bit of economic planning this culture is willing to admit to for the last ten years, and if I had been thinking, I'd have expected this." She shook her head slowly. "Aimeric, I am very glad you're here. I am quite sure I'm the only cabinet-level Pastor who is, however."

"I didn't think this would appeal to my father and his cronies," Aimeric said, and turned away from the screen to go pour himself a drink from the sideboard—beer, I noticed, the first time I had seen Aimeric take alcohol during working hours. "But this is all nothing. Wait till they hear what they have to do to avoid it."

By now I had grabbed a spare screen and finally gotten to see what they were talking about. The graph showed labor demand down forty percent within three years and production down fifteen percent; shortly after that, production would begin to rise rapidly, dragging employment up with it . . . but there would be two straight years of inflation over one hundred percent.

Six or seven years down the road it all stabilized at higher production, steady prices, and full employment, but until then the economy would be off on a wild roller coaster, first plunging and then soaring.

"Isn't this what happened in Nou Occitan?" I asked. "We got through that all right . . ."

"Sure," Aimeric said. "The shape of the curve is the same for every Connect. It's the magnitude that counts. On Nou Occitan it was almost an order of magnitude smaller in all directions. They just extended some people's vacation for a couple of years, and issued a little more cash through the central bank to help prices stop jumping. Biggest job we ever did at the *Manjadorita d'Oecon*, but still just a simple management problem. Here—half of the economy is rigidly controlled so that the market gives the theologically 'right' results, so it's too rigid to take the shocks. The other half is completely uncontrolled, again for religious reasons, so there's lots of room for the shocks to build up in. Plus St. Michael is very likely to be able to ride it out by exporting their problems—they've got the whip hand in trade on Nansen, and they've always been willing to use it. And again for theological reasons, I expect Caledony to be very slow and reluctant about self-defense. And on top of all that, the shocks are intrinsically bigger anyway, the biggest they've been since any inhabited planet had Connected. No, it's going to be bad all around, worse than anything anyone's ever seen before. I wish we had someone qualified here to handle this."

"Based on this report," Shan said, "I could get you anyone in the Thousand Cultures, almost overnight."

Aimeric shook his head, drained his glass of beer, and poured another as he explained, "I already checked that. Aside from my knowing my way around these people, and having family connections you can use, you have to remember that the *Wilson* Connect Depression—back in Nou Occitan—was the biggest one before now in the Thousand Cultures. I'm the best qualified there is." He sighed and drained the glass again.

The Pastor stood up and made a handsign at Aimeric, then turned and left.

Ambassador Shan had been left gaping. "Is she angry at me? Did I say something?"

Aimeric's voice had an odd sound, as if he were reciting something he had memorized long ago. "Did you see her gesture?" Aimeric showed it to us. "It means she's just taken a Silent Oath to pray and meditate. She can't speak again till she's done with that. So she'd gone off to the prayer room. You can com her later today."

Shan sighed. "I'll never get the hang of this culture. Never."

Aimeric made sure everything was locked and saved for the next day's work, gulped the last of his beer, and said, "Well, from her viewpoint, it's the only thing to do. And she may be right—because for all the good economic theory can do here, we might as well just break out the rattles and dance to drive off evil spirits."

FIVE

We got home exhausted, two hours after Second Sunset, but none of us could sleep, so we didn't try. Bruce had accessed a new collection of paintings, just arrived from Buisson in the

Metallah system, and was running up the holos of them for Bleris, so the two of them were unavailable for conversation. "Want to come over to my place for a drink or two?" Aimeric asked.

I said yes; with the sun down it was cold outside, though nothing compared to Utilitopia. We didn't bother with the cat, but we did hurry over to Aimeric's house. We had just poured wine when our coms chimed—personal letters for both of us.

It was from Marcabru, finally. I set myself to read it calmly; in Occitan, though you are honor-bound to your friends, there's a lot of rivalry and most people climb to the top over a lot of former friends. So if he were angry at me for any reason—and he might well be—or if he was just writing to brag, the letter might be nasty. It was part of the risk you ran by having interesting, ambitious friends.

> *Giraut, you silly toszet, .*
> *The big news comes first, of course—Yseut is to be the Queen for next year. And you are not here, for whatever silly reason. Did you actually do all that for the love of that flighty little beauty whose name, just at the moment, I can't recall?*

"Garsenda," I said aloud. I had not thought of her in days.

> *Well, you are the veritable* donz de finamor, *and I shall see to it that your reputation spreads far and wide, for as well you must know any glory I can give you will be returned to me as the friend of a legend. So you will surely have a place among the jovents when you return.*

Perhaps it was just having spent the day assembling the Center, but I suddenly felt a lurch of overpowering homesickness. I wanted to drink at Pertz's, to visit Raimbaut's grave, to be hiking in North Polar Spring and sailing on the wide seas of Wilson, or just to lie in the warm red sunlight on the beach south of Noupeitau. I wanted to get drunk, to cross

epees with someone over some trivial cause, to be in *finamor*,
to be back in my old apartment.

I blinked back tears and read on:

> Yseut is absolutely radiant as Queen-elect, and
> it's affected her writing in the most marvelous way,
> so that it's become (if such a thing indeed could
> ever be) even more artificial and epigrammatic,
> until it's just the sheerest scrim of beautiful shimmering
> words over an absolutely cold void, like a lace of
> frost crystals in space. As Queen, she'll surely
> publish a lot, and I shall immediately send you
> every volume.

> But you mustn't think that's our only activity. We've
> not even had time to go to the North Polar
> Mountains—this year the ice is literally exploding
> downward off the glaciers—some effect from the
> terraforming heaters. Artificial, of course, and thus
> not a fit subject for art, but what a splendid thing
> to see all that ice plunge into the newly rushing
> rivers. But we've had no time, for where one of the
> boring old men who would normally be King for
> this term would simply wear the suit-biz, Yseut
> must actually set fashions, and so she must decide
> what suits her best, describe it to designers, have
> it made—and in my nonofficial role as Consort I
> must do much the same thing ... it's exhausting
> and we do almost nothing but talk to tailors and
> designers and shop for clothes. I find that even though
> I have to feel that the exaggerated, primary-colored
> sleeve has about run its course, it will take one
> more fashion season to kill it, so I am ordering
> everything just as exaggerated as possible, sot that
> perhaps in six stanmonths I can suddenly, boldly,
> go some other way.

> I looked at pictures of Caledon clothes but it
> looks as if the only vus they permit were taken either
> in their prisons, or on mountain-climbing expeditions.

*At least all the interior was looked as if people
were dressed for the former, and all the exteriors
as if they were dressed for the latter. You couldn't
really be wearing such dreadful things, could you?
Please, please, in nomne deu, write and tell me that
you would never even think of it!*

*I must report that all is of course not well here;
what can you expect since we have acquired this
damned, damned infestation of Interstellars? They
have moved into and occupy two more of the old
familiar places in the Quartier des Jovents—I
won't tell you which ones, as they weren't places
we went commonly, but jovent places from a century
or more ago, enough to break your heart to see
them turned over to onstage sadoporn with all
the young beauties and the strong young men struggling
for their turn on the stage.*

*I confess that I did lie a bit above, and of
course remember Garsenda's name, and her person, perfectly well. I don't know whether you'll take
this as good news, or bad, or simply as confirmation,
but she is absolutely the social and performing
star of the Interstellars, with all their clubs fighting to get her. I do trust the news will no longer
bring you pain, and no doubt you've already found
some delightful young donzelha, her hair clipped
close like a man's and a vision of loveliness in
her thermal underwear, coveralls, and plastic boots
. . . now don't be angry, you know how I tease!*

*At any rate, the great problem with the Inter-
stellars is that they've raised the complaint that
none of their ugly lunatic donzelhas were Finalists
for the Throne. They tried to complain to the Embassy
but were brushed back immediately—that's exactly
the sort of thing, as I understand it, that the
Council has directed its agents never to interfere
with. So, thank heavens, even if their local imitators
have taken leave of their senses, at least the bu-*

*reaucrats of the Thousand Cultures know enough
to keep their noses out of such a fine, pleasurable
institution as the monarchy!*

*More serious, to my mind, is the fact that so many
of these rude Interstellars, having deservedly received no consideration in a contest that they
could not possibly have won, either on style or on
personal quality (I say nothing of enseingnamen because they have nothing of it!), now pretend there
was nothing to win and mock the winners! Really,
nothing stops them, nothing shames them, they do
whatever nastiness they wish and their poor battered
consciences lie dead or unconscious through all
of it. Yseut has already begun to wear something
a bit more decollete, and to favor (naturally—you
remember her coloring) the light lavender shades;
their vile girls wear the same colors, in roughly
the same cut, but exposing their nipples and the
horrible spiked studs with which they're pierced. I
would add that many of the Interstellar boys were
swaggering around in tights and boots quite similar to mine (with the exception of one dreadful,
obscene decoration that I can't bear to tell you
about—oh, all right, they sewed a quite real looking,
gigantic phallus to the seat of the tights, but if
you're my friend you'll boil with rage rather than
laugh)—*

I fought down the laughter, but found it impossible to work
up any rage at all. Marcabru was so resolutely, crazily hetero
that he had never even gone to bed with a man out of friendship or common courtesy. How the Interstellars had sensed
what he would be most offended by, I didn't know, but I had
to admire their perception.

I looked back to the letter

*—boil with rage rather than laugh)—but I have
dealt with that little problem of parody most thoroughly.*

*I encountered four of them on the street just
a few days ago, and though I was without friends,
I challenged them all to combat in serial. They
seemed delighted, but I promptly beat the first two
who came at me, leaving them thrashing and then
comatose there in the gutter. And then, in the most
cowardly fashion, with no trace of honor, the two
survivors broke their oaths to fight in serial and rushed
me together, with neither salute nor warning.*

That was where I did almost explode with rage, my hands
gripping the tabletop till my knuckles felt pierced. A friend in
danger, long odds, and me not there to share the glory? And
the cowardice of that attack—how far had things fallen to
pieces back home? Had I even seen it while I was there?
What would be left for me when I did return?

I scrolled down and read.

*And it was then that enseingnamen told, for naturally
I was far calmer and readier than they were. I saw
that the one slightly ahead, to my left, had all
the same characteristic scars as poor old
Raimbaut, and gambled everything on its meaning
that he was slow, vulnerable, and had been severely
scarred internally like Raimbaut. I ignored the
laggard and gave the scarred one three hard cuts
with all my strength, finishing with a solid thrust
to the heart. He went down without touching me.*

*I squared off with the sole survivor, calling him
every vile name I could think of as he seemed
to back away, white, almost fainting with fear, looking
for any way to break and run—but I had him cornered
against a wall!*

*It was then I heard the wail of the ambulance,
and knew how far I had succeeded. It swooped, just
as you imagine, and my last-finished opponent was
sprung off to the hospital.*

"I hope your friend is really dead," I said, "and

I do hope you'll be joining him soon, no doubt as one more bloody greasy turd to pass through the devil's shithole." With that I lunged and disarmed him—truly I don't think he had anything you could call a grip on his weapon, and of course none at all on his enseingnamen—*and then began to cut, administering some dozen wounds or so before I finally gave him a* coup de merce, *forcing him, between wounds, for the amusement of a crowd that was gathering, to confess to all sorts of incest and bestiality, to sing childish songs at the top of his lungs while they roared with laughter, and at last to beg and plead till the snot ran from his nose and he sobbed for breath. By that time he was on the ground, for I had severed most of his major tendons and so he thought he couldn't use his arms or legs. The last cut before the final one was a castration, and he screamed just as if it were really gone . . . a tribute to the engineering of the neuroducer, my last pigeon was. I finished him off with a long slow cut across the throat, so that it would take him a long time to believe himself dead, and turned to take a dozen bows before the cheering crowd.*

I have no doubt that, even after they release him from the hospital, he will find that the psychological scars are thorough and deep, and that he will ache for years to come.

Ah, Giraut, after a fight like that—it was then I longed for my old friend to be drunk with, to shout and laugh with, to celebrate it all! And where are you? Some six and a half light-years away, and not to return till after Yseut's glorious reign is almost all in the history books! Honestly, as I thought of that, my oldest friend, I nearly wept and spoiled all my triumph.

But at least those insulting costumes disappeared from the streets overnight, and I've noticed

*that more than one Interstellar has crossed the street
when he sees me coming. The bolder ones spit, angry
because their idiot, honorless friend really did
die—but then, surely he knew the risks going in?
Anyway, they took a bit of my honor off by ruling
it a neuroducer accident. On the other hand, the
one I tortured is still, as I understand it, hospi-
talized, and it may be literally years before he
is past the risk of flashback seizures.*

*Well, I have boasted and commiserated and told
you all the news, so now the only thing I have
left to do is to demand that you write me immediately and tell me what has become of you and
Aimeric and our angel Bieris!*

Fondly te salut,
Murcabru

I felt Marcabru's triumph myself; he had acquitted himself
beautifully, and moreover, gratified as he might be to have
paid the Interstellars back for Raimbaut, I had no doubt that
his thorough, systematic, drawn-out humiliation of that other
young ape had done even more to discredit them. My heart
ached to be with him and share it, and my throat closed with
sadness.

I wondered what my new friend Thorwald would have to
say about bragging of having killed someone, let alone
Marcabru's beautifully done torture of his last victim? I decided I would bring up such topics only when I had some
well-prepared students, and that perhaps I would put off the
traditional opening of dueling arts instructions—"cutting off"
the student's nose with the neuroducer, then reviving the student, to teach them not to fear it.

In fact, now that I thought of it, perhaps Raimbaut's life
would have been happier, and certainly longer, if only he'd
had more fear of the neuroducer, or shown more fear of it . . .

I wasn't sure where all these strange thoughts were coming from, and they rather disgusted me. Perhaps I was just

jealous of Marcabru's accomplishments, or more probably just exhausted and homesick. I swirled the warm, clear apple wine in my glass and inhaled the bouquet appreciatively—it was like the blossoms in Field Seven, just now hitting bloom in the rotation, and so sweet it almost pierced the nose, yet the wine itself was dry, without a hint of cloying. I resolved that, when I wrote back to Marcabru, I would also drop a short note to Pertz and tell him that he needed to import Caledon fruit wines—back home, they would surely sell well at almost any price, no matter what the cost of using the springer might be.

"Sounds as if Marcabru is as bloodthirsty as ever," Aimeric said, folding his terminal back up.

I nodded, and raised my glass in a toast. "Marcabru!"

"Marcabru," he said, curiously without enthusiasm. He must be homesick too. He raised his glass, and drank with me.

I realized, as I looked around his quarters, that they were contributing a little to my homesickness. Every artifact in there cried out for the rich red bricks and synthwoods, the intricate tight curves within curves, of Occitan architecture, but not even Aimeric's having tuned the lights a deep red could compensate for the off-white starkness of the walls (it only turned them pink) or for the lack of shadowing on the wide expanses of wall. Instead, the clean straight lines of Bruce's design made all of Aimeric's furniture and furnishings look overdone and somehow gaudy.

"It's almost cold in here," I said. "Do you mind if we turn up the heat a bit?"

"No problem, I was about to do it myself. More wine?"

"Always," I said. "You must really have missed this stuff when you were first on Wilson."

"I did," he said, seriously. "Nothing tasted right, either—you've surely noticed that food here is always richer, but with milder spices? It's much harder to go the other way, where the food always tastes too scant and too hot. No, it kind of surprises me to realize, after all this time, that one reason I was so antagonistic in my first few stanmonths in Nou

Occitan was that I missed home so much." He sat down beside me. "I suppose it's not so different for you, even though you know you'll be going home in a stanyear or two?"

I winced. "Is it that obvious?"

"I suppose so." He sighed. "I do keep feeling guilty about how you ended up here. Seems to me that if Bieris and I had just argued a little harder you'd have ended up back in Noupeitau, causing trouble in your accustomed way."

I shrugged. "Well, it's not so bad. A stanyear or even two of this isn't so much, and then I can go back and do all that joventry if I still want to. I suppose I probably will want to, at least at first, just to have something familiar to do on my return. But what place needs *us* more than this stolid, cold, stuck-in-the-mud world? I think of myself as a missionary on behalf of fun, grace, style, wit, beauty—passion! I assume that's how you feel—"

"I spent my youth trying to persuade Caledons to have fun. In, of course, a very Caledon, which is to say militant, serious, hard-headed, way. If they're going to get any of that from me this time, they will have to get it by example." His voice sounded tired and distant; he must be about ready for bed himself. Mentally I braced for the dash over to my place. "Besides, I need to get along a little more than you do. Part of my function is communicating with the old stiffnecks."

He was looking out the window toward the brightly moonlit orchards. With the light on the side of his face, I could see that his skin was getting coarser as he got older, and that his beard was beginning to show just the faintest touch of silver. By the time he got back, he'd have no place among the joventry.

"Bieris seems to be taking to it all right," I said, hoping to change the subject.

"Well, she's less lonely than either of us are, because she's already found such a good friend in Bruce."

"They do seem to be fond of each other," I said, judiciously. "Part of it is that they're both such visual people and they seem to share tastes on what things ought to look like."

"Part of it," he agreed.

Some part of me had been afraid from the beginning of the conversation that this would be about Bieris and Bruce.

"You can relax, Giraut," Aimeric said. "I'm not having an attack of jealousy. I'm just lonely myself." He poured another glass for each of us. "Besides, once you find out what we Caledon men do in such situations, you're going to be shocked and appalled."

"Really?" I said, sensing that this was some setup for a joke.

"You'll probably think it's disgusting and perverted," he added solemnly.

I nodded, a little bit drunk, and sort of sad, and waiting for the joke to come.

"We shake hands and do our best to stay friends."

I didn't see why that was funny, but I was tired. I turned down his offer of his spare bedroom, preferring the short dash across to my place. I thought that waking up in a fully furnished, red-lit Occitan room, then realizing where I was, might be just too much.

SIX

Two days later, less than an hour before the first classes were to start, I was sitting up in the solar making some notes to myself when my terminal signalled that there was a message for me. When I answered it, I was directed to com a Reverend Saltini at the Pastorate of Public Projects.

According to the information I could access in the next minute or two before not comming would have required an explanation, Saltini was about three layers down from Cabinet level—he certainly ranked me, anyway. I'd heard passing references to the PPP, and they sounded like people you wanted to stay clear of, and I half-suspected (correctly it turned out) that they were the "peeps" people referred to in whispers.

I called him at once, and had the usual brief exchange with

the call screener, a living human being again. (In Caledony, no one ever made small talk or established a relationship with minor functionaries—you were just supposed to tell them what you wanted and have them get it for you. Aside from being rude, it seemed grossly inefficient to me ... how could you ever build up the special relationships that make it possible to obtain favors and get things done?)

The screener agreed that I ought, indeed, to talk to the Reverend Saltini, and a moment later the image on the screen was of a small, bald man with what seemed a puckish smile. "There's something very peculiar in the list of people who have requested credit transfers to the tuition accounts at your Center for Occitan Arts. I think you may want to reconsider whatever it is you're planning to do."

"What I'm planning to do is public," I said. "It's right there in all those syllabi that I've made generally accessible on the planetary sharecom."

"Just so. Just so. You see, the problem is that it seems to be attracting—well, the sort of people it's drawing are overwhelmingly one sort. They are mostly intelligent young people who have failed the examinations for higher education several times, and overwhelmingly they are people who failed the examination in mathematical theology. There are a significant number who failed in natural sciences and in mathematics as well, but one suspects that their resistance to learning mathematics is at the core of the problem and that they don't learn math—to put it bluntly—because many of the problems they would have to solve in mathematics classes are in theology."

Before fleeing or fighting, always see if you can just step aside. "Nou Occitan doesn't take its religion very seriously, mostly it's all ceremonial, and so I really had not planned on touching on religious questions as such."

"We know that and we appreciate it. If it weren't true we'd never have approved the Center. No, I'm afraid this is in the nature of a very—let me stress very—very preliminary inquiry into the rationality of what you propose to do. Not at all a formal inquiry, you must understand; right now what I'm doing is accumulating a few facts for the files so that in the event of questions arising, those of us who would be answerable for them would have a reasonable basis for answering them."

He sounded exactly like the *qestora* did when they caught my father cheating on his taxes. This was just what I was afraid of; somehow I had fallen afoul of the local secret police, and I still understood so little that I had no idea what response, if any, could get him off my back, or even of what I might be accused or what he could do to me. Wherever you go, a friendly off-the-record inquiry is exactly the kind at which you have no formal rights and no idea of the accusations or evidence. That's why every cop in the Thousand Cultures would rather have a little chat than actually arrest you.

While I had been waiting, and getting more nervous, and figuring out that this was more trouble than it first looked like, Reverent Saltini had been sitting there watching me. Finally he seemed to decide that he might be able to get somewhere by continuing the conversation. "Well," he said quietly, "you do remember that one of your goals in setting up the Center was to facilitate communication and improve mutual understanding between Caledony and Nou Occitan. Now, at this point, it would appear that the course syllabi, as you've written them, are not attracting anyone who is suitable for such purposes. Clearly people who are out of the major route of promotion, however versed they may become in Occitan culture, are not going to be in any position where they can make use of their knowledge. Of course they can work as translators, or personal assistants, or perhaps as business agents—none of those positions require any special licensing or degrees—but then, as the people on the scene who actually do know what they are doing, they are very likely to come into conflict with their better-qualified superiors, and that can only result in unhappiness all around, don't you see?"

"Nop," I said, using one of my two words of Reason. It was true—I had lost him some time before—and besides, stalling might be as good a strategy as any. "And should the trade begin to expand until my students-to-be are all employed in trade with Nou Occitan, I'd suppose that the increased trade would give people an incentive to take the courses."

"But not before people who have no grasp of ethics or of man's place in the universe have already succeeded. You must see how that looks, to see the market rewarding vice and thus by implication punishing virtue. You can't really expect us to allow the will of the market—which we hold to be synonymous with the Will of God—to be seen doing something so ridiculous.

"And more to the point, by extending the initial loan, the Council of Rationalizers and the Pastorate of Public Projects have jointly committed themselves to your project as a good thing for Caledony and for all its citizens. You yourself did an admirable job of persuading us that it is. Now, to have the most discreditable—there are people who outrightly say 'useless,' though I think that is a bit harsh—to have these extremely, as I say, discreditable people so overrepresented in your first classes . . . well, again, can you expect us to sit by idly while such an important project, to which we have committed so much money and prestige, becomes associated with a group of people who are at the least looked on as inept or misfits, and despised outrightly by many? You must see our position on this."

There was no getting away from it. "What do you want me to do?"

That odd little puck-smile never left his face; it did not deepen or become more forced; it was apparently just there all the time. "We think that some delay, perhaps just a few weeks, in beginning the courses, accompanied with your getting some help from a couple of qualified people—say one in theology and one in market research, for example—would allow you to phrase things so as to draw an *appropriate* group of students. You do see what I mean?"

"I would suppose," I said, visions of spending the next year and half filling out forms and shoveling shit, as if there would be a difference, bouncing through my brain, "that if I change the syllabi, I will also have to change what I teach.

And I don't really want to do that. These are immersion courses; if people are going to be offended by Occitan culture, or baffled—or if they're just not going to be willing to make any kind of personal peace with it—then it's better that they find out right away. And for that purpose"—inspiration!—"it might even be better to offend people who are deviant from your culture. First of all, if I fail with them it's no great loss to you, and since they are members of the Caledon culture all the same, they're still a good test population—in fact, an exceptionally good one, because I'm sure they'll react but they won't necessarily be as outraged as your more mainstream citizens might be, and even if they should react in such a way as to give the Center bad word of mouth, all the same no one is going to believe them because of who they are. And of course if their talents do turn out useful, you could see it as a matter of your policy having redeemed some otherwise useless people."

I really could not believe the way I was talking. Maybe Saltini was contagious or something?

He said nothing, but his fingers flew over keys in front of him as I watched him on the screen. The smile never left as he looked at what I assumed were rows of figures, or perhaps dossiers of my students-to-be.

Why had I been talking like him? I was just desperately trying to speak his language, I realized . . . it seemed to be Terstad, but the more I heard of it the less I understood. Perhaps, like Aimeric's father, he had grown up speaking Reason? But old Carruthers was blunt to the point of rudeness, so surely Saltini's greasy vagueness wasn't intrinsic to the system.

He looked up and this time his smile did deepen. It made me nervous and I was sure it was meant to. "Well, now that you've put it in that light, it seems we have a happy accident here. I think you probably *should* exploit it, just as you say. And I'm sure you'll be happy to know that all seven hundred aintellects polled for theological correctness agreed with me on that. If I may say so, I think you've found a home here— you reason very well off the top of your head."

"I'm planning to start studying Reason soon," I said. It was true—I was curious, and Aimeric said that it wasn't particularly difficult to learn—and it certainly would not hurt me with Saltini to mention it.

"I'm not at all surprised. And now I've got to let you go; I have a lot to do, and you'll see when you check your files that the additional students who've been allowed to enroll may pose a bit of a problem." He blinked off, and I was alone again with my nerves.

I hadn't even looked at the number of students enrolled, or the number trying to, just assuming that things would start slowly and planning on classes of a dozen or so at most.

When I called up the file, I discovered that until one minute ago, when Saltini had cleared the rest of the applicants into the Center, I had actually had no more than five students in any one class, and a total of twenty-one students for the whole Center.

Saltini's held-back file had contained 264 students.

The numbers were incredible; if I'd known that the day before, I could have set up sections and rotations to accommodate everyone. As it was, I spent the whole day trying to get everyone onto some workable schedule, and for at least my first few months I would be putting in very long days and paying legally required bonuses to Bieris and Aimeric for the extra sections they would be teaching.

If I had known twenty-eight hours ago . . .

I could not get the notion out of my head that this was what Saltini had intended. "Of course it was," Thorwald said, later that day, when I took a ten-minute break to show him what the routine maintenance would be in the Dueling Arts Gymnasium. "I'm surprised you got as far as you did, and spent as long here as you have, without crossing with Saltini a couple of times at least. That's his job, you know."

"Creating chaos?"

Thorwald eyed me as if trying to decide something; then he said, quietly, "Everyone knows Reverend Saltini. Sooner or later everyone has to do some routine business with him. A lot of people think he's actually an aintellect hooked to a

realtime visual simulator, but my guess is he's real." Thorwald wasn't looking at me and might as well have been continuing our conversation about cleaning the floor and about
its different elasticity settings for *ki hara do*, *katajutsu*, fen-
cing, and freestyle. "If you want to talk about him, try not to
sound excited; the monitors pick up on vocal stress and if you
sound excited it's much more likely that we'll be audited."

I realized he was telling me the room was bugged. It was
like some grotesque acting class exercise, playing a scene
from the centuries before the Thousand Cultures, perhaps during one of the four World Wars or the three Cold Wars that
had preceded getting humanity reasonably organized. I could
not have been more surprised if he had warned me about
witches.

But clearly he was serious. I swallowed hard, consciously
relaxed my throat, and said, "Tell me."

"Well," he said, "he believes what he says. Or if he's actually an aintellect, somebody believes what he says, anyway.
It's part of doctrine—the market, as the one true instrument
of God, will reveal who's a good person and who is not.
Saltini's job is to make sure it does. And he's empowered to
do practically anything to get his job done. All right? I don't
much care to talk about this for any length of time."

He didn't say anything more. After a moment we got back
to talking about the gym, and then about the floor polishing
that would need to be done regularly for the Dance Room.

When I went back upstairs, I found 150 people there to
start Basic Occitan; I ended up splitting them into three sections, all still too large, and giving up a couple of lunches a
week, to accommodate all of them.

So far Thorwald was right—the only class that was staying
at one section was dueling arts. I couldn't imagine people
who didn't want to learn to fight, who found no confidence
in being good with weapons, but that was just the way they
were.

By the time I had gotten the administrivia taken care of, it
was already quite late, and I was very glad to have the apartment in the Center instead of having to drive back to my

house on Bruce's farm, especially since I had early-morning duties working for Aimeric the next day.

If I had known that I would not get back to the house for another six days, I might have given up right then and just sat down for a good cry. As it was, I just ordered some new clothes to be delivered to the Center, so I'd have something clean and decent to wear, and turned in for the night.

After a few days of teaching, I had made some notes about all these rebels and misfits who had so concerned the Reverend Saltini.

First of all, they were all docile. They appeared to *like* the boring repeat-after-me drills and memorized conversations in Occitan class (*"Bo die, donz." "Bo die, amico, patz a te."* A hundred repetitions of that in a day made me wonder if maybe there wasn't a positive side to shovelling shit that I had missed). None of them liked any kind of improvised conversation, not even the many of them who could already read Occitan.

In poetry class, no one wanted to keep talking once they had settled on the "right" interpretation; prosody was gibberish to them, except as a set of rules like those of a crossword puzzle. In painting, there were some good draftsmen but only Thorwald seemed to really paint, according to Bieris.

Music was either the best or the worst. After a brief exposure to Occitan music, about two thirds of the students had decided to take some other course or get their refund. As for the remainder, the problem was that there *was* a tradition of music in Caledony.

At Caledon music festivals, which were heavily publicized, there were no live audiences. Instead, musicians sat in soundproof booths and tried to duplicate, in live performance, the "perfect" performance generated from the score by an aintellect. Three other aintellects would compare them to the generated version and score them on it, deducting points for any deviations.

I had shocked the majority the first day by talking about improvisation, but my surviving students didn't seem to be especially bothered by it. They at least had the intuitive notion that there could be more there than the written score, even with all the complicated diacritical marks that Caledon music always had.

What did baffle them—and thus was taking up all my time in teaching the lute class—was the idea that you could "feel what it ought to sound like," as I urged them to do a dozen times per class. I could see the repetition wasn't helping but I really could not think of anything else to say. "Now, listen *this* time." I began to play. "This way is sad, a trace of melancholy, a twist of sweet sadness, *comprentz*, *companho*? Now I liven it up by picking up the tempo and perhaps even by syncopating."

Seventeen pairs of eyes—all my survivors, counting Thorwald, who was sitting in on the pretense that he was helping me—watched me as closely as if I were a demonstration in a psych lab, and had just gone mad and eaten the arms off one of the chairs.

"What *do* you hear?" I asked, trying to keep the despair out of my voice.

"The first one is slow. The second one is fast," the pudgy blond woman (Margaret—that was her name) said. I waited for her to say more but it looked like that was all she had to say. "I don't see how you can expect us to know the music is sad or not until we hear the words."

At least that gave me a different idea: "Let me play you all something—ah, two somethings." First I played and sang the *Canso de Fis de Jovent*, in Terstad translation; I flattered myself that some of them seemed a little moved. Then I swung suddenly into the bawdy *Canso de Fis de Potentz* (or the "It Never Came Up Again," as it's called in translation). "They're the same set of notes," I said, when I had finished, to the laughter of Margaret, Thorwald, and a big, brawny fellow named Paul. Most of the rest just looked embarrassed. "Now what can you tell me about that?"

"The first is sad, and it's slow. The second is fast, and it's funny," Margaret said. "But I don't think that being slow made it sad, or fast made it funny—it's the *situation* that's one way or the other."

I sang the first verse of *Canso de Fis de Jovent* to the "Never Came Up" rhythm.

After a long hesitation, Thorwald finally said, "Well, it's not as pretty."

Paul nodded agreement. "Doesn't go together as well."

"That's it exactly," I said. "The going together—or not going together—is what I'm talking about. And once you know that a song can have a mood that way, then the words don't have to be there, do they?"

They all nodded dutifully.

Hesitantly, Valerie, a tall, slender girl who seemed a bit shy, said, "You could probably do the same thing with some of our music. That might be sort of interesting."

The other students turned and stared at her. I wanted to beat them all senseless and then sit down and just talk to Valerie.

But before I could open my mouth to enter her defense, she went on. "It's an idea. The principle could be extended."

Thorwald asked "What would it sound like? I mean, how would you do it with a song that didn't have words to tell you what the feelings are?"

Valerie gestured toward the wall where my guitar sat on its rack; I nodded, unsure what she was going to do but eager to see somebody, anybody, on this cold world do something spontaneous. She got up and walked slowly toward the instrument; everyone watched her—or at least I know I did. I had suddenly noticed how huge her dark eyes were with her jet-black hair cropped close, and wondered what it would be like to look into them while I took that tiny waist in my hands.

She picked up the guitar and returned to her stool; ran through the tuning once, nodding with approval, and tried fingering a couple of chords silently. All her attention seemed to fall onto her left hand.

I was about to warn her that it was a male guitar when I noticed her fingernails were cut short, like a man's. So were a lot of other women's, here, of course, because so many worked on farms or at mechanical jobs, but still it was disappointing to see yet another plainness in her.

She began to play. At first it was just an arpeggio through the basic four-chord flamenco progression, precise but nothing special. Then her picking became harder, sharper, even staccato, and as it slowed, the melody acquired a mournful bleakness that rang of Nansen as nothing else had. It made me think of hard-faced people facing the cold wind and of the syrup-thick freezing seas gnawing at the bare rock continents. It was quiet and unassuming like Bruce, pitiless like Reverend Carruthers, empty and grand like the peaks of the Optimals, and as suddenly beautiful as the Gap Bow bursting from the fog of the Gouge.

I was moved, shocked, to find something like that here.

She finished and the room went up in an uproar. All of them were speaking very fast, several of them in Reason, and I couldn't understand any of it. *"Patz, patz, companho!"*

They all turned staring at me, then at each other. There was abruptly no sound at all in the room.

Now I had to think of something to say.

I drew a deep breath. The room stank of sweat and anger. "Would any of you, or perhaps all of you one at a time, mind explaining to me what you are all shouting about? I grant that the performance was beautiful and extraordinary—I never heard anything *bellazor*, more beautiful! *M'es vis*, we have a true artist, a real *trobadora*, among us."

Valerie had been sitting there, my guitar in her lap, staring at the floor, through all the commotion; now she looked up, as if I had startled her. I could see that her skin was worn, even at her young age, by the ultraviolet and the cold winds . . . but those eyes, deep and black as space itself, shining at me—*deu!*

Paul spoke very quietly. "Mister Leones, I don't see what any of this has to do with Occitan music. Especially I don't see what a performance like that . . . well, if you think music ought to be some kind of an emotional outburst or, um, something—then that's just completely irrational! What if she plays it like that at the contest? I realize you don't know this,

sir, but Valerie is a contendor for All Caledony Soloist this
year, and that's an obligatory piece. She shouldn't practice it
that way—it could destroy her performance."

Then they all started shouting again, this time even more
of it in Reason. And again, when I did get their attention,
they all fell into that terrifying instant silence.

"Well, someone at least gave me some information," I said,
thinking as fast as I could, knowing it couldn't be fast
enough. "Are there any of you who like Valerie's performance—no, don't start yelling again—" I found myself wishing
I had my epee here to keep order. "Let's do it by hand count.
How many of you liked it?"

About a third of the hands in class went up.

"How many of you didn't?" Another third. "How many of
you were yelling about something else entirely, and just happened to be in the room at the time?"

They all laughed, and the tension seemed to collapse. I
looked around at all these slightly embarrassed people, most
of them still holding lutes, and was struck by the oddity of almost all of them being my age or younger. I forced my voice
to get as soft and as gentle as possible, even though my heart
was racing. "*M'es vis*, it's for Valerie to decide what matters
to her—she is the true artist here. How was it to play in that
way, Valerie—do you feel damaged?"

She looked down; the brown of her face deepened, shad-
owed by her head, and it was disquieting to me to see white
scalp through the thin bristle of dark hair on her head. "No,
Mister Leones, I don't. In fact, at home, by myself, that's
how I usually play that piece, and I was doing that long before you got here. I just didn't have the words to talk about
what I was doing."

Paul seemed stunned. "Valerie—why would you do such a
thing?"

She turned away from him, carried my guitar back to its
rack, and set it carefully there before she said, "It just sounds
better. I think I'm a better musician than the aintellect is."

"You never told me you were doing that!" He sounded hurt
to the bone.

"I never talked with anyone about it, except Reverend Saltini of course."

Paul gasped. "Then they've been picking it up on the monitors—and you've kept doing it?"

She nodded. "As I said, it's the way it sounds right."

The uproar before was nothing compared to the uproar now. I had not heard so much anger and insult flying around a room since the night Raimbaut died. Almost all of it was in Reason, so aside from being unintelligible to me, it had that peculiarly irritating rhythm that always sounded like a bad stutter.

I found I was bellowing *"Patz! Patz marves!"* as if a brawl or a duel had to be stopped, and I was standing in the center of the room trying to glare 360 degrees at once.

Then there was that dreadful silence again, and this time they were all hanging their heads and blushing as if they'd just been caught committing some terrible crime. "We're really sorry, sir," Prescott Diligence said. A short, red-haired boy, he was the son of a Pastor of something or other—I had seen his mother on the Council of Rationalizers, sitting in the little corner of non-stiffnecks. "These emotions are absolutely uncalled for."

I looked around the room to see Thorwald and Margaret hanging their heads like beaten dogs, Paul scuffing at the floor, Valerie clearly in tears of shame. For the first time today I was really angry. "I was shouting for quiet so you could all hear each other. Because I'm your teacher and that is my job. But I will *not* permit any of you to apologize. You have *nothing* to be ashamed of. Art—pure raw disturbing art—is the only thing people *should* fight about."

Out of some neurons that had spent too much time with Raimbaut, I heard his quiet laughter. I myself had fought much more often for *enseignamen* or sheer thrill of the fight. I dismissed the thought.

"All of you had nothing more than your own honest reactions to what Valerie has made here. You are entitled to those reactions—they are yours. Nothing and nobody has the right to tell you how you ought to feel."

I said that straight into Prescott's face; he seemed rather shocked and startled. I fought down the childish urge to stick my tongue out at him.

"Let me be explicit. For some of you, the overriding fact of Valerie's work is that it has brought a familiar piece of your art into a direct, powerful connection to your feelings—and because you feel it as never before, you are impressed. For others, the intrusion of Valerie's feelings has marred the classic form. That is what you are fighting about, and it's as important as anything can be—you're fighting about who you are, and how you fit into the world you've received. So of course you're fighting all-out; how could you do otherwise?"

The room was now very quiet. Prescott was obviously in no mood to argue, and sat down. Now that I had recovered my lost temper, I hoped that he was thinking, rather than just hurt. Everyone else seemed, if anything, more embarrassed than before. I managed not to sigh or groan with exasperation, and said, "All right, now, let's get back to the lute. Prescott, you're up; let's hear the 'Wild Robbers of Serras Vertz.'"

I thought I detected a little passion as he played, and dropped a little praise on it before it became clear that he would only experience that as further humiliation. I let class wind down quickly, and then treated myself to going up to my room and writing a long, long letter to Marcabru, detailing Caledony as the culture that strangled its artists at birth, where people with no feelings punished anyone who dared to have them, and so forth. I sent it before I could think of moderating my tone at all.

Marcabru had not written to me in ten days. I had no time to go back to Bruce's place for at least another couple of days. I was more alone than I had ever been.

SEVEN

Some days after, as Aimeric presented and Bieris and I pointed to things on cue, the Council sat in solemn silence, nodding perfunctorily at the beginning of each subject heading—except Clarity Peterborough, who nodded constantly, with great enthusiasm.

At the end of the presentation there was a very long pause.

At last Carruthers rose to his feet, looked around the room, and said, "I think I do speak for all of us when I say that we badly needed to hear your presentation, Mister de Sanha Marsao. The issues here are very serious. I would like to adjourn to another room for discussion. Reverend Peterborough, I think you will want to stay with our guests."

They all got up and left, leaving Reverend Peterborough and Ambassador Shan trailing after us, embarrassed, not speaking or even looking up, to one of the small lounges.

There, Peterborough seemed to have an attack of feeling pastoral. "So sorry, there's no window in most of these rooms. Silly—light would be more cheerful—but I suppose they don't want to waste the energy and they don't value cheerfulness. Let's see—I think something warm and comforting is in order." She set the machine to make cocoa for everyone.

"How do you think we did?" Aimeric asked, holding his voice neutral and level like he usually did just before a really dangerous brawl.

Peterborough handed out the cups of hot, foamy stuff before answering. "You know, I wish that there had been more outcry. I wish they had tried to shout you down."

"Dad just sat there. But from what he said afterward, I'm sure he heard every word."

"Exactly." The Parson sighed and blew on her cocoa, then took a little hesitant sip. "I'm not sure I want to try to guess. The way they excluded me is probably not good. It means there are points of view they won't consider. But on the other hand, I think your father really did listen and really did believe you, and understood what the implications were. That's what we have to hope for."

Shan growled, "I don't understand one damned thing about this damned culture. If they understood Aimeric, why are you so worried?"

"Well," Peterborough said, "um—" She left it hanging in the air a bit too long before she said. "Well, maybe it's not such bad news."

Aimeric jumped in. "The problem is that they picked it all up so *fast* and accepted it right away. If they had argued we might have had a chance to steer their thinking a little and get them going our way. As it is, anything could happen. They *might* be all set to hear and embrace the policies I suggest, but then again they might commit to something completely unworkable."

"You really don't expect a reasonable response," Shan said.

I took too big a sip of hot cocoa, and it burned on the way down. Tears formed in my eyes and I had trouble breathing. As I recovered, Peterborough was speaking. "But that's exactly the point. They're so dedicated to logic and reason that common sense hasn't got much to do with it."

Shan shook his head hard, as if to get an idea out of it. "So all sorts of catastrophe might happen here, but since the locals will have picked the catastrophe for themselves, it won't matter."

"It will matter to the locals," Bieris said. "They aren't going to follow someone else's policy manual when it has nothing to do with the way they've actually lived all their lives. Whatever they come up with, whether it works or not, is going to be a *Caledon* solution."

I was nodding vehemently, surprised at my agreement with

her. "Doing it your own way is what the Thousand Cultures are supposed to be founded on. People have to be allowed to find their own ways, even if they're mistakes. Didn't something like this come up in Occitan, anyway?"

Aimeric nodded. "It did. But there the issue was just one of how crisis aid was going to be distributed. We had to persuade them that nobility *needed* to have higher income than commoners if our social system was going to function as it was designed to. The difference here is that it's not just distribution of aid. It's what they think should flow where, and how. A lot of archaic economic notions that disappeared centuries ago everywhere else have been written into doctrine. That's why you've got markets that depend on spying on consumers and ordering them around, and this whole notion that cash transactions are the only moral form of social communication. I would guess a good quarter of the real budget goes into making the economy behave as if their dogma were true. Well, there is about to be an economy uncontrolled by all that, and there is no way that the Council will give them money to maintain those fictions."

"Still, it's part of how they see the world and they have a right —" Bieris began.

"Horseshit. People who put principles before people are people who hate people. They won't much care about how well it works, just about how right it is . . . they may even like it better if it inflicts enough pain."

Bieris sat with her arms folded tightly across her chest and said, "Don't people have the right to make their own mistakes?"

"In principle, yes. In practice, the people who will suffer are not the ones making the decisions. If we can get them not to make this mistake, that's all to the better. I don't see any reason for them to exercise their right to be stupid by hurting a lot of innocent people."

Peterborough interrupted. "Well, in a sense, any solution they come up with will 'work' eventually anyway, because in six or seven years everything is supposed to come back on an even keel. And even if the stiffnecks want to pretend nothing has changed since Caledony Free State was chartered, things *are* different—for one thing, even with the worst imaginable policies, nobody is going to die of starvation or cold."

There was a knock at the door, so as junior flunky closest, I got up and opened it. Carruthers came in, very quietly.

"I owe you an apology," he said to Aimeric. "Your numbers verify completely. I understand some of your emotionalism, whether or not I agree that your display of it was warranted." Aimeric, several times, had raised his voice, and once had thumped the table as he made his points. The old man hesitated for a long time before he added, "I was very proud of you." Then, clearing his throat, he said, "We will be debating and praying for however long it takes, so we'll need access to you all next week—if that's not too much trouble?"

"Nop," Aimeric said. "That's what the Council of Humanity is paying me for. You're welcome to call at any time."

Carruthers turned quickly away from Aimeric and said, "Reverend Peterborough, let me apologize for your exclusion; it was an error in my judgment. Perhaps you would be good enough not only to join in our deliberations, but to brief Ambassador Shan afterwards?" He didn't wait for a response. "Then I think that's everything." He turned and went through the door; Peterborough followed, turning to give us a bare trace of a shrug and a raised eyebrow as she closed the door.

The cat ride home was silent, except for the normal whir of the levitated tracks and the faint crashing of the gravel against the underside. I drove, which gave me an excuse to keep my attention on the road and away from whatever Aimeric might be feeling.

Perhaps two-thirds of the way up to Sodom Gap, Bieris ventured, "Your father said he was proud of you."

"Didn't mean anything more than that apology he gave Clarity."

That was the conversation for the trip. At night there was no hope for a Gap Bow, of course, but moonrise was also hidden behind clouds. It was as drab as the Sodom Gap road ever is—which is to say the little we could see was spectacular.

Bruce had a big, really wonderful dinner waiting, and ushered us right in to it. Somehow that only seemed to make Aimeric more sullen, as if he resented Bruce's gift, and that in turn made Bieris snippy with Aimeric and by extension with everybody. I was working up a short way to excuse myself and get home. With my drive into Utilitopia the next day, I would have to be up fairly early, and this was my second night up late in a row. Then a com for Aimeric summoned him from the table.

When he came back, he looked thoughtful and worried. "It was Dad. They want me to come in and consult first thing tomorrow. They seem to have arrived at something they think is a solution. So, Giraut, can I catch a ride with you tomorrow? And does that mean getting up as early as I'm afraid it does?"

"Yes to both. Did he say anything about what this answer is supposed to be?"

"No. And that's not good. As you get to know us you'll learn that a Caledon only says things you don't want to hear to your face. Are you going back up to your place right away, Giraut?"

"I was thinking of it." I got up. "Want a ride? Bieris?"

Aimeric nodded and reached for our coats; Bieris shook her head and said, "I don't have to be up early tomorrow, and I'd rather walk home in a little while, when the moon's up a little more."

As I quickly spun through the short trip by Aimeric's cottage to mine, I noticed he was still out of sorts. "Four o'clock tomorrow," I said.

He grunted at me and got out. I thought of asking what the matter was, but it was late and whatever it was could keep until next morning. I headed the cat for home.

Not home. Home was my old apartment in the Quartier. I must not forget that.

When I got to the Center the next day, I had gained a little sleep by trading off driving with Aimeric. There were a lot of people milling around, and Thorwald was frantically trying to get enough information from them to get their registrations filled in. "Late registrations," he explained. "Since I was here I thought I should get this going."

"Absolutely right. Where'd they all come from?"

"Oh, looks like PPP held up a bunch of people's approvals to join, then released them early this morning. So we've got thirty-eight more people in addition to the overcrowding we had before."

"Saltini?" I asked quietly.

"Sure, I could use some breakfast. These things just have a way of happening, yes, I guess you could say that."

I was never, never going to get used to being spied upon, let alone having to worry about it, but since I still had no clear idea of how dangerous things might be for Thorwald or the others, I dropped the subject.

In about an hour we had fitted all of them in. Much to Thorwald's disgust, after they filled up the last few slots in dance classes ("at least that's harmless"), they all took the last standing opportunities—the dueling arts classes.

As he and I sat down to a quick breakfast before beginning the long day, he commented, "I'd heard some of them say that they would kill to get in here, but I hadn't thought that they meant it."

"We won't have any killings," I said, being patient because by now I was learning that Thorwald always complained a lot in the morning and it didn't mean much—he was actually one of the most pleasant, polite, and frivolous people here, one of the few of them who had any receptivity to culture or civilization at all—it was just that like many of us he did not endure mornings gracefully. "No neuroducers set at full—just tinglers—and of course the epees aren't real in any case."

"Very comforting," my assistant said, mixing together the nasty mash of boiled ground grain that passed for breakfast locally (he seemed to feel there was something hopelessly decadent in my preference for pastry and fresh fruit). "They *won't* kill to get in. Hurt people, sure, but not kill."

"There is some difference," I said. "I would think that your family would feel differently about my punching you in the arm than they would feel about my decapitating you."

He snickered. "Yap, they'd rather you decapitated me. It would rid them of me and confirm everything they think about offplanet people at the same time."

I laughed. Despite being tired and short of sleep, I felt good because we were getting morning sunlight. When the sun shone all day long, Utilitopia sometimes warmed up and dried out enough to resemble an unusually ugly industrial park.

"Why the big smile?" Thorwald asked. "Thinking of a new way to inflict pain?"

"Only on the willing," I said. "Anyway, you should relax a little—the dueling arts class is all *ki* and falling for the next couple of weeks. No real fighting yet at all. Maybe you should have more faith in your fellow Caledons—probably when we start actual contact and combat, they'll all be so revolted and nauseated they'll leave en masse."

"I wish I did believe that." He poured himself another cup of coffee and yawned. "I got up early this morning—good thing I did, considering that surprise influx—and the mats are all scrubbed down and the ballroom is in good shape."

"Real efficiency," I said. "Well, I've got to get down to the main classroom and start the Basic Occitan section in a few minutes. I guess the next thing that needs doing is the dusting, and then destaticking the vu surfaces. Have you done that before?"

"Yap. And I'll recheck the specs from the robot before I start. I certain wouldn't want to damage the art."

Perhaps it was only because of the good mood I'd begun in, but language class seemed a bit discouraging that particular day. They took well enough to simple repetition drills (conjugations and declensions mostly) and they didn't have any big problem with working through the sample conversations—

"Bo die, donz."

"Bo die, donzèlha. Ego vi que t'es bella, trop bella, hodi."

"Que merce, donz!"

But when it came time to improvise, in free conversation, they turned to stone. Perhaps we had not yet come up with a topic that they would all want to talk about . . . maybe when I began my lessons in Reason, the next week, there would be beginning conversations I could borrow to make it more interesting for them.

Still thinking of that, and badly frustrated, I went downstairs to get Thorwald for our morning workout. If he was to be my assistant for the dueling arts class, I had to keep him ahead of the class, so one of his four hours of required daily work was currently going into private lessons.

I knew I had been pushing him hard from the way he moved. He was obviously sore, but he didn't complain; probably the soreness was the only thing that allowed him to feel like he was doing work.

He had finished the cleaning and was dressing when I got there; I hurried to put on my fighting clothes myself, and then we went into the mat room for some quick stretches before beginning. We had just begun the unarmed portion of *ki hara do* the day before; we resumed it now.

"Venetz!" I said. *"Atz sang!* Inner leg attacks, first form. Facing the mirror. *Uni, do, tri . . ."*

I had been drinking much less alcohol since getting here, and the daily triple workout of Thorwald's lesson, dance class, and dueling arts class—all in eight percent higher gravity—was rapidly bringing me into the best shape I'd been in since getting out of school. Nowadays I knew a duel against anyone would be no problem; even most of the old neuroducer damage seemed to be repairing itself. My right Achilles tendon no longer hurt where Rufeu had nicked it in a barroom brawl, and the neuroducer scar on my forehead, which I had gotten while holding off two drunken bravos, had relaxed into invisibility.

We got through the full set of basic drills in less than half an hour. I was setting a very aggressive pace, of course, but really it was Thorwald's grim determination to keep up that made the difference.

"Bo, bo, companhon!" I said, as he finished the drill. "For

a man who doesn't want to fight you show a certain excess of *espiritu*."

"If that's Occitan for 'lung failure,' I agree," he said, bending over, hands on knees, and panting.

I laughed, which seemed to gratify him, and then said, "All right, the next part is the hard part of the lesson. Today we do a little limited sparring. I know you're going to hate it, and I know you'd rather not, but you're going to do it—we have to get you thoroughly used to it if you're ever going to be any help to anyone else. We'll wear gloves, helmets, and pads and take it slowly."

Slowly turned out to be accurate only on the average. It took him five full minutes to agree that he was properly strapped into his fighting gear, and that his mouthpiece fit. Then, suddenly, he seemed to commit himself to it and was up and ready to go.

I circled him, occasionally feinting and trying to encourage him to take shots at me. In a way his earlier resistance to the idea of fighting had worked to his advantage—so many beginners get through the drills by venting their aggression, and thus pound through by ignoring what they're doing. Thorwald had done the drills with the calm, patient focus that is the fastest way to learn anything.

His movements were quick, relaxed, and by the book, and when I could occasionally probe out a real spontaneous response, he pressed his attack as if he wanted to win. My experience and my feel for a real fight still gave me the overwhelming advantage, and Thorwald would have been harmless as a kitten against me or any Occitan male of his own age—but I could see that he wouldn't be for long.

Toward the end of the time it seemed as if even Thorwald was having fun. Of course, I was not about to mention that and risk offending him.

I stepped in to draw another attack from his right side, and he pivoted and socked me in the nose. My face felt like it was exploding, *"Patz!"* I gasped out.

"Did I hurt you?" He sounded like he might cry. "Your nose is bleeding."

"It's a fight *atz sang, companhon.* You won." I tried to force a smile at him, but I don't think it worked because my nose still hurt. "I just need to step into the restroom and splash some cold water on this."

He turned still paler. "Shouldn't you see a doctor or something?"

That's the kind of thing one says in Nou Occitan when one is suggesting that the other jovent is a hypochondriac or a mama's boy, and I was already furious at him for his silly response to winning the fight, so rather than say something to humiliate him, I turned and stalked to the bathroom. As I was splashing handfuls of welcome cold water on my face—and probing to discover that my nose was probably just badly bent—Thorwald heaved up breakfast into the toilet behind me.

"Are you all right?" I finally asked.

"Do people get used to that?" he asked, going to the sink to wash.

"You even learn to enjoy it. Drawing blood, I mean, not vomiting."

He shuddered all over, but he followed me meekly enough back into the *dojo* to bow out. And strangely, when we entered the *dojo*, he seemed to suddenly stand straighter and prouder; and his bow was crisp and proper, the first real one I had gotten him to do.

As I stepped back from the *sensei*'s line after accepting his bow, I happened to look up.

Margaret and Valerie were up in the galleries.

Even here in Caledony, nothing brought out *enseingnamen* like an audience of *donzelhas*. I had to admit that Bieris had a real point; somehow seeing it this way, though, made it funny rather than offensive. It was all I could do not to tease Thorwald about it as we showered off. It was also all I could do not to scream when I accidentally touched my nose.

EIGHT

I had planned to stay in town, partly to keep Aimeric company (he would be taking a guest room at the Center that night) and partly to get a few extra hours' sleep. Now that I had enough clothing here at the Center, it was no major problem. I didn't worry much about Utilitopia's nightlife distracting me because as far as I could tell, Utilitopia's nightlife consisted mostly of sermons. So, when late in the afternoon I sat down to review some administrative nonsense, I was more than a little surprised to find a note in my file of incoming messages, inviting me to "A Performance of New Works by Caledon Artists" in the city that evening.

The idea was at least intriguing—to hear of a Caledon artist was to hear of an exhibit of dry water or heavy vacuum—and perhaps one of my students was involved. I tried to check with Thorwald, but he'd already gone out for the evening—so probably he was.

Well, whatever it was, it wasn't common and I knew I didn't want to miss it. I commed Aimeric and discovered he had been sitting around all day, being bored and answering technical questions. He was more than ready to go to dinner; after the heavy workouts of that day, I was even looking forward to dinner at Restaurant Nineteen, Aimeric's favorite place in Utilitopia. We agreed to meet there.

I left the cat parked and took the trakcar, sitting back to enjoy the swift, silent ride up the steep hills into the city. It occurred to me that Utilitopia would really lose something with the coming of the springer, and not long ago I'd have sworn it had nothing to lose. Restaurant Nineteen had become so popular that the ferocious Pleasure Tax had forced it to locate less than two hundred meters from the front gate of the Municipal Sewage Works, which meant that by pure accident it had also acquired a view. It was hard to imagine how they had justified windows, but they had managed that as well.

Every thirty seconds or so the automatic voice reminded me that "Having the windows unshuttered and the heat on simultaneously is wasting power, sir." I didn't let it annoy me; I was watching the sun of Second Noon play on the icy summits of the Optimals. Somehow I was going to go climbing up there before I left.

Restaurant Nineteen's special was called "Shepherd's Pie." A rough translation of that would be "overcooked vegetables and chunks of undrained mutton buried in oversalted mashed potatoes." "I'm obviously going native," I said to Aimeric, as I took seconds. "I think I'm beginning to like this stuff."

"You're just acclimating to the colder weather," he said. "So where is this place you've been invited to? And who invited you? I guess things must have changed more than I thought they had—there sure wasn't anything of the kind when I was here."

"I don't even know what's being performed. The place is called the Occasional Mobile Cabaret. Anyway, the time specified isn't for an hour and a half yet, so we might as well sit here, kill a dessert, and catch up a little. We haven't really talked much since getting here, with everything we've had to do."

Aimeric sighed. "Not a lot to talk about and too much to do is a Caledon's favorite situation. I've got to say, Giraut, you've taken to it far better than I thought you would."

That hurt me, reminding me of Marcabru's last letter, complaining that I wrote as if I were "a stranger named Giraut."

Aimeric had been sitting there quietly, watching me think, and now he grinned at me. "Your nose looks kind of swollen."

"Accident with a beginner."

"Oh." He let that subject go.

I remembered that Aimeric had spent his first couple of hundred standays on Wilson as a rigid, angry young man, alternately plunging into Occitan life with a fierce gusto and re-treating into angry, sulking moralisms. He had then been four years older than I was now. "It must have been very different, growing up here," I said, quietly.

"Yap. I always explain to myself that I got to be an adult, and then I got to be a jovent. It was so bizarre, coming to Nou Occitan, to find out I didn't have to miss being a kid after all. If I hadn't gotten a slot on the ship, I might have ended up a minister like Bruce."

"I still haven't figured out what a minister is or what one does," I admitted.

Aimeric shrugged. "A substitute parent for grownups. Tells them what's right and wrong, comforts them when they're upset, interprets the world. Shames them into being good and coaxes them out of being bad." He sighed. "When it's a good, decent person like Clarity, there's probably no harm in it. That's why she has the biggest congregation in Caledony, I suppose."

"She *does*?" I said. "Then why do they all discriminate against her? Why doesn't she have more power on the Council of Rationalizers?"

"Her congregation is so big mostly because it's sort of an automatic gerrymander. She tolerates dissidents and nobody else does. So all those people get one representative—and every little orthodox congregation gets one. Dad's congregation is only about three hundred people, but Peterborough's must be upwards of two hundred thousand. Anyway, the decent gentle souls like Clarity are the exceptions." He took another long pull from his wineglass. "It's usually just ambition that puts them into it—and like any group of people selected for ambition and nothing else, they turn out to be a pretty bad lot. Like manda-rins in China, colonial administrators in the British Empire, lawyers in old North America, or the reconstruction agencies after the Slaughter—individually there are decent people who do some good, but as a class they're amoral, vicious leeches with a good cover story."

The bitterness in Aimeric's voice startled me. He added, "This hasn't been a good thing for me to say. Anyone who was overhearing us and didn't report it could be in trouble with the Reverend Saltini, and I don't want that to happen to anyone. We're safe, of course—as resident aliens—but there's something about taking advantage of our position, like that, that bothers me. And I just want you to understand that a lot of what is just amusement, or entertaining an idea for the fun of it, to you, is potentially very dangerous to your students."

"What do they *do* to people here?"

"Well, Caledony isn't Thorburg or Fort Liberty. They don't torture or imprison dissidents, if that's what worries you. What they do is shut them completely out of public discourse. Heretics spend years of living on nothing but naked anger, doing godawful jobs and never having anything more than basic material comfort, ignored by everyone except the other angry cranks like themselves—until one day in their midforties or so, they realize that their lives stink and there's no point in any of it anymore, and then they go in for a big public confession, recant, and get a belated slice of decent life. It's a lot more effective than police repression—they just demonstrate that they can live with being called names a lot longer than most dissidents can live with being invisible." He flushed, and I realized now that he was really drunk, had had a lot of wine before dinner and must have had some before I got there as well.

He began to tell stories of his old times with Bruce and Charlie. He kept going back to something that did seem a little surprising—Bruce had been the real hell-raiser and *toszet des donzelhas* among the three friends.

"Well, it doesn't sound like the Bruce I know," I said, after about the fifth story of his escapades I'd heard, "but it was a long time ago."

"I suppose it's really on my mind because . . . well, maybe I'm a complete idiot. It bothers me that Bieris is with him all the time."

I poured myself another glass and waited for Aimeric to look up and talk again; there was a hot little fire at the base of my spine as I felt drama coming back into my life.

"Well," he said finally. "I suppose you can see what runs

through my mind." But instead of continuing on, and confiding, he shook his head, stood up, and shook off crumbs. With the exaggerated care of the truly drunk, he then straightened his clothing. "Must not practice mere utility in front of these natives," he said gravely. "Have to keep up appearances, most especially style."

That made *me* itch, so I had to do it too. As I finished, Aimeric said, "More than anything else about my leaving, I regret the fact that it may have contributed to Bruce ending up as a Reverend."

I stood there, not moving, not sitting down, unsure what I could say.

"We'd best get over to this Cabaret if we want to get any sort of seats," Aimeric said, and it seemed clear the subject was dropped. Yet as we ran through the snow and wind to our trakcar, he suddenly said, "You know, if Bruce got a free springer ticket to Nou Occitan, he'd probably deplore everything he saw for six months, then suddenly move up to the North Coast and join a Neohedonist commune. And two years after he got there, he and I would look the same age."

With Second Dark, a storm had come howling in off the sea. I waited till we were in the trakcar and the door had dogged closed before I raised my facemask and asked, "Why aren't there trakcar stops underground, under the buildings? Why do we all have to run through the wet and sleet to get to them?"

"Because the distance between the building and the trakcar is short enough not to be truly dangerous, and merely being unpleasant is something a good Caledon should ignore."

I had realized it was a foolish question as soon as I had asked it.

The trakcar pulled up in front of a big multiuse building. The Occasional Mobile Cabaret turned out to be in a "utility space," a big room that anyone could rent for a short period of time for any legal purpose. A young man whom I didn't know was collecting admission with a thumbprint reader. It took a moment to authorize me, probably first checking the

whole Caledon and St. Michaelian populations before looking
through the file of resident aliens.

"How's the crowd look tonight?" I asked.

"Hard to say. It's the first time we've done it," he said.
"But we've broken even, already, so pretty clearly we're not
seriously irrational." He said it with just the mixture of enthusiasm and carefully pushed sincerity that means the person
talking to you thinks you're a cop. "Hope you enjoy the
show."

I nodded, and at that moment my thumbprint cleared, so he
let me in. Aimeric only took a moment. "The i.d. system
must have been smart enough to look for you in the same
place—or does it still know you as Ambrose Carruthers?" I
asked, as we strolled into the room and looked around.

He grinned. "I offered the doorkeeper a small tip. Often
works wonders."

I still had not caught on to the idea that for some services,
but not others, you paid additional to the person doing the
service. Probably he had assumed I was a cop because they
were the only people rude enough, by Caledon standards, to
not tip. I felt angry at Aimeric for not telling me and angrier
at myself for not knowing.

It was the first room I had seen in Caledony where lights
weren't either full on or completely off. There were a few
dozen standard industrial chairs and a square portable stage;
it looked much like a poverty-stricken community theatre
back home.

There were a couple of dozen people milling around, forming brief excited conversations and then moving on, too restless to settle into conversational partnerships yet. Somebody
shouted "Mister Leones!"

I turned around to see Thorwald and Paul approaching.
"Glad to see you," Paul said. "I hoped you would get the invitation."

"Obviously I did," I said. "I assume this *is* the Occasional
Mobile Cabaret."

"The one and very much the only," Thorwald said. "And
possibly the only one ever to be. It's a limited partnership,

and Paul and I have to show a big enough profit to prove that it was rational to go into this business."

"You're the owners?"

"Well, it seemed like if Caledony needs more excitement and art—and Paul and I agree that it does—then maybe someone can turn a profit providing it. Of course, once we do turn a profit, then they have to decide whether it's a morally rational profit, but I guess we can fall off that bridge when we get to it."

Paul grinned. "If nothing else, it will give us the opportunity to have been illegal traders—not too many people have managed to do that in Caledon history."

I had just taken my seat next to Aimeric when Thorwald bounded up onto the stage; since it was Caledony it would never have occurred to anyone to start late, even though people were still filtering in, finding seats, and stopping to buy food and drink at the table in the back. "Hello everyone. Thank you for coming to the Occasional Mobile Cabaret. We have four performances for you tonight—that's down from scheduled six, I know, but the management takes no responsibility for last-minute cowardice—"

There was an uproar at the back of the room. Apparently one of the people who had backed out was there, and his friends were noisily calling attention to the fact. I glanced at Aimeric, and he was grinning. "Never thought I'd see a rowdy crowd in Caledony. Maybe there's hope for the old place yet," he said.

"The performance in the back of the room, on the other hand, is unscheduled and so comes to you at no extra charge," Thorwald said. "And it's worth what you paid for it."

That quieted them down, in a burst of good-natured grumbling.

"He has a way with a crowd," I said to Aimeric.

"Yap. He'd make a politician or an art critic in Occitan."

I nodded—it was true—and since Thorwald seemed to be taking his time about getting any of the acts up on the stage, headed back to the food table to get wine for both of us.

Valerio and Margaret turned out to be the hosts of the table. I grinned at them both. "So they've dragged you into this as well."

Margaret smiled. "I'm just getting paid to sell food and drink. The tip bowl is right there, by the way. Val's the real violent case here—she's actually going to perform later on."

I ordered the wine, and then gave Valerie my most winning smile—after all, if Paul wanted to learn Occitan ways, he might as well learn to watch out for them. "I'm really looking forward to your performance. Are you going to play?"

"Yes, and sing." Her eyes did not meet mine, and I detected a very pretty blush.

"I'm sure you'll be the best act of the night." I collected the glasses of wine from Margaret, threw a tip into the bowl, and grinned at Valerie again.

She was deeply flushed now, and looking down at the table; Margaret seemed baffled.

As I rejoined Aimeric, Thorwald was just explaining to the crowd that the other missing act was held up by having to come in through the Babylon Gap. Higher and colder than Sodom Gap, that pass was unsafe perhaps three days out of ten, even for a fully equipped cat.

"One more reason they're going to appreciate the springer when they get it," I said.

Aimeric shook his head. "If they cared about ease and practicality there would already be automated roads running through tunnels under the mountains. That used to be Dad's pet project."

From the stage, Thorwald's voice rose a little with excitement. "And that's all I'm going to say about what you *won't* see tonight. Lights please!" The house lights dimmed. The crowd seemed to hold its breath. "And now, for the first time on any stage—and with a little luck not the last!—we proudly present Anna K. Terwilliger, for a reading of her poetry." He turned and left the stage, a little limply—obviously he'd never thought of the problem of making an exit before now.

A plump woman of about twenty-five stanyears, pale, weak-chinned, and acne-scarred, but with rather nice thick, frizzy auburn hair and big blue eyes, came out on the stage. In her hands she held a thick, old-fashioned book, the kind with paper pages that have to be turned, and she opened it with the sort of assumed importance that the priests always had on Festival Days back home.

"My first poem was written while I was in a trakcar," she said. "It doesn't really have anything to do with trakcars, though. It's just that that's where I wrote it." There was a sympathetic, amused rumble from the audience. "I guess what I was really thinking about when I wrote it was just that you get older, you know, and then you're eventually older than you ever had any plans to be, so you don't know what to do. It's called 'Getting Older: A Trakcar Poem.'"

She lifted the book and read:

> "The ending is not yet, and yet the beginning has
>   already been.
> No one understands that until they do. Too late
> And well beyond the time for which you wait
> You find you cannot do the same again.
> So all grow old, and die, and fall, and rot
> And everything degrades or else it breaks
> And nothing ever is found by him who seeks
> Except the thing beyond which he seeks not.
> So abstract reason unaided by the soul
> Cannot push back the curtains dark of death
> Nor taste the air before the tasting breath
> And so we face forever to the hole,
> Which blackly draws our eyes, our face, within
> Denying all. So do we not begin."

She read all that solemnly, with that strange upward turn at the end of each line and the heavy intonation that pounds into the audience that by-god-this-is-poetry. They all sat there quietly as each dreadful, monotonous, awkward line thudded into them; I bit my tongue to prevent giggles, and felt Aimeric silently shaking beside me. Clearly Anna K. Terwilliger was going to achieve note as the first Caledon poet, not as its best . . . unless she was also its only.

She finished and looked up, blinking, with all the hopeful shyness of any first time on stage. I liked that about her, and hoped the audience would not be excessively cruel.

First two or three, then a dozen, and then all sixty or so people in the room burst out in wild applause, some rising to their feet. The air was rich with cheers and excitement.

She beamed at them all, her eyes wet.

I glanced at Aimeric. "I've been away a long time," he whispered in my ear. "I really don't know how I'd have reacted to it as a kid. It's awful in technique, sure. But these folks don't know that. Taste later—experience first, Giraut."

I sighed. "I guess so. Maybe I just envy their excitement."

The room was quieting now. Anna K. Terwilliger brushed back her flying hair and read another work, the point of which was that everything that dies has its constituents recycled. Broken out of verse it might have made a suitable introduction to a child's ecology textbook. It got more applause, if anything, than the first one did.

Then something about god and reason and numbers that I couldn't follow at all brought the house down; then some very simple descriptive poems, at least not completely incompetent, about her family and where they lived . . . none of it would have gotten a passing mark in any class in Noupeitau. No three lines of any of it would have escaped a shower of nuts and beer at any Occitan reading club. I just hoped we were going to be more successful in exporting our culture than they were in exporting theirs.

At last Anna K. Terwilliger was off the stage, to thunderous applause, and Thorwald came back up. "And another first—I'm going to have to think up some other line if we ever do it again—here's Taney Peterborough."

He sat down, and again there was no applause. I was about to ask Aimeric if this was any relation to Clarity, but when he came on stage there was no question at all—it was obviously her brother or cousin.

From the costume and expression, I knew at once this

was someone who was going to try the ancient art of *statzsursum*, and my heart sank—to do it well takes years of training, to do it badly just a few moments of near-thought, and since there was no place here to get the training (maybe I should offer a course at the Center? But there was no one to teach it) I knew pretty well what I was going to see.

Taney Peterborough had a fairly engaging stage personality, and the crowd warmed to him right away. This was not a positive thing, because it encouraged him. His jokes were unconnected, merely a random collection arranged loosely by topic, and old besides—especially the political ones, which must have dated back a thousand years or more, and been told in every authoritarian regime, especially those with puritanical streaks. There were the obligatory ones about Aimeric's father and the Reverend Saltini, and about the system in general.

"Things must be looser than I thought they were," I said to Aimeric.

"He's got a free pass," Aimeric whispered. "It's rational for him to want his sister to succeed politically, so he can prove it's rational for him to disparage the opposition. So they can't get him for irrationality or commit him to therapy—and that's how all political crimes are handled."

"Is it rational for everyone else to be listening, laughing, or applauding?" I asked.

"That's a good question, which I have no doubt Saltini is working on at this very moment."

That didn't leave much to say, so I sat there and watched through all the excruciating jokes, and was amazed that so many people were brave enough to laugh without thinking first.

Finally it was over, and the applauses was respectable if not quite so thunderous as Anna K. Terwilliger's. Thorwald popped back onto the stage, a certain tension on his face, and said only "There will be fifteen minutes' intermission—then we'll be back with two more acts."

Aimeric shrugged at me. "Don't make too much of it. It may be nothing, or even an opportunity for the Pastorate of

Public Projects to signal some loosening up. Or they may just not care what goes on among these folks, anyway."

He knew Caledony, and I didn't. I still had a feeling he was just trying to reassure me.

On my way back to the food table—to get a little more wine and perhaps a little more Valcrie—someone tapped my shoulder. I turned around to find myself face-to-face with Bruce and Bieris.

"Hello! How'd you get here?"

"Someone left a message for me at the Center, after painting class," Bieris explained. "I gave Bruce a call, and he had time to come in with the cat, so he joined me. We saw you come in but there wasn't time to get over and say hello before the show started."

I doubted that somehow, and certainly the place was informal enough anyway that there would not have been any problem with them moving around. And had it been my imagination, or had Bruce dropped Bieris's hand just as I turned to speak to them? I felt the delightful shiver, deep inside, that said that everything was about to get tragic and complicated any day now. Perhaps I would be lucky and Aimeric would ask me to be his Secundo ... but then, they didn't duel here, so did they have Secundos? And if they did, was he simply the go-between, or was there some role in settling the matter of honor?

The idea of being Secundo between friends—well, I had always envied Raimbaut the occasion. The first time I saw him die he was my Secundo against Marcabru, back when we were teenagers and I caught Marcabru in flagrante delicto with my *entendedora*.

Bieris had been talking of a couple of students she was teaching in her painting classes at the Center that she thought had promise. "And of course Anna is in my class. She has a real feel for Occitan."

"She *does*?" I spoke without thinking—fortunately it looked like no one had overheard.

Bruce chuckled. "You weren't much thrilled by the poetry either."

Bieris glared at him and I realized there was a difference of opinion about to erupt, but before I could make a move to get out of the way, Bruce had excused himself to go get wine for all of us—which also, unfortunately, put Valerie out of reach for the time being. I turned back to Bieris, who was smiling more nicely than necessary, always a bad sign.

"You can't mean you actually liked that performance," I said. "I could understand all the sympathy Aimeric was giving to it, because he grew up here and he was impressed that it was happening at all, but when you consider the actual content and quality—"

Bieris's mouth curled up a little at the corner. "Giraut, I know perfectly well that if I argue now you'll put it down to my loyalty to my student. And no, it certainly wasn't the rhetoric, perception, technique, or performance that impressed me."

"Which is to say, it wasn't the poetry. What else is there?"

She bit her lower lip. "Two things, Giraut, and you're going to make fun of both of them. First of all, the event. These people care so much more about art than we do. They really put us to shame. And secondly, the woman herself. The fact that someone who looks like that is allowed to be a poet here impresses me a lot more than you can imagine."

"I can tell that you're serious, but I don't understand how you can argue that people who make no art care about it more than people who do nothing but make art. And as for the other—well, I must admit you're right. The writings of an ugly woman can never reach the level of poetry, any more than the writings of an ugly man can. What will her descendants think, if she ever makes a reading tape, and they see it?"

Bieris whirled away from me and went after Bruce. I stood there for a moment, realizing that the Caledons had really gotten to her. She no longer made any more sense than they did.

Before I could go after her, a voice spoke in my ear. "Quite an occasion. Is this your influence?"

I turned and found I was facing Ambassador Shan.

"I'd like to claim credit—a lot of these people are my students—but it's their ideas and their courage." Perhaps Bieris had managed to make me a little ashamed of what I thought of their crudity. Besides, now that I thought of it, there was something a little brave, and gallant, and foolish about the Occasional Mobile Cabaret, and I would not have been Occitan if that had not won my heart, at least a little.

"How did you find out about this one?" I asked.

"I'd be a poor Ambassador if I didn't know what was going on in Utilitopia—and a worse one if I told people how I found out."

"You'd probably also be a poor diplomat if you gave an honest review of the show thus far," I said.

His smile deepened. "Oh, not at all. I honestly find every bit of art I have ever encountered, in thirteen different cultures, since going to work for the Council, to be charming and delightful. It's part of my job."

He turned to talk to someone else. Just as well—the thought of *having* to like anything made me shudder.

Bruce came by with the wine. We chatted for a minute or two about things out on the farm before, to my surprise and delight, Valerie joined us.

"Hi," she said. "There's something I wanted to ask you, a really big favor, and it would be just fine with me if you said no."

Bruce chuckled. "Something tells me that's about the most irresistible offer Giraut is ever likely to hear."

"Something tells you right," I said.

Valerie blushed. "Well, I just feel stupid because I could have asked you before. I was listening to some Occitan music, and sometimes checking the annotations, and I noticed that you have a way of improvising together? More than one musician at a time, I mean? And what I wondered is, do you have to practice doing that, or can two people who've never played together before play together and sound good enough to be out in public—because what I'd really like you to do is to come up and—I mean after I do some songs, of course, but if I asked you to come up—"

"You're asking me to jam with you?" I asked.

Her eyes got wide, and even Bruce looked a little startled, and I realized I had just inadvertently acquired an expression in the local slang. I hastened to explain. "Anyway, the answer—at least to making music together!—is yes," I said. "Pickup playing is actually very common in Occitan clubs. I'd be glad to."

She blushed again, very prettily I thought, and said she'd look forward to it, before scooting back to the table to relieve Margaret, who seemed more baffled than ever. She whispered something to Margaret. From the way Margaret suddenly guffawed and slapped the table, it was probably about the little misunderstanding of "jam."

Bruce winked at me.

Just then Thorwald bounded up onto the stage again. "All right everyone—"

A voice in the back bellowed. "Let me get another beer before I have to watch anything *you* wrote!"

There was a roar of applause at this; Thorwald grinned sheepishly. "More time for intermission?"

It got one of the biggest ovations that night. Thorwald sat down, and people continued to socialize, although now they were drifting slowly toward their seats.

When I got there, I discovered that Margaret was now sitting on the other side of me from Aimeric. Aimeric seemed to be talking to his neighbor about something, so I took my seat and—with, I admit, a certain inner weariness—resolved to be courteous to this very plain girl.

I think Margaret would have been plain no matter where she was; no full set of Occitan skirts could have concealed her oversized rump, no possible top reshaped her too-wide shoulders and small, flaccid breasts, and no arrangement of hair softened the harsh planes of her face or concealed her lumpy complexion. But in the unisex clothes of Caledony, she was honestly hideous—her crewcut hair only amplified the shiny, unhealthy pallor of her face, the pullover only revealed her old-woman bust and belly, and the knee-high protective boots and baggy trousers only emphasized that her scrawny legs were capped by big, sagging buttocks. In Nou Occitan she might have made a forest ranger, or joined one of the survey teams for Arcturus's lifeless worlds, or perhaps sailed in the round-the-planet skimmer races—any occupation where most of the time she could be away from people. Here, she even seemed to be popular.

And in any case, whatever she looked like, I was not going to allow myself to be rude. "So are you enjoying the show?" I asked.

Her smile turned under just a bit. "I'm too involved, I guess. Everything that isn't perfect embarrasses me, and everything that works makes me want to jump up and cheer. Is it . . . is it really like this every night, I mean, are there really a lot of things like this, in Nou Occitan?"

Determined to stay polite, I dismissed every answer I had and simply said, "There are a lot of performances and a lot of art, yes . . ." meaning to leave it dangle there, and hope she didn't catch any other implications, but as I looked around the room, and saw all those people squirming and waiting for things to resume, not studying each other for later comment as they would have been at any theater in Noupeitau, I found myself, quite unwillingly, saying "I don't think we appreciate it as much as you do. When there's so much, it's just not as exciting to us . . . and of course, we're awfully apolitical, so there's just not the . . . *passion* there."

She seemed to think that my answer was a compliment, and maybe it was. And, plain or not, I liked her. I was glad that what I said had made her happy. For a moment, we were awkward and shy with each other, the way you are when a friendship is just forming. Then probably looking for something to say, she added, "Valerie is *really* nervous."

"She shouldn't be. She's likely to be the hit of the evening. But I suppose it's her first time in front of a live crowd, or at least a live crowd that she can hear."

"Yeah, but even more so . . . she's throwing so much away . . ."

"Throwing?"

"You didn't know? But I suppose there was no way you

would. The decisions about who gets to compete for the prizes are based on the average score of the last nineteen public performances or competitions. Since the aintellects will score this extremely badly . . ."

"Deu! She'll lose everything!"

"Well, she seems to want to perform this way. And as she points out, as long as she can sell tickets, all she has to do is please a lot of people consistently. And if not, there's always work, you know—we aren't barbarians."

I was silent. A girl like that, and an artist besides, could end up shoveling stables or scraping paint, merely because she thought she was a better musician than a machine . . . I was beginning to phrase my next letter to Marcabru already . . .

Margaret patted my arm and said, "It's really her choice, you know. And you didn't lead her into it or anything. Don't take it too hard."

I was spared the need for a reply by the lights coming down. Thorwald came out on the stage, and the same voice heckled him again: "Scared you off last time, hunh?"

"Paul, you're bad for business."

With a mutual snort, Margaret and I both realized that in fact it was Paul who had been heckling before. "He was right, though," she whispered. "We do have to give people time to do what they're doing. We really can't just make them all come to order on the clock . . ."

"You're sounding very Occitan tonight," I teased—and could see it was a mistake. She flushed the way Val did, which meant it had read as flirting . . . and flirting with someone you couldn't possibly be interested in is the worst sort of cruelty. I would have to be very careful for a while with Margaret—especially because I *did* want her friendship.

How would I explain her to Marcabru? I could present Thorwald and Paul as nascent jovents, Valerie as a *donzelha*, but Margaret?

The Occitan solution occurred to me. I would say nothing of her, but if he ever saw her, or pictures of her, and voiced a critical thought, I would offer him challenge *atz fis prim*, to the first death.

Life really was simpler, back home.

Thorwald was introducing Valerie; he seemed to think that this was going to be the most shocking act of the evening, so he was apparently trying to prepare the crowd adequately, stressing the "freedom and power of expression" that came from this "new—or new to us—technique of improvisation. You are going to hear things in the music that you have never heard before; it is our belief that they have always been there, that Valerie simply brings them forth." He went on in that vein for a while, long enough to have convinced me, if I hadn't known better, that we were about to see an exhibit in musical anthropology.

When Valerie finally came on the stage, she didn't get quite the applause that Anna or Taney had gotten, and "small wonder after that yawn-y introduction," Margaret whispered. I nodded emphatically.

Valerie had obviously decided to break them in gradually. She started with a few old ballads from the Scottish, Argentine, and Texan traditions—it was strange how, when they crossed over to Terstad, they seemed to become so similar. Her introductions were brief, usually just telling us where a piece came from and in what century—the most controversial thing she did, probably, was to play "Diego Diablo," an old ballad of the Southern Hemisphere League from the years right after the Slaughter that was thoroughly loaded with the traditional hatred of the Latin Americans for United Asia, throwing all the blame and blood of the destruction of the Plata Transpolis (and its 130 million people) on the "Butcher-King of Taipei," and glorifying the counterstrike that leveled Honshu Transpolis. Even after hundreds of years, on a world tens of light-years from Earth, it could stir and freeze your blood—I would have to point out to Thorwald how very natural the lust for a fight is in a human being.

It was when she broke into another piece that everything went crazy. She had taken one of Anna K. Terwilliger's poems, one of the ones that had made no sense at all to me but drawn fierce applause, and set it to what was apparently

another traditional contest piece, one that was supposed to be
instrumental.

The uproar when she began was deafening, and so many
people were on their feet that the rest of us stood up to see.
Most of the arguments were in Reason, so I had little idea
what was going on at the time, and I still don't really, but
it seemed to be that Anna had written a sort of Godel's The-
orem of the local theology in that poem, proving that if it
were true, there had to be true things that it could not com-
prehend—and that was heresy. To top it off, Valerie had set
it to a melody that was traditionally a dirge, played in some
ceremony where they contemplated . . . well, the Reason for
it translates as the "TradeOffNess of Life," and the title of
the piece is "You Can't Always Get What You Want"—
anyway, I still don't entirely understand it, and I don't think
a non-Caledon ever can, but the point was it was played at
many of their most serious religious rites, and dated clear
back to the legendary founders of their faith in the Industrial
Age, and *she was playing it in ragtime.*

In short, between the angry words and the mocking music,
this was bitter sarcasm hurled straight into the face of Caledon thought, and the riot that followed was probably about
the most restrained response that could have been expected.

Everywhere around me people shouted into each other's
face; you could see couples breaking up into furious acri-
mony with each other, Caledons pushing each other (Deu I
was glad I hadn't yet taught any of them to punch or kick effectively!), and one pale blond woman standing on a chair
screaming at the whole crowd—but though her mouth moved,
and she could not have been more than six meters from me,
I could not hear a word she said.

I turned to Aimeric and he wasn't there; in his place was
what looked at first like a redheaded child—it took me a moment to realize it was Prescott—who was shouting at Margaret on my other side. He drew back a fist as if to strike her,
and I swept his foot and dumped him to the carpet, hoping
that would cool him off and keep him out of trouble. I noticed that Paul and Thorwald actually moved up to stand in

front of the stage, as if they were bouncers and this some rowdy bar, and I flatter myself that their balance was just that much better, their assurance just that much stronger, from their dueling arts work—no one seemed to want to close with them. After a moment I saw that Aimeric and Bruce were joining them. I started working my way through the crowd.

It went pitch-black all at once, and then obviously a suppressor web was lowered into the space, because suddenly you could barely hear anything, as the ambient sound was erased. I realized it meant the police, and that was bad, but I was so relieved that for a moment I didn't care.

Then, out of the web, modulating its interference pulses, came the flat, emotionless voice of an aintellect. "There is evidence of serious irrationality in this gathering. We request Thorwald Spenders and Paul Parton to identify themselves."

"Here," they said, simultaneously. By now the room was quiet again, and the suppressors seemed to be slowly fading out, leaving the weird hum in the ears I always got when they were applied.

"Please develop some method of calming this assembly, on penalty of having this gathering and all similar ones declared a hazard to rationality."

The lights now came back on—full on, leaving us all blinking and uncomfortable—and I could see Thorwald thinking desperately; then Paul spoke up.

"We will provide, to everyone who wishes to leave now, a full refund of tonight's admission price, and if they wish, a free pass for any future performances."

There was a stunned silence, and then a little burst of applause—I didn't see why, since surely that was the simplest—

"Objection," the aintellect said. "It is not rational for you to do that. These people have already consumed more than half the performances you have offered."

Paul spoke slowly. "I understand that. But I also understand that many of them are quite disappointed because what they saw was not what they had hoped to see. This way, assuming there are any future performances, they will still be

rational in attending them as a speculative venture, on the
chance that they might like them."

"Objection. This supplies them with a means of defrauding
you."

"Yes, but as long as we maintain shows of sufficient quality, they will wish to see the last act through to its finish—
and if they see that, they will not be able to claim a refund."

"All objections withdrawn. Proceed."

It took Paul and Thorwald a few minutes to give refunds
to the twenty or so people that wanted their money back;
meanwhile I went up to talk to Valerie, partly to congratulate
her on her set so far and keep her spirits up, and mostly to
see where I could get with another round of flirting.

She was in surprisingly good spirits; apparently a large
crowd had not been nearly so frightening as she'd thought it
would be, and moreover, she was gratified that the whole intent of her song had been understood so immediately and
thoroughly. "Well," she said, "if I'm going to strike off in
this way, then at least I know that people will understand it.
Hate it, maybe, but understand it. And knowing that I'm
making sense counts for something."

"But—the risks you run—"

She smiled and shook her head. "What risks? I get to play
what I like; they can't stop my doing that. I can write songs
and rely on audience approval rather than what some aintellect thinks it ought to sound like—even if I have to *give*
the songs away, they'll get sung."

"But you could end up shoveling shit!"

She shook her head sadly at me. "Do you know how many
of the great songwriters of the past two thousand years have
worked with their hands? It won't kill me and it's a small
price for freedom."

I realized that pointing out that there was something perverse and profoundly wrong in the idea of a girl with a beautiful voice and the face of an angel doing that kind of work
would clinch the argument with an Occitan, but that a Caledon would just stare at me, so I contented myself with plan-

ning to write a very long, passionate letter to Marcabru as soon as I got home.

At that point Thorwald came up to tell us that we'd be starting again soon. "Margaret seems to think she's squeezed about all the utils she can out of the crowd, Val, so she wants you to know that you don't have to cause any more unplanned intermissions."

Valerie giggled and nodded; she suggested we simply do half a dozen Occitan pieces, "to keep things a bit calmer—I do think that we've given them enough excitement for the night, don't you?"

It struck me that as soon as the subject was music or performing—rather than flattery—her shyness disappeared. "Oh, certainly, if you wish," I said. "I hope they won't regard it as a letdown."

"Tonight nothing could be a letdown," Paul said, coming over and sitting next to Valerie. "Mister Leones—"

"Giraut, please," I said. "I've been meaning to tell you I prefer that you use my given name."

"Giraut, then. I don't suppose you can imagine what all this means to us."

I sighed. "I really don't suppose I can, either."

The lights were beginning to flicker—where had they learned that traditional signal for show about to start?—so Paul, with another nod, got down off the stage, and Thorwald brought up my lute in its case. "We had it expressed from the Center when Val told us," he explained. "I hope that was all right."

"It was splendid of you," I said, meaning it. "I always prefer playing my own instrument."

I had all the normal tension I get just before a performance, but packed into the five minutes of tuning while Thorwald made some veiled political jokes about the police and "what a night, friends—our first cabaret, our first poet, our first riot." The crowd seemed quieter and more subdued.

If I may say so, Valerie and I were brilliant together. Her instincts for improvisation were every bit as good ensemble as solo, and I don't think there have been very many finer performances of the dozen Occitan standards we went through.

And yet—warm and friendly as the audience was, good as the performance was—as much as I knew that in style and quality, we were far ahead of everything so far that night . . . I had a curious empty feeling about it. People were applauding beauty, which was as it should be—but somehow that moved them less than Valerie's defiant (and to me incomprehensible) anthem, or Anna's dreadful verses—or even, as I hated to admit to myself, less than Taney Peterborough's stale jokes.

I moved back to let Valerie take all the remaining bows, to applaud her myself. The applause was hers by right; I found that I resented the whole situation a little, and felt deep shame, like a spreading stain on my *enseingnamen*, that I could be so petty. I thought of some things Bieris had said to me earlier, and realized how silly some of my posturing must look to her . . . and to the students at the Center.

When at last we were permitted to sit down, Thorwald came onto the stage almost at once, as if afraid of any loss of momentum, and seemed edgier than before. The reason became clear in a moment: "Our final piece is by a playwright of such remarkable ability, and represents so major a breakthrough for him and indeed for all of Caledon culture, that I can only say to you . . . I wrote it."

The place roared with laughter and he looked relieved. I realized he had no idea how dependable that old joke was. *Deu*, he probably thought he had invented it.

"Let me point out that because this is the first presentation of this play anywhere, there are no accepted interpretations of any of the roles, so our actors have truly had to create from scratch." There was another scattered burst of clapping, probably from the more supportive friends of the actors. "What that means, of course, is that if they get it wrong, it's not my fault—I assure you it was written brilliantly." More laughter followed; I saw Thorwald check for a cue from backstage, and then he added, "All right, I suppose I really can't delay this any longer. If you have any questions I'll be out in the hallway, either biting my nails or throwing up."

A group of awkward people in mostly dark clothing, working in mostly dark that they didn't blend in with, lurched around getting two tables and four chairs onto the stage.

"Oh, uh, yap," Thorwald added, returning to the stage, "the play is called *Creighton's Job*." His exit was even more awkward this time.

The actors stumbled and thudded a lot getting into places in the dark, and there was a little tittering at that. When the lights came up, all the actors were scratching or shuffling to a new position, so of course things took a moment to start. I noticed they all wore prompter earpieces, so at least we would not be treated to the charming effect of watching them try to remember their lines.

As far as I could make out—there was too much laughter and applause too often, and apparently the play was set in the back country up beyond Gomorrah Gap, far to the icy south, so the accents were thick—the play was about Creighton, whose parents wanted him to get a good job and kept proving to him—using a blackboard at the dinner table, for example—that he wanted one. Then he would go interview, always with the same man (I was not sure whether this was part of the joke or a shortage of actors) and after a lot of complicated mathematics, and a lot of (apparently hilarious and possibly ribald) dialogue in Reason, Creighton's father would get the job.

After the second time this happened, the pattern began to vary and escalate—Creighton's mother got hired, the interviewer hired himself, the interviewer punished Creighton for applying by firing his father and marrying his mother. The little I could understand was very broad, low—and old—humor.

Just as the wedding ceremony was being performed, with Creighton's father officiating and Creighton running from function to function as simultaneous best man, maid of honor, choir, and flower girl, the lights went out completely.

The crowd had been roaring its approval almost continuously—Margaret had been so excited she was practically in my lap—but now they fell instantly silent, patiently waiting for what seemed to be a technical difficulty. I thought of see-

ing if I could get some stamping and booing and barking going, which was how an Occitan crowd might have responded,
except that frankly the whole thing so far had been so ama-
teurish and crude that the interruption seemed like more fun.

Then the speakers came on, and the lights came back up.
"It has been determined by the Pastorate of Public Projects
that this presentation in its whole and in its parts is funda-
mentally irrational. It has furthermore been determined that
the permission for this gathering is to be revoked retroac-
tively, and that police authorities who granted the permit, and
who failed to suppress earlier rioting, will be brought to trial
at the earliest possible date. Pursuant to this case and to others pending, all persons here are liable to subpoena for testimony against permit-granting authorities. A full copy of the
declaration of irrationality is available for offprint on request.
All persons are enjoined to leave this space within thirty minutes and to avoid any displays of irrationality in the near future under penalty of inquiry."

The room stayed unbearably quiet. No one looked up, I
think, except me. I saw a tear run down Margaret's cheek,
and her lower lip trembled.

Thorwald got up, looking as if he'd been kicked in the
groin, and said, "All right. You heard them. Apparently
we've managed to get the police into trouble—let's not make
them come out here to evict us. I make an official public
statement to any monitoring equipment now present: we will
be appealing these actions on all possible grounds as soon as
possible." A few people stood up to clap; the rest looked at
the floor. "But for right now, we have to get out of here
quickly." He looked around the room, obviously trying to
think of how to say what he had to say next. "Any and all
persons who wish to express a rational protest against the action of the PPP are invited to participate in the takedown and
cleanup as a way of voicing their disapproval."

Aimeric whistled, and whispered in my ear. "Brilliant.
They thought they'd stick the few promoters and employees
with the whole job, and then fine them for not doing it fast
enough. Now Thorwald has completely legitimated and ratio-

nalized people staying to help. No one can be punished for assisting without pay, now."

They did it all very quickly, and I noticed there was no bickering. "In Noupeitau you wouldn't have been able to hear the chairs crashing for the grumbling," I said to Bieris, as we both carried stacks of chairs to the back of the room. I noticed she was carrying more than I was, and congratulated myself on not saying anything stupid about the fact.

"Yap. If anyone had stayed to help at all."

"Well," Aimeric added, as he came up beside us with a box of audio gear, "it does enhance their defense if they're charged with irrationality."

"Crap," Bieris said. "They could get that by turning in their friends. These kids just have a ton of courage, Aimeric."

He didn't say anything, and I didn't either—it troubled me that except for Valerie, I hadn't been *able* to like any of the show. Still, I was glad I had come; it was nice to be on the right side of anything.

Margaret needed a hand with some of the stuff from the refreshments, so I helped out there next. As we were carrying out an untapped beer keg, I said to her, "I still don't see how it can be irrational to give people what they want, especially not when they prove it by paying for it."

She sighed. "As a pure debating exercise, I can see how their argument would go. They don't believe in allowing cultural contradiction. So it's for our own good that they won't let us use all this freedom, prosperity, and happiness to attack the source of all the freedom, prosperity, and happiness. The argument is that since rational markets make people happy—"

"It's an outrage, just an outrage," a voice said behind us. We looked back to see Prescott Diligence and Taney Peterborough carrying a table between them. "The PPP has grossly overstepped itself this time," Prescott said. "It's obvious that they're trying to undermine the whole Reform Bill twenty years after the fact. We're having a meeting tomorrow to get the Liberal Association restarted, if you'd like to come, Margaret."

"Yap, I would." She clipped the words out impatiently—probably she hadn't forgotten his trying to punch her.

"The proper authorities just don't know what's going on, and this has to be brought to their attention at once," Taney added, and Prescott nodded emphatically.

We dropped the keg off in the temporary storeroom, then stood aside as everything else was carried in after us. "That does it," Thorwald said, as the last of it came in. "Make sure you've gotten all your possessions from the meeting room. Thank you for acting in rational defense of your rights."

Now that the job had been done, everyone seemed to be heading for home. I offered to share a trakcar back to the Center with Thorwald, but he had some other winding-down things to get done, so I went on alone. Once again, I left the windows unshuttered so that we could see what there was to see of the city—quite a lot since there was bright moonlight. Strangely, there seemed to be parties of people out moving through the dark streets everywhere; hooded and masked as they were, I couldn't see who they were or what they were about. Once the trakcar crawled right through a long line of them that ran across a street. They all had their backs to me, so I saw nothing of them. A block later, another line of them, facing me, parted to let me through.

I got out, sprinted into the Center, and headed immediately upstairs to change into nightclothes; I felt a passionate need to just be comfortable and decompressed. As I was changing, I switched on the kitchen remote and ordered two warm sweet rolls and a cup of hot chocolate. A moment later, as I was fastening the front of my robe, there was the soft *ping* that alerted me to mail that had arrived. It had to be from Marcabru or my father, and either way it was bound to be news of home—home where things weren't so hopelessly weird, where you could admire an artist for style and grace and talent and not for anything so bizarre as courage or principles, home where I would be returning soon—

I padded quickly down to the kitchen, where my food was now ready, set myself up comfortably at a table with the rolls, chocolate, and reader, and called up my new letter.

The return address said it was from Marcabru—it had been quite a while since I had heard from him. As it popped up on the screen, I began to read eagerly:

Dear Giraut,

I am well and truly angry with you, which I can only think is what you must have intended since the Giraut I used to think I knew surely could not give such egregious offense other than deliberately. Has it not occurred to you that your entire reputation and honor here at Court has depended upon my defense of you, my keeping your memory alive after your inexplicable act in jumping off to that frozen wasteland—and upon my public readings from your letters?

And yet for the past four letters, nothing you have written has at all justified my public praise of you, for all you seem able to do is to gossip about your half-witted Caledon acquaintances, and not only that, but with neither fire nor acid to apply to them. You seem to take no interest in, or at least you choose not to comment at all about, the many changes of fashion that I, as Prince Consort, have begun—does it never occur to you that the Prince Consort actually takes time to write to you personally about these matters?

And what has become of your real work—no recordings sent us—and of finamor and enseingnamen? You write of your precious Center like some old drudge who thinks that drudgery is all life ought to be. You have grown as bleak and cold as that iceball to which you so foolishly fled and your deadly seriousness on behalf of those poor barbarians only proves what a cold-blooded earnest bore, like them, you have become.

I trust you must appreciate my situation, Giraut. I have extended myself to the utmost, risking frequent derision as a sentimental ass, to maintain a reputation for which you apparently do not care in the slightest, since you do nothing to help me maintain it. There has been nothing that I could cite in any of your letters to endorse my high opinion of you; have you truly become so un-Occitan that you do not remember, or do not care, that reputation demands constant defense?

Well, I am no longer willing to fight for you or your reputation when people are so clearly right to describe you as boring and worse. As you well know, but act as if you had forgotten, by your actions you place me in the impossible position where enseingnamen *forces me not to fight but to actually accept shame when the charge is obviously true.*

> *And it is, Giraut, it is.*
> *You may die for all I care,*
> *Marcabru*

I read it through, slowly, once more, gulping down the rolls and chocolate because I knew I would surely be hungry later. I could feel how right he was, and yet at the same time I could not feel that I had any power at all to do otherwise than what I was doing. I had done what he said, and it was cause for grave offense; even after an unlimited duel with him, there could be no friendship after this. My best friend had become my sworn enemy.

And yet . . .

I finished the stuff without tasting any of it, hurled the dishes into the regenner, and hastened upstairs to bed.

On my way up the stairs I met Thorwald coming down. "You look like you've had bad news," he said sympathetically.

"So have you," I pointed out. "Thorwald—is all this my fault? Did I stir you people up to it? Because if I did, maybe I should just take the blame and get myself deported."

"Are you that eager to leave?"

"No, not—well, yes, I really am homesick just now. But that isn't why I'm offering. I'm just concerned that it seems like I got here and all of a sudden all of you are in much worse trouble than you would have been without me and the Center and so forth."

"Depends on what you mean by trouble." He sighed.

"Did Saltini interrogate you yet?"

"Now you're thinking like a Caledon. No, not yet. I'm surprised because I was sure he would. How about you?"

I shook my head. "It just occurred to me that he probably would pretty soon, if he hadn't."

Thorwald nodded, then abruptly asked, "Can I ask you something personal?"

"I might not answer."

"That's all right. Did you just get a really rude letter from your friend Marcabru?"

I nodded.

"Because," he continued, "every time you get a letter from him it seems to make you sad and cross for a day afterwards, and right now you look like you're really in pain."

I was so shocked that anyone would be paying that much attention to me that I stammered out my first thought, which was that I hoped I had not taken out my bad feelings on Thorwald or his friends.

Thorwald shook his head. "Nop. You're pretty good about that. But it doesn't take that much effort to see you're unhappy, and—well, we all like you. So we try to stay out of your way when that happens, so you won't say anything you'll regret."

I nodded and went upstairs, unsure of my ability to speak. So, not only had I failed at Court; even these students at the Center had been simply extending charitable kindness to me, taking care of me because I could not look after myself. And with their tiny, fledgling artistic movement—well, if it was broken, they would have little need for me, and if it was not, they could make art for themselves—what *they* needed and liked, not some arbitrary attempt to meet my standards. I had nothing to teach them. It occurred to me that I had sat there sneering at them all night—and that while I had been doing that, and planning what cruel things I would say to amuse Marcabru, they had been the real artists in the room.

I couldn't wait to get home, despite knowing of the failure that surely waited for me there. At least I was in good physical condition for the dozens of duels I would have to fight.

I was feeling so sorry for myself that I must have cried myself to sleep, because my face was stained with tears when the morning prompter sounded its alarm and said, "Sir, today is the day of the presentation to the Council of Rationalizers, and my record shows you need to bathe, shave, and dress."

It was quite right. I jumped up, praising the aintellect loudly to reinforce it so that if anything like this ever happened again, it would do exactly the same thing. I stripped and stepped into the shower, shaved as quickly as I safely could, and flipped to dry the moment I was rinsed. I reached out of the stall, grabbed the remote, and ordered fruit, pastry, cheese, and coffee in the kitchen.

At least dressing was no problem—I had one formal Caledon outfit, which looked like all the formal outfits on Caledon—the coverall was black, the knee-high boots were black, the shirt was white, and the ridiculous little string tie was a pale silver color. I fastened on the white belt and was dressed; looking at myself in the mirror, and straightening my cuffs, I realized that I looked a bit peculiar to myself, since my hair was shoulder-length and I wore a beard and moustache.

Well, I would have to tolerate incongruity, anyway. And Bieris and I both would probably give far less offense than Aimeric, with his insistence on wearing Caledon clothing, undoubtedly would.

The food seemed tasteless, but I bolted it and gulped the coffee. This was no day to be late.

As I threw the dishes in the regenner, Thorwald came in and said, "I wanted to catch you before you left. Hey, you almost look like one of us in that—I hope the embarrassment doesn't kill you."

I managed a wan smile. "What's up?"

"I just wanted to point out that if by any chance you were

thinking of volunteering to take the blame for all of us, all that will do is give them an excuse to shut down the Center and then to interrogate you to see how many more of us they can convict. Really, I just wanted you to know there's nothing you can do to help, other than just sit tight and give them nothing."

I nodded, having concluded that myself. He wished me luck, and I was on my way.

In the trakcar, it occurred to me that I hadn't heard or read any news yet, and that given the events of the night, and the fact that this would be a vitally important meeting, there might be some report on something I was involved in. I switched up the news access in the trakcar—and discovered it didn't work. At first I thought it was a malfunction, but the unit was working fine on all other accesses, and when I flipped back there was a brief message:

CHRISTIAN CAPITALIST REPORTS
LICENSED NEWS MONOPOLY
REGRETS THAT IT HAS BEEN
NECESSARY TO SCHEDULE
THIS INTERRUPTION
PRAISE GOD
GIVE THANKS
THINK RATIONALLY
BE FREE

Hadn't Aimeric said that when he was a child they used to include those last four commands at the end of all public announcements? Maybe they were still using the old standard form for anything as unusual as interrupting a whole channel for this much time.

I lowered the shutters to see what there was outside, having no desire to catch up on "Pastor Rational's Children's Hour," "Classic Sacred Rational Texts," or "Sunrise Sermon."

We were almost at the government complex when the trakcar stopped unexpectedly. In my whole childhood of riding the things, I could never recall such a thing happening, and moreover, this was happening right after the equally unprecedented failure of the news channel.

As suddenly as it had stopped, it rose from the track and proceeded on. As I approached the government buildings, there was yet one more strange thing—a double row of what looked like short black posts surrounded the building. I thought at first it was some new system of traffic bumpers— but they couldn't have put them up overnight? Or did they grow them in situ? Then I thought they might be utility fixtures, for some unknown purpose, and then I saw one move and realized it was two rows of people, facing each other, a few meters apart, dressed in heavy black cold-weather gear. That anyone would stand out in the morning storm, more than anything else, at last made it clear that something was really wrong.

So I was a bit less surprised than I might have been to realize that both rows of men were armed with riot weapons. I passed through the lines silently, and into the parking area. Right now I'd rather have gone anywhere else, but I went into the building.

Aimeric and Bieris were already there, obviously nervous. Shan was sitting behind them, not speaking, but two Embassy guards flanked him. No one else was in the Council's chamber, but you could hear occasional angry shouting, faintly, from elsewhere in the building, echoing through the undecorated concrete corridors like an aggressive street lunatic in a bad dream.

We didn't say anything to each other. It was hard to tell what might or might not be trouble to have said, in the next few minutes.

When the Council came in, they came in a group. The biggest surprises were two: Clarity Peterborough was not with them, and Saltini was. I felt Aimeric start beside me, and on his other side, Bieris emitted an odd, strangled noise. I suppose it was partly what it portended, and partly that none of us was used to thinking of Saltini as physically real.

Aimeric's father, at the podium, looked gray and old, as if he had been up all night without food or rest. When he began the prayer, he seemed to be summoning himself for an effort, and now that I had begun to understand a little of the structure of Reason, and understood that the prayer was translated directly from it, I could tell that the parts where his voice rose and he looked up—on one occasion, his hands even shook before he grabbed the side of the podium—were the passages about understanding and mutual agreement, about reason and compromise precluding violence. As bad as that made it seem, it comforted me to have him thundering away like that—if only because nothing could happen until he was done, and at least there was clearly still some kind of contest.

When he finished, I noticed that one half of the room "Amen"-ed a lot louder than the other half. I had thought we were first on the agenda, but instead old Carruthers turned directly to Saltini. "Now that we are in session, as Chief Rationalizer I exercise the Absolute Right of Inquiry. Why are PPP guards still holding riot lines across the city when there has been no civil disturbance anywhere, and by what authority do they prevent the advance of the regular city police into those areas? Let me point out in this context that the set of demands you made last night have been entirely met."

Saltini spread his hands; if anything, that little half-smile was warmer, happier this morning than when I had seen it before. "It was not a set of demands; it was a perfectly constitutional request for authorization for certain emergency measures by the Pastorate of Public Projects, and as you may recall one provision was for whatever ancillary powers might be needed. We have reason to believe that the outbreak of irrationality—which we are specifically charged to guard government, church, and society against—has spread into police ranks, and since we cannot identify which members are at risk at this point, it is necessary to exclude them from—"

"Never mind that. Your answer is not satisfactory. Let the record show that I believe it to be false. Next question: You have been granted a Pastorate Without Congregation so that you may vote on the Council of Rationalizers; your first *demand* of last night. Since that time you have arrested four pastors, leading to the accession of assistant pastors favorable to your position—"

"Naturally," Saltini said, "since as I stipulated, this conspiracy for irrationality extended into the highest reaches of society—"

"Specifically including the Highly Reverend Clarity Peterborough, who we agreed would remain inviolate—"

"For any crimes committed prior to the time of the agreement. Since that time—"

"What do you expect us to believe she did during the middle of the night?" Carruthers roared the question at him, no longer hiding his fury.

There was a long, cold silence, as everyone seemed to wait; then Saltini simply said, "There are six offworlders present in this room, and the matter concerns the most urgent matters of—"

"Shit." The disgust in the old Chairman's voice was as thick and heavy as a wad of the substance itself, flung into Saltini's face.

The Reverend Saltini actually rose from his seat a bit, and said, "Perhaps the simplest way of settling all of this might be some sort of vote? Say, one of confidence, or perhaps a ratification—"

Carruthers sighed. "We have other business as well. We will proceed with it first."

"That's it. We're in real trouble now," Aimeric said, under his breath.

Bieris and I stared at him.

"The only thing that can mean is that Dad isn't sure he has the votes." He slumped down lower and stared at the floor, not looking at either of us. Bieris and I had a second to exchange glances; I hoped I did not look as frightened as she did.

Carruthers and Saltini were still staring at each other; then, slowly, they both nodded. We went back to the original agenda.

When Aimeric got up to speak, he seemed surprisingly calm to me. I had no idea where he found the strength, but he managed to go through it without any stumbles at all, just as we had rehearsed it. This time it was my turn to run the graphics board, and Bieris's turn to stand beside the screen and point at things as they came up.

Aimeric had laid out the standard plan for handling the Connect Depression in elaborate detail, being extremely careful to phrase everything in ways he hoped would be acceptable to the Council. The problem with that, of course, was that there wasn't that much that was acceptable about the standard way of doing things, which essentially was to pump money into the economy at the bottom by heavy government borrowing for massive public works projects. The resulting debt was then to be inflated out of existence by the soon-to-follow Connect Boom, especially since taxes were to be raised sharply as the Boom began.

The problem was that it was pretty hard to come up with any phrasings that would make a Caledon favor deliberate government debt, arbitrarily increasing the ratio of reward to work, or planning to devalue the currency.

The room got quieter and quieter as Aimeric went on, and by the end it was only his father who appeared to be listening at all.

As Aimeric said "I'm prepared to answer any questions you may have—thank you," I could see muscles standing out like ropes in old Carruther's neck, and in Saltini's, and they were looking at each other.

As the old man opened his mouth to speak, Saltini said, "As we can all see now, this conspiracy to destroy our faith and way of life extends to the very highest levels. I place you under arrest—"

Carruthers growled at him. "As you surely are aware, a legal tradition more than fifteen hundred years old prohibits police of any sort from legislative chambers—"

Saltini shrugged. "Shall we take a vote?"

From outside, there was gunfire. It was a few scattered shots, low thudding sounds, meaning probably that they were—so far—using Suspend cartridges to knock each other unconscious. Then there was a long silence, while no one breathed, a couple more shots, and the sound of feet running in the corridors.

Carruthers pushed his chair away from the table and got up. "Let me remind you that if nine of us leave, there is no quorum."

"The absence of members overcome by irrationality seems a strange basis for us not to act."

Two PPP men entered from one door; no one moved. There was a booming shot in the corridor, and everyone jumped. Then PPP men entered from the other door.

They led away Aimeric's father and four more pastors; Anna Diligence, Prescott's mother, was one of them. It took about three minutes for them to ratify everything Saltini had done, declare a state of emergency, and vote down Aimeric's proposals. Two minutes later, after another prayer, they were out the door.

A thought crossed my mind, something my father had said once when he sat in the legislature back home. "The way you can tell there's democracy going on is that nothing gets done."

We were left alone in the room, the three of us and the Ambassador, surrounded by PPP cops and not sure whether we could move or not. A long minute went by; from the uncomfortable way the cops kept shifting their balance, I realized they had no idea either. I was just contemplating getting up, walking casually toward the door, and seeing what happened, when Saltini came in. He still had that same smile, but it was taut and small.

He went straight to Ambassador Shan, ignoring us. "The remaining business is quite simple. You have your grants for the Embassy, and, frankly, I don't think we have the force to throw you out, since you could bring in an army through that springer on the Embassy grounds. Outside Embassy grounds, however, and along the line of demarcation, Caledon law is going to prevail."

"These matters can be discussed as they come up," Shan said quietly.

"And, as you might expect, we are immediately ceasing to pay for these so-called 'advisors' of yours—'agitators,' I think, might have been a better word. I truly believe that had you not forced them on us, none of this would have been necessary." Saltini seemed to be allowing himself a little anger, now that he was on top.

"You realize, of course," Shan said, "that this means they cannot return home. And I'm afraid I have no berths for them in the Embassy."

I truly enjoyed seeing Saltini shocked—so much that for a moment I didn't realize what Shan had said.

Saltini almost seemed to whine. "They are your people."

"They're salaried employees of your government. If you want them to go home, you are responsible for their fares. A springer trip of six and a half light-years for three, in any case, is no more than two days of your government's operating budget at the rate we'll charge you for it. I don't see what the difficulty can be. Of course, if they should wish to remain as resident aliens, I would assume you would have to accommodate them, as well, under their existing employment contracts with your government. Indeed, molestation of resident aliens, or denial to them of rights they possess on their homeworlds—such as full enforcement of labor contracts—is one of several possible grounds for the Council of Humanity's terminating the Charter of your culture."

"As a matter of fact," Aimeric said, "I've been rather homesick, and I hate to leave at midterm."

Bieris's face was unreadable; she did not pause at all before saying, "I want to stay."

I saw now what Shan's game was. He would gain three people, free to travel in Utilitopia, whom the PPP could not touch. In the maneuvering sure to follow on the heels of this coup, those might be invaluable ...

Or not. There was really no telling. Shan might have no real use for us, other than as an issue to harass Saltini with.

And god, there was a mess at home, in clearing my reputation, winning back my position—and last night I had actually *prayed*, seriously, for the first time since I was a child—to go home.

Besides, Aimeric and Bieris were staying. They would be enough, and Bieris at least liked it here better than I did, and Aimeric's knowledge would make him valuable to Shan.

What did I know? Music, poetry, and dueling—and even that, only with bare hands and neuroducers, not with any real weapons . . .

Moreover, there was an economic shitstorm coming, and probably Saltini would find a way to take the Center away from me, and I'd end up as a stablehand.

I became aware that Saltini was watching me intently, as if somehow fascinated with me. I realized that he had to know everything I had been thinking of, since no doubt he had been reading my mail, and probably could see more of Shan's scheme than I could.

To him, it must surely seem that I would have to be totally irrational.

"The Center is where my real work is," I said. "I can't leave when things are just getting established."

I guess I should have been hurt that everyone except Shan seemed to be surprised.

Saltini looked from one to the other of us with a burning glare. "I am sure you must realize that there is about to be some budget cutting. I suspect the post of Professor of Occitan Literature will go by the wayside soon. I think that a farmhand who is absent from a farm too often might find that she is declared superfluous. And as for that Center—I suppose you are counting on its being technically an enterprise, not subject to our budget cuts. All I can say is that your students, and their families, are at this moment being looked at for serious irrationality, and that they will have this fact drawn strongly to their attention. And with no one enrolled—"

He left, not bothering to finish the threat. He hadn't had to.

On the way out the door, Shan said quietly to me, "Thank you."

I wished it had made me feel better.

The trakcars were running smoothly again, and I had no trouble getting one back to the Center. There were still some PPP guards standing around on corners, but in the bright sun, the dark of the morning storm gone, their parkas thrown open or draped over their arms, they looked more like embarrassed ushers than the menacing figures they had been. I turned on the news, realized it was all lies except, probably, for the statement that seven city policemen were dead—even there, they claimed it was rioters, as if anyone would have been out looting in that black storm. I suppose it mattered more to them to get something said than that it be believable, and no doubt the story could be changed or erased later.

The trakcar glided into the lot behind the Center, extended its wheels, and drove up to the steps. I grabbed my parka, not bothering to put it on, and walked up the steps.

Thorwald was waiting for me at the door.

"Something pretty urgent's come up," he said, without preface.

"Yap, I know," I said.

"They've threatened to permanently bar every student at the Center from any assignment except general physical labor. Because we're all too irrational to be trusted with anything else. It came over right after you left this morning."

Naturally. Saltini had been sure I would go, but he had wanted to make sure. He probably had already ordered the wrecker nanos to take the building down, too. Well, it would be the shovel for me, then, for sure. Maybe, on the rare occasions when it got warm enough, I could sing on street corners or something. There was probably a local ordinance against it.

"Uh, some of the students wanted to see you about it," he said.

"Sure. I suppose I shouldn't com them. Are they coming here?"

"They're here. Up in the Great Hall." His voice sounded funny—I pictured two or three students, maybe Margaret or Paul—or dared I hope for Valerie?—sitting in that big, empty place, hearing the echoes of the empty Center, feeling it all go away. If they had come to say good-bye, some of them must have felt it was worthwhile. And that was a special kind of courage, to show that kind of human feeling.

As we came up the steps to the second floor, where the

Great Hall was, Thorwald asked, "Um, if you can keep the Center open—do I still have a job?"

"Always," I said, and threw an arm around him. He seemed startled—Caledons hardly ever touch each other—but after a moment, he hugged me back.

It was going to be a cold, lonely decade of shit-shovelling, but maybe Thorwald and I, and some of the others, could pal around together, and that might be all right . . .

We opened the door to the Great Hall. In a sense, I had been right, because Margaret and Valerie were there . . .

And Paul, and Prescott—and just about everyone. The room was packed.

"We just wanted to tell you," Margaret said, without preamble, "that we've taken a vote, and we're all willing to pay more per class to keep this place open and get your loans paid off."

"After we all came here, and the PPP saw why, Saltini had his conversation with you and the others broadcast live to us here while he tried to scare you back into the Embassy," Paul added. "We say you stand him down."

So much turns on a tone of voice, on the attitude they have when they tell you to do something you don't want to. A minor coincidence the other way, and my friends might all have been quietly drifting away, knowing I had run out on them.

I wasn't quite what they thought I was, and the only decent thing I could see to do—the only thing that would clear that hidden stain from my *enseingnamen*—was to act as though I were. I couldn't let them be wrong.

If anyone had ever told me, back in the Quartier des Jovents, that I would burst into tears in front of a whole crowd of people, and cry like a *donzelha*, and not even decently cover my face—I'd have challenged him, fought him, probably insisted on a fight to first death.

Here, though, when I could breathe, I just stammered out, "It's good to be home." And because I knew my display of emotion would bother them, I added, "There's a lot of work to get done—come on, now, *mes companhos*, let's not waste the whole day."

PART THREE

THE LONG,
LONG ROAD

ONE

For a long time afterwards, my main memory of the next few days was of a desperate need to sleep. Within four hours, Saltini's coup was complete, and the last independent ministers in the city of Utilitopia were under arrest and held incommunicado. As he gained control of the hinterland—not difficult since most of the more conservative outlying settlements had been on his side to begin with—communication was gradually restored.

For about three hours that day Bruce was under arrest, and Bieris spent some very frightening time standing in front of the Pastorate of Public Projects offices in the storm of Second Morning, trying to get to talk to someone and arrange bail. There were hundreds of friends and relatives of those arrested, there in the street, with PPP cats zooming through the crowd regularly, autocameras scanning them from the Pastorate steps, and peeps carrying stun sticks standing all around them. We had to call each other every few minutes, because the peeps did not approve of my trying to use Center funds for Bruce's bail and kept finding objections, which I would then answer, freeing the funds up again until the next objection, so Bieris had to be kept posted on whether or not she actually had any money to pay the bail with.

It was bad enough to deal with that sitting at a desk and arguing on the com; I could hardly imagine what it must have been like for Bieris, who wasn't physically large and not at all suited to standing out in three hours of freezing rain, having to keep her facemask open much of the time because the peeps deliberately turned their loudspeakers down. Tough as she was, and even used to working outside, when we finally got Bruce back she was blue and shaking with the cold. She had told me that her portable com's visual channel wasn't working, because she had been afraid I'd send one of the Center students to replace her.

It was certainly a legitimate fear, but I knew as well as she did that outside the Center all of them were at risk of arrest that day. Indeed, as the rules eventually became clear in the next few standays, the Center was actually no protection, but apparently Saltini was sufficiently shocked by Shan's firm response that he wasn't sure whether the Center was under the same protection as the Embassy or not. Probably he was made more nervous because within an hour of Shan's return to the Embassy, four companies of Council Special Police— the euphemism for "marines"—came through the springer, and Caledon Embassy employees, some of whom were Saltini's spies, reported that the CSP's said that they had been standing by for hours in case Council personnel had needed rescuing.

I only learned of that later, of course, which was unfortunate because I was frightened myself and if I'd known that there was that much help around I might have felt better.

Thorwald really proved himself invaluable. He informally deputized Margaret and Paul, and they saw about setting up some kind of system for sleeping spaces, and for notifying families, and for getting everyone fed something. We had almost two hundred people in the building, well over half the enrolled students for the Center, all afraid to return to their homes while the city continued under curfew and the PPP cats continued to roll through the city picking up dissenting ministers, people who had been members of the Liberal Association twenty years before, elders of Clarity Peterborough's congregation, and seemingly anyone who had ever mumbled anything unpleasant about Saltini into a beer.

Every so often there'd be a sharp wail from downstairs, or a little outburst, that would mean someone had just learned of a brother, a lover, or a parent arrested. It played hell with my concentration as I went through my latest argument with the aintellects . . . Bieris was critical personnel for the Center and she wouldn't be functional until Bruce was released—"Objection: Excessive regard for subjective feelings of employees is . . ." Bruce was a major contractor to the Center and it was in my interest to see the work not interrupted—"Objection: Substitution can be made at lower cost . . ." Bieris would sign a contract giving me extra hours at a substantial profit in exchange for my going bail on Bruce—"Objection: Bieris Real's connection with the arrested is not such that it is rational for her to expend this effort . . ."

They let Bruce go late in Second Light, along with hundreds of other people that they apparently had just wanted to scare, and that was when we found out where Aimeric was. As a naturalized Occitan, and Council personnel as well, he was as safe from them as Bieris or I, so he had been down at the Council of Rationalizers' main administrative office, trying to get his father and Clarity Peterborough released. He didn't succeed, but at least he was able to learn that the plan called for them to be released under house arrest within a day or two.

It was less than an hour till Dark when Aimeric, Bruce, and Bieris could finally catch a trakcar for the Center. Once I knew they were on the way, I went downstairs to see what was going on, and shortly I was looking over what Thorwald had set up and approving of everything, with Margaret guiding me through it—Thorwald was upstairs trying to get five last people settled into the solar.

"If we're lucky," Margaret said quietly, "Paul will manage to do the first illegal data penetration in Caledon history—I should say the first one we know of—and maybe we can find out who's liable to be arrested and who's not."

"Aren't you afraid of—" I gestured around at the corners.

"At least not of these," she said, grinning, and dumped a fistful of shattered electronics on the desk. "And they know what we're trying to do. The thing is, they've never been able to reconcile having to spy on people with the idea that this is what people rationally want. We're betting that for the first few weeks after taking over they'll be even more doctrinaire . . . and we hope that means that they won't be able to admit that these were PPP property, and so won't be able to bring themselves to charge us.".

"That's quite a bet," I said. It came out much more harshly than I wanted it to.

She didn't answer at first. Maybe it was a trick of the soaking-wet cold yellow sunlight bouncing around the room, but the highlights on Margaret's face shone like mirrors, giving her skin an amazingly clammy, greasy look; her close-cropped pale hair looked like fungus growing on her skull. I realized I was almost staring at her, and not in a flattering way, and glanced off to the side; when I looked back, I saw that she had noticed, and wasn't going to talk about it either.

I have never felt so ashamed, before or since.

After a moment she smiled at me, tentatively, as if afraid I would shout at her, and said, "Well, if they charge us, we'll go to jail. Historically we're in good company; Jesus, Peter, Paul ... Adam Smith was burned at the stake on Threadneedle Street, and Milton Friedman was eaten by cannibals in Zurich."

"Let's hope it won't come to that," I said hastily. I knew who the first three were, of course, and later on I was glad I had no idea and so said nothing about the other two, because they turned out to be part of the Culture Variant History—the mythic story that founders of cultures were allowed to load in as real history. Of all the silly things that happened during the Diaspora, that was one of the silliest, for it resulted in permanent deep cleavages among the Thousand Cultures; the first time that I heard an Interstellar making a speech on a streetcorner proclaiming that Edgar Allan Poe did not die in the Paris uprising of 1848, that Rimbaud had never been King of France, and that Mozart was not killed by Beethoven in a duel, I challenged him and cut him down like a mad dog. *Deu sait* how Margaret, emotionally and physically exhausted as she was, would have reacted if I'd contradicted her.

What she, Thorwald, and Paul had done was simply amazing; I'd never have imagined we had that many places for people not only to sleep, but to wash up and to sit down and eat. While I had been on the com, they had virtually converted the place to a well-run dormitory or hotel.

"Uh, delicate question coming up," Margaret said. "Thorwald and you have the last single rooms—"

"You can put a couple of cots in mine without cramping anything," I said. "Is there anyone left to accommodate?"

"Well, I've got one other room, but it's the guest room where Bieris or Aimeric usually sleep, and some of their stuff—"

I thought of the obvious affection developing between Bruce and Bieris, and the equally obvious difficulty Aimeric was having in considering it, and was about to say something when all three of them came in the door. They were dripping wet and cold, especially Bruce because he had been held in a courtyard and not given adequate clothing, and it was obvious that the first thing was to get them fed, warm, and into dry clothing. It's amazing how little personal things matter in some circumstances.

Margaret's efficiency was almost frightening; in two minutes they were all headed off to hot showers with changes of clothing in hand, and the kitchen had been notified of the need for a large pot of hot soup and some fresh rolls. "I'm afraid we'll have to charge them for it," she said. "It's the only way we've been able to get enough supplies to keep everyone eating."

"Not a problem," I said. "Who's in the kitchen?"

"Prescott. He seems to handle pressing buttons and ordering supplies pretty well; I might decide to think of him as a human being if he keeps it up. I asked Val to do it but she was busy being hysterical and having three men, none of whom is Paul, comfort her."

I'd never heard Margaret sound so snippy, but she was tired, and probably out of sorts.

Come to think of it, at home I'd never heard anyone criticize an attractive *donzelha*. On the other hand, nobody expected them to do anything, so it's hard to say what they could have failed at.

Margaret showed me the accounts. Probably thanks to her,

the Center was going to make more as a hostel and restaurant than it ever had as an educational institution. Further, she had set things up so that we could keep operating, even teaching the classes, indefinitely. "By the way, you're hired," I said.

"Hired?"

"All these extra bodies and so much extra work—I need another assistant," I explained. "Thorwald's a terrific assistant for many things, but I want you to do the business side from now on."

She started to protest, but I cut her off. "How else are you going to prove it was rational for you to do all the work you've already done today?"

She had no answer to that, but there was a deep red blush spreading up her throat to her face, and I realized this might encourage something I had promised myself I would discourage. Well, all the same, I needed her, and I surely would not hurt her any more than I could help, and maybe she'd get over it anyway. Perhaps with Thorwald—though he was young for it; Margaret was much closer to my age . . . time enough for that later, and I mustn't sit here and brood about her; that could be interpreted too many different ways.

The com beeped; Bieris had called us from the women's locker room. "Giraut, would you like me to be in your debt and your slave forever?"

"Superficially a generous offer. What appalling thing do I have to do to claim it?"

"Move Bruce into my room and let Aimeric know I asked you to do it. Take Aimeric in yours."

"I'd rather feed my genitalia to rats a piece at a time." I heard Margaret gasp and make a strangling noise behind me; I don't think she was quite used to the earthier side of Occitan humor yet.

"But will you do it?"

"Forever, you said, *companhona*?" I said. "'Backrubs. Cake on my birthday. Listening to me when I'm being an idiot.'"

"That last part is the hard one, but sure."

"Then I'll do it." We clicked off. That had been a very

strange conversation; in tone, it was much like the way we had talked till we were fourteen or so. And how had she known I would respond that way?

Margaret sighed beside me. There was something disturbingly romantic in the sound. "That won't be easy, will it?"

"It would be harder in Noupeitau. Aimeric would have to challenge, even if he didn't care, and there'd have to be a duel about it."

"But wouldn't it be all over once the duel was fought?" She seemed baffled. "I mean, the other day, when you and Thorwald—"

"Oh, *deu*, that was an accident. He was more upset than I was. Nothing to take personally." I shrugged and balanced the issues on my palms. "Aimeric and Bieris go back perhaps six stanmonths. That's a very long time to keep an *entendedora*. Perhaps, *qui sait*, they were even serious enough to think of marrying once she turned twenty-five. So he may be involved enough to take it with very ill grace. But the average Occitan . . ." it caused me pain to admit this, but I saw no way around it in all honesty, and couldn't imagine lying to Margaret. "Well, the average jovent pays no attention to his *entendedora*, really doesn't even know what she's like. The point is to worship and to serve, not to establish some permanent relationship . . . that's usually done later, after you move out of the Quartier. Of course it's not unknown to marry your *entendedora*—my father did—or for a couple to be friends as well as lovers. But none of that is expected, and it's more typical to be sort of . . . er, each other's hobby. *Finamor* is sort of like dueling—something to do while you wait to be a grown-up."

Margaret swallowed hard. "Um—is it too personal to ask—"

I laughed, and felt embarrassed about something that not long before I had thought as natural as breathing. It was an odd sensation, but I was still feeling very much as if I had been born that morning, when I had agreed to stay on Nansen and stand by my Caledon friends. One more novelty would not kill me.

She looked embarrassed too. Maybe the question was too near her own thoughts? Or perhaps the laughter had made her think it was a foolish question. "It's not too personal," I hastened to say, "and I'm only laughing because I just realized I wouldn't have understood the question before coming here. The answer is, I don't have any notion at all what was going through those *donzelhas'* heads; I can tell you a great deal about Garsenda Mont-Verai's body, and her exact eye color and what she liked to do . . . er, for fun"—Margaret was now blushing furiously and it had just occurred to me that I might be talking to the oldest virgin I had ever met—"but nothing really about how she felt or thought."

Margaret made a little face and shook her head, but said nothing.

"You were going to say something," I said, "and whatever it is, it won't offend me."

"Oh . . . just that it seems like there's always a catch. We could all use a lot of pampering and attention, but getting it from someone who doesn't even know who you are . . ." she shrugged and spread her hands. Her smile looked as washed out as the rest of her. ". . . well, I hate to sound like a preacher, but it sounds like there's always a trade-off."

"Probably. Some people are better suited to some cultures than others are, I suspect. There are people here who'd have been made miserable on Nou Occitan, and, well, there are Occitans who would take to this culture easily."

"I suppose." I almost liked her peculiar smile. "I suppose when springer prices come down—they say they will in ten or twenty stanyears—we can all go find the place that suits us. Always assuming it hasn't been destroyed by everyone else finding it."

We sat there quietly, together, for a long minute, and my eye kept trying to decompose her and find some way to rearrange her so that I could appreciate her, but with the best will in the world it could not be done. As definitely and finally as Valerie's appearance always led your eye to beauty and symmetry, Margaret's seemed to force your eye right to some flaw and make it overwhelm everything else.

As we were sitting there in the gathering awkwardness, Bruce came upstairs from the men's locker room, and I told him what the arrangements would be. He nodded, and did not look entirely happy, but took his bag upstairs without comment.

I wasn't sure what I would say to Aimeric, but before I could give it much thought he was coming down the stairs. I had just an instant to wish that I would not have to handle it in front of Margaret before I realized that she had somehow vanished into thin air—which gave me the fleeting thought that she might have been some help in the situation. As she had been saying, there are always trade-offs.

Aimeric gave me a wry half-grin. "So, has Bieris been down yet?"

"Not yet," I temporized.

"Listen, can I bunk with you? That leaves her the choice of either inviting Bruce to the guest room or turning it into a girls' dorm, whichever way she wants. I don't want her to feel like she has to tell me her choice directly."

In Noupeitau, I'd have said this man had no pride and was groveling to a *donzelha*. Here, I said, before I could think what I meant, *"Que merce!"*

He gaped at me. "You've really changed."

"Not that much." A thought left over from last night suddenly hit me. "Uh, when we get back—would you like to be my Secundo against Marcabru? He wrote me an incredibly insulting letter about my preoccupation with Caledon things, and it was just occurring to me that if we should happen to get home on schedule by some miracle, I can have the pleasure of assassinating the Prince Consort."

"It's a deal. His last few letters to me have been pretty insufferable too. But I don't think I ever had to fall out of friendship with him really; we weren't close. To tell you the truth I never knew what you saw in him."

I shrugged. "He was a *companhon* for a long time, and we had a long history. But I never really knew him. I've seen enough in his letters since I came here—which is why I'd like to take him on."

"Then I'm your Secundo. Challenge that dickless little po-seur, and cut him down." He slung up his bag and we headed up the stairs together, his hand resting lightly on my shoulder.

The feeling I had, as I was climbing the stairs, I later turned into a song, one that many people say is my best, but at that moment it simply overwhelmed me, and I fought down a hard, chest-stabbing sob, and did not manage to suppress the rush of tears from my eyes.

Aimeric's hand tightened onto my shoulder like a claw. "Giraut, what is it?"

I sniffed a little, and had myself in hand again. *Deu*, I had cried in front of people twice in one day; what sort of jovent was I anymore? "Oh, just a thought that crossed my mind. We four—you and I, Marcabru and Raimbaut . . . I never re-ally knew Raimbaut, either, until I wore his psypyx, and it was only then that I found what a delight he used to take in things, or found out what a dark sense of humor he had. I felt more loss when he began to turn inside and fade than I had when he died; there was more to lose, if you see what I mean. And just now I suddenly wished I had known him, re-ally known him, as a friend and not as another jovent *com-panhon*, while hc was alive."

Aimeric nodded. He looked a little silly—his bald spot was bigger than ever, and his Occitan clothes had gotten hope-lessly disheveled—after all, except for outdoor gear, we nor-mally change clothes three times in our twenty-hour day, and our clothes are just not made to be worn hour after hour the way Caledon clothing is. He looked like the old drunks who hang around their Quarter, trying to get attention with the sto-ries of the jovent days, because they have failed as adults . . . but now as I stood here on that long gray staircase, the last buttery sunlight splashing off a column above us, and really looked at him, I saw that he knew perfectly well what he looked like, and refused to care about it because he knew he had come by the appearance honestly. It was more than most people were capable of, and at that moment I loved and hon-ored him for it, and for a lot of other things, some many years back. "From now on, when people cross my path, I'm going to know them," I said.

"I think we never know enough about other people," he said, finally.

"I'm so glad you'll be my Secundo. Do you think I should challenge without limit?"

"Why not? Teach the sadistic bastard what it's like." The grin that swept across his face would have been equally at home on a shark; I was sure mine was similar. Our hands clasped, and some loop that had opened with his arrival at my father's house in Elinorien closed around both of us at the moment.

"How are they bearing up?" I asked Aimeric, as we got a cot set up for him, and another for whomever, in my room. "Your father and Reverend Peterborough, I mean."

"Dad is taking it like a martyr ... but that doesn't quite mean what it would in Nou Occitan. I mean he's very conscious of other people in the past who've endured a great deal for what they believed. And he's ... trying to live up to them." Aimeric sighed. "On the other hand, Clarity ... she's not doing well at all, Giraut." He sat down at my breakfast bench and I could see some of the tension run out of his muscles, not because he felt better, but because his body was realizing that there was nothing to fight and nothing to achieve. "Her whole view of the world—what she's always told her congregation, and how she's always approached things—well, it's all built on the idea that the Caledon system is basically a good, fair, rational one that only needs a little tinkering, that the whole problem was a few stiffnecks, or some rigidly moral people who wouldn't let the system work as it should, or something like that. For that matter, she really did believe in that gentle, reasonable, loving God ..."

"And now she doesn't?"

"Praise God. Give Thanks. Think Rationally. Be Free. Queroza's Four Articles ... and what Queroza taught was that they were all the same thing; we praise God by imitating Him, since He's the supremely rational being, and we give thanks to Him for being rational, and by doing all that we no longer must struggle against the rational world we live in, and therefore we're free. Free in the sense of a body in free fall, you see; you don't experience gravitation if you do just what the gravity wants you to." He sighed and shuddered, whether from cold or from sympathy I could not tell. "Clarity believes in all of that. Because she's—well, you know her. Generous and kind and loves everyone—because she's that way, those ideas take on a particularly important meaning to her. She doesn't know—I don't think you *can* know if you live in Caledony all your life—that it wasn't that she was good and kind because of the words, but that the words meant those things because she was good and kind." His eyes got far away again, and suddenly I knew more than I ever had before about that first stanyear of his in my father's house at Elinorien—how he must have been astonished to see people behaving decently when what they believed was absolute anathema to him. His swings between anger and debauchery were as explicable as Morning Storm here was.

"So what's she doing?" I asked after a long moment.

"She sits much too still. She barely talks. It took me a long time to get her to agree to even send a message via me to her congregation. And the things she says . . . I don't think right now she wants to live, Giraut. She's about given up on God, at least as she's always known Him. Saltini's coup —carried out by the most devout believers in Caledon—has made her think she's been wrong all her life. When they let her out, I think she won't be any threat to them at all; she'll probably just sit at home and stare at the wall. There's just no fight left in her; that's what happens when you really believe in something, and find out that it was never true." He stood and began to undress. "I'm too tired to eat. I've got to sleep. Anyway, *Dad* is fine; the only thing Saltini's done is turn him into a blazing liberal. I'm glad to have the old dragon on our side—he'll be a real asset."

"I hadn't thought of us as having a side, yet," I said.

"Oh? Well, we will." He tossed his tunic into the laundry fresher. "In any society there are reasons galore for being unhappy with the existing order. As long as everyone has a substantial stake in it, though, that unhappiness never focuses into anything coherent enough to make much difference. Classic mistake—economic game theory of coups—when one little faction grabs the whole works, it takes on everyone's unhappiness. My bet offhand is that in three years Saltini will be beating down Shan's door begging for asylum and safe passage offworld."

Sitting, as I was, in a city of many millions, in one of two buildings not in Saltini's hands, with a force made up entirely of a couple of hundred unarmed, frightened, and exhausted social misfits, my conclusion was that hypothermia had set in on Aimeric. As he was tossing his boots into the corner and getting into his pajamas, Thorwald showed up at the door with soup and rolls for him. Aimeric accepted them and sat down to eat as if he were a child just come in from a long day playing in the snow. "And right to bed after you're done," Thorwald added, for all the world like somebody's mother. "Mr., um, that is, Giraut, some of us are having cocoa in the small kitchen if you'd like to join us to talk things over."

"Certainly," I said, and we left Aimeric in there to finish his dinner and get to bed. As we closed the door, I said, "I'm quite impressed with what you accomplished today, Mr. Spenders."

He grinned. "I'll get the habit of using your first name in a little while—Giraut. I might even get used to your nasty habit of teasing."

I laughed and didn't deny that I'd been doing it; apparently the laugh was all the apology required. As we went down the big stairway, I could hear an unfamiliar buzz; in a moment I realized that even in a very large building, a couple of hundred people make enough noise so that you're always aware of them. To my surprise—I had thought one thing I liked about the Center was that it was so perfectly shaped to my own mind—somehow the intruders, while creating some mess and confusion, made the place seem much more warm and human than . . . well, than any place I'd ever lived.

It was a stray thought, no more, but it was the second idea

for a good song I'd had that day. There was a prespaceflight poet, I remembered, Wordsworth, who had gotten a lot of the spirit of his work from having been in France when the *Ancien Régime* fell . . . maybe I would at least come out of all this with something to sing about, which might put me ahead of many another Occitan performer.

The kitchen turned out to contain just me, Paul, Thorwald, Margaret, and a huge lasagna that somebody had baked. My stomach rolled over and I suddenly realized I had not eaten since before First Dark. The situation was general; at first all we did was gobble the wonderful hot food down.

"All right," I said. "Officially, Paul, since we're finally face-to-face, you're hired too. I assume you at least guessed that was going to happen."

"Sure did," Paul said. The tall young man leaned back and sighed. "If anyone had ever told me I'd be glad to have a job that was this much work . . ." He grinned. "You're certainly doing a good job of teaching us all not to be rational."

I took it as a compliment, and asked, "So how did your attack on the PPP's databases go?"

"No luck, I'm afraid. The generic aintellects available commercially have all been asimoved to the nth. Not only can they not hurt people, they can't help people violate any religious precepts. And it's really carefully woven into them—no way to get it out of them while you're customizing them. I'm afraid I drove two of them stark insane before I realized it just couldn't be done." He took a big gulp of the warm red Babylon Basin wine that Thorwald had found a couple of jugs of. "And they've got a lot of aintellects that are over a hundred stanyears old working for the PPP, some of which have spent all their time running simulations. Within twenty seconds of my trying to penetrate, they had gone from almost no defences to a complete set of self-improving ones. To get anywhere against that, we'd have needed ten thousand aintellects from somewhere outside the culture in a coordinated attack."

I shrugged and nodded. That had been the story of data raiding for a thousand years; a thousand parts of offense could be turned back by a thousandth part of defense. Still, it had been worth a try. I suppose any good burglar tries all the doors and windows, just in case one is unlocked, before he breaks anything.

"I did pick up one set of files, but it's only sort of half useful," Paul said. "It looks like Saltini and his merry men are all Selectivists."

"What?" Thorwald said, his mouth hanging open.

"What did you find?" Margaret asked.

"The files had a list of things the Council of Rationalizers was going to ratify in the next three months. Most of it was just regularizing Saltini's 'emergency measures' into permanent policy, plus some of the Sabbath regulations they've been pushing for all these years. But they're also going to make Selectivism doctrine—which is just about the best thing they can do from our standpoint. Talk about stirring up rebellion—"

"If it's not too much trouble," I said, "I'd like to know what Selectivism is."

Margaret grinned. "Life evolves faster in the presence of mind, and even faster in the presence of rational mind."

I must have looked baffled, because Thorwald jumped in. "It's a crackpot explanation that some of our ultrareligious people use for why this was already a living planet when we got here. They say it's because the rational purpose of life is intelligence, and so when there's intelligence around, life develops faster. So because this world was predestined to be the home of Rational Christianity, just that predestination was enough to make planetary evolution run one thousand times faster than it would have otherwise."

I found it hard not to snicker, but I had vowed not to laugh at anything Caledon.

Paul sighed and said, "Incidentally, any half-witted theologian could knock it down; since God is infinite intelligence and is omnipresent in the universe, if Selectivism were true, everything—rocks, stars, and vacuum itself—would be alive."

"So they're going to actually make it doctrinal?" Margaret asked, as if she still couldn't quite believe it.

"Anyone want to tell me what difference it makes?"

"You have to swear you believe all the doctrine before you can take communion," Thorwald said, "and you have to have taken communion within three days prior to voting."

"So they're going to disenfranchise all but their own crazy supporters? That doesn't seem like it's progress for our side—"

"Hah. Wait till you see what happens when the average stolid churchgoer has to swear an oath that he believes in obvious bullshit before he's allowed to vote against tax increases. Paul's right. We couldn't have better recruiting from them."

I took his word for it; Caledon politics, even when I was up to my neck in them, always seemed to slip away from my mental grasp.

"So is there anything else, besides seconds, that we need to consider tonight?" Margaret asked, as she cut another slice of lasagne. "Informally, I guess we're the nearest thing to the executive council of the resistance there is at the moment."

Thorwald grinned and said, "Well, I have a slightly silly idea, but let's see if you all like it. I think what we should do is launch an artistic movement."

The idea fell incredibly flat. Even I, an Occitan, could hardly imagine a less worthwhile project. But Thorwald's lopsided little grin meant that there was something in his mind.

We all ate; the lasagna was good, after all, and we were all still hungry, and we had very little desire to give him the satisfaction.

After about three more bites, with a glance at both of us, Paul said, "Okay, Thorwald, I can't stand it anymore. Why an artistic movement? Why don't we start a sewing club or an elevator racing association?"

"Those might work too," Thorwald agreed cheerfully. "But consider the following: What is it rational for an artistic movement to do?"

"Seek acceptance," I said. "I think I see what you're getting at. So it might be possible to say all kinds of things—and perhaps to *do* all kinds of things—under the claim that what you're doing is art. But didn't they shut you down for good after last night?"

"Ah, but we had no manifesto at the time," Thorwald said.

"And now we do?"

"We will tomorrow," Thorwald said, cutting himself a third large slice of the lasagna. "By the way, if this is an example of what Prescott Diligence can do, I'd like to suggest that Giraut hire him as chef first thing tomorrow."

In fact, cooking class had been the one thing Prescott was any good at, and I had already thought of it, but it was impossible to say all that with my mouth as full as it was just then, so I merely nodded vigorously.

"So just who is going to write this artistic manifesto?" Margaret asked. "I happen to be exhausted, and my current plan is to run down to the locker room, take a hot shower, and then race to whichever spare cot remains, in about five minutes." She finished off her glass of Babylon Basin red and tossed her dishes in the regenner. "Unless we actually plan to start the revolution tomorrow morning, there's going to be a lot of things to get done."

"There's just two cots remaining," Thorwald said, "the one in my room and one of the two in Giraut's, and Margaret and Paul, you're the only unallocated bodies. Anyone have a preference?"

Margaret started to turn purple—the drawback of very pale skin—and I knew perfectly well what her preference was, but before I could think of what to say (invite and thus encourage her, but make her feel appreciated? invite Paul and hurt Margaret's feelings right now while she was tired and discouraged?) Paul pulled out a coin and flipped it high. "Call it, Margaret."

"Heads."

A slap as he laid it on his wrist. "You're with Aimeric and Giraut. That room has a shower, so you can just go straight up."

"Thanks." If she'd left the room any faster there'd have been a sonic boom.

"Which way did that coin come up?" I asked.

"Tails, of course. Poor thing lost." Paul's expression of innocence would not have fooled a two-year-old.

"Yap." I guess I didn't look perfectly pleased.

"Giraut," Thorwald said.

"Yes?"

"You don't have to fall in love with Margaret. You just need to be very kind to her. You're the first fellow she's ever been interested in at all; even if you have to let her down, do it gently." He grinned at me. "Otherwise I might have to *try* to break your nose."

"You don't have the skills," I pointed out, glumly, as I tossed my dishes in the regenner.

"No, but if I force you to beat me up to defend yourself, the guilt you'll feel will be worse than anything I could do to you anyway."

"The horrible part, Thorwald, is that you're right. But in any case, Margaret is a fine person, and I won't hurt her deliberately. New hearts are tender, though . . ."

"Yap, understood." He solemnly extended a hand, and we shook on the arrangement. At just that moment it occurred to me that I probably had more real friends here than I had ever had in Nou Occitan.

On the other hand, I realized as I went up the stairs, I had also been maneuvered into a position where pursuing Valerie would be nearly impossible, and Paul had done the maneuvering.

I was going to have to stop underestimating the Caledons at the grand game of *finamor*.

When I got into the room, Aimeric was sleeping like a corpse, and so was Margaret. I made the resolution to remember the power of exhaustion as a defense, just before my head touched the pillow and I was asleep.

TWO

The prompter shouted into my ear. "Time to get up! Time to get up!" I might have gone back to sleep after I hit the shut-off, except that Aimeric was groaning his way off the cot and stumbling around, and Margaret was repeating the same five not-very-imaginative obscenities over and over.

As I stood up, I realized that I had chosen roommates very poorly; Aimeric had already beaten me to the bathroom, and Margaret was securely second in line.

She wasn't any more impressive in pajamas.

Mufrid was not yet up, but the moon was shining in through the narrow windows, so it was quite bright already. I staggered over and hit the light switch, causing Margaret to blink painfully. "Oh, God," she said, "we've got a whole day ahead of us."

"Maybe we can get a long nap at First Dark," I said, without much hope. On second thought, though she wasn't any better looking at this hour or in the pajamas, unlike Garsenda or any of my family, she had the common decency to be grumpy and out of sorts in the morning.

Aimeric emerged, and the moment Margaret was in there tried to hurl himself into his clothes before she finished. If I had been in the mood, it might have been very entertaining; as it was, when she emerged, modesty had been served but dignity had disappeared somewhere into the tunic that was now flapping around halfway down over his head, his arms groping for the sleeves like blind pigs in a sack.

"I'd have been willing to step out into the hall," Margaret said, one corner of her mouth twitching.

"Not me," I said. "I wouldn't have missed this for anything."

Aimeric's head popped out of the tunic at last, his long hair so fallen about his face that it wasn't immediately apparent whether we were looking at the front or the back of his head. As he pulled the hair back, he commented, "I *hate* people who are cheerful in the morning."

I hated realizing I was becoming one of them. I ducked in and did the necessary, and when I came back out Aimeric was combing his hair and Margaret was mostly dressed. Maybe they were more casual about nudity than we were? I would have to ask Aimeric, privately, but for right now—

"I think I hear a unicorn in the hall," Margaret said. "Better go out and take a look at it." She stepped out the door, still brushing her hair, though what difference it could possibly make to run one set of bristles through another was beyond me.

As I dressed, I whispered the question to Aimeric. "Er—well," he said, "yes, Caledons are often nude around family members. Or around people who are, um, too old or too young to be of interest."

So his reason for looking embarrassed was entirely different from mine, I suppose. Sort of like the first time a clerk addresses you as "*senhor*" in Nou Occitan; you suddenly feel hopelessly old.

In a moment I was dressed, and we were all heading down to breakfast in a still-slightly-grouchy but generally pleasant mood. Margaret had posted shift times for eating, and we all were getting first shift—today it would mean being that much shorter of sleep, but there was no getting around the fact that the Occitans and the Caledon staff had to be awake and ready for anything today.

Anything did not take long to surface. As we were finishing breakfast in the smaller, private kitchen (I was disgusted to notice that Bieris, just as she had always been on camping trips, was very alert and cheerful), there was a ping from the com.

It was Prescott, who had been fielding calls from the

kitchen phone in addition to supervising a small crew of cooks. "Sorry," he said, "I was hoping you all could eat in peace, but it doesn't look like it. I think we have to be prepared for some real bad news; Saltini wants to talk to Giraut in five minutes. He says anyone who wants to can listen in."

Well, at least that meant he didn't expect to be able to cut any private deals with me. I took that as a compliment, gulped the last cup of coffee, and set the com in the little room for wide angle so that we could all see him and he could see all of us.

"I might have expected to see all of you together," Saltini said sourly. It was the first time I had ever seen him without that nasty little smile. "Though I'm a bit surprised that you are all up so early in the morning."

Puritans down through the ages have always thought of the early morning as the virtuous time, I suppose. I fought down the urge to tell him we'd been up all night doing round-robin sodomy, and said, "Is there some matter that's urgent?"

"Oh, a little change of policy, effective six hours from now. We think that many of the people who have taken up residence in the Center are very probably negative, disturbing, irrational, and anti-Christian forces within their families. As you must know, because many of them were unable to qualify for higher education, a rather disproportionate number of them had been living with parents, even though many of them are well past the normal age for it. Such I suppose is always the situation with social misfits. At any rate, it seems to us that since many of those homes have been weakened by the damaging presence of those people, and since providentially they have been removed from those homes, that this is a desirable situation we will want to preserve. Therefore we have decided to seek—and the judges have been good enough to grant—a blanket injunction prohibiting the list of people we will download to you momentarily from further contact with their families, and from moving back into their family homes. So to begin with, you are to be congratulated in that you have gained many of your guests in long-term tenancy, as opposed to the short-term you had expected."

"Well," I said, "speaking purely as a businessman, I can always use the additional revenue." And thinking as a human being, I would like to have you alone in a room for five minutes, just to see how many times I could punch and kick you while still leaving time to strangle you before my time was up.

The spectacular pretty cruelty of Saltini's action fascinated me; it was art in the same way that Marcabru's torturing a defeated opponent was.

"If I may, sir, I have a question," Thorwald said.

"Let me see—Thorwald Spenders, I believe—pending case arising from the incitement to riot at the performance of the Occasional Mobile Cabaret?"

"Pending case arising from unjustified police interference with a legitimate public entertainment, yes, sir, that's me. My partner, also," he added, gesturing at Paul. "But my question does not arise directly out of that event."

"Well, then, I suppose since it does not involve a pending court case, the Chairman of the Council of Rationalizers might legitimately give you some advice on whatever's on your mind. Do remember I'm quite busy at the moment."

"Yes, sir. I myself have duties to get to, here at the Center." Thorwald might have been making pleasant, if somewhat formal and stilted, conversation with anyone of his parents' generation. I avoided looking at the screen because I was afraid some of my admiration for Thorwald's straight face might leak through. "My question was, I'm unable to find any rule or procedure for properly registering a new artistic movement with the authorities. Should my next step be to petition the General Consultancy, or should it be presented as a request for a private bill to the Council of Rationalizers?"

It was only later that day that Aimeric managed to explain to me what was brilliant about Thorwald's question. The General Consultancy was a vast collection of aintellects, the same one that had often ruled on Center policies, which judged whether activities were rational or not. It could be subverted only over time; if Saltini stayed in long enough, the body of case law would eventually warp the General Consultancy's policies. At this moment, however, the General Consultancy was going to interpret Caledon law very much in the traditional manner, and that meant it might be relatively easy to get a ruling that would not suit Saltini at all, which—if he wanted to hang onto his paper-thin claim of legitimacy—he would have to follow.

On the other hand, if he allowed the issue to come in as a private bill request, he would setting a precedent that in principle artistic movements were permissable activities—and from then on the General Consultancy would follow that precedent. Moreover, when he turned back the application, grounds would have to be stated—and by avoiding or reversing those grounds, the next attempt could probably sail through the General Consultancy.

So essentially Saltini could either take his chances with what the General Consultancy might do right away—and thus risk having the whole issue put outside of his intervention—or be forced to construct a policy on the issue and hope we wouldn't be able to turn it against him.

The cunning old Pastor had not reached his present position by hesitation; he smiled, although it looked more like he had a toothache than anything else, and said, "Hmm. I do see what you mean. There are no precedents. Well, let's just let it go to the General Consultancy; if there's any problem with what they do, then we might think about taking it up as a private bill." As Aimeric explained to me later, it was a bold gamble; if the General Consultancy crushed Thorwald, Saltini would win, but if not, Thorwald would have a free hand. Saltini was simply choosing to play for the stakes that would settle the issue once and for all.

"Thank you, sir." Thorwald's smile and nod were coolly correct; I thought I detected a little whiff of the *dojo* in the style.

"If there's no further business—"

There was none, so Saltini nodded politely to us and was gone from the screen, leaving us with the problem of telling more than a hundred frightened young people that they were legally enjoined against getting in touch with their families. I was certainly glad that Margaret had managed to get word out to every family the previous night, so that at least parents knew where their children were, and knew that they had reached a relatively safe place, even if they could no longer talk to them.

The first hour or so of First Light was exhausting; I felt as if I needed ten extra ears and four extra brains. Had I not had Margaret to help me, I don't doubt I'd have ended up back in my room, under the covers, whimpering. First of all, it turned out that no one outside the Center knew that we had notified *all* the families that their children were with us; therefore, a hundred or so people whose relatives had disappeared had to check in with us, and be turned away with the bad news that we did not know either. Several of them were in fact students at the Center, but hadn't made it here yet; four were to turn up dead later that morning, skulls beaten in or having drowned in puddles, after being stunned in some alley. Naturally all four were supposed to have been attacked "probably for purposes of robbery by unknown assailants during the recent brief civil disorders." For one of them, a young woman named Elizabeth Lovelock, we had to arrange a funeral at the Center, because her family refused to know anything about her.

She was the worst case. Someone, probably several someones, had raped her and bashed her teeth in with a "blunt object" (which was a clever way to avoid saying stun stick), and she had received a severe stunning after all this, which had caused her to drown in the blood from her mouth. ("What was she doing for them to give her a max dose like that? Resisting arrest by screaming too much?" Margaret had exploded as the facts became apparent.) Naturally the PPP said it was trying to find out which city policeman had done it, and the city police had been given no information about the case at all.

The body was to be delivered later that day. The Highly Reverend Peter Lovelock sent us a brief note saying that since we had encouraged his daughter in her "sluttish, disobedient ways" we could deal with the "foul garbage that was left of her," and that was all we ever heard from her family. I put him on my mental list for some sort of personal vengeance, but in fact I never met him. I would prefer to report that he came to a bad end, but given that he was Pastor of a small outland congregation far north along the coast, I suspect he probably retired as the most respected and valued member of his community. Justice has a way of not arriving where and when you wish it.

We also discovered that now that we had a subsidiary business as a hostel, we had to establish credit with a bunch of food wholesalers. It quickly became apparent that this was purely a matter of politics—and Bruce, who seemed to know everyone, was invaluable, steering us to suppliers who leaned liberal politically and could be expected to cut us some slack, and away from reactionaries who might try to tie us up in red tape, tight credit, and late deliveries.

It was not yet First Noon when I got a moment to run upstairs and see what the others were up to. The last thing I expected to find was Thorwald and Paul engrossed in drafting "The Inessentialist Manifesto." I fought down my irritation, though it was difficult when I thought of Margaret downstairs doing enough work for *deu sait* how many people. "Inessentialist" seemed to be the perfect description of this particular two-person movement. *"Companho,"* I said, as reasonably as I could manage, "is there a reason this cannot wait?"

"Well," Paul said, "I guess, um—"

Thorwald shook his head. "Paul, if I can't get the idea across to you, I guess I should just give up. Giraut, if we draft this properly, we'll have a legal shield to hide the whole dissident movement behind. Without that, Saltini will slowly strangle us out of existence, one arrest and one gag order at a time; with it, we can eventually pull him down. And I've got to get it set up before he figures out a way to head it off. I know you're overworked and short of sleep, *companhon*. So am I, and so is Paul, and poor Margaret must be dead on her feet. But if I don't get this done and submitted to the General

Consultancy within a couple of hours, Saltini will beat me to the punch, and we'll be locked out of the communication channels for good."

I was almost staring at him. He was a teenager, after all; even earlier that week he had still behaved much like a very new jovent, with all the explosions of temper and lack of discipline. The crisis had made him—well, admit it, more of an adult than I had been a scant hundred standays ago. And as such, he was entitled to the basic respect I would give a trusted friend. "If you say what you are doing is necessary," I said, "then I trust that it is. But there's a couple things you should know about."

Briefly, I told them about the Lovelock case, having to begin over again once, because Aimeric came in just then and had not heard. (I noticed that I became more, not less, enraged with each retelling.) I suppose that as an Occitan, I was partly inured to violence by the frequency with which I had encountered it in hallucinatory form, but the thought of such real brutality to a *donzelha* turned my stomach, and I could see that Thorwald and Paul were shocked beyond all bounds. The cold rage in their eyes when I finished with the news— and the deep blank stare of Aimeric—told me more than anything else that whatever Caledony had been before to my Caledon friends, it was now changed utterly.

"I'll have to tell Dad and Clarity about this," Aimeric said at last. "It might put some fight back in Clarity—and Dad may have some ideas about what to do. I've just been on the com to the PPP, and apparently most of the major political prisoners will be released sometime in the next couple of hours, generally out to house arrest, which means I'll be able to visit them but they won't be able to go anywhere. I'm supposed to com Ambassador Shan, soon, too. I assume I should fill him in on everything."

We all nodded. So far, the Council of Humanity had been about as strongly on our side as we could have dared to hope.

"Well, then I'd best get to it." Aimeric stood slowly and nodded at Paul and Thorwald. "You make sure that manifesto is airtight. If there isn't some way for me to speak, with things like this happening, I'm liable to do things that will get diplomatic immunity revoked."

They turned back to the page in front of them, and I went downstairs. There were five more crises exploding, and Margaret was on top of all of them; she pointed out another one. "We need to see if we can resume classes soon—otherwise the PPP can start forcing people to ask for refunds. Would you have time to figure out what we'll have to do to get the Center functioning as the Center again, in addition to being Utilitopia's leading Heretic House?"

Call it just natural *merce*, or maybe I just needed to keep my skills at flattery in shape, but I told her that what she asked me for I was incapable of refusing. She blushed yet again and her eyes wouldn't meet mine, but she was obviously overjoyed at the attention. I realized that I deeply enjoyed giving her the pleasure, and that as delighted as she was, she was almost physically passable.

Almost.

I was upstairs at a terminal in my office, trying to work out where we could move all those bodies so that all the classes could meet at their regular times, when there was a gentle tap at the door. *"Venetz."*

Valerie came in very hesitantly; she looked as if she might break and run. "Are you busy?"

"Incredibly, *midons*, but there's always time for you."

"I just wanted . . . well, to see how you were doing, and maybe to find out, oh, just how things are."

The difference between Valerie and Margaret, it occurred to me, was that both had Caledon skill at flirting—which is to say, none at all—but where Margaret simply communicated as best she could, Valerie actually *tried* to flirt and failed miserably at it. Still, as I looked at the clear skin, the immense luminous eyes . . . and the curves of her body . . . I thought skill and communication might be highly negotiable.

"Well," I said, "I'm exhausted because I haven't slept much, and there's much more work in front of me than I can reasonably do. But at least so far the PPP can't touch me personally, which is a better situation than most of you are in, so

I try to hold my share of things up." It came out much more tired and duty-bound than I had meant it to; more Caledon, if you will.

Her smile was still warm, and by lowering her eyes a little she managed to give herself some look of mystery; it would have been unusually crude for a pubescent Occitan, but just the attempt was remarkable here. "I know how much you've been doing for all of us. Have you . . . er, had even a chance to think a little about . . . when we—jammed together?"

She emphasized "jammed" just enough to make sure that I would remember what it meant in local slang. There hadn't been any real danger that I would forget.

"Well, it *was* just about the last pleasant thing that happened to me," I said. "Was there anything in particular about it you wanted to discuss?"

"Just that I'd love to . . . perform with you again. And since Paul and Thorwald seem so determined to launch this Inessentialist Movement, that means more chances to perform, and—well, you know. I wanted to know if you felt about it the same way I feel about it."

"Sort of the ultimate in unanswerable questions, isn't it?" I wasn't sure why I was teasing and fending in quite this way—perhaps I was afraid that she might make a more explicit suggestion soon, or perhaps I was afraid that she would not and I would be confronted by my own arrogance. Certainly I did not want her to leave, and I was enjoying the sight of the little flush spreading across her cheeks, not much caring whether it was embarrassment or excitement. "Anyway, until they get their manifesto done, how are we to know, as true artists, whether or not we are Inessentialists?"

If the peeps had a bug left, that might give them a bit of a headache.

"Oh, but . . . well, I think all artists are. Paul was telling me about it; his eyes were all full of light, and just to listen to him . . . what he said was that it's about the idea that art doesn't serve a purpose, art is a purpose, that's the only thing I can remember exactly." Her eyes were fairly "full of light" in their own right, and the mention of Paul's name had triggered a couple of thoughts in me. First of all, I was in the middle of a genuinely dangerous political crisis, in which Paul had been useful and Valerie had not, and from what Margaret had told me, I sort of strongly suspected that Valerie had been creating a certain amount of chaos among the people staying with us, and probably giving Paul one more thing to worry about.

The second thought, which practically blinded me, was that although I was certainly excited by her face and body, and the purity of her voice and the passion of her playing were magnificent, I did not know her very well, and what I knew I didn't like.

It had never occurred to me that I might like or dislike a *donzelha*. Maybe Marcabru *had* been getting letters from a stranger named Giraut, after all.

I don't know what exactly I did in that long moment of thought— toused my hair, I think— but something in the way I did it must have given her the feeling that she wasn't getting anywhere, because after a minute or two more of small talk she excused herself and disappeared.

The pile of problems in front of me claimed my attention immediately; if we put everyone sleeping in the dueling room onto shift two, then the kitchen work would be slightly screwed up but on the other hand—

Margaret arrived with lunch brought up from the kitchen. We had now thrown bail for about a dozen students, and we had them plus one other person as new residents. "They're just added numbers in the existing problem, fortunately," I said.

She poured coffee before answering, and handed me a sandwich. "It's early to eat, but we might not be able to when the remains arrive."

I had almost been able to forget. "It's just Elizabeth Lovelock we have to bury?" I asked.

She nodded. "The problem of finding a Pastor to make it legal, however, is solved. The Chairman—I mean, Aimeric's father, he's not Chairman anymore, but—"

"He'll always be the Chairman to me, too. At least compared to what's sitting in the chair right now. He's agreed to do the funeral for us? That's terrific politically if it doesn't get him sent to prison."

"Even if it does," she said, chewing quickly, "it's still a pretty good thing politically. But it's more than his agreeing to do the funeral. What I wanted to ask you was whether we could convert one more space and afford to grow a sink and toilet in there, because I'd like to give Chairman Carruthers a private room."

"He's here?"

"Yap. Enrolled for Occitan cooking, Occitan poetry, and Basic Occitan. Says he knows too much about God's will to attempt painting or music, and that dancing and dueling are not things for a man his age."

"Hmmph. I'm not so sure about dueling. He must have given this as his address to get his house arrest set up here. How are we going to get it cleared for him to go with us to the cemetery for the burial—or do we only need him for the funeral here?"

"What's a cemetery?"

It was a Terstad word, so I was quite surprised. "Um, where you bury people."

"You mean—literally?" She seemed more than a little shocked.

I had a suspicion I would be much the same in a moment. "In Occitan we put their bodies into the ground, yes," I stammered. "What do you do here . . . cremate them, or—"

"Well, we . . ." Her voice got very soft, and she looked down at the floor.

"It's all right, I'm almost a grown-up, you can tell me."

"I just realized—we saw that extended vu of your friend—Raimbaut?"

"Raimbaut," I said. "You mean of the burial service on Serra Valor. I realize you must do things differently here—"

"Yes, but when you hear *how* differently, I think you're going to be horrified, and even though I really like you, Giraut, sometimes you're so prissy about things, and make them so complicated—"

"Wait a moment here, *companhona*. I'll grant you that I often react badly to your customs, but give me the privilege of reacting badly for myself."

She looked like she was about to flare back at me, but then she swallowed it and nodded, apparently deciding my request was fair. "All right. There are no cemeteries here because we don't keep corpses around after the funeral. After the funeral a few of Elizabeth's close friends—if she had any here, and so far I haven't found any—will take her body downstairs to the main door on the regenner system and put her in there, along with all her personal possessions."

"That's disgusting."

"I knew you would react like that."

I got up from the chair, but with the cots in there, there was nowhere to pace, so I ended up with my rump on the desk and my feet in the chair, still eating. After a moment she said, "I'm sorry but you had to find out sooner or later and it *is* what we do."

The image now taking up all of my brain appalled me. *Everything*—kitchen scraps, floor sweepings, dirty dishes, *the toilet!*—went into the regenner system, where an ultrasound gadget converted it all to something you could mix with water, and the slurry was then piped away and fed into the city's fusion torch, so that literally every atom of refuse in the city could be reused. I suddenly realized what Anna's poem had really been about and was glad that I had not known while I was listening. Elizabeth's poor battered body would be stripped down to ions and mass-spectographed; most of her would end as fertilizer or simple fresh water, some bits as valuable light metals . . . and on the way she would mix with the city's garbage.

Finally I sighed. Raimbaut was mummified in his stone chamber, which was quite waterproof and on the dry desert side of Serra Valor. We had left a little device that induced ferocious shortlived radioactivity an hour or two after he was covered, so that there was literally nothing in the hole to eat him; whenever the Grand Academy elected a dead artist a saint, even generations later, and they dug him up to make relics, the bodies were always perfect preserved. My own lute had cost me a year's allowance because it contained three knucklebones of Saint Agnes shaped into tuning pegs. (Saint Agnes the painter, to be sure—musician relics made into instruments were out of my financial reach and always would be unless I somehow earned a peerage in perpetuo.)

I wondered how a Caledon would have reacted to knowing that. Would it strike them as sensible recycling, or as homage the way it did me, or—would they have found the idea of carrying bits of corpse around with us revolting?

"I'll get over it," I said. "It's taking me a bit of time to adapt to your ways, and you've got to allow me an occasional reaction, but I will get over it."

I don't think Margaret had expected that. She gave me a small smile and said, "Well, then, good, because we may end up being Elizabeth's friends for the burial. At this point I think we might even have to deliver her eulogies."

"How many does she need?"

"Our custom is three, but one is from the Pastor and one from the family, normally. We'll have to find things we can tell Pastor Carruthers about her . . . and all we've got for family is one distant cousin who can't remember ever having talked with her. Luckily it's Thorwald. You, or I, or somebody is going to have to be the friend, I'm afraid. She doesn't seem to have had any."

"Poor girl." I shuddered. "And she was here at the Center?"

"She enrolled first thing. As far as I can tell it was her one and only act of rebellion ever, unless you count attending the OMC—and the overlap between those must be ninety percent. So she had a regular job, and because she wasn't deviant she got everything she asked for: Aimeric's poetry class, the one on reading it that is, and Basic Occitan from Bieris, who just remembered her face, and doesn't think she ever did much individual conversation—and your music appreciation class."

I ran my mind over the thirty people in the class, and finally settled on her as one of three people who sat in the back, seemed to listen intently, and never spoke. "Do we know anything else about her?"

"She was an only child. Apparently very shy. Her academic schedule matches that of one young male coworker that she may have had a crush on, but he didn't go to the OMC and he's one of the few who asked for a full refund of tuition. She'd never had a copy made for psypyx after the age of eighteen, when they stop requiring them, so she's three stanyears out of date, and they can't find anyone to wear her that she was close to. I might have to volunteer, or maybe I can talk Val into it if she'll get off this hysterical act she's been doing and volunteer to be useful."

"She came up to see me and seemed normal enough. Very much Valerie, but normal."

Margaret sighed and scratched her head; there was something distinctly apelike about it to me. "Well, I guess that's progress."

"She didn't get anywhere," I said, softly. Perhaps I just wanted to see how Margaret would react to that piece of information.

She grinned. I liked that. "So you've noticed that she's developed a fascination with everything Occitan, also."

"I confess I could return the fascination, but Paul is so much . . . er . . ."

"So much more valuable? He certainly is. And she's certainly managed to upset and hurt him more than enough over the years."

"He helps her to do it," I pointed out. "In a way it's a shame I can't give him a crash course in Occitan approach to such matters. As a point of *enseingnamen*, he'd long since have dumped her—because we make ourselves so vulnerable to each other in *finamor*, we also have a well-developed art of storming out in a fury."

"He could certainly use it," Margaret agreed. A thought seemed to hit her, and before the shy smile I could see starting had a chance to turn into an awkward question, I said, "So poor Elizabeth Lovelock seems to have been a person from nowhere. How in the world did she end up as she did?"

Margaret's expression shifted as quickly as I had hoped it would. "It looks like it was just a case of being in the wrong place at the wrong time. There was a tiny little anti-Saltini demonstration by some ultraorthodox believers—not more than twenty of them—in the street near her home, and the city police tried to protect it from the peeps. At least four policemen died when the peeps jumped them; some of the demonstrators are still in the hospital. Elizabeth Lovelock was coming home from the OMC—the timing suggests to me that she was actually one of the people who helped us stack chairs and tear down, and *still* none of us noticed the poor thing—and between the trakcar and her front door—well, they grabbed her and the rest happened. I don't suppose we'll ever know much more than that. Several of the autopsy details are just horrible, Giraut, things that the coroner said indicated 'systematic torture aimed at sexual humiliation.' I think the coroner is liberal and must have been trying to make sure there'd be indictments. Poor girl. It must have seemed to her that she suffered eternally before they finally killed her."

There were tears forming in Margaret's eyes, and without thinking I moved over to her cot and sat beside her, putting an arm around her. She almost fell against me, but it wasn't desire; she was simply exhausted and had been looking after far too many people for far too long, with no time for her own feelings. "This is stupid," she said, still snuffling into my shoulder.

"No, it's natural. You've been carrying too much of a load for too long, and we can't do anything to lift it off you, and what happened to Elizabeth would wring tears from rock."

"I just keep thinking—if she had had even one friend, someone who might have been with her or delayed her even a few minutes . . . or if there were just someone to speak for her now—"

I held her close, and gently rubbed the back of her neck, and wondered how I had ever gotten into the kind of world where these sorts of things could happen. She held on for a long time, and when the grip broke it was because Margaret sat back to wipe her face. "Well," she said, "now, that was a total loss of dignity."

"I won't tell anyone," I said, and handed her a tissue to wipe her face. "Don't give up yet; keep looking. She might have a friend as quiet as she was. And there has to be *some-one* whose arm you can twist to wear her psypyx. The way you feel about her couldn't be good for her anyway—too likely to get her into self-pity. Though *deu sait* if anyone was ever entitled to self-pity . . . now, don't start again, or I'll join you."

She sort of forced a happy face, for which I was grateful, and left. It occurred to me that I had held plenty of *donzelhas* in tears in my time, but this was the first one where there had actually been something to worry about, let alone where I had worried about her after the tears were over.

Well, after all, I had come to Caledony, in part, to have experiences that were new to me.

I got the rest of the course-scheduling finished in an hour or so and looked at the clock to see that I had now used up all the time I had allotted for the First Dark nap, and moreover had not been downstairs in quite a while. In a real crisis someone would have called me, of course, but as the person ultimately responsible I did not want to learn of things only when they became real crises. With a mournful glance at my bed, and no more than a splash of water on my face and a quick brush of my hair, I headed downstairs.

THREE

The first thing I discovered on my way down the stairs was one more thing to work into the schedule; very apologetically, Aimeric's father stopped me on the stairs and asked if there would be any time at which he could have one of the larger rooms for chapel. That, at least, was fairly simple to fit in, so I made a quick note in my pocket unit and told him I'd have an official time for him soon.

"Thank you. I'm—er—sorry to deal with what was really a very small matter first, but I'm afraid a life of government and administration has biased me that way. The other reason they sent me up, and did not use regular communication, was to let you know quietly that young Lovelock's body has arrived. Thorwald and Margaret are moving it down to a cold storeroom below the kitchen."

"You've seen . . . her?"

Carruthers nodded, and his face was set in iron. "I have. I've proposed, and the others have accepted, that we not have her embalmed or restored, and we let her casket be open. The essential correctness of the decision, I think, is verified by the fact that the Reverend Saltini has commed me four times in the last hour to accuse me of 'politicizing' her death, and of 'creating martyrs where there is only misfortune and irresponsibility.' "

I exploded. " 'Irresponsibility!' After what his goons did to her—" I was too furious to speak further.

Carruthers lip twitched a tiny bit, as if he had seen humor he would not admit to. "I must confess, I reacted the same way. Furthermore, and more to the point, the General Consultancy agreed that it was rational for me to do so, thus losing Saltini his chance to have me committed as insane or senile. To quote a politician whose style I've always rather liked, now that Saltini has gotten onto the tiger, let us see if he can ride it."

By the time I got down to the loading dock, mercifully, the job was done and Elizabeth Lockwood's body decently covered. Thorwald, Paul, Aimeric, and Margaret were down there, badly upset, and it took some coaxing to get them upstairs and away from the situation. "The funeral will be early tomorrow," I pointed out, "and after that we can probably get classes back under way. Everyone here could use a little normality."

Aimeric sipped his coffee and nodded. "If no one needs me here, I'm going to go over and visit Clarity. I've commed her, and she sounds a little better, but I'd like to see for myself." He left very quietly—a great weight seemed to have settled onto his shoulders, and he bore it, but the strain was still evident.

Classes did not resume the next day, despite the best intentions in the world. First of all, the funeral was more upsetting than I think even Carruthers, who wanted an uproar, had intended to make it. Not cleaning or embalming the body, "burying" Elizabeth in the clothes she had come to the morgue in, had left three inflammatory facts in full view: her brutally crushed mouth and broken jaw, the blood that had soaked her torn clothing everywhere from knees to waist, and the expression of terrible agony on what remained of her face. You could not see it without wanting to scream or throw up.

Carruthers took full advantage of that; his condemnation of the coup tied it directly to the crime even in Terstad, and the portion of the eulogy he delivered in Reason made what many people felt was an airtight case that Saltini himself was directly responsible for what had happened to the young woman.

Then Valerie, of all people, stood up, and I wondered how she had come to be a friend of Elizabeth Lovelock's—until I saw the fresh scar at the back of her neck. Obviously Margaret had turned up the pressure; at least Valerie would be doing something useful for a change, I thought sourly.

Valerie's eyes were cast down at the floor; she seemed shyer and quieter than she had when she performed. "I think . . . this funeral is very . . . well, unusual. I've now known Elizabeth for just a few hours. Uh, actually, she wants you to know her family always called her Betsy, and that's—how she'd like you to remember her. She's had to do a lot of catching up; remember her last personality copy was made before the springer even opened. But . . . well, things are, uh, working very well, the doctors say better than it normally ever does. We've kind of experimented, and, if you can all be very quiet and not startle me, I can sort of . . . lend Betsy my voice so she can talk to you herself."

The room was so silent that I suddenly wondered if they all

were holding their breath, or if perhaps everyone was concentrating on breathing silently. Then Valerie's voice began to speak with a slightly different accent, sometimes not in perfect control, but quite intelligibly. "I—I just wan-ted ... I just wanted to s-say that I was very lonely all m-my life and it seems like it was because of the way we Caledons live. This is a very c-cold culture, and we are not a h-happy people. And I look at Valerie's memories of the Center and the C-Cabaret and even though I cannot remember it for myself I f-feel so happy to know that those things were in my life before I died. They will t-try to tell you that the Saltinis and the peeps, and the men who did-did-did this to my b-body, are the exceptions, but they are wrong. Reverend Carruthers or Reverend Peterborough are the exceptions, people who t-treat people decently. This thing you see in the casket that w-was me is what h-happens when you try to make people fit to ideas.

"I was very shy but I will try to talk to more of you especially because now that I have Valerie with me I am not so afraid. And I will try very hard to b-be someone they can g-grow a body for the d-doctors say I'm doing well. So I expect-pect-pect to be back with you again in the flesh and meanwhile please w-win so the world will be f-fit to live in. That's all-all I want to say."

The voice had been a little whiny and a little ashamed, as if Betsy had been one of those souls who is crushed almost from birth, whether by external force or internal weakness. Yet she had affirmed her dignity, claimed her place among us, and in perfect absurdity, the funeral went up in a roar of tearful applause.

Maybe our response was all political; what she had said would be carried on the news channels, and would damage Saltini deeply, and we knew that instantly. Maybe it was simple courage that we admired, seeing a personality so badly out of date find its footing and choose its side so quickly.

But suggest either of those reasons to me and you'll face a challenge *atz sang*, even today. I think we applauded because when human beings are forced to hear—to really hear—a cry for love, they don't have much choice but to give it. At least that's what I'd rather believe about my species.

In a way it was an anticlimax, but when Thorwald, as relative, stepped up, there was another surprise, for he was carrying a lute.

He wasn't a really accomplished musician, but he was good enough, and well-practiced enough, to be adequate, and what he sang was a loose translation of the *Canso de Fis de Jovent*. Normally I hate to hear the standards paraphrased or altered for some transient cause or occasion, even though that's quite common in Nou Occitan. This time, however, he had begun from the translation, and what he had done seemed wise and appropriate—removed the specifically Occitan places, changed the gender to neuter, and emphasized the aspects of courage in the face of loss, of waste. It had real power; certainly all of us wept without shame.

On the way out of the hall, everyone stopped to look into Valerie's eyes and greet Betsy. Then, finally, we took that poor broken body down to the recycler, and fed it in.

I had about decided to cancel classes anyway—I couldn't imagine that much learning would go on that day—when the com *pinged* for me. I pulled my unit from my pocket and found myself looking at Ambassador Shan. "You would seem to be the logical person for this announcement; please post it to the Center. The Bazaar will open on the Embassy grounds in six hours—just at the end of First Dark."

"Isn't that early?"

"Very."

"And I thought there was going to be more warning—"

"There was. There isn't now. And unless Saltini has this line bugged, he doesn't know yet. He's last on my list to call. Make sure word of that gets around as well, please?"

"Yap," I said, like a real Caledon—that is, doing my best not to let anyone know I was enjoying it.

"And—er, if I may mention, Giraut, the funeral was magnificent. Simply magnificent."

"I just provided the building. Other people did the work."

"Pass my compliments along to them, then. I have many others to com; I'll talk to you at greater length soon."

And with that he was gone.

I got on the public address system and made the announcement; in six hours all the wonders of the Thousand Cultures would be on display in the Embassy. Saltini's evident fear of the Council of Humanity meant that as long as everyone travelled together going to and from the Bazaar, it was unlikely that anyone would encounter much trouble.

I had half assumed I would have to declare a holiday for the Bazaar opening; I hadn't realized the half of it. An hour before it was due to open, my students were forming a line outside the Embassy; twenty minutes after that they were no more than five percent of that line. I had seen one Bazaar, as a teenager, and been dazzled and astonished, but naturally every Bazaar afterwards is larger, since more and more cultures are added to each one. This was a good third larger, for Nou Occitan had launched a crash program to get a springer built, so that even though we were remote, we had made Connect before many other cultures. Most of the outermost colonies were only now making Connect, like Caledony, and a few like St. Michael had not done it yet.

There were actually 1238 cultures in existence, and more than 1100 were represented. Many just had simple booths with one or two bored attendants ("THORBURG. PRESERVING THE MILITARY TRADITION . . . BECAUSE WE JUST MIGHT NEED IT AGAIN. ASK ABOUT OUR FOREIGN LEGIONS" was doing relatively little business; there were a lot of people at the JOBS IN HEDONIA booth until they discovered that what the Hedons wanted was people raised in sufficiently traditional cultures to be actually unwilling, and preferably even shocked, for abuse at orgies). Others—notably the United Cultures of Dunant, an amalgam of the heavily interblended cultures of the oldest settled colony planet—had full-fledged pavilions with incredible mixtures of products on display.

I found myself chatting with Major Ironhand at the Thorburg booth mostly because I felt a bit sorry for him—people were swinging around his booth as if he had a gang of thugs hidden under the table waiting to leap on them and force them into uniform. "Nou Occitan," he said. "Yeah, I was stationed at the Bazaar there for a few months. We actually had a few recruits, and I'd have to say it was a fun place; loved the simulated fighting, and it was certainly pretty."

A little further conversation determined that he'd actually been to some of the same places I had; Thorburgers wear their hair braided down their backs "in time of peace"— which of course is what there's been for six hundred years, so nobody has any idea what they'll wear if a war breaks out— and he'd apparently just stuffed it down the back of his neck and gone out to be a jovent. He seemed to have a good feel for music and poetry, so it wasn't purely as a brawler, as I had feared at first. On the other hand, I couldn't help noticing that it had been very easy for him to fit into Occitan society (most offworlders stayed on Embassy grounds there) and that he had successfully raised several companies of Occitans, enough to form their own Legion. "Best-looking uniforms in the army," he said, grinning, "god knows what history book they got them out of. Wild people to get drunk and stupid with. And they're smart and disciplined on duty." Thorburg was practically a pariah among the Thousand Cultures—even the many cultures that shared their planet with them didn't like them much—and it seemed unpleasant to me that we Occitans got along so well with them. When I talked with Aimeric later, he claimed it was because we were the only two really Romantic cultures.

After establishing that Major (it seemed an odd name to me, but I could tell that he liked being addressed by it) would be around for a year or so, and thus I'd have many more chances to talk with him, I took a stroll around the main concourse.

"Giraut! Giraut Leones!"

I turned around to find myself facing Garsenda. My jaw must have dropped like a brick, because she giggled and said, "Hi. We've got to talk. But come on over to the Occitan booth—I'm the only one there and I can't leave it unattended."

In a sort of daze, I followed her. She was wearing traditional Occitan clothing, but her jewelry seemed more Interstellar.

"So how have you been?" she asked, as she handed me a strong mug of coffee, stuff that tasted amazingly of home. "I mean, we all know what you've been doing, but how are you feeling? Do you ever get a chance to perform anymore?"

"You all know what I've been doing?"

Garsenda smiled and winked at me. "Listen, first thing . . . you knew when we went into *finamor* that I was a climber, didn't you?"

I nodded; I supposed I had. Few things are as flattering as having someone who is trying to elbow her way into good society decide that you are a logical doorway.

"Well, I have to say, I'm not an awfully competent one; I went and lost you just before you came here, and considering what your status is like back home—especially since Marcabru has made such a fool of himself as Consort—"

"Er, I've only been getting letters from my father about the weather and his tomatoes, and letters from Marcabru."

Garsenda snorted. "I can imagine. Sit, sit, thanks to your Center, everybody's seen Occitan stuff and nobody bothers coming here, although the aintellect tells me that tons of music and art and clothing patterns have been ordered. I'm going to look *brilliant* without having to do very much."

"How did you end up with this job?"

"Well, they wanted someone who had lived Oldstyle, and was willing to do it again at least a bit. And you'd be amazed how few are left or willing to admit it. Marcabru and Idiot Girl were trying to impose a cutoff from the Council of Humanity, or at least severely restrict contact, in order to squelch the Interstellars. That idea didn't stand a chance—too many people like Fort Liberty coffee, sporting goods from Sparta . . . well, you know—still, our monarchs managed to do a lot of petty harassment, and practically destroyed the Oldstyles because most of *them* can't stand Marcabru. Even

Pertz's has gone all Interstellar, just because they've managed to make it this embarrassing hyperconservative thing to be. So I was one of the few applicants—maybe partly because I, uh, well, had made quite a reputation as an Interstellar.

"As for how we all know what you've been up to, of course Marcabru was always reading your letters out loud at Court—oh, I didn't tell you, but we finally got a few Interstellars in at Court, and even though Idiot Girl practically fainted—"

"She *is* the Queen," I said mildly.

"No, *he* is. She sits in her room and writes verses that no one else can understand, and he wanders around the Palace in a weird Oldstyle outfit—much more extreme than anyone else ever wore—challenging everyone he can find to fight. Anyway, as I was saying, Wilson stayed in its orbit even after Interstellars got in."

I shook my head slowly. "You know, I think you've talked to me more in the last five minutes than you ever did while we were in *finamor*."

"Well, there's more to say now than there was then." She brushed her hair back and I saw that the scarring on her ears had healed.

"So have you gone back to Oldstyle for good, or—"

"No, this is more or less a costume," she said. "Let me finish the story, because it's something you need to know, and I'm afraid time to talk may get short later. So at first Marcabru was making a lot of capital out of the idea that you were finding out what the rest of the Thousand Cultures were like, and they were all gray ugly artless places, that we were the last outpost of civilization . . . but then after a while . . . well, the things you said about these people . . . Giraut, don't let it upset you, please, but you're a hero to the Interstellars. So is Bieris—there must be five hundred painters trying to imitate her—but you're the real hero."

I wasn't sure I was still breathing. "Me? What did *I* do?"

"Those letters. You really brought the Caledon culture alive to us; even through Marcabru's sarcastic readings. There's at least twenty people I want to meet here—

Thorwald, and Paul, and this marvelous Valerie you talk about—we just met Ambassador Shan this morning and he's *exactly* like what you describe."

Her eyes were shining and she was so excited that I asked, "But—surely you've had a chance to see what Utilitopia itself looks like, or the Morning Storm, or—"

"I won't get to travel much—I'm so frustrated that I'll be within a few kilometers of the Gap Bow and probably never get a chance to see it, or even Sodom Gap . . ."

I began to laugh, softly, because the whole thing just seemed so absurd; and yet, I had to admit, even having named the two ugliest things I could think of first, that part of me wished we had about a week to just go out and see some of the sights. Call it loyalty to my Caledon friends, or just to my own experience.

"All right," I said. "So, after you go back, should I write to you? I just dropped Marcabru a challenge without limit last night, so I won't be writing to him again."

She shrugged, and all that beautiful dark hair swirled around her face. "I'm really a rotten correspondent, Giraut, but for you I would try to make an exception. Especially . . ." she smiled at me, and I saw a ferocity that I would never have realized was there in the old days ". . . since I'm sure it can be turned to some account socially."

"At least one of us has really changed," I said.

Garsenda smiled. "Both of us, but I'm glad. I think we could be friends now."

It was true. "Well, what's become of you?" I asked.

Those blue eyes were so full of laughter—maybe a slightly decadent laughter, but I still liked it. "Goodness, the last time you saw me—well, I saw it on the playback. You were certainly upset and I suppose you had a right to be. That was a strange time for me too. But I don't suppose you know about the ongoing uproar among the Interstellars, because I would bet Marcabru hasn't told you."

She told me. Of all the Thousand Cultures, Nou Occitan had been one of the most extreme in enforcing gender differences, and had some of the most rigid and elaborate codes of courtesy. When Connect had triggered upheaval and change there, like most cultures it had at first lurched, not in the direction of the mean of the Thousand Cultures, but toward its own repressed side. "So you might say a lot of us *donzelhas* were just acting out what we'd all been afraid of in our own culture. Sadoporn is a minority taste on Earth, and in practically every other culture—the people at the Hedon booth tell me so far they have about three orders from all of Caledon, and they're all for pretty mild stuff. But in a culture like Nou Occitan, with its emphasis on gender difference and violence—well, did you know that was one of our major cultural imports right after Connect? It's just implicit in things. So a lot of us acted it out at first, the same way you go through a phase of being hyperconformist just before you drive your parents berserk. But there were a lot of other ideas floating around out there, and pretty soon it began to occur to a lot of us that maybe being rape objects getting actually raped wasn't much of an improvement over just being rape objects."

I was reasonably sure she hadn't come up with all of that by herself, but it was obvious she believed it and understood it . . . and worse yet, I had reached a point where I understood it, even if I was a bit uncomfortable with the phrasing of the whole thing. "Er—" I began, "that is, did you know . . . um, I would watch the symbolic language right now. You know we have a political crisis in process here, and there's been a coup?"

She beamed at me as if I were a star student. "Of course I do. Just before I came I was in a demonstration trying to get the Council of Humanity to intervene against the Saltini regime."

"Well—" I told her about Betsy Lovelock. "—so, you see, 'rape' is a more loaded than usual word locally."

She nodded, sensibly, but then she said, "Giraut, did you even *know* that real, violent rape was common in Nou Occitan?"

My mouth started to open; and then I found myself trying to think—*deu sait* I had never threatened a woman myself . . .

well, perhaps I had wrestled once with an unwilling virgin, but she was willing enough by the time that we ... still, did I know what had been going on in her mind? Perhaps she had just been frightened into submission.

And certainly I had known jovents enough who, armed with the neuroducer, against *donzelhas* who were not ... Marcabru himself had boasted to me once that he had gotten a "little ice princess" to "open her pretty mouth and satisfy me like the whore she really was" by threatening her with his epee, telling her he would use the neuroducer to give her the sensation of having her breasts slashed off, and of being sliced from anus to vagina. He had done it because he wanted to fight her *entendedor*, knowing that if he carried out his threat she would experience it as if real—I had thought of it as wildness, as a cruelty I would not have practiced myself, but I had also shaken my head with a certain admiration. Bloodthirstiness is a part of *enseingnamen*, after all.

Garsenda had been sitting quietly watching me, and finally she said, "I see it came as news to you?"

"Not when I thought about it."

"You know, you were my fourth *entendedor*, Giraut, and the first one who never forced me." She sighed. "I just wanted to ... well, not thank you exactly. You weren't wonderfully nice to me, but you did treat me with, oh, a little bit of dignity. Gave me an idea I might be good for something, perhaps, besides being sighed over between bouts of abuse. So when I went into the Interstellars, it didn't take long for me to ... you know. Find the *really* new ideas. You were part of my path to where I am now, and I guess that was a big help, and what I really wanted to say is that you looked so miserable when I saw that autocamera shot of you ..."

"I was, I suppose. But it was part of my education too." I got up, feeling strangely light-headed. "I'll try to visit a couple of times before you go back. And if you get any time at all, come over to the Center and meet everyone, please. Um—when I get back ... let's look each other up. And see if maybe we can't be friends."

She stood and hugged me. Her wonderful body, fitted

against mine, brought back a lot of very awkward memories, some of them physiologically expressed, but I think I managed to conceal that problem from her.

When I ran into Bruce and Bieris, they were strolling around openly hand in hand, and I was happy that they were now willing to let us all see that. I sent them over to talk with Garsenda, who I knew wanted to meet Bruce. Besides, it occurred to me, it was always possible that she and Beiris could be friends now, if Beiris could get over the impression we'd all had that Garsenda was a fool.

There had to be ten thousand people here at the opening of the Bazaar, and I hadn't the faintest idea what any of them was thinking about; but now that I thought of it, I had never really known as much as I felt I had.

There in the bright glare of the amber lighting, I suddenly felt a great surge of tiredness that seemed to come out of my bones and weigh my muscles down. For an instant I thought it must be the arrival of some new awareness, something I must capture for a song, and then I realized it was just that I had not slept enough. Moreover, for once, back at the Center, it was likely to be quiet, with few crises erupting. I saw Thorwald passing by and tossed him the top card so that he could take people back in the Center's cat, then got myself into a trakcar and went back home. A hot shower all to myself was an amazing luxury, and to slide between clean sheets and set the alarm for ten full hours in the future—that was paradise itself.

I woke suddenly in the dark with a distinctly wonderful sensation going on; I was a bit disoriented, but I reached down my body to find a close-cropped head and to take Margaret's hands in mine. She came up for air and whispered "It's all right. Aimeric is staying overnight with Reverend Peterborough."

I bent down and kissed her. "Margaret, that's lovely, but what on earth—"

"Garsenda told me you like to wake up that way, and sort of, uh, what to do, exactly . . ."

I should have guessed, I suppose. "I love it. I'm just a bit surprised. It's not ... oh, not much like my idea of what you're like. Even though I'm delighted," I hastened to add. *Deu*, what else had Garsenda told her? There's an Occitan saying—never introduce your current to your previous *entendedora* until you're sure one of the three of you is going to die immediately.

"Well, I was afraid you'd never get the idea otherwise. I'm not any good at this flirting stuff. And it's not like it's something I haven't thought about, even before I met Garsenda." She hesitated. "Am I doing it right?"

"Perfectly." No doubt Garsenda had given detailed directions. I was still trying to decide whether I should thank her or kill her. Probably both. "How do *you* feel about it?"

She didn't answer, but she seemed to withdraw into herself a little. My fault, love should not be interrupted. I drew her up toward me and began to caress her, whispering gently, almost baby-talk. Margaret was an adult, and not particularly frightened, but it was the first time, at least between us, and I could tell she was much more excited and anxious than I was, so the comforting and the tenderness were going to be up to me.

I found that I was enjoying it a great deal. Her breasts were small and flaccid, her thighs thick, her hips wide, her buttocks flat, noticeably so even in the dark, but they were *hers*, and that mattered more to me than I would have thought. By the time I mounted her I think I must have been as excited as she was.

At least Garsenda had not taught her to behave like an Occitan in every way. Margaret didn't thrash, scream, or make a display of being carried away by desire, or shout anything poetic (I had always found that distracting anyway). The frantic sincerity of her response could not have been faked; it was much more exciting than anything artistic the average *donzelha* might have done.

So it was probably only nine hours of sleep, but it was still wonderful, and when we got up the next morning I felt utterly, irrationally happy. And I wouldn't have missed Margaret's smile for anything.

FOUR

The best thing about what happened next was that for tens of days nothing especially unusual happened. Bieris and Bruce moved back out to Sodom Basin, now that they apparently could count on safe passage. According to Aimeric's report to Shan, almost half of one percent of Caledony's money supply had disappeared through the Bazaar in forty-eight hours, and by the end of the third day there were officially some unemployed people, though so far there was insurance to take care of them. About half the people staying in the Center, the half who had places of their own or were not banned from their families, moved back home, but most of our core group stayed around; with a little stretching and arranging, Margaret and Paul had rooms of their own, and Thorwald got his apartment back.

Margaret slept in my room most nights, and got into the habit, whenever we were together, of leaning against me or resting a hand or arm on me somewhere. I was surprised to find how much I liked that.

Betsy and Valerie got so proficient at sharing Valerie's body that people began to just address them as two people. Betsy, of course, had never attracted male attention, and Valerie had never been able to get enough of it, so they set about driving the male population of the place crazy. There was a brief and evident pass at me once when Margaret was off on an errand, and I was deeply astonished to find that I not only didn't have any trouble resisting it, I was in fact rather irritated by the whole thing.

I also discovered something else that Valerie and Betsy

shared. They both sulked when they were disappointed. One more reason not to be involved.

One of Valerie's roommates told me later that the oddest thing was that you could sometimes hear Valerie's voice, talking in her sleep, carrying on a spat between the two of them; whatever their private differences, Betsy and Valerie were certainly a united front out in public.

Classes resumed, and I found out just how much of the unreceptivity of students had been due to the watchful eyes of the peeps, for although the PPP was now in charge of everything, it was widely known that most of the bugs had been pulled (and more were being pulled as Paul and Margaret tracked them down), and in any case every one of the students was ripe for jail and reeducation, and thus it no longer mattered whether they put their normality on display. It wasn't exactly an explosion of creativity—people were still very much just finding their feet—but there was a lively interest in things and a willingness to argue and test that had not been there before.

Of course those days were really just a brief calm before more storm could break out, but even so, I appreciated it. Aside from the opportunity to collect my energies, and to settle into the new order of my life, it was also a time for a gathering of forces.

Inessentialism, as Thorwald and Paul had framed it in that manifesto, was a perfectly wonderful idea if you were a Caledon, and painfully self-evident for an Occitan. The central tenet was that art *should* be inessential, that art consisted in doing all the things besides bodily functions and working that could give pleasure, and thus by definition art was an attack on pure functionalism . . . but *in the name of greater pleasure and higher rationality*. The aintellects of the General Consultancy fought back and forth about that for a truly amazing amount of machine time, but with the help of Aimeric's father (who seemed faintly amused by the whole business) they had made an airtight case, and the Inessentialist Movement was registered as a legitimate, rational tendency within Caledon thought.

I don't suppose anyone thought that one of the major corollaries was going to matter quite so much as it turned out to; there was an argument implicit in Inessentialism that one ought to do a certain number of things on whim, just to experience them, particularly if no one else had ever experienced them. As Aimeric pointed out, if there had been Inessentialism when he was younger, he, Bruce, and Charlie would have had no problem getting permission to hike over Sodom Gap.

"Indeed, and quite a number of other good things might have come of it," old Carruthers said. We were all gathered in the Main Lounge, as we now always did in the last hour before bedtime; it was an occasion for campfire-style singalongs, or trading jokes and stories, or occasionally for political and religious arguments that I had a hard time following despite Margaret's best efforts to get them explained to me. This particular time no one had yet pulled out a musical instrument, and most people were just talking in little groups so far. I had gotten my preferred corner, and Margaret had slid onto the bench next to me, so that I could rest an arm on her shoulders while we talked.

Aimeric seemed astonished. "I thought you were *opposed* to our making the trip, and didn't like anything we were doing—"

The old Reverend grinned and sipped his beer. "Of course I was. I was a stiffnecked old swine at the time. Some of us take decades to acquire any youth, and some of us require a terrible shock."

Clarity Peterborough had recently gotten permission to come to the Center to visit on occasion, so she was there as well, sitting close to Aimeric and constantly glancing at him as if he were her bodyguard. "You're exaggerating the difference between then and now, also," she said. "Be honest, Luther. Much of the clash between you and Aimeric was just because you had two males in one household—"

"And no woman to mediate, yes, I know, I used to say that regularly," Carruthers admitted. "It was true too. You know, I've never thanked you for coming to visit so often in the first few years after Ambrose—sorry, but at the time you still *were* Ambrose—had left. I was dreadfully lonely, and your visits were very good for me."

Peterborough smiled, and somehow twenty or thirty stan-years vanished. "The pleasure really was all mine. Oh, I know a young apprentice minister is supposed to spend a lot of time with her mentor, but you know how rarely that's actually the case—most of them end up as unpaid personal servants. In the first place, you really did help me form my own vision of what I ought to be doing, and since I really was learning something, it was natural for me to stick around. And in the second place, it was my main way to get any news of Ambrose."

Aimeric sat up as if he'd unexpectedly gotten a splinter from the bench.

Old Carruthers grinned even more, and took an uncharacteristically long pull on his beer. "I always sort of suspected that might be the case."

Once again, Aimeric's relatively youthful appearance, due to suspended animation, a quarter century less exposure to ultraviolet, and perhaps most of all to having led a less embittering existence, had fooled me into thinking of him as younger than he was. He had to be almost the same age as the Reverend Peterborough. Just as I was making that connection, she said, "Oh, yes. A terrible crush on the local rebellious heretic ever since I was about twelve. Good girls who get scholarships and do all their homework and want to get everything right have a certain fatal interest in smart bad boys."

"I don't think I've ever seen Aimeric turn quite that color before," I said casually. Margaret stuck her elbow into my ribs.

Thorwald was tuning up with Valerie, and to my pleasant surprise they started to play some ballads from my Serras Verz group, doing some very nice duet work on them. We all turned to listen and appreciate.

As they finished the group, Thorwald gestured to me to join them. I was about to politely decline—I was enjoying their work too much, and having taught two music classes and played for the appreciation class that day my fingers were a bit sore and tired—when Valerie's face went briefly slack and then reshaped slightly, "D-do Oc-citans really do tha-at? Go on long walking trips out in the forest just because it's nice and it's pretty?"

"Yes, Betsy, they do," I said. "It's one of those things that's hard to explain the attraction of until you've actually done it—and then once you have done it, and do understand, you can't explain it to anyone else." I don't know whether my own songs had made me a bit homesick, or whether it was just the awareness that if I had stayed home I would probably be up in Terrbori to see the first wildflowers on the southern coast and fish for freezetrout in the roaring rivers right about then, or just a desire to hear myself talk, but I started describing a few adventures out in the boondocks, some of them trips I had made as long as twelve stanyears previously with my father. They seemed to enjoy the stories, so I kept going. Then Aimeric joined in and told about his trips with Charlie and Bruce, as well as more hiking trips. It killed most of the hour, and at the end of it I was really sorry that I hadn't just kept Valerie and Thorwald singing.

So often big things have small beginnings; the next evening, what everyone wanted to talk about was an idea that Paul had proposed as an "artistic experience." His idea was that since large passenger cats always carried a few bunks in case they were stranded overnight, that it might not be too much trouble to refit a couple of cats as rolling bunkhouses, and then to make an overland trip out to the "Pessimals," through one of several passes that could be identified from satellite maps, and finally down to the sea. The west coast was generally fairly sunny and warm, by local standards, which is to say it was like a chilly fall day on one of the islands off the polar continents on Wilson. The plan was to spend a day or two playing on the beach, perhaps hunting chickens or gathering crops gone wild, and then return through a different pass. Total trip time would be around twenty of the local twenty-eight-hour days, if we drove only in daylight.

I'd have thought that in the middle of a revolutionary situation, the idea of a camping trip wouldn't have mattered a bit, but Aimeric pointed out that plenty of revolutions had broken out over very minor questions. Within a day, they had drafted a plan and put it through to the scheduling bureaus, and received in exchange a list of over four hundred objections from the aintellects. They turned the list around within two of the local days by dividing it up among working groups, hitting the aintellects with a complete response. They also leafletted on the Bazaar grounds—something Shan allowed them to do—and thus turned the attempt to get permission for the expedition into a public squabble.

One media corporation owner, who had been a prominent elder in Peterborough's congregation, proposed to finance the whole thing by having the participants make sight-and-sound recordings of the trip, which would then be edited for consumption as a regular entertainment program. That gave the aintellects fits; they could see no rational reason for letting people buy irrational programming, and were as near as a machine can get to being dismayed when almost a million Utilitopian media subscribers flooded the system with requests for such a series of programs.

We hadn't even really tried to arrange for those million requests to happen, or at least not for *exactly* that to happen. It just grew out of the expedition permission application's being one of the major issues covered in our daily news leaflet, which had become unexpectedly popular. Every day, thousands of people went to the Bazaar to talk freely about their fury at the new regime, and went home bearing whispered stories of covered-up and censored peep excesses—and our leaflets, which were often recopied and scanned for transmission. Paper media were supposed to be insignificant—the city of Utilitopia had given up keeping track of them centuries before, because circulation was so small, but according to one report that Paul and Aimeric were able to extract in a data raid, the third most-used news source in Utilitopia was the leaflets that originated on our printer. Apparently anyone who was angry enough wanted to hear from us.

And the number of the angry was growing rapidly, with Caledony caught in a classic depression. In fewer than ten days, prices had dropped an average of thirty percent, putting one in every eight firms out of business and destroying jobs so rapidly that the unemployment insurance fund reputedly would be used up in less than a stanyear, after having accumulated for generations. All those shocked and angry people who with traditional Caledon stubbornness had opposed the coup not because they disagreed with Saltini's theology but because they did not see why rational persuasion alone would not have sufficed—and who saw the new order dawn with unprecedented economic disaster—were rapidly discovering that they had been secret liberals all along. Thorwald even got a friendly letter from his parents, and Margaret ended up having a long, warm conversation with her mother, who defied the injunction and commed her.

Thus, where ordinarily most Caledons would have regarded a petition for permission to rent equipment for a camping trip—or to record and produce media programming about it—as absolutely irrational and of no interest to them, the fact that Saltini was saying no to a potentially profit-making enterprise that apparently harmed no one made it all into a grand cause. It wasn't safe to attack doctrine and say that the necessities of life could be produced so cheaply that people should simply receive them free while the Connect Depression lasted, or to attack Saltini's policies and argue that if there wasn't enough work for people then unemployment should be shifted onto robots even at a further cost in lost efficiency, let alone to actually say that using people to do robot work was silly. Any voicing of such ideas, especially to a crowd in public, was good for a trip to jail, and although the PPP had had to release the first wave of political prisoners fairly quickly because they had flooded the prison system, after all it only took a few standays to grow more prisons, and now the peeps were able to lock up as many people as they wanted.

But to say that Inessentialism was a recognized school of thought, and that this particular Inessential activity would do no one any harm and would probably finance itself, and that therefore it was crazy of the regime to say no, was to oppose the regime on perfectly legal grounds, ones that could be defended to the hilt as rational.

So Saltini and the PPP kept objecting, and people kept lining up in our favor mostly *because* the regime objected, and as a not-surprising consequence, a million households were persuaded that they actually wanted to see the program. At that point the aintellects decided it was just one of those inexplicable pleasures that human beings insisted on indulging in, and reversed themselves, leaving Saltini little choice but to give in.

Thorwald ticked it off that night at the victory party, as we all took a break from singing so that everyone could get more to drink. "First of all, we've demonstrated a procedure that can force the Saltini regime to do things they don't want to do, and right now any situation in which they aren't completely in control is major progress. On top of that, we've established a major precedent for the General Consultancy to follow in the future, so that the law and tradition have been pulled a little more in our direction. And finally, we've established that it's possible to oppose the regime publicly and stay out of jail. At this point, I don't believe I actually care about going camping anymore; I'm already so happy that we've won so much—"

I was surprised when Paul said, "Well, I didn't care much originally—it was just a harassment issue—but now I really want to go on the trip, and I think even the people who just want to look over our shoulders *do* want us to go now. I think we accidentally stumbled on something people really did want, even if they didn't know they wanted it."

"What did they want?" I asked.

"Well, do you realize most Utilitopians have never been out of Utilitopia, for example?" Paul leaned back against the bar. "And Utilitopia is not really a highly varied place— there's the hills and the valleys, the waterfront side and the mountain side, and that's about all. It doesn't really have 'neighborhoods' or 'districts' per se, the way that cities in Nou Occitan or St. Michael do. So they've either been in the same place all their lives, or gone to the little towns up and down the coast that look like broken-off chunks of Utilitopia, or maybe they've been over to Sodom, Babylon, Gomorrah, or Nineveh. That's it. Otherwise there has never been any variety of environment. For that matter, the trip out to Bruce's place a few days ago was the first time in years I had gone beyond the city limits, and the very first time I had ever passed through Sodom Gap. I had a hard time believing that anything I saw was real!" He was beginning to gesture excitedly. "All right, now, I know people say I always talk like a calculating businessman, but do you see what this means? There's some kind of human need for visual or environmental variety, and if we can find a way to supply the need—"

"We could be richer than God," Thorwald said, trying hard to appear casual while blaspheming. He wasn't very good at it just yet.

Paul winced but grinned. "Yeah. Of course, there's this major problem that so many of the aintellects think that any pleasure they can't trace back to a full stomach, a good orgasm, or regular church attendance is highly suspect. But with the success we've had in persuading them that there are previously unconsidered forms of human pleasure, we may well be able to bring them around to it."

Margaret scratched her head. "Paul, I think you might be the most revolutionary of all of us. Doesn't that get very close to abolishing deciding which pleasures are rational, and which are not?"

"It does indeed," Carruthers said, coming up behind us. From the way Thorwald started, I could see that his career as a blasphemer would be developing slowly; he seemed to be reacting as if what he had said a minute ago was hanging around in the air like old flatulence.

There was a tense little pause, and then Carruthers added, "And I don't think that's entirely a bad thing. Giraut, you would not be familiar with it, I think, since you've only begun to study Reason, but in fact there are just under one hundred forbidden theorems in our mathematical theology, all of which are demonstrations that one axiom can be brought into conflict with another. It's part of the basic creed that somehow those contradictions are resolved within the Mind of God, and in fact the forbidden theorems, at least until recently, were one of the major causes of ministers electing to leave the pastorate. Well, nearly every significant one—forbidden theorems eight, twelve, thirteen, thirty, and forty-two, if memory serves—involves exactly the problem of rational pursuit of irrational pleasure."

"And by 'significant' you mean—?"

"Significant as a source of dissension and heresy. A question the Church has historically not had a good answer for." He smiled at all of us. "My, the things that cross one's lips once one embarks on a course of dissent, however unwillingly."

Thorwald flushed but I don't think Carruthers noticed.

The old minister went on. "So if I were placing a wager, it would be that if the General Consultancy loosens up on the issue of irrational pleasures it will actually just shift the grounds of controversy, rather than trigger a wholesale overthrow." His eyes twinkled. "And a good thing, too, because I'd certainly hate to have to learn a whole new theology at my age." With a final warm smile—I was finding it harder and harder to reconcile Carruthers now, not only with Aimeric's account of him years ago, but even with the way I had seen him when I had first arrived—he wandered off to talk to Shan, who seemed to be enjoying some sort of elaborate story Prescott Diligence was telling.

"The world is getting inexplicable," Aimeric said, with a sigh. "So you're going, Paul?"

"Yap. For one thing I'm the promoter—all those specialized cats are leased to me, and I have to make sure property I'm responsible for doesn't get damaged. For another, well, I already said I'd just like to see the other side of the hill. I wouldn't think you or Giraut would have trouble understanding that."

Aimeric ignored the teasing and asked, very seriously and pointedly, "You aren't worried about what might happen while you're gone?"

Paul shrugged. "I'm in business. My interest in liberty is in making money off it, or in enjoying it for myself. I get into politics only when I'm shoved in." It was almost funny—it seemed almost a parody of a few hardshelled Caledon capitalists I'd met at receptions and while out doing interviews to get data for Aimeric—and yet it wasn't, because I saw as he said it that he didn't just believe it to be true, he regarded it as part of himself like his eye color or his height. I was looking at a man not yet twenty who knew exactly who and what he was, and what that implied about his course through life—and it occurred to me that I had seldom seen a man, or a grown person, not yet twenty. Certainly I had never been one. While the rest of us looked for who we were, Paul had found it and gotten started.

The twinge of jealousy I felt was inexcusable, so I forced my attention back into the conversation. Paul was being, I thought, unnecessarily apologetic for the narrowness of his focus, but he seemed to need to say it, so we all listened as he wound down, and then Aimeric turned to Thorwald and said, "So, will you be going?"

He didn't hesitate. "I've got to stay."

I was not sure what Aimeric was interested in, but he seemed very intent on something. He glanced at Margaret, and she said, "I want to go. I'll have to think about whether or not I can afford to do it."

There was a long silence before Aimeric said, "Giraut?"

"*Companhon*, I'm not sure why you are taking this little poll, but you know me well enough to know that if time and duty permit I'd be delighted to have the chance—the notion of crossing so many kilometers of virgin territory, especially land that has truly gone wild since no one has planned the wildlife for it . . . I would regret not going very much. But it also occurs to me that I am not really here as a tourist, there is duty to be considered both to all of you, and to the Council of Humanity, and that must determine my answer. Now,

Aimeric, would you mind telling us why this question is so urgent for you? Are you hoping to get a cheap seat at the last minute for the trip?"

He smiled a bit at the joke, but when he spoke his face was still serious. "*Companho, m'es vis* we may have been had. There was really no reason why Saltini could not have simply declared that all those petitions on our behalf amounted to a prima facie case that there was a mass epidemic of irrationality. Then he could have simply declared martial law and thrown everyone in jail except Giraut, me, and Bieris. So I started thinking about what Saltini and his merry band could be up to in granting this request."

"There's a way it could hurt us?" Thorwald asked. He seemed to have trouble believing it.

"Maybe. It all depends on how smart they are, and how lucky. But we shouldn't forget that at least at present they have a good deal of control over their luck, because they're the ones who set the timetables—so far we're mostly just re-acting to what they do. So, if they are smart enough, they can *make* themselves lucky."

All around us the party still swirled in a confusion of happy chatter, clinking glasses, and bursts of music; yet now the room seemed cooler and smaller, and everyone in the celebrating crowd seemed far away, as if an icy fog had crept out of the stones and filled the room, muffling the sounds, killing the smells of food and wine, and dulling the colors.

Our little cluster of people had fallen silent, and after a long breath or two Aimeric said, "I seem to have killed our party. And it's possible that I'm wrong. Can we all sneak off to a side room, perhaps to the private kitchen, for a quick conference? If I'm wrong and you convince me I am, we'll have that much more to celebrate; if I'm right we should probably decide what to do about it."

There wasn't really any such thing as sneaking to the private kitchen, because somehow or other the five of us had become known as "The Committee"—of what or for what wasn't clear to me at all—and there was some kind of belief among all of them that whatever The Committee did was always something vital, so the fact that we were all disappearing together convinced a third of them that some new crisis was in the offing, another third that we were about to go make the next set of plans for the revolution—and when had there gotten to be this belief that there was going to be one, let alone that our little group was planning it? I only hoped that the rumors didn't get all of us jailed—and the last third that we were headed off to a somehow better private party (as if someplace in the Center we had an entirely different set of friends who were somehow superior and that no one had ever met). So as we left, nodding politely to everyone, we triggered a buzz of conversation that rose to a roar as I closed the door behind us. Margaret rolled her eyes at me, and I gave her a quick, one-armed hug; we had both gotten tired of the rumors that began flying every time me and my three Caledon employees got together to discuss the problem of cleaning some of the big sleeping areas, or what should be served at a party, or whether or not there was enough enthusiasm for Occitan Social Dance to add another section of it.

She and I followed the others, hand in hand. It seemed to me strange that a few weeks before I had believed the Center could function without someone like her—or for that matter that I could.

The silly attention focused on "The Committee" had a positive side. People were afraid to interrupt us whenever we all went to the private kitchen; they seemed to think it was the Top Secret Conference Room, when in fact it was simply a place with enough chairs, lots of sunlight in the mornings, and cocoa and coffee available.

We closed the doors, got comfortable, and all looked at Aimeric. Without prelude or warmup, he began:

"The whole key to it, if I'm right, is to try to look at it from the viewpoint of the peeps. Suppose they don't allow the expedition to the west coast. Then, in the first place, they keep the opposition going by letting us organize around an issue that the General Consultancy has already declared to be rational, and in the second place they let us keep winning rulings that will be useful in future cases. They look increas-

ingly unreasonable, because it really *is* a small request, and
finally it all happens right here in Utilitopia; the Center is the
most noticeable building in the waterfront area, and every
Utilitopian who passes through this part of town is going to
be reminded of the issue. So the longer they keep it alive, the
worse for them.

"Now, suppose they let us make the trip. First of all, it cools
off the hottest issue we have, and *companho*, you are surely
aware that it will take us considerable time to find another one
and build it up. Moreover, at exactly the time when we need
to be launching the new campaigns, some of our key people
will be on the other side of the continent. And that brings me
to the second point, the important one, which is that they've
now given themselves a twenty-day window—more than
twenty-three standays—in which they can do something without our being able to react effectively. Especially because our
more prominent members—prominent in the media, I mean—
will be exactly the ones on the expedition. That opportunity
for sowing confusion in our ranks is, well, exactly why I think
they agreed to it. In fact, I would bet that the reason why they
resisted so much was merely to set the hook; now we've
fought so long and so much for this peripheral issue that the
expedition can't *not* go. We're stuck—they know exactly when
they can do something big and we won't be able to give them
much of an effective fight—and so, to repeat, *companho, m'es
vis*, we've been had." He leaned back in his chair and looked
around the room, pausing to make eye contact with each of us.
"Now will someone please talk me out of that suspicion?"

Thorwald cleared his throat; he was drawing some invisible picture with his finger on the table, and did not look up
as he spoke. How had such a young man gotten to look so
mature so quickly? He looked too old to be a jovent, back
home . . . come to think of it, I caught a glimpse of myself
in the mirror, and so did I. He cleared his throat again,
seemed about to speak, then sighed. "Well, it's an obvious
point, but I can think of most of the answers to it very easily.
After all, the expedition will be taking along full media facilities—in fact there will be two paid staff positions operating

cameras, recording equipment, and the uplink to the satellites. So it should be perfectly possible for anyone on the expedition to make an immediate statement. The problem, obviously, is that since Saltini can physically seize control of the media and com links to the expedition, he can keep the people on the expedition from knowing anything that's going on, and he can keep the media from putting out statements from anyone on the expedition. Someone here in Utilitopia can always go over to the Bazaar, and start handing out leaflets or set up a podium and make a speech, but anyone on that expedition is completely dependent on Saltini's tolerance to be able to communicate."

Aimeric made a face. "And for that matter, one way to divert attention from events in Utilitopia would be to keep the expedition from knowing anything about them, and devote a lot of media time, including both the volume of headlines in the surface channels and the length of pieces in the depth channels, to 'happy news' from the expedition. That way even if they've got the whole movement in Utilitopia locked up incommunicado without bail, to the average viewer it would appear that civil liberties are still in force."

"Well, then," Margaret said calmly, "we've really only got two little problems to solve; it's not that big a matter, Aimeric, even though it's important."

One of his eyebrows crept upward, but he gestured for her to go ahead.

"Well, look, we need two things. We need a private way, that Saltini doesn't control, to com the expedition, with some kind of 'dead man' arrangement so that if everyone here is jailed the expedition will know something is up. And we need some way for the expedition to get a public statement back to Utilitopia so that the peeps can't get away with the things Aimeric is talking about. Solve those two problems and we not only don't have to worry about the PPP—we may even have the advantage of surprise and be able to hit them with something they aren't expecting."

Aimeric looked a little more hopeful, but he held up his

hands as if balancing weights in them. "You're right, and it might be a major opportunity ... but it would have to *work*."

"That applies to anything," Paul pointed out. "And as you say, we're going to have to go through with this expedition anyway. At least I feel better knowing we might have a couple of cards up our sleeves, to match the ones Saltini's got."

There was a knock at the door. I got up, opened it, and Ambassador Shan and Reverend Carruthers came in. *Now* the rumors would really start, I supposed, but then for once there was a gram or two of truth in them. As I closed the door, Carruthers said, "I think we have something important to discuss, friends."

Aimeric sighed. "Seems to be the night for it. You tell us your ideas, we'll tell you ours, and then we can all be depressed together."

Shan seemed to allow himself a trace of a smile. "Oh, I don't think you'll be depressed by this news. Rather the contrary. May I sit?"

Embarrassed, we all said yes at once; Caledons never asked, and neither did Occitans, the former because it would be irrational for anyone else to have a preference about the matter and the latter because that sort of petty concern for others' feelings was quite possibly effeminate and in any case *ne gens*. I've since learned that makes both cultures rude by the standards of most others.

"To give you a brief explanation of why I haven't been able to speak of or do anything about this before," Shan said, once he'd settled in and accepted a cup of cocoa from Thorwald, "I should probably tell you a bit about the relations between the Council of Humanity, its Ambassadors, and the Thousand Cultures generally. Understand first of all that the inner sphere of worlds—Earth itself, Dunant and Passy in the Centauri system, and Cremer, Ducommun, and Gobat—have almost ninety percent of the actual human population and about four hundred of its cultures. That's just six out of thirty-one planets, and if any of them were to rupture with the Council, we'd be deeply in trouble. Now, unfortunately, it happens that they had more than their share of peculiar founding cultures, and although they interbred more than the other Thousand Cultures, they had far more contact with each other as well, and unlike the situation out here in the frontier—I know you've been peaceably settled for almost as long as the core worlds, and you are quite as advanced and urbanized, but from the Council's viewpoint you are a frontier world in that you are far away and have low populations—well, I've delayed saying it as long as I can. There are a very large number of potentially explosive traditional hatreds in the inner sphere. That was one reason why priority was placed on getting springer contact with the Aurigan frontier worlds—the chain of isolated systems leading out to Theta Ursa Major—before we turned our efforts to getting springer contact out here, on the Bootes-Hercules frontier. It so happened that Thorburg was in the Pollux system, Chaka Home on Theta Ursa Major itself, and New Parris Island in the Capella system, and we needed to make sure that the military cultures were available to the Council to keep order if need be. Especially since, to put it bluntly, you had so many of the more offensive religious and cultural groups out here.

"Now, the way we were able to get a Council with enough teeth to prevent internecine warfare among the Thousand Cultures was that we did some classic deal-making, some of which we knew we'd regret later. So in addition to the cultures themselves, there are representatives from the most heavily inhabited worlds who hold permanent cabinet seats on the Council and who—just like the old UN system, I'm afraid—also have veto powers. And *their* biggest concern is that no matter how much trouble is happening out on the frontier, local cultural rights not be trampled on, because that might create a precedent for other cultures to try to get the Council to endorse their traditional positions, and perhaps even to force unwanted things onto their neighbors. So I've had to operate under very strict regulations in what I can and can't do here.

"Opposing that has been the fact that we also cannot allow a culture, once it has made contact, to drift out of our influence and control—for exactly the same reasons we can't trample on their rights. So when it has been possible to do so, we have been perfectly willing to treat a culture's original charter as a binding contract, and to enforce upon them various things they did not wish to do, in order to prevent their becoming an isolated pariah among the Thousand Cultures.

"Now, it so happens that I have been petitioning the Council of Humanity, ever since I got some idea of the situation here, to allow me a certain latitude in interpreting the original charter of Caledony, and in enforcing it. This has been because, to put it bluntly, the traditional Caledon culture was very likely to be painfully annoying to many of the Thousand Cultures, and given its obnoxiousness, it seemed best if it were severely weakened at home. Thus if liberalizing tendencies were encouraged in it, it might become easier to deal with for everyone concerned. I stress, because I think honesty is most likely to get the response I want, that the Council does not really *care* about civil liberties here—there are plenty of cultures that are far more oppressive that we leave alone. What we do care about is the need for every culture to have a basic tolerance of the other cultures, and that no culture be likely to turn messianic or millennial. In short, we don't want the Saltini regime to fall because they are a repressive dictatorship, but because they are a gang of stubborn bigots of the kind likely to ignite conflict elsewhere."

He looked around the room and saw that everyone was nodding and no one seemed to be terribly upset. "Oddly enough, I tell you these harsh, blunt truths because I like all of you. I want to make sure that you do not think the Council of Humanity is about to solve your problems for you; we will be intervening on your side in the next few days, but we will not necessarily always do that, even though there may be times in the future when morally the case might be far stronger. So do not count on any such thing to happen more than just this one time, and do not plan on any backing beyond what I'm about to tell you.

"It so happens that in the original Charter, drafted by Queroza, there is a provision about 'maximizing the welfare of individual citizens.' What Queroza actually meant by that, one of your theologians might be able to tell you, but the question is irrelevant to the Council. The important thing is that *we* are able to interpret it to mean that Saltini will not be able to solve his economic problems by disemploying a large number of people, cutting them off from their salaries, and thus lowering consumption and cutting back on the demand for imports. We're going to force him to either begin a massive social welfare program, or face the loss of the Charter."

There was a dead silence, until Paul gave a long, low whistle. "So either he jumps through exactly the hoops you order him to, out in public, or else you just seize power outright here?"

"One or the other," Shan said, the smile never leaving his mouth or reaching his eyes. "With a bit of luck we can get all but the most extreme stiffnecks convinced that intransigence won't work. Of course, along the way, it removes the whole *raison d'être* for the Saltini regime, which will very likely fall, since it's only staying on top by force. And any new regime will almost certainly have to cut some sort of deal with the opposition ... we have a number of suggestions, including that representation of congregations be proportional to population ..."

"Which would mean Clarity's congregation would dominate the Council of Rationalizers," Carruthers pointed out.

Aimeric nodded. "Just out of curiosity, would Saltini have known that you'd won your case?"

"He'd have found out the same time we did at the Embassy, since the issue was being fought out as a suit in a Council of Humanity court, and the decision would have been sent to all parties at the same time."

"What time was that?" Aimeric seemed almost ready to spring from his seat.

"Let me think—we got the message at fourteen o'clock—"

Aimeric snapped his fingers. "We've got it, then. They granted the request for the expedition at half past fifteen." He looked around at our baffled expressions, and then said, "Don't you see it? We have the missing part of the puzzle. We know what it is he wants to get our leadership scattered and mostly out-of-town for. When he goes to comply with that order, the public outcry is going to be tremendous—and with us on the sidelines it will all be from his diehard supporters. If he manages it right, he'll be able to claim almost unanimous support for himself—and if I remember the rules right from the nobility cases in Nou Occitan, if popular support for his position is close enough to unanimous—"

Shan stared at him, baffled. "Well, yes, then he could get the order rescinded. But one of the reasons we waited to bring this in front of a judge was to make sure that there was a sizable, strong opposition waiting in the wings—"

Aimeric shook his head. "If it works the way Saltini has planned, the opposition will be locked up in the dressing room. Margaret, you were absolutely right; we've got to come up with some kind of back channel communication between the expedition and our people here. Otherwise Saltini is going to make himself into the heroic defender of Caledon independence—and be in power forever."

FIVE

By the time we set out on the expedition, there were actually three separate ways for them to contact us, and two for us to contact them. We hoped that would be enough. We had subscribed to a remote voice line out of St. Michael, so that theoretically they could com us voice only, or we them, via Novarkhangel. Because I was a Council of Humanity employee, Shan had a pretext for installing a direct voice link to the Embassy on the cat I would be driving. Finally, we had a secret account for a widecast video antenna on a synchronous satellite over the proper area; the service was normally used by the more remote farms in Nineveh and Gomorrah for access to media programming, but we were able to rent an unused channel and get a scramble permit for it, and the footprint of the broadcast was wide enough to reach most of the way to the Pessimals.

We hadn't been able to find any decent covert way to secure video, stereovisual, or holovideo channels either for reception or transmission, but at least if Saltini shut down the legitimate channels we'd be able to get public statements made, even if not with pictures of us making them. We had to hope that would be enough.

Although we had loaded up all four cats the previous night, we had decided to wait for Morning Storm to clear, and thus give everyone at the Center time to have breakfast with each other and to suffer the inevitable dozen attacks of "I almost forgot's." There were either twenty-seven or twenty-eight of us, depending on how you counted Valerie/Betsy. Margaret had vacillated for days and finally decided that she'd rather go.

Paul really had to go and wasn't going to miss it anyway, and Thorwald probably wouldn't have gone under any circumstances—the idea didn't interest him except as a convenient stick to beat the peeps with. Aimeric had shrugged and said he wouldn't go on this trip but he expected to be in Caledony for a while; gossip was in part that he didn't want to go without Clarity Peterborough, and she was still under house arrest.

In many ways the biggest surprise was that Bieris was *not* going, but she apparently had a new series of paintings she wanted to complete first, and so she would be staying back in Sodom Basin.

Finally, we got everyone out into the street, as the sun came out and the last of the icy water was running off the Center. As long as I stayed there I never got tired of the sight of the graceful convolutions of the Center covered with the clear water, shining off of corners and diffracting little spectra everywhere, against the abrupt burst of amazing deep blue that marked the end of Morning Storm whenever a strong enough wind blew in. I drew deep lungfuls of the tangy, freezing air and found myself thinking that this was the first time I'd started a trip out into the woods without a hangover since . . . well, since I'd lived with my parents. And there really hadn't been enough trips to the woods when I had lived in the Quartier.

"Bring 'em back alive, Olde Woodes Hande," Aimeric said, dropping an arm around my shoulders and giving me an unexpectedly hard hug.

"I'll do my best, yap," I said.

"What a great crowd," Thorwald said. "Anyone would think you were setting out for an unexplored planet."

He was right; friends and families brought the crowd around the cats, each of them emblazoned with "PAUL PARTON'S OUTFITTERS AND EXPEDITION SERVICE" in bright blue on its visibility orange surface (color theory was still a bit hard to get across to a Caledon, like wine appreciation to a teetotaler who had just become alcoholic). There was a lot of hugging and good-natured joking going on, and sometimes people would laugh a little too hard, as if they were a bit nervous or jealous. "This means more to Caledons than even the Caledons are willing to admit," I said, suddenly, before wondering whether I might give offense.

Apparently none was taken. "It's something that we're doing just because it's happy and fun," Thorwald said. "It's Inessential and no matter what happens, now that the Inessentialism is an allowed tendency, there's some hope that there will be something more to life than work and prayer and reason. I look at this and I think, we've already won. Look at the kids running and playing around the cats, and the banners, and the flags flying from those cats. Those children will remember this all their lives, and nobody's going to be able to tell them that they were attached to the wrong values, or that mere appearances don't matter. I wonder if Saltini knows he's already lost? From here on, it's all what Major Ironhand would call 'mopping up.' "

I wasn't sure he was right, but I wouldn't have questioned or argued with him then for anything. I had a funny split vision, for one part of me could see that this impromptu parade—four vehicles that normally would have been hauling intercity passengers, or furniture, or bread, painted in gaudy colors, decked with crude clashing pennants, with a bunch of people in cold-weather workclothes around them was small and almost squalid in the ugly gray streets of Utilitopia. But while my Occitan vision was undimmed, my Caledon vision could see the same street shining with fresh meltwater, and the bright colors thrown defiantly against the grays and pastels, and the bold laughter of youth, of people who would no longer be told what to enjoy, or why, or how much. I chose to see it in the Caledon way.

Margaret, beside me, suddenly shrieked and waved. "Garsenda!"

She was coming up the street in a long, fur-trimmed cape, which swung open to reveal a matching purple costume, a soft baggy affair with a darker vest and billowing pants that hung down over the black kneehigh boots they tucked into. I noted a stir around me; the garment was so clearly an Occitan styling of Caledon clothing, and yet with her black hair flying out behind her and the whole soft composition ruffling and folding in the wind I had to admit that it was spectacular.

A spontaneous round of applause burst around me. *"Bella, donzelha, trop bella!"* Aimeric shouted.

Garsenda grinned in a way that I would once have thought oddly mannish, and dropped a small curtsy, carefully keeping the cape out of the soggy street. People turned back to their conversations, but I noticed they kept stealing glances at her.

"Companhona," Margaret said, "I'm so glad you had time to come by, but there are two questions I've *got* to ask you. Where in God's name did you get such beautiful clothing, and do you think I could get something like it for myself?"

Garsenda smiled and tossed her hair; a few months ago I'd have been captivated, but I very much doubted she'd have done anything so informal and so boyish in my presence. "Maggie, there's a whole collection now available through the Occitan booth at the Bazaar. It turns out that some of the most popular young Interstellar designers decided to try to design just from Giraut's written descriptions. Believe it or not, by Occitan standards this is very simple and plain; I don't think they could quite believe what they were being told. Since I've got your sizes, if you'll permit me I'll just put in an order for the pattern and have them make it up so it's waiting when you get back—my gift to you."

"Oh, nop, nop, that's too much for—"

"Oh, goodness, I still don't understand Reason," Garsenda said, winking at me over Margaret's shoulder. "Especially not an ugly word like 'nop.' Especially not from someone who's made me so welcome here."

"You're going back?" Margaret asked; it looked like Garsenda had successfully distracted her, anyway.

"For a couple of dozen standays. Business is so brisk that I'll be going back and forth for ages; the Caledon trade turns out to be the royal road to riches, and I'm beginning to find I like being rich, especially when you consider what I have to do to get rich this way, and what I would have had to do to get rich by marrying it." She smiled. "Don't worry, Mag, we'll see each other many times again. Now take your gift like a *companhona*, not like a stiffneck."

As I was thinking, wondering how the word "companhona" had so quickly become acceptable for adult women, the two of them hugged, and Garsenda went on to explain, "Besides, I'm making a couple of speeches as soon as I get out of the springer in Noupeitau. There are several big support demonstrations going on for the movement here, and I'm supposed to go speak to them. Occitans haven't changed *that* much—if I don't look absolutely stunning, *tropa zenzata*, they won't listen at all. And there's so much to tell them . . . oh, well, we all have to get going. I'll be in Noupeitau in three hours; isn't that strange?" She turned to me. "Any messages for home?"

I grinned. "Love to Pertz and to any other old friend you see; tell Marcabru the challenge I sent him was an understatement and that I want revenge because his mother gave her pubic lice to my best hunting dog. And—uh—those poor jovents I cut down in Entrepot—"

"Don't you dare apologize! You *made* their social careers!" Her deep blue eyes twinkled; how could I have spent so much time with her and never known her? "I'm getting presented at Court when I get back; I'll give Marcabru his message out in public. Anything to say to Queen Idiot?"

I shook my head. "I don't think it's Yseut's fault that her *entendedor* is a rude, drunken fool, or that he probably only wanted her because of his mama's-boy mammary fixation. So I have no grudge against her."

"I'll be sure to quote you exactly," Garsenda said. "We wouldn't want her to think you felt any *malvolensa* toward her, so I'm sure both of them will want to hear your explanation."

Margaret and Thorwald were staring at us open-mouthed, and Aimeric broke in. "I think you're shocking our Caledons."

I was about to offer some confused explanation, but Garsenda beat me to it. "Well, then I might as well horrify you further. This is all career advancement. Giraut can't afford *not* to have a certain kind of reputation, and a blood grudge to fight out with the Prince Consort is the kind of thing that will make his reputation. It may seem silly to you, but those are the rules we live with—and at least it does tend to select against hot tempers and people who are easily rattled, which is an asset in the leadership." She grabbed my face and, before I had time to think, gave me a quick, hard kiss, not erotic at all, just a fierce sort of physical "I like you." "Now take care of yourself and get back in one piece," she said. "And when you make Prime Minister I want to be *Manjadora d'Oecon*. Maggie, keep this maniac from killing all of you. I'll see you all a few standays after you get back."

There was one more round of hugs, and she was gone, the cape and hair swirling and flying behind her.

In a few minutes, we'd actually gotten everyone in the cats who belonged there, and we were on our way slowly up the street, an impromptu parade of well-wishers running along beside and behind us. I hardly dared take my eyes from the street in front of me, for some of our enthusiasts were small children and I was afraid one would run in front of the cat; maglev treads made it possible though unpleasant to stop instantly, but you had to hit that brake hard, and right away, to do it.

As we went, doors were constantly popping open and people rushing out to wave; Margaret, beside me on the jump seat, waved back enthusiastically.

"I didn't know you'd seen that much of Garsenda," I said. "I guess since you were going to the Bazaar every day—"

"We really did spend a lot of time together." She lowered her voice so that only I could hear; Paul was sitting quite near us. "She's sort of like Val without the neurosis or the nasty aggressive streak. I really love her."

"Where is Valerie?" I asked, turning up the outside mikes a bit so that everyone could hear the crowd noise better and incidentally to mask our conversation.

"In the tail-end cat. Waving like a queen, I'm sure. With some gorgeous boy who just got lucky from the waiting list a couple of days ago. The waiting list for the expedition, I mean, not Val's waiting list. The waiting list for Val is longer but the line moves faster." There was a certain pleasurable spite in her voice.

I snickered but kept my eyes on the road. Margaret didn't look anything like an Occitan's idea of a *donzelha*, but she certainly could gossip like one. Perhaps if I'd been raised in a kinder culture, or a more hypocritical one like Caledony, I'd have been shocked, but to me it was one more thing to love about her.

"I didn't know people called you 'Maggie,' " I said.

"My family does. My mother came by the Bazaar and Garsenda picked it up from her. I used to dislike it because my family did it, and besides I've noticed you usually call us all by our full names."

"Well," I said, "Margaret is not only pretty, it's almost the same pronunciation as the Occitan 'Magritza.' "

She leaned against me, I suppose risking the lives of children in our path, but I didn't much mind. "I think whatever you call me, I'll like."

"On the other hand, if you ever call me Gary, let alone 'Raut," I said, quoting the two nicknames I seemed to have been given by name-droppers pretending to know me, "I will probably—"

"Scream," she said. "It's what I do when people call you those names. I'm afraid Caledons are natural shorteners and nicknamers; the one I really hate is 'Thorry' for Thorwald."

I had to laugh at that one myself.

There was one jarring note as we drove out of town. I was handling the second cat, behind the lead cat driven by Anna Terwilliger, who normally spent her four hours as a freight-cat driver. (I could only hope she was a better driver than poet.) I couldn't quite see why she suddenly slowed down, but I was right on top of it and managed to keep a decent interval. Anna's cat shook hard twice before I saw that she was "jigging," flinging the tracks parallel to each other, hard to the side, which after several hard yanks allowed the cat to move at almost ninety degrees to its usual direction of travel and thus straight over to the other lane. I didn't know why she was doing it, but I followed suit all the time, and a glance in the rearview showed the other cats were following as well.

Then she had enough clearance and went around into the other lane, and as I followed her I saw what the matter had been.

There were almost fifty of them chained to the lampposts, stretching their chains out to lie down in the street, with PPP cops standing around watching them. They all had signs or banners, and they shouted at us and the people following us, but all of the signs and most of the shouting were in Reason, which the extremists had taken to using exclusively, so I couldn't follow. As we went around, almost climbing onto the sidewalk to do so, I was able to spare Margaret a questioning glance, and she translated. "They say they're on hunger strike. They're unemployed, and they'd rather die than accept the 'dole' when their insurance runs out. Some of them are demanding that insurance be abolished so that 'the unfit' can die more quickly."

"Do they mean it?" We passed the last of them and I swung the cat back into its proper lane.

"I'm sure some of them do." She sighed. "And some of the

rest of them don't but will be pressed into it, now that they've made public statements like that."

"But how can they call themselves 'the unfit' if they're pious enough to die—"

Margaret sighed and shook her head. "My cousin Calvin—distant cousin, I only met him a couple of times and his parents were on bad terms with mine—lost his job ten days ago and shot himself with a hunting sluggun. It's not a sin, you know, to realize that you aren't part of God's evolutionary plan for the universe, and removing yourself before you spread your unfitness is perfectly rational. I'm sure when Calvin pulled the trigger he was certain his eyes would open on heaven. And some of the protestors outside the Embassy were carrying Calvin's last vu, holding it up to the trakcar windows as we entered and left, within a day of that; he probably had the vu taken the day before he did it."

"How can they—I mean . . ."

"They just think of it as duty, Giraut. That's all. The way we're trained you can do practically anything as long as it's your duty to God."

I nodded; the concept was as foreign to me as *enseignamen* was to her, and we had occasionally quarreled about both ideas, and I didn't want to further spoil the day by fighting. "I'm sorry we saw that."

"I'm not," Paul said, coming forward to join us. "It reminds me of the kind of human waste that we've been causing in Caledony for ages. I know I pretend to be the apolitical businessman a lot, but the reality is that like anybody who's interested in getting people together with the things they need and want, I have an agenda. I want people to get what they want, and I want them ideally to get it from me, but most of all I want them to be free to want it and to make offers to get it. Those poor stupid fanatics have been sold on the idea that what they want is the ability to give themselves little priggish congratulations over having done the right thing. They'd rather be right than happy. More importantly, they'd rather that I be right than happy and they're not about to leave the choice up to me. I say, let 'em die, and I hope it's slow and it hurts."

Margaret tensed; I thought she might have the argument with Paul that I had managed to avoid. And I had to admit that I felt nothing like Paul's passion on the subject; they seemed foolish to me, but not despicable.

Margaret, however, said nothing, and Paul could tell he had given offense, and I think had not meant to upset Margaret, so after a long, awkward moment of standing there, he returned to the back where someone was starting to sing what I had assumed was an old Occitan hiking song, though I have since heard it in many places. *"Valde retz, Valde ratz"* means "the most real things are the most sincerely imagined," to give it in bland Terstad, and it is one of the first proverbs most Occitan children learn, so that it had seemed naturally to me that, hiking through waist-high scrub pine, and envisioning the oaks that would be planted a century after our deaths, tall and covered with moss, we would sing those words.

After a long interval, Margaret said, "Sorry. Effects of upbringing."

"We none of us escape them," I said. Rather than waiting to see what we would find in the open country beyond Nineveh and before the Pessimals, I had already been making it up and writing a song about it.

Oddly, perhaps, after a day spent getting out through Nineveh Basin, the first four days were so uneventful that there was nothing much to remember of them. We fell into a rhythm of driving during Second Light and exploring our surroundings on foot during First Light. The major thing we discovered was something that could have been seen by satellite, probably had been, but no one bothered to record it. The huge visibility-orange chickens could feed on lichen, but they flourished on grain—and escaped strains of wheat and maize now covered the fields east of Nineveh. There were chickens in enormous numbers, everywhere; now and then when we would spook a flock of them, they would darken the sky with their wings.

The stream banks seemed to be ideal locations for pear trees, which gave huge, succulent grainy pears that were sweeter than anything I'd ever tasted before—perhaps the wild trees were being strongly selected for freeze resistance. In a couple of days we had all given ourselves traveller's dysentery, necessitating stops whenever the two toilets in each cat could not deal with the six or eight people, but we managed to live through it, though I think Paul at least, if he'd been given a choice during the worst of the attacks, would rather have not.

The two media people, who associated with the rest of us very little, cheerfully recorded everything, though Margaret managed to prevent their taking shots of the row of men on one side of a cat and the row of women on the other during one pear crisis.

In the evenings, there was so much driftwood in creek bottoms that it was very easy to put together the makings of a campfire, so we had one every Dark, two per day. Anna Terwilliger would recite her new poems; she'd gotten into just writing them in Reason, and for some strange reason the media people always made sure they got pictures of her speaking the poems around the fire, or in a grove of trees, or as she walked along a streambank.

I saw some of the pictures they were making, and they were sort of pretty, although Anna surely wasn't. It seemed to me that her poems were considerably improved by being in a language I didn't understand well, but since Margaret was a major enthusiast for them, I didn't say so.

I asked Margaret to explain the appeal of the things, but it seemed to turn on Reason being used in a way that Reason never had been before, which was to say that I not only didn't understand the innovation, but that I didn't even understand what made it innovative.

On the other hand, I understand perfectly why they liked to get Valerie playing and singing against the same backdrops. I heard through Paul that she had made so much from added sales of her recordings since beginning the trip that from her standpoint it was practically paid for already. She always gave Betsy a few minutes to talk politics to the media reporters, but they rarely ran any of that in the programming.

For the rest of it, I slept more, got in some hiking time, did a little bit of very light *ki hara do* sparring at every stop with a couple of students who were beginning to develop some ability, and made quiet intense love with Margaret at every opportunity. I didn't drink at all, ate heartily, slept as I hadn't since I was a child, and generally felt so good at it it didn't seem like anything could ever really be the matter.

Meanwhile, Thorwald and Aimeric had no problem in calling us directly whenever they wanted to. Saltini's people were mounting more and larger protests against the Council of Humanity, and there were now almost a hundred hunger strikers in front of the Embassy; some of our people would no longer go to leaflet the Bazaar because they could not bear the sight of some friend or relative, gaunt with hunger, deliberately dying there.

There had been four deaths so far, although all of them were technically exposure rather than starvation, and it was a rare day when the bright, sunny part of each Light in Utilitopia did not have parades carrying the photos of the martyrs. Betsy scored off them by pointing out that she had not chosen to be dead, and the quote actually got distributed. The next day when she picked up her electronic mail file it had over a thousand letters in it, most of them addressed to "Betsy the Whore, Irrational Woods Expedition" and the like. Valerie said she was angry about it, naturally, but delighted to have provoked such a response.

"I don't know about it," I said to Margaret privately later, as we were sunning ourselves on a high boulder, taking a rare opportunity to be mostly naked. "I'm worried about what's going to happen when Betsy's in a kid's body and doesn't have the wherewithal to fight back; she's been a real heroine of a martyr—*que enseingnamen!*—we couldn't have asked for a better person, but I don't want anything like that to happen to her again."

"You don't think the peeps would—"

"Not so much them as the people who sent those letters. I would bet Saltini was pretty disgusted with his own cops over the murder and rape, but once you've set up as the all-knowing dictator you've got to protect your own. But the people who sent those letters calling her ... well, we know what they said—"

Margaret nodded and stretched; I was distracted by the way her small, soft, pendulous breasts rolled on her chest. They might not be up to Occitan esthetic standards, or even Caledon ones—she had been so embarrassed by the fine hair curling around her nipples that we had made love several times before I ever saw them uncovered—but I had grown very fond of them.

She grinned at me. "Are we going to talk more depressing politics, or are you going to quit ogling me and get down to business?"

After all, to turn down any kind of polite invitation is always a bit lacking in *merce*, and often outrightly *ne gens*, and no matter how many other Occitan customs I might violate, I would never be able to bear feeling myself to be discourteous. When we had finished, and spent the required time whispering and cuddling, we got dressed and climbed down to take our turn building the campfire for the oncoming Dark.

By now, at every sunset, the sharp, high range of the Pessimals was nearer. They were tall—Nansen had only just been assembled from the solid core of its gas giant recently (by geological standards) and the tectonic plates were still only newly risen. The collision—actually, the outright overrunning of a small plate—that had produced this range had been savage, compared with the glancing blow on the other side that had formed the Optimals. Some of the higher peaks were in space for all practical purposes, and there were a couple of passes that Paul was planning future trips through that would require the cat to carry an air supply rather than rely on compressors. Moreover, between the clouds that blew in from the wet side of the Optimals, the evaporation from the inland seas, and the storms that blew in off the ocean on the other side, they received much more than their share of water, and that plus glaciers had chewed deep crevices and channels into them, so that the terrain there had to be as rugged as any human beings had ever encountered.

At the next Light, we'd be leaving the warm interior of the continent, and there would be no more sunbathing or making love outdoors for a while. I was glad we'd taken the time.

Gathering firewood was really more just a matter of cutting it; there was a wide bend in the river near camp, and a pile of driftwood from the mountain vines in the canyon up above had accumulated there. We cut a sizable batch of it into small pieces with the vibrating monomolecular saw, had the waiting robots pick up the load, and took it back to camp. One thing I would never introduce here was the Primitive Camping movement—I had used a real axe a few times, and the idea of spending hours of time and gallons of sweat to get what could be gotten in two minutes was absurd.

That Dark, just after supper, when Margaret and I had just lit the fire but people hadn't yet gathered and there was still a little reddish glow behind the blue peaks of the Pessimals, the news came through that Saltini had declared being unemployed to be proof of unfitness and announced that anyone who didn't find work would be imprisoned.

"Clever," Margaret said. "Now the hunger strikers can eat because prisoners always get meals. And at the same time he can reinforce Rational Christianity by locking up people who violate it."

"There are two or three people at the Center who will be going to jail," I said, as we sat down and watched the fire get going. "Though I don't think any of them are vital to our work."

"I wonder how they'll deal with Valerie?" Margaret said.

"I hadn't known that she was unemployed. Have they—"

"They already phoned me," Valerie said, taking a seat on a log next to us. "I go under house arrest as soon as I get back. Then I go to jail after they transfer Betsy to her new body, which will be about four more months." Her face went slack for a moment, and Betsy said with disgust, "They're putting me into the new body at the physical age of two instead of six, just so they can save six months off the process and put Valerie in jail that much sooner. I'll have to live with rotten fine motor control for years, and I can't believe how long it's going to be until I can have sex again—I suppose I could start looking for perverts." The slackness flashed across her face again. "Supposedly you won't feel the urge until the body goes through puberty." And again. "Did I mention they're also sending me through puberty again?"

Both of us laughed at that, and it was hard to tell whether it was Valerie or Betsy grinning at us. "You'll miss each other," Margaret said.

I still wasn't sure which one said, "Yes, we will."

SIX

There was no road through the pass, and the satellite surveys had only been able to tell us where it was flat, and not encumbered by the vines; there had never been any reason to remote-sense the kind of surfaces there. A couple of centuries of having the vines—some of them were thicker than a man's waist, and knotted into astonishing convolutions that reached to twice the height of the cats—had caused a great deal of gravel and loose rock to be retained on the gentler slopes, and it spattered outward, sank, slipped, and generally made difficult going for the cats. Often we took turns driving lead, switching off at every wide-enough stable spot, and the trip ceased to feel like a casual drive in the woods and much more like a real expedition. In two days we had covered about half as much ground as we had planned to cover in the first day, and we had already decided that coming back we would circle the continent southward along its beaches until we could get to a shallow, gentle river valley that would take us back into the interior.

The beginning of that Light was like all the others so far; the peaks around us suddenly flared into sunlight, golden fire bouncing off the glaciers, blocks of ice and streams of water gleaming in the sun as they fell down from the heights. The cat smelled slightly too strongly of cooking and of human bodies, for it was bitter cold down in the shadows and no one wanted to venture out, let alone open the cat up for ventilation. After a quick breakfast of cereal and eggs—I still found the local gruel a bit disgusting, but appetite was living up to its reputation as a sauce—we were on our way, Anna's cat leading.

We had tried to com the Center in Utilitopia but were unable to reach them; the message said the channel was unavailable, which could mean anything from the whole Center having been seized by the peeps to the much more probable problem that we weren't quite at the right angle for a synchronous satellite to focus its extra antenna on us, and because our communication wasn't considered urgent the com company wasn't going to reorient just to pick us up; hence any noise from our part of the world on our usual frequency was being answered by a burst of widecast to tell us that they wouldn't be talking to us.

The canyon was so narrow that although some of the peaks ahead of us were in sunlight, if you looked straight up you could still see some of the brighter stars, including the great fiery eye of Arcturus, a scant six and a half light-years away in space, an instant by springer, and a lifetime in experience. I had a couple of rhymes and an image, and was looking for a motif that fit the image so that I could work up a song about seeing Antares from the Pessimals. For once there was little gravel or loose stone, and the ledge we were running along was well-sheltered from falling rock, so that all we had to watch out for were patches of ice and snow.

My cat had just taken over second spot. We were only making about twenty kilometers per hour, but that was about as much as we'd attained since leaving flat ground, and the driving was fairly easy. I saw Anna slow down to make sure of her traction on a snow patch.

Her cat vanished. In its place there was a great, gaping

hole. A gap in the ledge, no longer bridged by its thin skin of ice and snow, yawned before us.

I must have been shouting into the mike before they hit; in fact, Anna had had her mike open, and so all of us in the other cats heard the screams and a nauseating series of thumps and thuds, the long scrape as the cat slid down one wall of the crevice on its roof with everyone aboard shrieking, and finally hysterically sobbing. I snowplowed the treads to yank my cat to a swift halt fifty meters short of the edge, grabbed the hand com from the dashboard, and burst out through the heatlock, leaving both doors open in my haste.

The lead cat had probably started bouncing along the wall within ten meters of beginning its plunge, and had come to a stop on its back about sixty meters down after its long slide. One tread was all the way off the maglevs and lay across the rocks above; the other continued to spin lazily, floating above the lifters, indicating that at least the main power system must be intact and that the Seneschal tubes were still making anti-protons to feed the generator.

"Can anyone answer me? Come in lead cat. Come on, somebody pick up the fucking com, I can hear some of you . . ."

The voice that answered was Valerie's; she and Paul had been in there, I remembered, along with the media people. "I'm scared."

"Of course you are," I said, in the voice I'd learned ages ago in Search and Rescue Club back home, before springers. "What's going on down there? We'll get you some help just as soon as we can."

She started to cry, long shrieking gasps that cut her off every time she tried to speak. That made me really afraid for the first time, perhaps just because now there was nothing to do until she could answer. "Valerie?" I said, keeping my voice level, *deu sait* how. "Valerie, speak to us? Come on, Valerie, we need to know what's going on."

Margaret was beside me now, her mouth open wide in horror, just staring at the shattered cat below us. "Keep the others back," I told her. "We don't want panics or people charging in to do anything stupid."

Give Margaret something to do and she was instantly functional again. She turned to go do as I'd asked.

"Come in, Valerie. Please respond." I could tell more voices than hers were weeping or moaning. Why hadn't a transponder activated—where were the rescue birds and why were they not here already—

Because we were on Nansen, and they had no rescuers, and no springer ambulances, and not only were we out here on our own, but there had been no channel that morning, and the equipment for our two secret channels was down there in that wrecked cat.

The realization hit me like a hard kick in a relaxed gut. I drew a long breath; this was as bad as anything had ever been. Voice level, keep talking, get someone on the line, they had said in Search and Rescue Club a million years ago, and so I simply kept saying "Valerie? . . . Anyone?"

"Giraut it's B-Betsy s-sorry I c-c-can't talk w-well f-fighting Valerie for control of her voice." The last words came out in a rush. "Trying to calm her. Uh, I think Anna is d-dead, looks l-like a broken neck. She wasn't belted in got thr-thr-thrown against the r-roof. I-we're the only ones not hurt b-bad m-media people were in b-back sounded like stuff back there shifted can't open the door there too much weight against it the other voice you can h-hear is P-Paul and I think his b-b-b-b—" There was a long, raspy breath, a sound like an asthmatic seizure, and when Betsy spoke again her command of Valerie's voice was complete. "Giraut, Paul's back is broken, maybe a kidney ruptured, certainly some internal injuries, he's in a lot of pain. I think Valerie has passed out or something, I seem to be alone in the body right now. I've gotten out the first-aid kit and put a neurostat on Paul, and the foam is forming around him right now to hold him still. We have power here and the cabin's warm."

"Keep talking, Betsy," I said, "and try to hang onto Valerie's body. I'm going to need your help."

Margaret had returned and had been listening.

"Get the rappelling gear from the tail-end cat," I told her. "I'm going to have to go down there. Bring up the cat to about here; looks like it's solid almost to the edge, and I'm going to need something to work the belay from."

Betsy's voice broke in again. "Giraut, I'm sorry, I've checked with the neuro-read, and Anna is really dead. I think besides breaking her neck the impact fractured her skull. And there's still no movement or noise from the rear cabin."

"How's Paul?" I asked. *Deu, deu,* all we had to do was get him to any modern hospital and they could have him on his feet in a week, but if he stayed here in that condition he could just as easily die—

"Blood pressure is steady but low now. Maybe just shock; the instruments don't show hemorrhage. I c-can feel Valerie stirring now; I'll t-try to keep her calm—I'm s-sorry but if I try to use neural pacifiers I might—"

"Don't even think about that," I said. "You could wipe your psypyx by accident. You're just as important as anyone else, Betsy; Valerie will just have to deal with the situation."

Back home I wouldn't have even bothered with the rappel equipment—it would have been easy enough to get down there with simple threepoint climbing, and that's what I did most of the way, but as the only experienced climber in the party, I was taking no chances. It took me a good ten minutes to reach the cat, all the same, and by the time I did Valerie was back in charge of the body, sitting on the ceiling of the upside-down cat sobbing and being completely useless. I could see her in there, but she didn't even move to help when I tried to open the outer heatlock door and found I couldn't.

The sun had probably never penetrated here, and it was unbelievably cold now that I was no longer doing hard physical work; when I got home, I promised myself, I would spend the first week sleeping in the sand on the beach by day, then taking the hottest showers I could bear, and then sleeping under a down comforter . . .

I had just worked up the meal that Margaret and I would order in Pertz's, and a few details about the backrubs we'd give each other in front of the fire in my parents' guest house, when they finally managed to get the line lowered to where I could grab it. Right now I was wishing for Johan and Rufeu and a dozen others like them from the old club.

Once I had the line, though, it was pretty simple; they passed me down the drilling equipment and I got a good, secure powered zipline running between me and them. Margaret came down, and a couple of others, with power tools, and shortly we had Valerie out of there and riding back up; from the way she shut her eyes and clutched herself into the bosun's chair, she was going to have a prize case of acrophobia for a while, but I suppose she was entitled.

Paul seemed to be stable, and in a real pinch I suppose we could have moved him—the foam had hardened and now you'd have needed a power saw to budge his shattered spine one millimeter—but until there was something better up there than we had down here, there was no reason to take chances on injuries that our limited equipment couldn't spot.

The biggest nightmare by far was the two media people, who turned out to be dead when we finally got to them; we had all gotten very lax about securing gear, and a couple of tonnes of their stuff had landed on top of them, crushing them horribly.

By the time Dark was falling, we had a couple of people sitting with Paul in case he might wake up, Valerie/Betsy under a chemical sedative, Anna and the media people lay outside the cat so that the cold could preserve their bodies— and no response at all from Utilitopia. Not even "channel unavailable." The gear for reaching the secret receiving stations was hopeless hash; Prescott Diligence, and one or two others, were slowly picking through the mess, trying to figure out what kind of transmitter we might be able to rig.

"We have plenty of power," I pointed out to Prescott as he, I, and Margaret huddled in the back of our cat that night. "And Utilitopia still uses broadcast for a lot of voice channels. Why can't we just rig up a radio transmitter and scream for help on some frequency close to a commercial station, so that people scanning through the voice frequencies are bound to pick it up."

"Because Nansen doesn't have a Heaviside layer worth speaking of," Prescott said. "Radio won't go over the horizon."

It took a long moment for that to sink in. "So you mean . . . we can't talk to them at all?"

"It looks like we're right between places where we could hail synchronous satellites," he said, with a coldness in his voice that took me a moment to place; he had been brooding about this for hours and would rather have talked about anything else. "The mountains block a lot of angles and the whole planet really only has two clusters of satellites, both over on the other side, above Utilitopia and above Novarkhangel. If we sent one cat back about one Light's journey or so, they might be able to raise one of the satellites, but chances are they'd have to go farther if they wanted to get it for sure."

I doubt anyone slept that night, but we all pretended to for each other's sake. I heard Prescott rattling and banging around in the radio gear and parts all night, and suspected he might be disturbing people in the narrow confines of the cat, but I didn't have the heart to tell him to stop.

Next morning I was glad I hadn't. He'd come up with a simple stunt that at least offered some hope. The moon was big and a good radio reflector; we knew our position, and Utilitopia's position, and we had a couple of dish antennas available. With a string of amplifiers it was possible to put out a reasonably high-powered signal to bounce off the moon as it passed through the right part of the sky every ten hours or so, on a frequency where anyone scanning between the weather and the news would be bound to run into it. The windows during which the technique would work were around twenty minutes long; shortly we had a five-minute recording giving all the necessary information put together, and a robot detailed to keep our calls for help going out. Allowing for bureaucratic inertia, within a few hours of the first message they should get an antenna swung around to us, or a temporary satellite up, so that we could work out what would have to be done.

I had too much time to think while this was going on.

Whatever I'd thought of her work, Anna Terwilliger had been these people's poet, and now she was lying under a tarp next to the smashed cat, frozen stiff. And she had been both popular and on the right side.

It was not just through dueling that the traditional Occitan culture had wasted lives. Until the springer and Central Rescue, hikers and climbers, skimmer pilots and sailplaners, had died in astonishing numbers, now that I thought of it. Serra Valor was a crowded place for a culture with a deliberately small population and only a few centuries of existence; we were the culture of the *Canso de Fis de Jovent* because we slaughtered our young, not merely by exposing them to terrible dangers, but also by teaching them to love those dangers, to seek after them, to hold themselves cheap if they did not constantly risk throwing themselves away.

Had I brought that idea here, like a virus?

I knew that if I voiced the idea around any of my Caledon friends they would tell me no, never, not at all ... and I would still wonder. I wished desperately for some offworlder, Aimeric or Bieris, or even Garsenda or Ambassador Shan, to talk the idea over with.

At last the time came for the signal. I had nothing to do with it; Prescott played the recorded message six times through, beginning early and ending late in case of errors in calculation or navigation, and the bright white moon hung in the east just as it always had, its light making the snow and ice glow and turning the folds and crevices of the raw mountains into bottomless black pools.

I carried crates and tried not to think too much about it. In case bouncing the radio signal didn't work, I had started the process of clearing out one of the three remaining cats so that it could make a dash—well, so it could hurry—down to the flat country where we could com Utilitopia. Doing that without a backup cat following would mean running a great deal of danger, we knew now.

I had volunteered to drive it as automatically as I breathed or walked, and thought grimly that there was this to be said for the Occitan tradition—we did not let our friends run our risks for us, and however *enseingnamen* might lead us into foolishness, once there it kept us from behaving like fools.

The hours crept by, Mufrid came up in its fiery yellow glory, a sleet storm battered the huddled cats and drove everyone inside, and the time neared for the next transmission. There was no response from Utilitopia.

"It could be the radio didn't work as I thought it did," Prescott said, huddled with me and Margaret, his skin a translucent white against the blazing red of his hair, dark circles under his eyes. He gulped coffee and added, "The sensors did pick it up at the right strength about two hundred meters away, but all that means is we have the right sidelobes, not that the main signal was doing what we wanted. We're going to try to get a sensor up on an extensible pole right into the main signal path this time. But it's past the middle of Second Light in Utilitopia—there won't be many people listening—the last time was much more likely to turn something up."

"You're doing great work," Margaret said. "Once you've got it established that the main signal is doing what it should, you're going to get some rest. And no, you aren't going with Giraut in the cat, and neither am I, though we'd both like to. You've got to tend the radio and somebody's got to be in some kind of charge here."

Prescott nodded gloomily. "What I'm afraid of is that we're getting through loud and clear, and that there've been big changes in Utilitopia. That they're just going to leave us out here because we don't matter anymore. If we still had the secret com and tried to contact the Center, I wonder who would answer?"

"Thorwald," I said firmly, because Prescott had voiced my own fears.

As he began transmitting, this time in bright daylight, the sun and moon came out together and two overlapping rainbows formed in the canyon above us to the west, a vividly bright one from the sun and a ghostly pale one from the blazing sliver of the moon. I stood there on the stony ledge, yet another crate of supplies straining at my arms, looking around at the immense walls of rock and ice, at the torn and battered cat below us, and at our little party, currently all outdoors shaking out bedding and trying to let enough fresh air into the two remaining cats to make them smell marginally better, and for the first time since I'd been sixteen stanyears old such a scene did not summon one line of poetry or measure of music to my mind.

SEVEN

Again, the message had brought no response after some hours, though Prescott said the main signal was even stronger than he had planned for it to be. The cat that was to go for help was almost ready, but I was so sleepy I was in no shape to drive, and in any case it made more sense to depart right at the beginning of the next Light, especially since the Moon would be waxing at the beginning of the Dark that would follow, which would extend our light by about two hours before it set in the east. So I lay down to try to get ten badly needed hours of sleep, and Susan and Robert, two of our surviving alternate drivers, did the same, though with luck we'd be down out of the mountains before either of them needed to take over.

I actually got seven hours, and then woke unable to sleep any more. Margaret was sound asleep beside me, and must have gotten into the bunk we were sharing sometime fairly recently, so I didn't disturb her, but got up and dressed and went outside for air and thought.

There were lights on in the wrecked cat, so I took the zipline down there and relieved Petra, who was sitting up with Paul. She seemed grateful, which was not surprising since the two of them had never liked each other and now that Paul had recovered consciousness, he tended to wake at odd hours and to be alternately truculent and pathetically dependent. Part of the problem was that the pain was leaking through the neurostat unpredictably, often as a ferocious itching in the immobilized parts of his body.

He was asleep when I got there but woke up shortly after, in much better spirits than I had seen him in the last couple of days. For a while we just talked of things in Utilitopia, and what meals he would order when he got to the hospital and which ones we'd have to smuggle in to him, and he joked a lot about the damage to the image of his business that this was going to cause. "Maybe I should let someone else launch the expedition and outfitting business, and instead start Paul Parton's Remote Springer Ambulance Service."

"It really might not be a bad idea," I said. "But you Caledons aren't very superstitious, and most of you won't dismiss the whole idea because of one freak accident no matter how bad it was. I don't think the idea of these trips is gone forever, and as soon as you get ambulance service and a reliable com link available, you'll be able to start running regular tours. And I'm really glad you all made psypyx recordings just before we left. With a little luck Anna will have nothing more than what feels like mild amnesia, and she'll be able to look at a lot of recordings of her last few days so that the gap will be minimal."

He grunted; Paul was used to punctuating everything he said with emphatic head motions, and every time he tried he was reminded that he was now locked in the hardened support foam. "*If* her psypyx takes. I've never seen anything like Valerie and Betsy before." We had slowly and carefully rerigged him into a reclined sitting position with appropriate spaces for bodily functions, but we hadn't set him up with any way to nod or shake his head, and it frustrated him as surely as it would an Occitan asked to talk with his hands tied down.

"Er—Giraut."

"I'm right here."

"Sorry to do this while you're here, but I really have to um, defecate. At least that's usually what it means when it feels like the backs of my shins have severe athlete's foot."

"Fine—not a problem. Just a half second—" I moved a waiting bucket under the hole in his chair. "Coming up now."

What made it humiliating for Paul was that there was a

limited override on the neurostat that let us control those functions, leaving fewer places for pain to leak through, but also giving him the odd situation of being unable to go unless someone pulled a switch for him. We usually did it a couple of times per day whether he felt the need or not; it was probably a good sign that he could feel the need in any form.

The process was not at all one of fine control. When I threw the switch he emptied completely and violently, and I was glad that he could only feel a pale ghost of the experience. The smell was overpowering as well. Probably we hadn't been giving him enough peristalsis, so I made a note and cranked that up a notch or two. "I'll drain your bladder, now, too, if it will make you more comfortable," I said.

"Sure."

I slipped the drain tube over his penis and turned on the gentle suction, then turned back to the neurostat's controls.

"Think you could get that machine to give Val lessons?" he asked.

It was so unexpected that I all but fell over laughing, then said, "It might be easier to teach Betsy, and let Valerie profit by her experience."

He snorted agreement. "Unfortunately they have a deal. Valerie runs the body with me, Betsy with everyone else." Rumor had it that that second part wasn't true at all, but I saw no reason to mention that to Paul. "And they both claim they never peek. Okay, Giraut, let 'er rip."

I tripped the switch and an astonishing quantity of urine vanished up the tube; he must have really been sucking down a lot from his drinking tube. I refilled the reservoir there while he finished—"At the moment I seem to be mostly a device for contaminating water," he commented—and then when he was done set about the job of cleaning up.

A little bit from the bucket went into the medkit's stool analyzer, and the rest I flushed down the toilet we'd taken from the now upside-down water closet and gotten working again; there was a soft splashing as the water recycled, and the quiet thud of the sanitized block dropping into the hopper.

Of course what he had really been embarrassed about,

other perhaps than my having to handle his penis, was that I now had to douche out his rectum and clean his anus. It wasn't such a terrible job, really, but I could imagine how he must feel about it. As I was doing it—the angle was very awkward, so I ended up with my face closer to it than either of us might have chosen—Paul spoke again. "Giraut?"

"Right here, *companhon*."

"I'm really glad you came to Caledony. Even with everything that's happened." I thought for a while that he had fallen asleep after saying that, and finished wiping and cleaning and started to dry him off, but then he said, "We were headed for much worse things than this. Saltini would have taken over eventually and when he did there'd have been no escape, not even any thought of resistance. Most of us would have just killed ourselves as unfit." He gave a long sigh. "God, that's better. You wouldn't think ordinary discomfort could leak through the neurostat so much more than the real pain, but it does. You'll see, anyway. Anna will come right back from the psypyx, and they'll have me up and walking in no time."

I wasn't sure about the former, and if we didn't get help soon there might be degeneration so that his spine simply wouldn't regrow as well as it should, but I didn't argue with him. I finished drying him off carefully.

"Giraut?"

"Yap."

"Why doesn't Valerie come down and visit?"

The real reason was because she was lying under chemical sedation up in one of the cats; once a day we gave her a scrubber to wake her up, and to give Betsy a chance to work a fully operational brain, but within an hour or two Valerie was always back in hysterics and we had to shut her back down.

"Valerie patched you up after the wreck," I pointed out, "and some people have a hard time looking at their lovers when they're hurt." As I said it I felt myself lying. I knew that however badly Margaret might be hurt, I would never avoid her, and for that matter when Azalais, my *entendora* before Garsenda, had taken a stray hit from a neuroducer, I had stayed by her bedside constantly for the first few days ... badly hurt people rarely can imagine how little trouble they seem to be to those who love them.

Unfortunately Paul had a perfectly good sense of when he was being lied to, and he trusted me more than he did most of the people who had been sitting up with him. "No one will tell me, Giraut, but I know. It was Betsy that took care of me down here, wasn't it?"

I knew I would hate myself for whatever I said next, so I chose the truth and said yes.

"It doesn't matter," Paul said. "It really doesn't matter. Valerie must have been really frightened, and it's hard for her to face fear, or even just the memory of fear."

He paused for a long time; I thought about what the situation actually was, considered telling him for some perverse reason I didn't want to name, and fought the urge down. It would do no good. He would simply worry about her. And to have Paul worrying about Valerie would be just too much.

"It doesn't matter," he said again, his voice soft and far away. I think he fell back asleep about then, because his voice slurred, and he said no more after that. When I moved around to where I could watch him comfortably, there were tears on his face.

After a while somebody came down to relieve me—actually to relieve Petra—and I went back up the zipline, joined Robert and Susan in the stripped down cat, and set off down the road. There was still no word from Utilitopia; we might as well have been alone on the planet. My two relief drivers went to sleep in the back almost at once, as they were supposed to do; now there was just me, and the faint days-old tracks of the expedition, as I worked my way carefully along, making sure that we suffered no slips at all, but at the same time descended swiftly.

I hadn't covered five kilometers before I realized this job was going to be even worse than I had feared. The tracks we had left behind were often obscured, and many times the procession of four cats spinning out over a gravel bank or descending a slope of loose stone had made the surface considerably more slippery and dangerous than it had been before. Sometimes we had skated down a surface that now resisted climbing; often our climbing had done so much damage to the surface that I now could not follow the same pathway in descent, for fear of losing control. The more I saw of it, the more I had to admire Anna's driving in getting us through it in the first place—the collapse of the path under her had been the sheerest bad luck, and if skill had determined all, we'd have been perfectly safe.

Another few kilometers, and the sun rose, and I had settled more into the rhythm of things and realized that, though terrifying, it was largely controllable. Twice when I could not go over the same gravel we had come in over, I had to cross patches of snow and ice, which I first probed on foot with ultrasound, carrying a long pole in case anything should break through under me. The rock below was solid as far as could be told, though in places the ice was ten or twelve meters thick. Even so, as I would drive over the surface, keeping between the lines my footprints had made going and returning, it was hard not to hold my breath.

Even with all the problems, I was making somewhat better time on the way down than we had on the way up, and by the time Robert woke up and came forward to keep me company, I had passed the previous campsite. He tried the com but we could get nothing, not even a "channel unavailable." It was still many kilometers to the campsite we had used on our first night ascending the canyon, where there had been no problems with the com.

If the gravel slope of the bank we had to go down had not been so badly shredded by the passage of the expedition, we'd never have swung as far toward the cliffs as we did—it was dangerous because the constant melting and refreezing meant that there was a slow but steady rain of rocks from up above—after all, all that gravel and loose rock had come from somewhere. But since we had no choice, we were edging along next to the cliff when Robert very calmly said, "Stop a minute."

I did, thinking he'd seen some safety hazard; instead, he said "Look at that. What is it?"

I had had eyes only for the road, but now that he pointed I was startled myself. We had been running along a palisade of jumbled and broken rock, perhaps four times the height of the cat, that roughly paralleled the main wall of the canyon, and if I thought about it at all I simply assumed that it was the edge of a huge rock step.

But to the left, in front of us, there was an opening, and two astonishing sights. First of all, there was no mistaking the way that opening had been made—laser-cut rock simply looks different from anything that occurs naturally, even after time and the elements have had their way with it. Someone had cut a straight path through the meters-thick rock to the depression it enclosed.

And down that sharp-edged channel, there was a stone wall, twice the height of the cat, with a large arch at its center and a tower on either side of the arch, for all the world like a castle in an old picture book.

Robert and I looked at each other, trying to decide what to say. I saw his fingers dance over the keyboard as he made sure the location was recorded—the cat's inertial navigation was hardly perfect but it would at least get anyone who found the records back to somewhere near this site.

"What's going on? Why are we stopped?" Susan was coming forward from her bunk, rubbing sleep from her eyes. When she saw what was visible through the cat's front window, she gave a little gasp.

"We have a lot of distance to make yet today," I started to point out, but she and Robert were already grabbing up cameras and recorders, and clearly I wasn't going to win this argument. Besides, it would be a chance for me to uncramp a couple of muscles, and it looked like the stone was probably warmed enough by the sun for this little spot to be pleasant, at least more pleasant than where we'd been the past couple of days.

On the other side of the arch, we found the city—really no more than a small town, but something about it made you call it a city anyway. Most of the buildings clung to the walls of the natural depression, something like pictures I'd seen of Cliff Dweller houses on Old Earth, but there were a couple of long stone buildings, their roofs long since fallen in, in the middle, and a wide round basin that I suspected must have been a fountain. Susan systematically scanned the whole thing once and then turned back to me and said, "Sorry, but this was something we couldn't afford to lose. We can go now—I just had to make sure there was enough of a record to get someone back here."

We hurried back to the cat; it had only been a matter of minutes, but no matter how justified the delay, it had still been a delay. Once again, we began to pick our way down the slope as fast as possible.

"What do you suppose it is?" Robert asked.

"Maybe some crazed hermits from St. Michael?" Susan didn't sound convinced. "It seems uncomfortable enough for them. But why would they be trespassing on our continent? They've got plenty of bare rock in their own. And the way those stones had fallen in from the roof—that wasn't originally vaulted or domed. There must have been timber supports or something like that in there, and I didn't see anything."

"Which would mean?" I asked, never taking my eyes from the track ahead, but glad enough to have some distractions from the thoughts I had been alone with for hours.

"Well, maybe the supports were too valuable to leave behind, so whoever took them along. Or maybe they were made of something that decayed before we happened along."

"Nothing there has decayed for millennia," Robert objected. "It's all been frozen. The Pessimals have been losing ice since the asteroid strike, but only from high peaks and surfaces that get a lot of sun. Nothing in that little pocket valley was warmed up enough to even start to decay, especially nothing like timber. If there were clothes, or even bodies, in those houses, or caves, or whatever you call 'em, at the time of the asteroid strike, they'd still be in there, probably in decent shape."

Gravel skittered under the treads and both of them fell silent, watching as I jockeyed the machine slowly around a corner. Surely both of them had been handling cats longer—

But probably not over anything like Sodom Gap, I realized. Oh, well, if I wanted an excuse to not drive for a while I would have to say I was tired—and I wasn't.

"Of course if the supports had decayed before the planet froze . . ." Susan said, and let it hang there in the air.

"But Nansen has been frozen since—well, we think it's been frozen since it cooled down after the Faju Fakutoru Effect formed it out of the bones of a gas giant," Robert objected. "But I suppose if it wasn't always frozen—"

"You two are hinting at something," I said, "and my brain doesn't have room for puzzles right now."

"Maybe the site was old before it froze. Maybe we've found out what the source was for the bugs that pre-terraformed Nansen."

On any other occasion I might have jumped or started or something; as it stood, I kept my hands on the controls and my eyes on the road. "That would be pretty impressive, if true."

"That would blow a big hole in Selectivism," Robert pointed out. "Make lots of trouble for Saltini. Bring in thousands of offworld experts, if it really is the first nonhuman archaeological site, and I'd like to see him try to enforce Market Prayer on that many Council of Humanity employees. It's not as important, right now, as getting down to com range, but it sure could change things in Caledony."

"Change things in all of the Thousand Cultures," Susan corrected. "It's almost funny; we might have just found something humanity has been looking for for a thousand years, and unfortunately we have something much more urgent to get done. But I suppose—"

I never did find out what she supposed, because Robert let out a shout just as I snowplowed our cat to a rapid stop—no mean feat if I do say so myself, on that steep downgrade.

Coming up the trail in front of us was another cat—and one I recognized even before I was able to get a glimpse through the glare off the windshield and confirm that Bruce was driving.

◼ EIGHT ◼◼◼

"I thought four portable springers might be overkill," Bruce said, "but they pointed out I wouldn't want one that was broken when I got here, and we really needed both a big one to bring the main party home and a specialized medical one for Paul and uh, the um remains, and they're not normally field equipment and we have no one who can fix them, so I had to bring two of each. Which means I'm afraid we don't have a lot of bunk room."

He looked exhausted, and from the way Bieris hung on to me I sensed she was in terrible shape as well. "Could you run the springers in, say, eight hours, if you could sleep till then?" Susan asked.

"I probably could run them in my sleep, which seems like a magnificent idea right now," Bieris said. "These aren't locally built jury-rigs; these are standard Occitan models that the Council of Humanity brought over."

"Then you and Bruce take the bunks in our cat, I drive lead cat, Robert drives yours, and Giraut sits up with me to point out the trail. We can be back up to the camp in about eight hours, and everyone can be home in ten." Susan wasn't the type to waste words once a decision was made, so she headed for the cat we had come in.

"She's right," I said, because I saw Bruce was about to raise some fuzzy objection. "Susan and Robert both just got up after a full night's sleep less than three hours ago. And I won't be good for much else but I can certainly tell Susan where the trouble is. If Robert stays close to our tracks there should be no problem. Both of you look half dead—now get into those bunks, you can tell us what's up when we get there. How long have you been awake, anyway?"

"More than one full day," Bruce mumbled, as he staggered

toward the cat and the bunk. "A bit over one Light more or so—"

At least forty-two hours? And a rescue expedition that seemed to have been outfitted from Bruce's farm and the back door of the Embassy?

I think Susan, Robert, and I all figured out at that moment that some terrible things must have happened, but we could also see that no good would come of standing around talking about them. At least there were springers, and apparently somewhere to spring to.

As the bright blaze of the moon came up above us in the west, we started back up the trail. Susan was a good driver, good enough to know that you went faster by being cautious, so I had very little to say to her. Bruce and Bieris didn't wake or stir in the back. They had lain down almost without speaking, fully dressed on top of the covers, and been asleep before Susan and I had belted them in.

The moon climbed steadily, waxing as it went, and soon all but the brightest stars were gone. Arcturus itself was no longer impressive, but merely a red star brighter than most. I thought idly that the canyon would have made a fine subject for Bieris to paint, all silvers, blacks, and blues with the jagged edges of the rock stabbing up into the void, but no doubt if things worked out there would be time for her to come this way again, and if they did not it would not matter.

I had assumed that there would be some kind of catching up on news when we got back to the encampment, but again that was not to be. The main springer took so little time for Bieris to set up that the group was barely awake, dressed, and packed before she pronounced it ready; Bruce stepped into it and disappeared. A moment later he came back, accompanied by half a dozen CSPs—a medical team, I realized. They carried yet one more portable springer, a medical lift one— "Won't have to worry about whether the ones they carried took any damage from vibration," the officer said brusquely—and they were down the zipline to Paul in a matter of minutes.

I found myself standing around in a state of bewilderment, along with everyone else, checking for the tenth time that I had my lute and guitar and duffel bag, reminding Betsy to make sure Valerie's instruments were properly packed, carefully not looking into the crevice as the medic team uncovered the frozen corpses and sprang them ... where? No one had even told us where we were going.

Paul was already in a hospital somewhere, I realized, and I would be gone from here before I drew a hundred breaths. I looked around, maybe trying to find some image I could take with me, but all there was to see were the parked, shut-down cats, slowly cooling, the bright lights of the med team in the crevice, and the uneasy line of people. The moon shone on the rocks, and far off to the east the first glints of dawn were beginning. It was a beautiful sky, and a beautiful place, but nothing in it stirred me to compose in the old, automatic way.

The zipline whined again, and soon the medic team was back up. "Nothing more to stay for, is there?" the medic officer said. "And the springer checked out, and we've had a test trip in it. All right, then, everyone line up with your gear, and we'll send you through in batches of three or four."

I'm not sure why, but automatically I shuffled to the back of the line, and Margaret joined me there. "Bad trip?" she asked.

"Frightening. Hard work. It's hard to believe the worst is past us now."

Just ahead of us, Susan darted out of line, ran to the stripped-down cat we had descended the canyon in, and came back a moment later carrying several record blocks under her arm. "This is the stuff we took at the ruins," she said, turning to me. "Somebody's going to want it."

Then her group went in, and vanished; and the last of us except the medic team got into the springer, and the Embassy appeared around us, with Ambassador Shan himself waiting to greet us. Aimeric and Carruthers were with him.

We stepped forward into the rest of our group, and porter

robots took our stuff and carried it off somewhere. Behind us we could hear the medic team arriving.

"If you will all follow us," Ambassador Shan said, "we'll go to a meeting room where I can tell you something of what has been happening. I'm afraid a very large part of it is bad news."

There was no sound as we went down the hall; we were no fit sight for an Embassy anyway. There seemed to be an astonishing number of CSPs around, and most of them looked busy.

They gave us hot drinks—unnecessary, really, for we hadn't been hungry or cold—and had us all sit down, and when the Ambassador spoke, it seemed that he tried to leave out every word he could, to simply give us the undecorated truth.

"First of all: The Council of Humanity has dissolved the Caledon Charter and has placed the city of Utilitopia under martial law. Elements of the former government—mostly groups of PPP police—are continuing resistance in isolated pockets, but the city is in our hands and we expect to end the last resistance before sunset. The Reverend Saltini himself has been arrested and is being held offworld while awaiting trial.

"Secondly, during the outbreak of civil disorder and fighting that led to this situation, there were a great number of deaths and injuries in civilian areas—just at the moment several utility buildings are serving as temporary hospitals to accomodate the overflow, and serious cases, including your friend Paul Parton, have been sprung to the facilities at Novarkhangel in the culture of St. Michael, where they are being given the best possible care. A few critically injured patients, and some victims of neural abuse, are in Noupeitau, where physicians with a more extensive experience with both whole body and neural trauma are available. In a few moments we'll make com lines available for you to try to contact your friends and families, and we'll give you every assistance we can with that.

"Finally, I must tell you with a heavy heart that the disorders began with a physical attack by an armed mob on the Center for Occitan Arts. The building was virtually gutted, and in the fighting there Thorwald Spenders was killed while preventing the mob from attacking people who had taken shelter in the Center.

"Moreover, one of the several crimes the Reverend Saltini is charged with is that, during his last hours in office, he ordered PPP agents to seize the personality preservation records at several insurance companies, and deliberately destroyed all copies of many personalities which had been connected with the opposition movement. Among the personalities apparently lost permanently are Thorwald Spenders and Anna K. Terwilliger."

"They're dead," Margaret said beside me. "Really *really* dead."

It seemed to take many ages for us to learn the full story. Partly it was because I was very short on sleep and so didn't always grasp things readily, and partly it was because there were things I did not really want to hear.

There had been perhaps ten people inside the Center who were supposed to be arrested for being unemployed. Thorwald, probably because the authorities had not touched the Center yet, had tried to give them sanctuary.

The PPP had used that, in turn, as a cause to stir up anger at "meddling offworlders," and to surround the Center with protestors, so that every cat or trakcar pulling in or out was greeted with a shower of rocks and bottles. Supposedly for the protection of the Center, the PPP had set up riot lines, but people Saltini approved of crossed them freely, and they seemed to be much more interested in identifying everyone coming or going. A couple of routine food shipments were deliberately torn up and left in the mud by PPP guards, and the Center received a whopping fine for "poor sanitary practices."

The crowds grew almost by the hour; even during Morning Storm, they hardly seemed to diminish. At first they had taunted and shouted; then they had thrown stones; during the last Light, according to people who had been in the Center with Thorwald, they had barely spoken at all, and did not move, until someone would try to drive into or out of the Center. Then they would close in, pushing and shoving against the cat or the trakcar, until very, very slowly the PPP guards would stroll over and clear a path.

People said their faces were contorted with hate, and a weird hunger that reminded them of media horror shows.

This would last until the vehicle door opened and the driver and passengers ran the last six or seven meters to the door; then there would be several rocks, aimed, thrown hard and flat to hurt or kill.

Again, slowly, so slowly as to make it clear to everyone else how they felt, the peeps would move in front of the already-closed doors, raise riot shields, and make a show of holding back the silent watchers.

Inside, they said, Thorwald displayed no emotions other than compassion for those who were hurt and frightened, and a certain cold anger that one of them said was "frightening— but made me glad to be with him."

In the last two hours of Second Light, the mob had begun to press in closer to the Center. Thousands of receivers in Utilitopia had picked up our distress message, and somehow there was a rumor among the crowd that a big protest march, or a rescue mission, or something, would set out from the Center as soon as it was dark. They had not known it, but the rescue was already under way; Bruce and Bieris had been among the last people to drive out of the Center, Bruce taking a bad hit that later turned out to have cracked his ribs. They had driven to a warehouse Shan had sent them to in the city, where, somehow or other, the springers and supplies were waiting for them. Already at that time, taking turns driving, they were roaring up the river valley, making all the speed they could for us. "It must have been a stretch of the rules for Shan to do that out of the Embassy budget," I said to Bieris, after she told me about it.

"Shan had a pretext in that you're his employees, and then he simply told the Council of Humanity that it would be intolerably bad public relations if he didn't rescue the whole party. Not that they really cared as long as he gave them excuses that would sound good enough." Bieris sighed. "He did his best, Giraut. You know, I think he was really fond of Thorwald . . . maybe of the Center as a whole. He used to really seem to enjoy being there, and I think he was sort of recruiting Thorwald for Council of Humanity service. This all hurt him terribly."

I nodded; I knew in an abstract way that I was hurt, too, but also that it might be months or years before I really felt the torn and shredded edges of the huge, aching void the Center—and Thorwald, and even Anna—had left in my soul.

Bieris went away without talking more, and I went back to sleep.

The end of the story was something I heard from, of all people, Major Ironhand, almost ten days later. He had come by, he said, because I'd done such a good job of making him feel welcome the first day, and because he thought as a matter of honor there were things I should know that other people might not have told me.

When it became clear the building might be stormed, not counting on the PPP guards, Thorwald had taken some of the neuroducers from the dueling arts kits, had someone technically proficient defeat the safeties so that they would put out really dangerous signals, and mounted them on mop handles. "As an improvised riot weapon," Ironhand assured me, "it was damned good. But there were just too many of them. No one could have held against that mob in that building. There were more than a thousand of them storming the Center. It was never meant to be a fortress, and your friends had no projectile weapons to keep them back. I don't think I could have held that crowd off in that building with anything less than a fully armed platoon."

The mob had rolled over the PPP lines like a lawn mower over a snake; four guards had died and several were badly hurt. The doors had come down just from the pressure of the bodies.

Thorwald and some of the larger people had tried to hold the spiral stairway leading up to the main spire; it was about the only place in the building narrow enough to defend.

"They killed him with a rock," Ironhand said, looking down at the floor, I think unsure of what my reaction would be. I know I was unsure myself. "With that mop handle gadget he'd brought down six of them—amazing, really, for a kid with barely any training. Your people might say '*que enseingnamen,*' and mine might just say 'guts,' but all we really would mean is that we don't understand how he did it. But finally he couldn't hold, no one could have, and he got hit hard enough with a rock to fall down, and—well, they beat him to death with broken pieces of furniture, we think. And they headed up for the next kid, what's his name, Peterborough, the one still in the hospital, and would have done the same, except that's when the Occitans finally got there."

By a very elastic reading of the rules, Shan had at last managed to declare the Center under his protection, apparently by claiming that since my personal effects were in there, and since some of the people who worked there worked for me ... it didn't matter. Probably the Council just approved of what he had done after the fact, and he could just as well have said that he did it because he felt like it.

He had already hired several units of troops from Thorburg, including the Occitan Legion. That unit was actually only six companies, but they were trained to fight in the urban environment, and perhaps more importantly their costumes looked vivid and threatening. They were on standby when Shan commed for help, and in minutes the helicopter carrying their portable springers had rolled through the springer at the Embassy, extended its rotors, and flown to the Center. Occitan troops poured out of the springers and into the Center—

And found an angry mob that had already beaten one brave young man to death, and was in process of burning every tapestry and painting, wiping every vu, and crushing musical instruments into scrapwood.

I'm told a Council of Humanity report later concluded that although there was no alternative available at that instant to Shan, sending Occitan troops into such a situation was a mistake that still should have been avoided, never mind how.

For about ten minutes discipline collapsed. Reports later called it a "police riot," a technical euphemism centuries old for "the forces of law and order go berserk and attack the civilians." At the end of it, the people who had sought refuge up in the spire were safe, and were quickly brought out of the building; the Occitan troops were yanked and beaten back into their ranks by the Thorburger officers . . .

And eighty of the mob were dead, and because of the lost time, the Center could not be saved from the fire.

Whether true or not, a rumor raced through PPP ranks that Saltini's agitators had caused the riot—and it was certainly true that the first casualties had been from the PPP. Two hours later, still within that single long Dark, at least half the city's PPP security forces were in open mutiny, and the city police, still bitter from the coup, joined on the rebel side. As fighting intensified, Saltini gave a series of orders; he wiped the records needed to revive any dissidents, sent loyal units of the PPP to attack the Embassy, and cordoned off the always-rebellious waterfront area, apparently planning to lay siege to part of his own city.

It was the pretext Shan had wanted for many days. The Council of Humanity jumped in with both feet, and the city was now under martial law. The cultural charter was revoked, and the Council of Rationalizers dissolved. In a few days Aimeric's father was to form a government, with himself as President and Head of State. It was an open secret that Aimeric would be the first Prime Minister of Caledony.

I heard all this and I lay there and stared at the ceiling. Now and then they came and hooked me to machines or gave me pills, and I complied. As often as they would let us, Margaret and I would go outside, into the courtyard of the hospital where they had us, and sit and hold each other in the blazing yellow sunlight. When we could, we cried.

I understand that Thorwald and Anna went into the regenner to the sound of hundreds of people singing his version of the *Canso de Fis de Jovent*. I don't think he'd have been displeased. I can never know, of course.

PART FOUR

M'ES VIS, COMPANHO

ONE

There was a new procedure, just out from research in the Inner Sphere of settled worlds, called "accelerated grief," and they brought out a specialist in it, Dr. Ageskis, a tall blond woman who spoke very little. I remember it as the time when I slept twenty-six or twenty-seven hours per day, and endured dreadful nightmares. In them, Thorwald and I had terrible shouting matches, and Raimbaut followed me around pestering me with his self-pity, and Anna pointed out in public that I had never understood her poetry . . . it went on and on like that. A hundred times I saw the lead cat drop into the crevice again, and Thorwald crawl out of the regenner just as we were sitting down to breakfast, his head as mangled as Betsy's had been. I wept and screamed, woke to be fed and exercised, went back under to more nightmares.

And slowly the nightmares diminished. The neuroprobes built healthy, though sorrowful, acceptance around the losses, triggered the waves of anger and then prevented their bonding onto the memories, found the crazy spots and excised them from the natural loss. I don't know how many days it was before they began to put me under for only two "maintenance" hours per day, but by that time I seemed to sleep through "maintenance" without difficulty, and after more days, they began to merely keep a running probe on me for "observation."

Apparently they liked what they observed from me, and from Margaret, but they had to wait a few days to make sure nothing more would come screaming up.

I had just reached the point of being really bored with being in the hospital, and of taking some interest in Aimeric's doings as Prime Minister—many stiffnecks were quietly coming around to him because he was working so hard to get cultural autonomy restored—when there began to be far too many visitors to the hospital. All of the them were offworlders from the Embassy, scientists and scholars of one sort or another, and they all wanted to talk about the ruins that Susan, Robert, and I had seen up in the Pessimals. Had there been any evidence, to my perception, that the gateway into the city was more recent than the dwellings? Or that it was less recent? Even though I had not approached the buildings, how tall did I think the doorways were? Had I noticed anything at all unusual about the shadows, the stonework, the regular curves of the doorways, the spacing of the doorways? Had there been anything lying around loose on the ground? Was I lying, and had I actually gone into one of the "dwellings"? Was I sure I wasn't lying when I said I wasn't lying? The endless procession of them asked the same questions again and again, as if none of them ever communicated with any of the others.

On our first day out of the hospital, the Council of Humanity put Margaret and me up in the best of the local hotels, a building that had not existed when we'd departed on our trip—some hotel chain out of Hedonia had grown it in the interim, and it still smelled slightly of new-building dust. It was now the tallest building in Utilitopia, but in the tradition of hotels, it was perfectly rectangular and looked like a child's building block rammed on end into the city around it.

The room, however, was comfortable—trust the Hedons for that!—with an enormous temperature- and resistance-controlled bed, a couple of different baths and showers, and several other amenities. We had only had a few minutes to explore it when the door pinged, and I opened it to find Aimeric.

"The Prime Minister has nothing better to do than visit pricey hotels? Do the taxpayers know about this?"

He grinned. "Moreover, he brings pricey wine with him—" he held the bottle aloft, and I saw it was some of Bruce's best private issue—"and he's already ordered an expensive meal to come up here with him. Corrupt as they make them—he learned it from his old man. May I come in, or shall I eat and drink it all by myself out in the hall?"

The set-up for dinner arrived almost at once, so our conversation was fairly limited for a while, but at last Aimeric said, "It may have occurred to you that it is fairly odd for a Prime Minister, even one whose culture is actually being run by the Council of Humanity at the moment, to have this much time on his hands. The first piece of news I have is part of why that's true,—and it also might help me prepare you for the big news.

"There will not be any Connect Depression in Caledony. Or rather, it's all over already." He let us think about that for a moment, then went on. "The reason is that vast quantities of offworld cash are being spent here, and the reason *that* is happening is because we have something like eight thousand scientists and scholars crawling around the ruins you found up in the pass in the Pessimals, Giraut."

"Does that include the two thousand who interviewed me and always asked the same questions?"

He snickered. "I realize it must have seemed that way to you. There was a reason for it. They had to make sure that you were telling the exact truth as you knew it. They went so far—this was very much against my wishes and I've filed a protest on your behalf—as to put in a tap on some of the neural work that you were having done."

I vaguely remembered a dream or two of the ruins. "So now they've decided I'm not a liar. How comforting."

"Giraut, *I* know you tell the truth, and so does everyone who knows you, but this was too important for the Council's experts to take our word for it. And luckily for you Robert and Susan are equally truthful, or they might have kept you in till they found out for sure who wasn't. It was vital that they make sure those ruins could not have been forged. What you stumbled across is—and I don't exaggerate at all—potentially much more important than anything connected with Caledon or Council politics ever was.

"Now that they're sure they've got every bit of testimony

they can from you, you're going on a tour of the ruins to-morrow—sorry but it's an order, and Shan will back me up on it if necessary—to see if anything there will jog your memory. They have to get you there right away, before you have a chance to hear any rumors—and believe me, there are plenty. So I hope you weren't planning to go out tonight—"

Margaret grinned lewdly and in a mock-husky voice said, "Have you looked around this room? We'll be hard pressed to get to all the surfaces in here."

Aimeric made a face; for some reason, this was serious to him. Since he clearly could not have a sense of humor about it, I said, "Well, then, what springer do I report to, and at what time?"

He told me; I was a bit surprised it was so late in the day, until I realized that I would be springing two time zones west—even after all this time, because you could see the Pessimals from Sodom Gap, I tended to think of them as "close," when in fact the parts you could see were virtually sticking out of the atmosphere.

There was little enough to say after that, but Aimeric and I were Occitans, so it took us an hour or so to say that little. After he left, Margaret and I treated ourselves to some very slow shared massages and lovemaking, and then had another light meal, and finally just fell asleep like any two lovers with no other cares. It was wonderful. I dreamed of Thorwald and Raimbaut that night, but though it was sad when I awakened and they weren't there, the dream itself was pleasant. I woke up saying "I love you," not sure who I was saying it to, but it woke Margaret, so I said it again to make sure it was for her.

Our guide was a middle-aged man named al-Khenil, from New Islamic Palestine, a culture on Stresemann. He was a pleasant, scholarly sort who didn't seem to be much inter-ested in answering questions. I realized after a few of them that he *wanted* to answer—was probably dying to talk to someone who didn't already know the ruins as well as he did—but must have been under orders not to give me any information that might slant my answers to the questions he was asking.

It seemed as if he had a question every three meters. They had marked all our footprints in the dust, and first he had me slowly rewalk the path I'd taken, but I saw nothing new; at the time I had mainly been trying to get Susan back to the cat so that we could get going again. In the better light, I saw that the fountain was a fountain sooner, but that was the only real change. I had not realized that the stonework on the fountain and on the dwellings had been laser-fused together, but considering the laser-cut pathway into the space, that really didn't surprise me much.

One thing that did was that the space was considerably smaller than we had realized; all those doorways were only about a meter and a half high, and ceilings in the rooms behind them no taller. The doorways all had identical holes in them, in identical places, as if some sort of standardized hardware had once been mounted there. Al-Khenil volunteered that they had found traces of copper and zinc in all the deeper holes, meaning probably that there had been brass fittings.

Inside one large, low room, there were carvings, partly covered with soot. "Perhaps they burned sacrifices in here in their later, degenerated days, who can say? Or maybe they used tallow lamps for light. But X rays have seen through the soot, and praise Allah that the soot is there."

He pulled out a sheaf of pictures and showed us the carvings that the X rays had revealed. "This one, you see, seems to be the periodic table of the elements, but arranged right to left. This seems to be their numbering system, which was apparently to the base sixty and always done as scientific notation—that triple arrow mark apparently is the equivalent of 'E' in our numbers. Much of the rest of it we don't yet understand, but at least they apparently tried to provide us with clues."

"You said the soot covering the carvings was—"

"I said praise Allah that it is there. Microscopic examination makes it clear that it built up, year after year, layer after layer, on the carvings, and was never disturbed in all that time. For at least two of Nansen's millennia, they came here and burned animal fat of some kind, although the rapid decreases in quantity for the last three hundred years suggests something was going terribly wrong by then. The Nansen year, is, of course, three-point-two stanyears, so we have more than six thousand stanyears of authenticated occupation here."

"*Deu!*" I said, shocked. "Then they were here in the time of ancient Sumer—"

He shook his head. "Long gone by then. Whoever they were, whatever they were, the outermost layer of soot carbon dates to around 20,000 stanyears ago—just under 17,000 BCE."

"But how—this planet is not old, and it only had unicellular life, and—" I was sputtering; I could not dare to hope for what this might mean.

Al-Khenil shook his head again. "No doubt they will make trouble for me because I am telling you this, but it seems to me a terrible thing for the discoverer himself to be kept in the dark. Because Nansen was already living, and neither Caledony nor St. Michael wanted any further terraformation, many routine surveys were not done, and many more were done and recorded but never analyzed. Now that we know where to look, and what to look for, in reanalyzing the data we have found coral under the seas, and chains of impact craters used to divert rivers, and we have some hopes that we may even find some of their machinery out in the Oort cloud or in the asteroids. Nansen was terraformed, however unsuccessfully, once before our civilization did it. The question at hand now is whether we have found the equivalent level civilization—twenty millennia too late—or perhaps, just possibly, remains of a previously unknown high human civilization that somehow collapsed before the last ice age on Earth." I imagine he must have been a fine teacher at his home university; certainly he had plenty of authority and presence as, with a sweep of his outflung arms, he indicated the whole site and said, "The question we are faced with, now that we know this is not a fraud, is which of humanity's long-sought goals we have found—whether we are looking at relics of the Martians, or at Atlantis."

After we returned, I had a long conference with Shan; he wanted me as a Council of Humanity employee, in permanent regular service, which seemed very strange to me considering the number of things that had gotten smashed up with me around. He said that he didn't think anyone else would have done any better, and pointed out what I would have missed by not coming.

I wasn't sure why I resisted the offer, but since I did, perhaps to give me more time to change my mind, he got around to mentioning that due to hardship and injury, I had accumulated special leave and a free springer ride to and from Nansen, and could therefore go back and visit Noupeitau for a few weeks if I wished. Moreover, if I declared that Margaret was my fiancée, she could come along. It seemed like as good an excuse as any, ans she really did want to see Nou Occitan.

TWO

Garsenda met us at the springer, with a big hug for each of us. "You're wearing my gift to you!" she exclaimed to Margaret.

"Yap. Only thing that might make me presentable. Since supposedly we're getting presented."

"Oh, you are, of course." Garsenda said. "Not that the Prince Consort is thrilled with the idea, but important people from an offplanet culture, and moreover a general-purpose hero like Giraut here, rate too high for him to ignore. We could spring to the Palace directly if you'd like, but the presentation won't be for another hour and there's time to walk if you'd rather see some of Noupeitau."

I was deeply grateful to Garsenda for meeting us, because as we walked from the Embassy up the hill toward the Palace, she and Margaret caught up on all the things friends do, and I had time to be alone with my thoughts. Arcturus burned as red as ever, and the colors and shadows were rich and deep, but I had never before seen the extent to which the landscape of Wilson was really only three colors, pitch-black where the sharp-edged shadows fell, deep red on stone or soil, and an odd sort of blue-gray where living plants grew. After so much time on Nansen, when I looked again at my home, though there was more variety, the variety seemed to be only of subtleties; had I not grown up here I might have thought of the landscape as almost monochrome.

People passed us in the street, but the few who recognized us were warded off with one fierce glance from Garsenda; Occitan *merce*, at least, was not altogether dead. Margaret's modified Caledon costume was echoed on many young women, who I assumed belonged to this new mode of Interstellar that Garsenda was describing—I overheard her mention in passing that carrying small neuroducer projectile weapons was now so common that "derringer pockets" were an indispensable part of the style, and was amused to realize Margaret had been equipped with seven different places to conceal a small equalizer.

I had to admit that while the *modo atz Caledon* did not display the unusually beautiful to particular advantage, it tended to flatter most of the rest—the streets of Noupeitau were no longer apparently filled with a few blazing beauties at which men stared, and a great quantity of "all other" which they ignored.

As we passed through the Quartier, I saw no one else in Oldstyle costume, and began to feel more than a little prehistoric. I had to admit that what I was wearing had become steadily less popular in the last couple of stanyears before I had gone to Caledony, but all the same I had never expected to see its complete disappearance.

Or, really, to care so little about it. My main concern now was to make sure that after the presentation, we did some shopping, so that I could get out of these conspicuously unfashionable clothes.

I had been to Court many times with my father when I was younger, and the ceremony of presentation was familiar, but again there were things I had never noticed as a child—the bored expressions on many of the courtiers, the gaudy over-statement of the soaring decorated arches of the chamber, even the fact that the fanfares were hopelessly overdone, so that the whole thing resembled nothing so much as the Court of Fairyland in a badly done low-budget children's show.

Yseut, moreover, looked like a mess. She was well-enough dressed—the gown had been chosen to accentuate her large bosom with its deep cleavage while hiding her weak chin with a clever, soft, detached ruff. Whoever had put it on her had done her best, but it was not clear that Yseut knew entirely where she was; she seemed to be disoriented, as if this were all a dream.

Garsenda leaned over and whispered in my ear. "There's a rumor he beats her, and that he's frightened her into keeping him as Consort."

I wasn't sure about Yseut, but I also figured out during the ceremony that all the other people of the Court, most especially including Marcabru, were at least moderately drunk. Some of the looks of boredom and inattention were coming from people who couldn't quite focus their eyes, in fact.

In part, I saw all this because I remembered how splendid Court had seemed to my childhood eyes. Margaret, afterwards, told me that she was utterly enchanted, and besides she had to remember all the proper forms and when to curtsy and so forth, so she didn't see much except the glamour.

I was glad for her, and gladder still because something about the modified Caledon costume allowed her to be—not pretty, or beautiful, she would never be either—but handsome and dignified, someone that no one would dare to mock.

At last the ceremony was over, and we were allowed to depart through one of the private south gates. I knew I would have to find Marcabru by himself, since Aimeric could not be here to go Secundo for me, and play through the challenge, but that could as well be done later. For right now, Garsenda, Margaret, and I were going to dinner at the Blue Pig, a favorite place of mine on the edge of the Quartier, which both Garsenda and my father's last letter had assured me had not changed one bit.

The choice was not mine, however. When we came out of the exit from the Palace, into the Almond Tree Yard, Marcabru was waiting for us, with half a dozen hangers-on in Oldstyle costumes. A glance showed all wore a *Patz* badge; Marcabru at least intended to fight solo.

I pressed back with my arm and found empty air; the corner of my eye saw Garsenda already dragging Margaret over to a bench and compelling her (I heard the whisper) to "sit *still* and don't distract him, he'll be fine."

Since the *donzelhas* under my guard were safe, I turned my attention to pressing matters. I made sure of my footing, and that if I backed up there was flat wall and no stone bench to trip me, and spoke to him in Occitan. "Ah, how pleasant, and ah, what a homecoming, to see the Prince Consort in all his besozzled glory. Do you know, Marcabru, you dear old friend, I never thanked you for the letter in which you described the Interstellar parodies of that quaintly tasteless costume of yours . . . you remember the letter and the parodies, no doubt, the giant phallus dangling from the seat? I laughed for what seemed a full day as I thought of that, for if only they had known how six or seven of us jovents used to take you up into the bedroom in your father's house, and share you as our woman, and how you used to weep and squeal because there were not enough of us—"

It was all unnecessary, for I had already challenged him without limit in my letter, but the old wild fight-lust was bursting in my heart, and the drunken rage in his eyes drove me to new heights of creativity. His maniacal hetero masculinity was just the easiest target to hit; this *toszet* had made himself a parody of the Occitan jovent, one that embarrassed us all, and it was as such a parody that I would bring him down.

"Why, do you know, my oldest friend of oldest friends, you owner of the best buttocks ever buggered, I do believe you are more fun in bed than the Idiot Queen, and you have even been had by more men, hard though that is to imagine."

He drew then, the neuroducer extending out from his epee hilt with a loud bang, glowing at me in the shadows, and said in Terstad, "Your bitch is very ugly, and I used to fuck Garsenda half an hour before she would meet you."

"And your words, the poetry of your Occitan, *que merce*, old friend." I did not switch languages; I could see that he was having a little trouble following his own culture language, and anything that added to his confusion was in my favor, for though I was sure I could defeat him, I needed to make it seem completely without effort. He took a step toward me, but I popped out my neuroducer and he held a moment, which gave me the chance I wanted to enrage him further. "Another man might have composed some clever phrase and shown off, but our Prince Consort shows us that, however slowly and belatedly, he has mastered the simple declarative sentence—nay, is able to join two of them with a conjunction. *Que merce*, I say *que merce*. You must have been spending some of what you've made peddling Yseut on the street on a tutor, my clever, my darling, the favorite whore of all my friends."

I had gotten matters where I wanted them. His rage drove him straight onto me with neither subtlety nor strategy. Like many drunks he was preternaturally strong because his saturated nerves no longer gave him feedback enough to know he was overstraining his muscles, but with the epee strength matters little, grace and speed are all, and those were completely on the side of my healthy, well-trained body.

I turned his point as a bullfighter does the bull, flinging his arm out to the side, and slashed his cheek before he could return to guard.

Bellowing his fury, he lashed out with still greater force, so that my parrying epee bent almost double before slipping through again to scar his other cheek.

He leapt back dramatically, trying to pretend that he was not injured, but his facial muscles betrayed him; he must be hallucinating big flaps of flesh depending from each cheek.

I closed slowly, giving up a little reaction time to keep him off balance.

When had I ever thought of him as formidable? I supposed it was only because I and all our opponents had been in the same condition he now was.

There was a moment of utter clarity, his black shadow falling on the cobbles of the pavement, his entourage staring open-mouthed at the swift destruction visited on him, his bloodshot piggy eyes locking onto me, the rich folds and drapes of the costumes. For one moment it was like some High Romantic play of two centuries before, a moment of pure Occitan drama and grace—

He lunged. This time I delicately turned him once more and then slashed the tendons of his blade hand with sure finality. His weapon clattered on the pavement, and, sensing that his hand was no longer on it, retracted an instant later. I slashed his chest lightly to make him back up, and stepped over his dropped epee. He was disarmed, wounded, helpless.

I must give him some credit. Whatever wreck of a human being he was by then, he still had *enseingnamen* enough. He took one more step back, clasped his hands behind his back, raised his chin, and stood with feet apart. Since it was a fight without limit, he expected now to be tortured, humiliated, or both, and he was making virtue of necessity by refusing to plead for mercy.

I spoke in Terstad now. "You demanded things of me you had no right to demand, and condemned me for not being what you wished me. If I have insulted you, it has been because you would not listen to me otherwise. If I have defiled your name, it is only so that you will face me, me as I am, and not insist that I wear a mask of your choosing. I wish that this battle of ours may be *non que malvolensa, que per ilh tensa sola*. Therefore I offer you honorable terms—either honorable yield or honorable death, your choice, with first the handshake of peace between us."

It was generous of me by Occitan standards, but my generosity was all calculated, for if he accepted my offer I would have far outdone him in *merce*, and if he refused, though it showed great *enseingnamen* on his part, my own *merce* would still be praised for years to come. In that, it was as cynical a bit of career maneuvering as any I had ever done.

"*Ages atz infernam,*" he said, firmly.

"*Per que voletz.*" I strode to him, drew a cord from my belt, and bound his hands, shaming him by indicating that I did not think he could hold them in that pose himself.

Then, as the crowd gasped in shock, I jerked down his breeches, forced him over a bench, and beat his buttocks with my bare hand until I was sure he would be badly bruised. Then, and it was at this point that Occitan opinion held that I went too far, I walked away without giving him the *coup de merce*, thus not giving him an excuse to hide in a hospital for the several days it took to be revived. Let him face, now, having to stand up, cover himself, and go home. Let him have to keep his afternoon appointments with the humiliation fresh upon him.

As we sat over lunch later, Margaret stared at her plate and picked at her food; I realized how it must have seemed to her. We barely spoke; toward the end of the meal, Garsenda suggested that she and Margaret might want to go shopping, and I added one more to the uncountable pile of favors I owed my old *entendedora*. I myself headed up to Pertz's, now a prominent Interstellar hangout, after buying conservative street clothing. No longer dressed like the old vus of me, I wasn't recognized by anyone but Pertz, and he and I spent a pleasant time catching up on gossip.

Most of the gossip was about people who had hung up the epee and moved from the Quartier.

Margaret never really spoke about the fight with Marcabru. I don't know what Garsenda said to her, if anything, but a day or so later Margaret seemed the same as ever.

I freely admit that I lacked the courage to ask.

The day we got on the coaster ferry to go visit my parents in Elinorien, Garsenda came down to see us at the docks. "By the way," she muttered in my ear, "I know you wouldn't have believed a thing he told you, but I wanted the pleasure of saying that Marcabru made passes at me several times while you and I were in *finamor*, and I turned him down every single time."

I grinned at her and said, "I assumed as much."

Margaret and I had a marvellous time taking the coaster up to the little port, and she got along fabulously with my mother. I spent a lot of time walking with my father, along the many trails that wove up from the coast to the mountains, and he even got me to help a bit in the garden. He wanted to know everything about the mountains and trails of Nansen; it occurred to me, to my deep surprise, that after all the man was only in his early fifties, and that if Shan was right and springer prices were low enough for routine tourism ten stanyears from now, my father and I might yet get a chance to hike through Sodom Gap together.

Margaret and my mother spent all their time over at the university; my mother was in fact the only reason anyone knew the name "Leones" in the Inner Sphere, for she was an authority on archived cultures—the groups that had not been able to raise enough money fast enough to launch colony ships during Diaspora, and so had been recorded extensively and then quietly, regretfully, but inexorably assimilated during the Inward Turn. I had grown up with my mother's constant talking about the Amish, the Salish, the Samoans . . . and now every night in the guest bungalow, Margaret seemed to echo it, though her fascination was more with how the recording had been done.

It hadn't occurred to me until we'd been there for about a week that my mother was hinting about the fact that she and my father could not possibly come to Caledony for the wedding. I thought, for one moment, of saying that after all we had affianced entirely to get Margaret a ticket here—thought about it, and decided it wasn't true.

It wasn't legally binding, since neither of us was of age under Occitan law, but we had a very pleasant ceremony in my father's garden, looking out across the tomato plants down toward the gray sea, just as Arcturus sank into Totzmare. Garsenda sprang up for it, vowing that she would be at the one in Utilitopia as well, and put out enough energy and noise to constitute the whole bride's side by herself. Pertz came, and a few of my other old jovent friends also, but mostly the occasion was for my parents and their friends.

The party afterwards was wonderful. I was a little surprised to realize how interesting all my parents' friends were, after all this time. Somewhere in the course of the evening people got the idea that this was also the farewell party, and that night, after getting around to consummating the marriage, Margaret and I agreed that it was time to go back.

I still did not know what answer I would give to Shan; I could tell that Margaret was getting caught up in the romantic idea of roaming the Thousand Cultures, and the fact that she would be delighted was one more argument in favor of taking the job, but I myself felt somehow past romance.

Though not at all past happiness, I thought to myself. As I lay there in the utter darkness, facing the big window that faced the sea, Mufrid came into view, yellow and brilliant. It was the brightest star in our sky, just as Arcturus was the brightest in theirs. I slipped my arm further around Margaret, without waking her, and let the warm bed and the deep peace carry me back to sleep.

THREE

Garsenda had bought out the contract to operate the Center, with Paul's company as her local management, but it wouldn't be ready until the nanos got done cleaning and clearing its insides, and restoring the structure itself. In any case, there were too many memories there. So we were married in the legislative chamber itself by the President of the newly chartered Caledon Republic—Aimeric's father, who was grinning quite uncharacteristically the whole way through. It figured, somehow, that in Nou Occitan, where social standing was everything, we had had a small, private ceremony with friends and family, and that in much less society-conscious Caledony, we had the President officiating, the Prime Minister as the best man, and an immense array of prominent politicians in the house.

Valerie was maid of honor at the wedding, and I'm told, but did not stick around to see, that she disappeared from the reception with some attractive male or other, leaving Paul once again in the lurch. I think we'd have been disappointed in her if she'd done anything else.

Betsy, in her new two-year-old's body, was a perfectly charming flower girl, though it did occur to me that she was a remarkably plain child. Perhaps by the time she hit puberty, there would be adequate plastic surgery available in Caledony, or she would be able to travel to Hedonia or Nou Occitan for a rebuild. "Or perhaps character will tell anyway, and she will be one of those handsome women who are devastatingly attractive through force of character, the sort that only sensible, discriminating men are interested in," I said to Margaret that night as we watched the moon come up over the sea, from the enclosed balcony of the Parton Grand, the first resort hotel on the west coast, the first springer-equipped hotel in Caledony, and the first million utils or so of Paul's indebtedness. Currently it was jammed with archaeologists and paleontologists of every kind, but somehow a suite had been found for us.

"I'm just glad she didn't trip and fall like she did in the rehearsal. That's all I'd need, would be my mother having a story like that to tell for years afterwards—the adorable little flower girl that landed on her face and got up saying, 'Goddamn these short legs!' "

I leaned back and laughed. "Do you ever wonder—if the cat hadn't wrecked, if the expedition had gotten out here on schedule—what might have happened?"

"Sometimes. It's sort of unknowable, isn't it?"

"Yap." I took her arm and we went up to our room.

The last day we were there, Shan came to see both of us. "Now that your personal decisions are made," he said, "would you both like a job? I'm now in a position to hire you as a couple. Before you answer, let me say that I'm sure you're aware that Aimeric, or for that matter Paul Parton, or any of a dozen others would hire either of you in a minute, and probably for more than the Council of Humanity could afford to pay you. You'd be wealthy eventually. Within a few years you could commute between your home cultures. So I shall tell you up front that I want to make my offer first before you have any idea what you're worth."

His friendly grin made it easy enough to ask.

"So, what do you have to offer us? Travel, I assume."

"To everywhere. We've found that people from frontier worlds tend to work out well on other frontier worlds, so of course we'd use you there. But if you're to function well on behalf of the Council of Humanity, you'll need to understand the Council's problems, which mostly originate in the Inner Sphere, so you'd be spending time there too. Everywhere and anywhere."

"Doing what?" Margaret asked.

"Officially," Shan said, leaning back in his chair and accepting the drink I had poured for him, "you will administer and oversee all sorts of functions in Embassies around the Thousand Cultures. Be bureaucrats, if you will. You'll also have a 'secondary contact' job, which only means that we expect you to spend as much time as you can out of the Embassies and in the culture you're visiting."

"That doesn't sound like anything you need us in particular for," Margaret said. "But you said 'officially,' which is your secret phrase for 'don't believe this.' "

"Unofficially," he went on, in the same tone of voice, "you would be in the Office of Special Projects. Reporting to me, no matter where you happened to be. My standing in the Office is something I'm not at liberty to discuss, but you'll find the Office itself in the organization chart of the Council of Humanity, reporting only to the Secretary General and the Executive Cabinet."

"And what does the Office do?" I asked. "I might mention I have very little desire to be a politician or a spy, after having coped with too many of them."

Shan made a face. "Not that. If we want to keep humanity

together, we have to make sure the bonds are loose enough not to chafe." He sighed. "In a sense we began before we had a purpose, thirty-two stanyears ago when the springer came out of nowhere. You know, at that time there were probably fewer physicists than there had been on the Earth a thousand years ago; it was a solved science. No one and nothing expected the Council to be anything more than a ceremonial body, ever.

"We had not had a request for a new colony—not that we had anywhere to launch one to—in four hundred years. Humanity was closed in on itself, and we comforted ourselves with the thought that if there were anyone else out there, they no doubt were living in much the same way.

"But the moment instant travel became possible ... well, have you considered that a robot ship can get its fuel through a springer, so that it can get very close to the speed of light? All the structural problems with handling antimatter in quantity are repealed. And when the ship arrives, another springer on board can bring through a full expedition, and they can send back for anything else they need. In fact, once you get a ship carrying a springer moving outward at light speed, it can drop off probes and expeditions as it goes, so that it need never decelerate. There will be new expeditions in all directions, and in a very short time humanity will be on the move again, expanding outward at the speed of light.

"*Unofficially*, we have more than ten thousand proposed new cultures making their way through our review process. *Unofficially*, it has occurred to us that if we can find the springer, so can anyone else out there, and that we have to be prepared to meet the equivalent level civilization within the near future—indeed, the mystery of where they are and why we haven't met them yet is all the deeper. And *very* unofficially, the fact that there are now billions of uncontrolled channels of communication in the form of springer-to-springer contacts means that there is now a tremendous centrifugal force acting on humanity; we are very likely to be pulled apart and scattered, just as we are getting ready to meet other sentient species for the first time. So the Office of

Special Projects has in fact just *one* special project—to bring humanity together, gently and by its own choice if at all possible, but to bring it together." He gestured toward the rise of the Pessimals east of us. "And now we find that the special project is more urgent than ever. Who were they? And where did they go?"

"And where did they come from?" Margaret echoed.

"Oh, that we have. At least one quite obscure and unimportant G star, twenty light-years away, seems to be strongly indicated in the carvings; why else would they include so many pointers to it? The first of the new springer ships will be heading that way, from here, in a matter of less than a stanyear. But why did they never come back? And how did a terraformed planet apparently overpower a civilization capable of star travel, and revert to an almost pristine state? You see how much there is to know."

For a long time, neither of us replied. Shan sipped his drink and watched us intently.

"Well, I wouldn't object to seeing the rest of the Thousand Cultures," Margaret said at last, "while there are still only around a thousand of them. And if they do find somebody out there, then perhaps a senior, experienced diplomat—which I would be in twenty years—might be among the first to meet them."

Shan's smile deepened. I got up and went to the window, not sure what I wanted to look at, but needing to rest my eyes on something outside the room. The jagged, cruel peaks of the Pessimals stabbed straight up into the sky. Mufrid was already sinking in the west, and soon Arcturus would rise over the Pessimals, and the moon over the sea.

"Style and grace," I said, finally, and whether they understood at once, or were just letting me work out the idea, I didn't know, because I did not look around. "The question is not just, 'will humanity be united?' but 'will it be united around anything worthwhile?' You know, of course, that I come from an invented culture, one that was founded by a small group of eccentrics fascinated with the romance of the *trobadors*, who sought a place far away where their mad romantics could live the life that seemed to them best and most beautiful.

"But the *trobadors* themselves, the model from which we were made, were wanderers, bearers of culture, teachers and news carriers. It was they who taught Europe to care for fashion and trend, art and love, style and grace ... for all the ephemera that make us human, and not merely for the politics and economics that are expressions of the needs to fuck and eat.

"*M'es vis, companho*, a humanity brought together by bureaucrats and administrators alone will be a humanity made up of petty clerks; a humanity organized only around banks and treasuries would not be one worth meeting or knowing.

"*M'es vis, companho*, there is need for a little style and grace among the stars. We are going to have guests, soon, and we must look our best. Ambassador Shan, I would be happy to accept the commission."

Margaret was beside me then, taking my hand, and behind me I could hear Shan's dry chuckle, which went on for so long that I realized he was really amused, rather than making his usual polite diplomat-noises. "They told us that when we looked for agents for the Office of Special Projects, we were not to recruit merely proficient or talented people, but people who might bring us some vision—for now that humanity is turning its eyes outward again, it will be vision we will need. They added that such people might not seem like ideal employees. I know now I was right to recruit you," he said. "I've already begun to regret it."

After arrangements had been made over coffee, and Shan had sprung back to the Embassy, we went down to sit on the balcony over wine, listen to the crowd chatter, and watch the sunset and the ever-changing sea and sky.

We stayed there a long time, not speaking, smiling to each other at things we overheard, looking out into the immense empty spaces around us. "Giraut, do you suppose we'll have time for this sort of evening very often?" Margaret asked at last.

"Style and grace, *companhona*. *M'es vis*, how often we

have them will not matter much as long as when we have them they are like this. But here—accept more wine, and give me your hand, and let's make sure that when people look at us, they'll smile at how happy we look."

We stayed to see the moon come up, but did not linger after that.